SPITFIRE GIRL

Lily Baxter

SPITFIRE GIRL

arrow books

Published by Arrow Books 2011

2 4 6 8 10 9 7 5 3

First published in Great Britain in 2011 by
Arrow Books
Random House, 20 Vauxhall Bridge Road,
London SW1V 2SA

www.randomhouse.co.uk

Addresses for companies within The Random House Group Limited can be found at:
www.randomhouse.co.uk/offices.htm

The Random House Group Limited Reg. No. 954009

A CIP catalogue record for this book
is available from the British Library

ISBN 9780099562634

The Random House Group Limited supports the Forest Stewardship
Council® (FSC®), the leading international forest certification organisation.
All our titles that are printed on Greenpeace approved FSC® certified paper carry
the FSC® logo. Our paper procurement policy can be found at:
www.randomhouse.co.uk/environment

MIX
Paper from
responsible sources
FSC
www.fsc.org   FSC® C016897

Typeset by SX Composing DTP, Rayleigh, Essex
Printed and bound in Great Britain by
CPI Mackays, Chatham, ME5 8TD

For Gay and Tim

Chapter One

Primrose Hill, London – December 1940

It was midnight but the sky over London was alight with fire and flame. Susan stood on Primrose Hill, watching in horror as the bombs fell from the sky and showers of shrapnel cascaded down like fireworks on bonfire night. Audible even at this distance, the roar of the German aircraft engines and the ear-splintering explosions were enough to terrify the bravest soul, let alone the small creature shivering at her feet. 'It's all right, Charlie,' she said, bending down to scoop him up. She cuddled him in her arms, rubbing her cheek against his soft fur and inhaling the warm puppy smell as if it were the most expensive French perfume.

Charlie made soft grunting noises as he snuggled up beneath her chin, raising his head in an attempt to lick her face. She could feel him trembling even now and she turned resolutely in the direction of home. 'Let's get you back into the warmth, little chap. But I want you to be a very good boy and keep absolutely quiet.' She retraced her steps along Elsworthy Terrace, turning right into Elsworthy

Road. In the red reflected glow of the fiery sky, the Edwardian terraced houses bore an air of shabby gentility, not least the one where Susan lived and worked. She climbed the front steps and let herself in, making as little noise as possible. She would never normally have been wandering around this late at night, especially in an air raid, but Charlie was not yet fully house-trained and his needs were more pressing at this moment than her own safety.

How long she could keep his presence a secret from Mrs Kemp and her daughters was not something she dared think about. London might be falling about their ears, but for the first time in her eighteen years she had something that belonged to her and her alone. She tucked the Labrador puppy under her jacket and headed for the back stairs which led to the lower ground floor. Feeling her way in the darkness, Susan's fingers touched the cold glass of one of the framed watercolours that lined the narrow hallway. She was glad that she could not see the enigmatic faces of the Japanese warriors who glared stonily into space. Stepping carefully, she negotiated her way around the mahogany half-moon table where a rather angry-looking Buddha sat cross-legged next to the old-fashioned candlestick telephone, which was just another relic from their past that the family refused to give up. The late Graham Kemp had been a minor official in the British Embassy in Tokyo, although to hear Mrs Kemp speaking about him anyone would think that he had held a far superior position. Their glory days, living the lives of ex-pats, might be long gone but the family continued to believe that they were in all ways a cut above the rest.

Jane Kemp, as Susan had found out to her cost, was a snob and a bigot. Her daughters were not much better. They made it perfectly clear that a girl such as herself, an orphan raised in a children's home, was less than nobody. She was a servant and as such should be invisible. She was paid a weekly wage that barely kept her in stockings and shampoo, but she was supposed to be grateful for her bed and board and the two uniforms she was compelled to wear when on duty. As she only had one half-day off a week, this meant that she was almost constantly garbed in one or other of the unflattering outfits provided by her employer. Susan loathed the brown cotton dress and beige apron and cap which she wore in the mornings. For afternoon wear she had a black number with a frilled white apron and headband, which was little better. Neither of the garments could be classified as being in the height of fashion, and the accompanying black lace-up shoes were both ugly and uncomfortable.

Cuddling Charlie, she made her way carefully downstairs to the large, old-fashioned kitchen, which could not have changed very much since the house was built shortly after the turn of the century. A deal table stood in the centre of the room and the original cast-iron range still held pride of place, although Mrs Kemp had recently, and somewhat unwillingly, invested in a more modern gas cooker. It was second-hand, but Susan much preferred cooking on instant and controllable heat. The range was large, temperamental, and guzzled wood and coal like a hungry giant. It needed constant feeding and cleaning, and once a week she had to apply a coating of blacklead to the cast iron in order to prevent it from rusting. It was a dirty, thankless task and one that she would have been happy to relinquish.

When she first came to the house in Elsworthy Road, the Kemps had employed a cook-general and a charwoman. The cook, a kindly woman who had been with the family all her working life, had given in her notice at the outbreak of war, choosing to retire to the country and live with her married daughter. The cleaner had taken up well-paid work in a munitions factory.

Susan set Charlie down on the floor, and checking first that the blackout curtains were drawn, she turned on the light. A forty watt bulb emitted a feeble glow but Mrs Kemp now had the excuse of doing her patriotic duty by saving electricity. Before the war it had simply been her parsimonious nature that had led to such economies. Susan went to the larder and taking the milk jug from the marble shelf, she poured a small measure into a saucer and placed it on the floor in front of Charlie, but before he had a chance to lap it up a ball of grey fur hurtled across the room and sank its claw into the puppy's nose. Charlie yelped with pain and fell over backwards in his attempt to get away from the growling Siamese cat.

'Binkie-Boo!' Susan said crossly. 'You horrible creature.' She bent down to comfort Charlie, but she did not attempt to wrest the saucer from the malevolent feline who was now lapping contentedly, having won that round. She took a fruit bowl from the dresser and put it at a safe distance from the irascible Binkie-Boo before filling it with milk. Charlie slurped it down in seconds, eyeing the cat warily.

Susan stood guard, ready to pounce on Mrs Kemp's spoilt darling should he decide that small Labrador puppies were fair game, but, having slaked his thirst, Binkie- Boo stretched, exposing his sharp claws as if it were necessary to remind anyone that he was armed and dangerous. He sat down and proceeded to wash himself.

Susan shook her head. 'You're the most horrible, pampered animal I've ever come across,' she said conversationally. 'But, on the other hand, if I hadn't had to take you to the vet this morning, I wouldn't have found Charlie.' She smiled down at him and he wagged his tail in response. She picked him up and headed for her own room, which was tucked away behind the pantry and the gardener's lavatory. It was small and simply furnished with a single bed, a chest of drawers and a bentwood chair, but it did boast a window that overlooked the large back garden with the grassy hump of Primrose Hill beyond.

She put Charlie on the bed and sat down beside him, stroking him until he curled up in a ball and closed his eyes. 'No one must know you're here,' she said softly. 'I mean it, Charlie. You must be very, very quiet. Mrs Kemp doesn't like dogs and she would be horrified if she knew I'd brought you into the house.' She sat for a moment, frowning as she remembered the scene in the vet's waiting room. There had been at least a dozen dogs with their owners, and all the animals appeared to be healthy, even if some were obviously quite old. What was even stranger was the fact that none of them had emerged from the consulting room. Their owners hurried off alone, and some of them were in tears.

Susan had had to wait until almost last, and the only occupants of the waiting room had been herself with Binkie-Boo in his wicker cat basket, and a large cardboard box containing one very small, yellow Labrador puppy. It was still there when she came out after Binkie-Boo's consultation with the vet. Having explained the cat's symptoms, or rather Mrs Kemp's version of her pet's condition, Susan had known exactly what the response was likely to be and she was not disappointed. The vet had raised his eyebrows and said that he had rarely seen a healthier specimen. Nursing a large scratch on his hand inflicted by the indignant Siamese, he had advised a light diet and a total ban on giving the overweight animal the cream skimmed off the milk. 'There is a war on, you know, young lady,' he said, glaring at her as if she were the culprit.

She had left the consulting room with Binkie-Boo who was still emitting low threatening noises, having suffered the indignity of a thermometer inserted into part of his anatomy that he obviously considered personal and private. Susan had put the cat basket down on the floor, and after juggling with her gasmask case she had taken her purse out of her handbag. The receptionist handed her the bill, which Susan paid with money given to her by Mrs Kemp. 'Demand a rebate for cash,' she had said. 'Make sure you get it.'

Susan had been here before. She angled her head and the receptionist met her unspoken question with a smile. 'Don't even ask,' she said, counting out the change.

'I gave that up ages ago.' Susan slipped the coins into her purse. 'There's one thing though. What happened to all the dogs? At least a dozen went in and none came out. Is there some awful canine epidemic?'

'You could say that.' The receptionist's smile had faded. 'It's the same all over London. We've put dozens of perfectly healthy animals to sleep. It's the war. People either can't afford to keep them or they're afraid of the air raids and they don't want their pets to suffer. I don't understand it at all.'

Susan glanced anxiously at the sleeping puppy. 'Not that one, surely?'

'I'm afraid so. We found homes for the rest of the litter, but he's the littlest. You might call him the runt. If no one wants him by the end of the day, I'm afraid he'll go the same way as the others.'

That had been enough for Susan. She had emptied her purse on the counter, regardless of the fact that sixpence three-farthings belonged to her employer. She would say she had dropped the threepenny bit and the smaller coins and they had rolled down a grating. She would rather face an irate Mrs Kemp than leave the little fellow to his fate.

Charlie snuggled deeper into the eiderdown, making soft grunting noises, and Susan stood up slowly, not wanting to disturb him. She knew that she had done the right thing. She had been horrified to learn that people were destroying their pets in fits of temporary madness. She would share her last crust with Charlie. He belonged to her now, and she would do anything to protect him. She turned with a start as she heard someone calling her name. She hurried from the room, closing the door behind her.

In the kitchen, Virginia Kemp was standing by the table staring down at the empty dishes and the telltale splashes of milk on the floor. 'What have you been doing, Banks? I thought the vet said that the beastly cat should have less cream. Are you trying to kill him?'

Binkie-Boo stalked over to Virginia, arched his

back and rubbed himself against her legs. He looked up at Susan and she was certain that he was smirking. She snatched up the offending articles. 'I'm sorry, miss. I forgot to pick one up earlier.'

Virginia shrugged her shoulders. 'You'll be in trouble if Mummy sees that mess on the tiles when she comes in.'

'Yes, miss. Was there anything else?'

'Mummy wants tea and biscuits. It looks as though it's going to be a long night. Pam and I will have cocoa. No sugar for her, she's too fat as it is.' She turned on her heel and made for the back door. 'Bring it out to the shelter, and don't forget the blackout.' She switched off the light and let herself out into the darkness.

Susan waited until the door closed before switching the light back on. She sighed. None of them seemed bothered by the fact that she was left alone in the house. No one had banned her from the Anderson shelter, but on the one occasion she had ventured into the corrugated iron construction dug into the ground and covered with turf, she had felt unwelcome and slightly claustrophobic. Anyway, she would rather take her chances indoors than spend the night with Mrs Kemp and the two furies, as she had nicknamed them. Pamela was not too bad. She was all right when she was on her own, but when she was with Virginia it was a different matter. Susan could only hope that one day soon there would be conscription for women and she herself would be called up to join one of the women's auxiliary forces. As far as she could see it would be her only way out of the present situation. Ever since her birthday in August she had given serious thought to enlisting in the Women's Auxiliary Air Force, but had abandoned the idea when she found out that she would never be allowed near an aeroplane. Inspired by reports of Amy Johnson's remarkable exploits, Susan's secret ambition had been to learn to fly a plane, but of course it was out of the question for a girl like her.

She set about making a pot of tea and heating milk for the cocoa. When it was ready she loaded up a tray and took it down the garden to the shelter. Primrose Hill was a dark hump silhouetted against the red glow in the sky. She could smell the acrid smoke from hundreds of burning buildings, and she could hear the crump of ack-ack guns interspersed with the roar of aeroplane engines and the percussive explosions as bombs rained down on the East End and beyond. It felt like the end of the world. The noise must have reached Mrs Kemp's ear as she was moved to invite Susan to join them in the shelter but she demurred, using the excuse that she had not locked the back door, and she was not certain that she had turned off the gas. She retreated with Mrs Kemp's caustic words ringing in her ears. 'Stupid girl. I don't know why I keep you on.'

She spent the rest of the night curled up on her bed with Charlie nestled in the curve of her body.

She awakened early next morning to take him out into the garden before he could disgrace himself. A dusting of frost iced the grass and the bare branches of the apple tree at the bottom of the garden. Late chrysanthemums were shrivelled with cold, bowing their heads into their dying leaves, and a pale buttercup coloured sun struggled to part the featherbed of clouds. Apart from the lingering smell of burning, and the faint crackle of fires raging somewhere to the south, it might have been a perfect winter's morning.

Susan set Charlie down on the grass, hoping that he would take the opportunity to relieve himself. He pottered about, nose to ground, sniffing the smells undetectable to human noses, and she waited nervously, keeping a wary eye on the Anderson. 'Hurry up, Charlie,' she whispered. 'Get a move on, please.'

He wagged his tail and cavorted round her feet, but then he seemed to realise what he had come out to do and obliged. He had barely finished when the shelter door opened and Pamela stuck her head out. Susan swooped on Charlie and slipped him into the pocket of her dressing gown.

'Oh. It's you.' Pamela squinted at her short-sightedly. 'Bring us some tea, will you, Susan?' She ducked back into the shelter, leaving the door ajar.

'Yes, miss.' Susan retreated hastily to the kitchen, taking Charlie out of her pocket and setting him down on the floor. 'That was a near one, boy. Thank

11

goodness Miss Pamela is too vain to wear her specs.' A giggle rose to her lips from sheer relief. 'We'll have to be more careful in the future.'

While she waited for the kettle to boil, she crumbled some bread into a bowl and covered it with milk. She placed it in front of Charlie, glancing anxiously at Binkie-Boo, but he was still ensconced on his velvet pillow, seemingly uninterested in the proceedings. However, Charlie's enthusiasm for his breakfast roused the cat from his state of lethargy, and in one sinuous movement he rose from his bed and stalked across the quarry tiles with obvious intent. This time Susan was ready for him and she moved Charlie out of the way before pouring the cream off the top of the milk into the bowl. 'There you are, fat cat,' she murmured. 'Eat up and enjoy it, because you won't get any more.' She took Charlie to the safety of her room. 'This is going to be difficult,' she said as she closed the door, shutting him in.

Her only thanks for taking a tray of tea to the shelter was a scolding from her employer. Mrs Kemp emerged from the Anderson, her head bristling with curlers and her face naked and pale without makeup. She glared at Susan. 'Why aren't you dressed, girl? What would the neighbours think if they saw you parading round the garden in your nightclothes?'

'I'm sorry, madam,' Susan said meekly. 'Miss Pamela asked me to fetch tea.'

'Don't blame my daughter. For goodness' sake

make yourself decent.' Mrs Kemp snatched the tray and disappeared into what looked like the bowels of the earth.

At that moment Susan could quite happily have filled the hole in with soil and left them there to rot, but she merely sighed and trudged back to the house. *Thank you* did not seem to be words in Mrs Kemp's vocabulary, but after four years of waiting hand and foot on the family Susan had become resigned to being treated like a serf. One day, she thought, I'll pack up and go. It was just a question of where and when.

She went to her room and put on the hated brown dress, which would have made the most beautiful woman in the world look dowdy. She brushed her fair hair until it shone and secured it in a snood before pinning the cap to her head. Fastening her apron round her waist she gave Charlie a final pat before leaving him once again. He attempted to follow her but she placed him on the bed with a firm instruction to stay there until she returned. Of course he did not understand a word she said, but there was little else she could do. She hurried to the kitchen and began preparing breakfast.

Despite the carnage and destruction of part of the city, life went on as normal in the Kemp household. Having complained that the porridge was lumpy and the toast not done to her liking, Mrs Kemp retired to the drawing room where she spent most of her time perched on the window seat, watching the world go by, or seated in an armchair by the fireplace reading back copies of the *National Geographic Magazine* and *Woman's Journal*.

Pamela left early to open up the small bookshop in Swiss Cottage where she was manageress, and after a leisurely breakfast Virginia set off for the golf club. Having inherited a small annuity from her father, she had no need to go out and earn her living. She had let it be known that she was unofficially engaged to Dudley Thomson and was soon to be married, although Susan often wondered if Virginia had let him in on the secret. Dapper, urbane and suffering from flat feet and asthma, Dudley Thomson had been declared unfit for military service. He was assistant manager in the local branch of the Westminster Bank, and rather fancied himself as a ladies' man. After a distressing episode when he tried to kiss her under the mistletoe last Christmas and had allowed his hands to wander to her breasts and buttocks, Susan took care never to be left alone in his company. Even so, her obvious antipathy to him seemed to have little effect on Dudley's ego. When he visited the house, which was too often for her liking, he treated her with cheerful bonhomie, adding the occasional pat on her bottom as confirmation of their close friendship. She suffered in silence, knowing that any attempt to denounce him would simply stir up trouble in the household. She suspected that he had put Pamela through a similarly humiliating experience, as she blushed whenever she saw him, and she too avoided being left alone in his company. That, in Susan's book, could not have been a coincidence. Given half a chance, she suspected that Dudley would have made a play for the younger, prettier sister, but Virginia had seen him first and her claw-like fingernails were firmly dug into her prey. Dudley might wriggle like a rabbit caught up in a hawk's talons, but he was well and truly hooked. Susan could only hope they would live unhappily ever after.

The breakfast table cleared and the washing-up done, she was free to get on with her chores. She began by making beds and slopping out chamber pots, which the family still insisted on using even though there was a perfectly good lavatory on the first floor adjacent to the bathroom. She dusted the rooms and swept the floors with the Ewbank carpet sweeper. It was not her day to polish the heavy mahogany furniture in the dining room, or to blacklead the range, but she needed to go shopping for groceries.

She had found an old bicycle that had lain neglected and rusting in the garden shed for years, and she had resurrected it. Now cleaned up, polished, oiled and with tyres inflated, it was a useful means of getting about, although Mrs Kemp made it clear that it was not to be used for recreational purposes. There was to be no galli-vanting about on Susan's days off, such as trips to Hampstead Heath or further afield. Walking was good for one; it developed the leg muscles and deep breathing helped the circulation and kept the heart strong. Susan often wondered why Mrs Kemp never took her own advice. She rarely left the house and even then it was usually by taxi unless she was accompanying Virginia and Dudley on one of their jaunts into the countryside in his motor car. Mrs Kemp still believed in chaperoning her girls, even though Virginia was pushing twenty-four and Pamela had just attained her majority. Sometimes, but not very often, Susan actually felt sorry for them, but then she remembered Virginia's caustic comments and Pamela's constant carping, and her sympathy evaporated like morning mist.

It was late afternoon by the time Susan finished shopping. She had queued for hours, first at the baker's and then at the butcher's. She had waited in line at Waitrose for their meagre rations of butter, cheese and bacon at one counter, and at another for tea, sugar and biscuits. Mrs Kemp insisted on having a digestive or a custard cream with her cup of tea, and Pamela had a sweet tooth; she was addicted to chocolate and missing her pre-war habit of eating at least one bar of Cadbury's fruit and nut every day. Pamela at the best of times was not a happy soul, and deprived of chocolate she became positively suicidal.

Susan emerged from the greengrocer's carrying a string bag filled with potatoes and a large Savoy cabbage. The basket on her bike was already full, and she had to balance carefully as she set off with the string bag hanging from the handlebars. She was vaguely aware that a large red ball had rolled into the road just ahead of her, but she did not see the small child who ran after it until too late. She applied the brakes sharply, skidded and fell off amidst a shower of King Edwards, which went rolling into the gutter to join the ball and the cabbage. Howling piteously, the little boy ran to his mother.

'Are you all right?'

Nursing a scraped elbow and a bruised ego, Susan struggled to her feet aided by a helping hand. 'I'm fine, thanks.'

'You're bleeding.' The young man, wearing what Susan took to be RAF uniform, pulled a clean white hanky from his trouser pocket and placed it gently over the injured limb. He bent down and picked up the ball, handing it to the sobbing boy's mother. 'You should keep that child under control, madam. He could have caused a nasty accident.'

'When I want your advice I'll ask for it, mister.' The woman grabbed her son by the scruff of the neck, slapped him round the legs and dragged him into the nearest shop. His yells echoed down the street.

'She should have been holding his hand,' Susan said shakily. 'The kid might have been run over.'

'Are you sure you're okay?'

'Yes, thanks. I'm fine, just a bit sore.' She lifted the bike, glancing ruefully at the front tyre. 'It looks as if I've got a puncture.'

'This might sound like a line, but my old man's got a cycle shop in the next street.' He grinned, and his hazel eyes twinkled.

Susan leaned the bike against a lamp post and bent down to retrieve the vegetables from the gutter. 'Thanks, but I've got to get home.'

The sudden wailing of the air raid siren was followed by the sound of running feet as people hurried to take shelter. Taking the string bag from her, the young officer helped her pick up the last of the potatoes.

'My dad really does own a shop round the corner. We've got a shelter in the back yard. Come on.' Without waiting for her to answer, he thrust the bag into her hand and taking the bicycle handlebars he started pushing it in the opposite direction.

Susan was left with no alternative but to follow him. She knew the cycle shop well, having spent much of her hard-earned wages on bits and pieces for the bicycle, but she was still suspicious. Mrs Kemp had imposed a curfew on her from the start and she was not allowed out after eight o'clock in the evening, making it almost impossible for her to mix with people her own age or to have a boyfriend. Mrs Kemp had made it clear that she frowned on young women having followers, and that included her daughters. Pamela dutifully obeyed her mother's rules, but Virginia took pleasure in flouting them.

Susan quickened her pace in order to keep up with him. 'It's probably a false alarm,' she said anxiously. At this moment she was more concerned with what Mrs Kemp would say if dinner was late than she was about getting caught in an air raid. And then there was Charlie. He might start whimpering or scratching on the door. 'They don't drop bombs this far from the docks,' she added breathlessly.

'John Lewis store bought a packet recently. Baker Street caught one too, and Pimlico.'

'I ought to go straight home.'

'Don't worry; my intentions are quite honourable, young lady.' His chuckle was infectious and he hurried on despite her protests.

All around them people were scurrying towards the public shelter and the entrance to the tube station. The blood-curdling sound of the air raid warning echoed through the rapidly emptying streets, and the sense of urgency and panic was infectious. It was a relief when they came to a halt in front of the cycle shop, but Susan was still wary. It seemed a humble place for a young officer to call home, but her new friend did not hesitate. He pushed her bike down a side entry and opened a gate leading into a back yard. They arrived just as a bald-headed man emerged from the building carrying a mug of tea. His lined features creased into a delighted smile. 'Hello, Tony. This is a nice surprise. I wasn't expecting you until later.'

Susan was well acquainted with Mr Richards and he turned to her with a friendly smile. 'Hello, love.

Bike come to grief again, has it? Or has my boy been touting for business on my behalf?'

'Nothing of the sort, Dad. She had a bit of an accident and the front tyre's got a puncture.' Tony hugged his father, causing him to slop tea onto the concrete. 'But never mind that now. Let's get you into the shelter.' He held his hand out to Susan. 'Come on, Miss . . . sorry, I don't know your name.'

Susan hesitated. For the first time in her life she was faced with an attractive young man who was treating her like a grown-up. She was desperate for him to think well of her, but he was an officer and she was little more than a skivvy. All the doubts and insecurities she had suffered in the past came flooding back to spoil the moment. She was a nobody. She had been unwanted and unloved. Banks was the surname of the policeman who had found her abandoned on the steps of a Methodist chapel. The only identification she had possessed was a piece of paper pinned to her shawl with SUSAN printed on it in pencil. 'It's just Susan,' she murmured. 'How do you do?'

'Tony Richards. How do you do, just Susan? I take it you do have another name.'

She took a deep breath. She was desperate for him to think well of her. 'Of course.' She forced her lips into a smile. 'It's Kemp. Susan Kemp.'

Chapter Two

She had told a whopper. She could almost feel the hand of God about to strike her down, but she had done it now. She had stolen her employer's name and claimed to be a member of the family who despised her. She eyed Tony doubtfully, wondering if he had seen through the lie, but he was smiling.

'Hello, Susan Kemp. I'm delighted to make your acquaintance.' He took her by the hand. 'I've a feeling this is the start of a beautiful friendship.'

'Never mind the sweet talk,' Mr Richards said, shaking his head. 'You'll be a goner if the Jerries drop a bomb on Swiss Cottage and you're standing here acting like Beau Geste.'

Susan looked from one to the other. 'Who's Beau Geste?'

'It's a great movie.' Tony ushered her into the shelter. 'I saw it in Southampton last week. Maybe you'd like to come and see it with me, if it's still on locally?'

Susan blinked as her eyes grew accustomed to the half-light. She took a seat close to the entrance. 'Maybe. But I hardly know you.'

He sat down beside her. 'There's only one way to remedy that, Susan.'

She cast an anxious glance at his father, but Mr Richards was busy polishing his spectacles on the tail of his shirt. 'Are you home on leave?' she asked by way of changing the subject.

'He's a pilot,' Mr Richards said proudly, without giving his son a chance to speak. 'A First Officer in the Air Transport Auxiliary.'

Tony shook his head. 'I'm a flying instructor, Dad. There's a difference.'

'He's still a pilot,' Mr Richards said proudly. 'You'd be flying sorties if it hadn't been for that back injury.'

Tony shrugged his shoulders. 'It's much better than it was after the crash landing,' he said casually. 'I'm more or less back to normal, although it's bad enough to prevent me from being aircrew.'

'You're a real pilot,' Susan said, gazing at him in awe.

He grinned. 'I earned my pilot's licence before the war. Flying was always a passion of mine, so now I teach.'

'And you're alive.' Mr Richards huffed on the lenses of his glasses and gave them an extra polish. 'You might not be here today if you'd still been flying a Wellington. You're doing a fine job as it is.' He cleared his throat noisily.

'It must be amazing to fly a plane,' Susan said, changing the subject. She could see that Mr Richards was embarrassed by his overt show of emotion. 'Just to be up there in the sky, free as a bird; I can't think of anything more exciting. I'm sure your work is vital.'

Tony pulled a face. 'It is, I suppose, but it's not glamorous. I train pilots to fly all types of aircraft for the Air Transport Auxiliary, and that's all I can tell you, I'm afraid. The rest is classified.'

'It's still really thrilling,' Susan said, clasping her hands together in genuine admiration. 'I think it's wonderful.'

Mr Richards put his glasses on and stood up. 'There you are, Tony. You've got another admirer besides your old dad. Speaking selfishly, I'd rather have a live son than a dead hero.' He paused, cocking his head. 'That sounds like the all clear. Must have been a false alarm. I'd best get back to the shop. This war's costing me a fortune in lost business.' He stepped outside, pausing on the threshold. 'Give me ten minutes or so and I'll have your bike fixed, Susan.'

'No, really. I don't want to take up your valuable time,' she protested, jumping to her feet. 'I really should go home. I can push the bike and bring it back tomorrow or the day after.' She did not want to admit that she could not pay for the repairs. She had not a penny to her name until Friday when Mrs Kemp somewhat grudgingly paid her wages.

'Don't worry, ducks,' Mr Richards said, patting her on the shoulder. 'It won't take me long. I could

23

mend a puncture in my sleep.' He had gone before Susan could think of a valid excuse for leaving.

Tony stood up and stretched. 'Let's get out of here. I hate these damned places. I'd almost rather take my chances out there than spend the night in here.'

Susan needed no second bidding. She stepped outside, taking a deep breath of frost-laden air. 'I feel exactly the same. I hate being underground.'

'It seems we've got a lot in common.' He followed her out into the back yard which was littered with empty crates, piles of rubber tyres and skeletons of bicycles, some without wheels, and others minus their saddles. 'It's a bike graveyard,' he said, following Susan's gaze. 'I'll have a bit of a clear-up for my dad while I'm home. He's got enough to do with running the shop and looking after himself.'

'Does he live on his own?'

'Mum died when I was ten. It was a hit and run accident. They never caught the driver.'

'I'm sorry. That must have been awful for both of you.'

'I saw it happen. One minute she was holding my hand as we crossed the road and the next . . .' He turned his head away. 'It was twelve years ago. Sometimes I have difficulty in remembering her face.' He shot her a sideways glance. 'That's terrible, isn't it?'

She slipped her hand into his, giving his fingers a gentle squeeze. 'Not really. You were very young.'

'You're a nice girl, Susan Kemp.' He met her gaze with a serious look in his hazel eyes. 'How old are you, if you don't mind my asking? I'm twenty-two and I wouldn't want to be accused of cradle-snatching.'

'I'm eighteen.' She felt a hot blush rise to her cheeks and she withdrew her hand. Was he flirting with her? She had no experience in this sort of thing and already she was out of her depth. She backed towards the gate. 'I really do have to go now.'

'Wait. You've forgotten your shopping.' He disappeared into the shelter and came out again holding up the string bag. 'This is heavy. I'll walk you home.'

'There's no need, honestly.' She unlatched the gate that led into the passageway. 'I'll go and see if your dad's finished with my bike.' She headed for the front of the shop with Tony close on her heels.

'I haven't said anything to upset you, have I, Susan?'

'No. Not at all. I just have to get home to Charlie.' She had spoken without thinking and the moment the words left her lips she regretted them.

'Who's Charlie? Your boyfriend?'

She had already lied about her name; another little fib would make no difference. 'Yes,' she said, taking the easy way out. 'That's right.'

'Then I suppose taking you to the pictures is out of the question.'

She had reached the shop entrance and she hesitated. 'I'm afraid so.'

'Fair enough.' Tony opened the door and held it for her. 'But I'll still see you home. This bag is heavy and we don't want you taking another tumble. You might not be so lucky next time.'

She murmured something beneath her breath as she entered the shop. She would have refused outright, but she sensed that his over-protective attitude might have something to do with his mother's tragic death. Perhaps seeing her sprawled on the road had triggered unhappy memories. It was hard to imagine how he must have felt when he saw his mother mown down in front of him. She struggled to put the image of a bereft ten-year-old boy from her mind as she approached the counter. 'How's it going, Mr Richards?'

'Almost done.' He took the cigarette from his mouth and placed it in an ashtray. 'There you are, ducks. As good as new.' He lifted the hatch and wheeled the bike out.

'How much do I owe you?' Susan asked anxiously.

'That's all right, love. No charge.'

'It doesn't seem fair.'

He smiled. 'We've had the pleasure of your company in the Anderson shelter; that's payment in itself, Susan.'

She was about to protest but Tony took the handlebars and started towards the door. 'Don't worry, he'll probably charge you double next time.'

'Cheeky young blighter,' his father said fondly. 'Hope to see you again soon, Susan.'

'Yes. Thank you for mending my bike.' Susan leaned over the counter and kissed him on the cheek. He smelt of cigarette smoke, Brylcreem and lubricating oil. He was nice, she decided. If she could pick someone out of the blue to be her father, it would be a man like Mr Richards; kindly, generous and loving. She had seen precious little of any of those qualities since she had been taken in by the Kemps. She turned away and realised that Tony was watching her with a smile of approval.

'Come on, Susan. We mustn't keep Charlie waiting.' His tone was neutral but she found herself wishing that she had not told such a preposterous untruth.

They walked along in silence for a while. Susan was trying desperately to think of something to say by way of explanation, but she had given Charlie a human persona and it would sound childish if she were to admit that she had simply panicked. It would lead to all sorts of questions about her family and she would be forced to tell him that she had lied about her name. She had dug herself into a pit of deception and there seemed to be no way out.

'Tell me about your job,' she said in desperation. 'The bits that aren't classified, of course.'

'It's quite simple,' he said easily. 'We take volunteers who already have a pilot's licence and at least two hundred hours' flying time and train them to fly anything from a Gypsy Moth to a four-engine bomber.'

'And you teach women as well as men?'

'I don't at the moment. The women ATA pilots are stationed at White Waltham, but I believe they do a damn fine job.'

'And do they fly Spitfires?'

He met her eager look with a smile. 'Is that your favourite?'

'I should say so. Not that I know much about aeroplanes,' she added hastily. 'But I've read about them in magazines and the newspapers. Spitfires have such a lovely shape.' She felt herself blushing again. 'I suppose that sounds silly.'

'Not at all. I think they're amazing.' He eyed her curiously. 'Is Charlie interested in flying?'

Stifling the urge to giggle at the thought of a puppy with wings like a bird, Susan shook her head. 'No. He's a feet on the ground sort of chap.'

'What does he do? I mean, is he in one of the armed forces?'

'No.' She hesitated, thinking quickly. 'There are physical reasons why he can't be.'

'I'm sorry. I didn't mean to pry.'

He sounded so embarrassed that Susan wished she had never started the conversation in the first place. She came to a halt outside the Kemps' house. 'This is where I live, Tony.' She held out her hand to take the bag of vegetables from him. 'Thanks for everything. I hope you enjoy your leave.'

He hooked the string bag over the handlebars, staring in awe at the imposing frontage. 'This makes our flat above the shop look like a doll's house.'

'I'm sure your home is very cosy.' At a loss for anything better to say, Susan held out her hand. 'Thanks, again.'

He shook it solemnly. 'It was a pleasure.' He pulled a notebook from his jacket pocket, and a fountain pen. Taking the cap off, he scribbled something on the pad. 'If you and Charlie are ever in Hamble, I can recommend some good pubs. The Bugle puts on a super lobster dinner, or you can sit and look out at the water in the King and Queen or the Victorious. It's a pretty little place, even in wartime, and you'll see plenty of Spitfires. I've written down the phone number of the Victorious. The landlord's a good sort and he'll pass on any messages.'

Susan took the paper from him. She knew she would never go there, but it sounded like heaven. 'Thanks, Tony. If Charlie and I are ever down that way we'll definitely be in touch.' She pocketed the slip. 'Goodbye, and take care of yourself.'

He tipped his cap. 'It was nice meeting you, Susan.'

She watched him as he walked away, and a feeling of sadness almost overwhelmed her. She had met a man that she really liked and she had made a dreadful mess of things. Not only had she lied about her name and made herself seem more important than she really was, but she had let him think that a yellow ball of fur was a human being. She hurried up the side entrance that led into the garden. She stowed the bike in the shed and headed for the back door. She opened it, hoping and praying that Charlie's presence had not been discovered.

She was met by the ferocious jangling of the bell labelled *Drawing room*. She sighed. Mrs Kemp would be demanding afternoon tea, and she had not had time to bake scones. It would have to be bread with just a scraping of butter and a generous amount of jam, which thankfully had not yet been rationed. Susan took off her raincoat and hurried to the drawing room to face her employer's wrath. She paused by the hall table to straighten her cap, checking her appearance in the mirror situated on the wall just above the Buddha's head. Her heart sank as she recognised the unmistakeable cut-glass tones of Mrs Kemp's friend, Mrs Girton-Chase. Mrs Kemp never missed an opportunity to show off in front of this particular guest, whose family tree was rumoured to go back to William the Conqueror, although she now lived in a home for retired gentlefolk overlooking Regent's Park. Susan thought privately that Mrs Girton-Chase's illustrious family were probably glad to get rid of the old witch. She braced herself to knock on the door and enter.

Mrs Kemp glared at her. 'Where have you been, girl? And why aren't you wearing the correct uniform?'

Her chance meeting with Tony and her concern for Charlie had put everything else out of her mind.

Susan clasped her hands behind her back. 'I'm sorry, madam. I've only just got back from the shops. I had to queue for ages and then the air raid warning went.'

'Excuses,' Mrs Girton-Chase said, shaking her head. 'You can't get the staff these days, Jane.'

Mrs Kemp chose to ignore this pronouncement. She pursed her lips. 'Change your clothes immediately, Banks. And then bring tea. I fancy scones with plenty of jam. I don't suppose you were able to get any cream?'

Susan reached for the doorknob. 'No, madam.'

'She should scald the milk.' Mrs Girton-Chase pointed a gnarled finger at Susan. 'That's what you should do, my girl. Heat the milk to blood temperature and leave it overnight. In the morning skim off the cream. Use your initiative, if you have any.'

'She doesn't,' Mrs Kemp said, dismissing Susan with a cursory wave of her hand. 'Orphanage children are a lost cause, Margot. I thought I was doing my civic duty, but sometimes I wonder if it was worth all the trouble.'

Susan left the room, closing the door behind her. She had heard it all before, but Mrs Kemp's harsh words still had the power to hurt her. Sometimes she wanted to stamp her foot and shout at her alleged benefactor. A few home truths would not go amiss, but they would probably fall on stony ground. Mrs Kemp was convinced that she was right in everything she said and did.

Susan went to check on Charlie before she did anything in the kitchen. What difference would it make in the great scale of things if Mrs Kemp had to wait an extra five minutes for her tea? Nothing mattered as much as the welfare of her small charge. She found him curled up on her bed with her woollen bedsocks for company. There were several small puddles on the linoleum but nothing worse. He opened his eyes and yawned, exposing a pink tongue and tiny pointed teeth. He wagged his stumpy tail and leapt up to greet her joyfully. She picked him up, cuddling him and whispering baby talk. She could feel his heart beating as she held his warm, soft body in her arms, and he made small whimpering noises as he licked her cheek. Reluctantly, she set him back on the bed while she changed into her black dress. He sat there watching her expectantly, and she had not the heart to leave him again so soon. She tidied her hair and secured the frilled headband before picking Charlie up and making her way to the kitchen.

Binkie-Boo was thankfully absent. His afternoon siesta was usually taken in the drawing room with his mistress, and although she had not seen him, Susan thought he was probably ensconced in one of the armchairs. Even Mrs Girton-Chase would think twice before shooing the Siamese off any seat he chose to make his own. Binkie-Boo showed no mercy when annoyed, and sometimes he hid behind an item of furniture in order to strike out with his talons at any person unlucky enough to come into range. Susan had the scars on her legs to show for such attacks. She took Charlie out into the garden and left him to romp around on the lawn while she set about making scones and a pot of tea for two. She had a narrow escape when Virginia burst into the kitchen to announce that she and Dudley would also require tea. 'And bring the rest of the fruitcake,' she added as she hovered in the doorway. 'If you've scoffed it I'll be furious.'

'I haven't touched it,' Susan said, forgetting her place in a moment of anger. 'I don't even like fruitcake.'

'Don't speak to me in that tone of voice, girl.' Virginia tossed her head. 'There may be a war on but there are plenty more like you in the orphanage who would give their eye teeth to live in a house like this.' She swept from the room without waiting for a response.

Susan stuck her tongue out. It was a childish gesture, but it went some way to relieve her feelings. 'Horse-face,' she muttered beneath her breath. 'Stuck-up bitch.' She thumped the dough down on the floured board and was rolling it out when the drawing room bell jingled yet again. She sighed, knowing that she could not win. Whatever she did was bound to be wrong. She would take it on the chin, as she had done for the last four years. The family might treat her like dirt, but she knew that she was better than that. One day she would walk out of the house and leave them to cope without their personal slave. It amused her to imagine them trying to look after themselves. Neither Virginia nor Pamela had even so much as washed out a pair of stockings, let alone lifted a duster. Mrs Kemp would not know a saucepan from a frying pan, and left to their own devices they would have to live on bread and cheese – just like a family of house mice. The image that conjured up made her giggle. She put the tray of scones into the oven to bake and filled the kettle. The bell rang again, twice, but she ignored it, taking her time to lay up a tray with plates, knives and cups and saucers. She took embroidered linen table napkins from the drawer, making sure that they were the small ones used only for afternoon tea or a light luncheon. Mrs Wilson, who had been cook-general until she retired, had been a kindly soul. She had taught Susan the rudiments of cooking and had shown her how to lay a place setting and how to fold table napkins for a dinner party. She had been the only person in the household who had treated her with any degree of humanity and compassion. Susan had loved Mrs Wilson and still missed her.

While the scones were cooling, Susan went outside to find Charlie. He made ecstatic noises and bounced up to her, his eyes shining. She took him inside and gave him a bowl of bread and milk, which he demolished in seconds. She watched him anxiously. 'I'm not sure what you should be eating, Charlie.

I'll have to go to the library and find a book about dogs,' she told him, and at the sound of her voice he wagged his tail.

The bell rang again and she hastily piled the warm scones onto a plate together with a dish of jam. Butter had become a luxury with only two ounces a week allowed for each person, but there was plenty of homemade blackberry jam in the store cupboard. Mrs Wilson had been delighted to pass on her knowledge of making preserves to Susan, and she had become adept at making pickles and jam, as well as baking. Cooking was something she enjoyed doing, which was more than she could say for the rest of the dreary household chores.

She picked up the tray and took it to the drawing room.

'About time too,' Mrs Kemp said, frowning. 'If you'd taken any longer it would be dinner time.'

'You just can't get the help these days,' Mrs Girton-Chase reiterated. She eyed the scones. 'I hope they're not heavy. If they are I will suffer all night with dreadful indigestion.'

Dudley and Virginia had been sitting side by side on the window seat, but he sprang up to take the tray from Susan. 'Allow me, my dear,' he said, covering her hands with his and winking. 'I prefer a piece of crumpet myself.'

'Put the tray down, Dudley.' Virginia rose with the grace of a panther about to leap on its prey. 'That will be all for now, Banks.'

Susan beat a hasty retreat to the kitchen.

There were some narrow squeaks during the next few days, but the closest happened just a week after Susan had brought Charlie home. Pamela had been sitting at her dressing table one morning, putting on a dash of lipstick, when she spotted Charlie gambolling about on the lawn, but by the time she found her glasses and put them on he had disappeared into the house. She came down for breakfast complaining that the pet rabbit belonging to the children next door must have escaped from its cage and found its way into the garden. 'There isn't much left for it to eat at this time of year,' she said, munching a piece of toast. 'But you'd better go and see if you can find it before it does any damage, Susan.'

'Yes, miss.' Susan refilled Pamela's cup with tea. 'Will there be anything else?'

Pamela shook her head. 'No, thanks. I've got to go now or I'll be late opening up, and Mr Margoles is coming to do a stock-take today.' She took a swig of tea, patted her lips on her napkin and rose from the table. 'What's for dinner tonight? I hope it's not stew again.'

'I don't know, miss. I'm going to the shops this morning. Perhaps the butcher will have some sausages left, if I get there early enough.'

'Do that. Leave everything and don't wait for my lazy sister to get out of bed. Let her get her own breakfast for a change.' Pamela grabbed her handbag and hurried from the dining room. 'I'm counting on you, Susan,' she called from the hallway. 'Don't let me down.'

The sound of the front door opening and then closing again confirmed that she had left for work. Susan cleared the table and set places for Mrs Kemp and Virginia. They would get up when it suited them, and she would have to wait until they deigned to come to the table. It was nothing new. She was quite used to their little ways. She took the dirty crockery to the kitchen and fed what was left of Pamela's porridge to Charlie. He lapped it up eagerly, but then hearing sounds of life in the bathroom, which was directly above them, Susan picked him up and took him to her room, exhorting him to be quiet. 'I'll take you out after dark,' she promised, closing the door and locking it. As far as she knew no one ventured into her private domain, but there was always a first time. She had been living in fear of someone discovering Charlie and it had been a near thing this morning. It was fortunate that Pamela could not tell the difference between a pet rabbit and a puppy.

An hour later, having gained permission from Mrs Kemp to do the shopping before she had completed her household chores, Susan set off on her bicycle. She queued for an hour at the butcher's only to be told when she finally reached the counter that the last of the sausages had just been sold, but she could have some liver and kidneys as offal was not yet rationed. She bought a pound of pig's liver, four lamb's kidneys, and a pound of tripe, which she loathed but Mrs Kemp liked it cooked in milk and served in an onion sauce. She went next to the greengrocer's and was about to go on to the baker's when she saw Mr Richards standing outside his shop. He was chatting to a prospective customer who was examining a second-hand bicycle with the air of someone who considered himself to be an expert. She was going to walk past but Mr Richards spotted her and beckoned. It would have been rude to ignore him, and she propped her bike against the shop window.

'Won't be a minute, Susan,' Mr Richards said, taking the cigarette from his mouth and exhaling a plume of blue smoke. 'If you'd like to wait inside the shop we can have a nice cup of tea and a chat. That is if you've got time.'

She could hardly refuse without seeming churlish, and anyway she still owed him for mending the puncture. 'That would be lovely, Mr Richards.' She went into the shop and waited while he finished dealing with the customer, who walked off without apparently completing the purchase.

'He's thinking about it,' Mr Richards said cheerfully as he re-entered the premises. He rubbed his hands together. 'It's a bit parky out there. Come through to the back, love. I could do with a cuppa, and I expect you could too. Those queues are a blooming nuisance.' He hurried through to a small kitchen at the rear of the building and Susan followed him, making her way between racks of spare parts and bicycles, some in the process of being repaired and others obviously brand new. There was an air of ordered chaos on this side of the counter, but the tiny kitchen could definitely do with a woman's touch. The Belfast sink was stained with tea and there was a musty smell in the air, mingling with a definite odour of sour milk. Mr Richards picked up a bottle and sniffed it, pulling a face and then tipping the semi-solid contents down the sink. 'It goes off quickly,' he said apologetically. 'I've got some powdered milk somewhere. Would you like to fill the kettle, while I go through the cupboards?'

'Of course.' Susan filled the kettle at the sink before putting it on the gas ring. 'Can I do anything to help?'

Mr Richards was systematically going through a wall cupboard, sending showers of tea leaves onto the tabletop to mingle with breadcrumbs and what looked suspiciously like mouse droppings. 'I'm not much good at housekeeping. I've got a bit better at it since . . .' He paused, glancing at Susan over his shoulder. 'I suppose Tony told you that we'd lost his mum, years back.'

'Yes, he did. I'm so sorry.'

He uttered a murmur of triumph as he came across a tin of powdered milk tucked away behind a can of 3-in-One oil. 'I knew I had one somewhere. Now where did I put the tea caddy?'

Susan had already found it beneath a crumpled newspaper. She handed it to him. 'How is Tony?' she asked, steering the conversation onto safer ground. 'Do you hear from him often?'

'He phones once a week. He's a good son; he never forgets his dad. I'm really proud of him.' Mr Richards emptied the teapot into the sink, adding a mound of soggy tea leaves to the lumps of sour milk. 'He liked you, Susan. But he told me that you'd got a young man.'

She was quick to hear the note of regret in his voice, and the feelings of guilt that she had pushed to one side came flooding back. She could not bring herself to tell him that she had lied to his son. 'We're just good friends,' she said, staring down at the floor. There was definitely a mouse hole in the skirting board. She wondered if she ought to draw his attention to it, but decided against saying anything that might upset him. She knew from experience how much it hurt when people like Mrs Girton-Chase said things that made their subject want to shrivel up and die from embarrassment.

'Well, that's how it goes,' he said, sighing. 'I'd like to see my boy settled with a nice girl, but he's very choosy. I think losing his mum like that has made him hold back from getting too involved with anyone. But he's young. There's plenty of time.'

He took the bubbling kettle from the hob and

poured hot water into the pot, swilling it round and tipping it down the sink. He was about to make the tea when the telephone in the shop rang, making them both jump. 'I'll bet that's Tony,' he said, putting the kettle down with a thud. 'This is about the time he usually rings. I'll tell him you're here, shall I?'

'No. Please don't.'

But he had rushed into the shop and picked up the receiver. 'Hello, Tony. Guess who's just walked in.'

Chapter Three

Susan snatched up her gasmask case and handbag. She squeezed past Mr Richards, shaking her head and pointing to the door. 'Sorry. I didn't realise it was so late. Must fly.'

He put his hand over the mouthpiece. 'Just a quick word with Tony?'

She lifted the hatch. 'Say hello for me. It was lovely meeting him.' She escaped from the shop not daring to look back. It had been a mistake to accept the offer of tea. She should have simply acknowledged Tony's father and walked on. One day they would find out that she had lied to them. Pretending to be part of the Kemp family had been a foolish thing to do, and she was ashamed of herself. If Tony found out he would be quite justified in thinking she was just a silly girl who should have known better. She mounted the bike and set off in the direction of home. She did not like leaving Charlie for long periods of time, and quite soon it would be impossible to conceal his presence. He seemed to have grown, even though she had only had him for a week, and although he was content to take naps like a human baby, she knew this would not last. She had visited the library and studied a book on rearing dogs. If only she had realised that Charlie would mature into such a large animal she might have thought twice about taking him on, but it had been love at first sight. She knew in her heart that she would have rescued him from certain death even if she had known that he would grow to the size of a Bengal tiger. She pedalled harder.

As the days went by it became more and more difficult to keep Charlie hidden from the family. The constant air raids forced the Kemps to use the Anderson shelter every night and quite often in the daytime as well. If the siren went while Susan was letting Charlie have his run in the garden she had to act quickly in order to hide him away. Occasionally this entailed both of them sitting out the air raid in the shed amongst the plant pots, garden tools and spiders' webs. Each evening when her work was done, Susan took him for a walk on Primrose Hill, regardless of the danger from falling shrapnel. The sight of London burning was appalling and deeply distressing. There were thousands dying beneath the rain of German bombs. Homes were wrecked and whole swathes of the East End razed to the ground. It was definitely the worst of times for the city, and yet the spirit of the Londoners remained unbroken. Susan read the daily reports in the newspapers after Mrs Kemp had finished with them. She wished that she could do something for the war effort. She had tentatively put this suggestion forward one evening after dinner when the family were assembled in the drawing room for coffee. She had been met with a firm refusal.

'Fire watching! Are you out of you mind?' Mrs Kemp spluttered, having swallowed a mouthful of hot coffee. 'You're forgetting your place, Banks.'

'You should let her go, Mummy,' Virginia said, smirking. 'Let her do something useful for once.'

Susan stood stiffly to attention. It had been during one of her nightly excursions on Primrose Hill with Charlie that she had come up with the idea. She could combine dog walking with being on the lookout for the increasing number of fires caused by incendiary bombs, and put her time to good use.

Mrs Kemp put her coffee cup down on the side table with a decisive thud. 'Certainly not. She'll use it as an excuse to go out at night. She's probably got a boyfriend waiting for her as we speak.'

Susan was used to being talked about as if she was not present, but this was too much to bear. 'That's not the reason I want to do this, madam.'

Mrs Kemp turned her head to glare at her. 'Speak when you're spoken to, Banks.'

'I can't see that it would make any difference to us,' Virginia said, taking a cigarette from the silver box on the coffee table and lighting it. 'And it looks as though we're all going to be in it soon.'

Pamela choked on a mouthful of chocolate. Susan

had observed that she hoarded her weekly ration as carefully as any miser, allowing herself one tiny chunk each evening. Susan also knew that Pamela was not above using her sister's points to satisfy her craving for sweets. She had had to search for Virginia's ration book several times, and on each occasion had discovered it in Pamela's room, tucked beneath her pillow. Luckily Virginia was too figure-conscious to consume anything containing sugar and considered it beneath her to shop for groceries, so the pilfering went unnoticed.

Pamela swallowed convulsively. 'I won't be conscripted. Not with my poor eyesight.'

'Don't count on that to save you.' Virginia flicked ash from her cigarette into the fire. 'We'll all have to do something. Dudley says it's just a matter of months and women will be called upon to do some kind of war work, if not actually conscripted into the forces.'

'Stop it, girls.' Mrs Kemp heaved her considerable bulk from the armchair. 'I don't want to hear any more. I won't have my daughters mixing with the hoi polloi. Your father would be turning in his grave at the very thought of you in uniform, or doing any sordid war work.' She picked up her ebony cane, leaning heavily on it. 'As for you, Banks, voluntary work is out of the question.'

'Yes, madam.' Susan moved swiftly to open the door for her.

Mrs Kemp paused on the threshold. 'I don't want

to hear any more about it. I'm virtually crippled and I need you here. D'you understand me, Banks?'

'Yes, madam.'

'So no more of your nonsense.' Mrs Kemp limped from the room and made her way towards the staircase.

'I'll have another cup of coffee, Banks,' Virginia called out as Susan was about to leave.

'Yes, miss.'

'I'll have one too,' Pamela said, moving from her seat by the window to take her mother's place by the fire. 'And, Susan, before you disappear.'

'Yes, miss?'

'I think someone must have let their dog stray into our garden. I trod in something very nasty on my way to the shelter this afternoon.' Pamela grimaced, shuddering. 'And it wasn't rabbit's thingies.'

'Yes, Banks. You really must make certain the side gate is kept shut,' Virginia said crossly. 'Anyone could be lurking outside in the darkness.'

'We could be murdered in the air raid shelter,' Pamela added, glaring at Susan. 'And it would be your fault.'

'Yes, miss.' Susan left them discussing the dangers of living without a man to protect them, and she returned to the kitchen. She took the kettle from the range and added more hot water to the coffee in the percolator. Although it was not rationed, it was expensive and often in short supply. Given the unenviable task of balancing the household budget for groceries, she had to be careful when she went shopping. Mrs Kemp scrutinised every receipt and counted the change in a manner that would have been applauded by Scrooge.

Binkie-Boo yawned, exposing two rows of sharp teeth. He rose from his bed and stalked over to Susan with intent. Eyeing him warily, she filled a saucer with milk diluted with water and placed it on the floor in front of him. He lapped a few mouthfuls and with a disdainful shake of his head retired to his cushion to wash himself, casting baleful glances at her as if to say that he was not so easily fooled. Brought up on the cream off the top of the milk, Binkie-Boo was finding rationing hard to bear. Charlie was not so fussy. Susan had allowed him to remain in the kitchen, safe in the knowledge that neither of the Miss Kemps would offer to help with the washing-up. He finished off the contents of the saucer and chased it round the floor with his nose, making certain that not a drop was missed.

Susan was about to pour the coffee when the air raid siren almost caused her to drop the pot. She put it down on the hob and grabbing Charlie by the collar she dragged him to her room, only just making it before Pamela and Virginia burst into the kitchen. They were closely followed by their mother, who moved with surprising agility when faced with the threat of the Luftwaffe's bombs.

'We'll have our coffee in the Anderson,' Virginia

shouted as she wrenched the back door open. 'And bring my cigarettes, Banks. I left them on the table in the drawing room.'

'Yes, miss,' Susan murmured. 'Three bags full, miss.' She sat down on her bed and stroked Charlie. He licked her hand and looked up at her with such adoration in his liquid brown eyes that it brought a lump to her throat. She picked him up and gave him a hug. 'You're worth more than the lot of them put together.' Reluctantly she put him down. 'Stay there like a good boy. I'll be back in two ticks.' She set about finding Virginia's cigarettes, not forgetting a box of matches, and she put them on the tray with the coffee, adding a plateful of rich tea biscuits for good measure.

Having satisfied their demands she returned to her room and made herself ready to face the cold on Primrose Hill. Charlie recognised the signs as she pulled on a woollen hat and scarf that she had knitted under Mrs Wilson's guidance, and he bounced up and down, making excited whimpering noises. 'Come on, Charlie,' she said, clipping on his lead. 'Let's get out of here.'

It was a cold, crisp night and a bomber's moon shone down on the city. Standing on the top of the hill Susan could see the red glow of yet more fires, and the criss-crossing of the searchlights etched patterns on the black velvet sky. The all too familiar sounds of aircraft engines, gunfire and explosions reverberated like the most terrible thunderstorm it was possible to imagine. She pulled her hat down over her ears in an attempt to deaden the noise as she stood watching Charlie gambolling about on the grass like a spring lamb. His joyful yelps were lost in the reverberating crumps and thuds that literally shook the earth.

She did not hear approaching footsteps, but suddenly she sensed that they were not alone. She spun round to see a man coming towards her. He wore a flat cap and a scarf partially obscured the lower part of his face. She felt the hairs prickle on the back of her neck, realising that she was alone and defenceless. She whistled to attract Charlie's attention but he had found a series of interesting smells and was scurrying away from her, nose to ground. She followed him, quickening her pace, but she could still hear the footsteps behind her. They seemed to be getting closer all the time, and then to her astonishment someone called her name.

'Susan? Is that you?'

She stopped and turned round. She recognised the voice. 'Mr Richards?'

He hurried up to her. 'I thought it was you. What on earth are you doing out here in the middle of an air raid?' He pushed his cap to the back of his head, peering at her through the misted-up lenses of his spectacles. 'Why aren't you in a shelter?'

'Why aren't you?' Susan demanded, her relief turning to anger. 'You scared the living daylights out of me.'

He took off his glasses and wiped the lenses on the tail end of his scarf. 'I'm sorry, love. I come up here because I hate the ruddy shelter, and because this is where I used to bring Tony's mum when we were courting. But you shouldn't be up here on your own.'

She was about to offer an explanation when she realised that she could no longer see the puppy. She panicked, calling his name. 'Charlie! Here boy!' She imagined him running off into the darkness and getting lost. She called him again and he bounced out from behind a tree, scampering towards her as if playing a delightful game. She bent down and picked him up. 'You bad boy, Charlie. You gave me an awful fright.'

'Charlie?'

She had almost forgotten Mr Richards' presence and she turned slowly to face him. 'Yes, this is Charlie.'

'So it is.' Mr Richards' eyes twinkled and his lips curved in a wry smile.

'I can explain.' She set Charlie down on the grass. 'It was all a misunderstanding.' The successive explosions of bombs falling somewhere to the south-east of them made her shudder. 'Poor things,' she murmured. 'I feel so sorry for the people in the East End.'

'They're certainly getting the worst of it.' Mr Richards took her hand and slipped it through the crook of his arm. 'Tell you what, Susan. Let's go and sit on a seat and pretend it's a lovely summer evening with no war, no bombs and no German aircraft flying overhead. You can tell me all about yourself, if you've a mind to, that is. If not, we'll just sit and make small talk until the raid ends. Because I think there's a lot more to you than meets the eye.'

The sudden urge to cry rendered Susan speechless for a moment but she allowed him to lead her to a nearby bench and they sat side by side, watching Charlie as he recommenced his exploration of the deep shadows. She had to suppress a sudden urge to tell him everything. She could not remember anyone having shown such interest in her past before. It was a new and confusing experience and she did not know quite how to handle the situation. 'I don't know where to begin,' she said, shaking her head.

'Well, you can start by telling me why you're out here all alone in the middle of an air raid. I mean, won't your family worry about you?'

She clenched her hands in her lap, digging her fingernails into her palms as tears stung her eyes. 'I haven't anyone close to me.' She shot him a sideways glance. 'I lied to Tony. I told him my name was Susan Kemp. It isn't.'

'Might I ask why?'

'He was nice. I wanted him to think well of me, and when he saw the Kemps' house I knew he was impressed. But I'm not one of them. I just work for Mrs Kemp. I'm a servant.'

'That's nothing to be ashamed of, Susan. My father was in service, and so was my mother.'

'I don't know who my parents were.' This time she turned to face him, lifting her chin and meeting his steady gaze. 'I was a foundling, left on the steps of a church and taken to an orphanage. Mrs Kemp took me on as a maid when I was fourteen. I've been with the family ever since.'

Mr Richards laid his hand on hers. 'Is she good to you, love?'

'I get two uniforms a year and all my meals. She pays me weekly, so I suppose that answers your question.'

'But does she treat you well? That would be my idea of someone who was a good employer.'

'Mr Kemp was a civil servant and they spent most of their time living abroad in British embassies all over the place. Mrs Kemp was used to having servants at her beck and call.'

'And so she treats you like a skivvy?' Mr Richards' eyes gleamed with humour. He patted her hand. 'You don't have to tell me. I can guess the rest. But whatever the woman is or was, you're still a minor and she is responsible for you. She should look after you.'

'I can take care of myself.' Susan rose to her feet. 'Thanks for listening to me, Mr Richards. I'm sorry I lied to you and Tony. I should have spoken to him on the phone, but I was embarrassed.' She shivered as a cold wind laden with the smell of smoke and burning buildings blew in from the east. 'I must take Charlie home. He's just a puppy and it's getting too cold to be out at night.'

Mr Richards stood up, straightening his cap and wrapping his scarf more tightly around his neck. 'Call in at the shop any time you're passing, Susan. I'm always pleased to have a bit of company.'

She hesitated. 'You won't tell Tony about me, will you?'

'Not if you don't want me to. It'll be our secret, but you can trust my boy. He'd understand and wouldn't think any the less of you.'

She called to Charlie who obeyed her this time and ran to her, jumping up excitedly as if life was a huge game. She clipped his lead onto his collar, and was about to walk away but she hesitated, turning to Mr Richards. 'Shouldn't you be going home too?'

'I think I'll stay out here for a while. I feel closer to my Christine when I'm up here on the hill.'

'Goodnight then, Mr Richards.'

He held out his hand. 'The name's Dave. Young people calling me Mr Richards makes me feel a hundred and one.'

She smiled and shook his hand. 'Goodnight, Dave.' She left him staring up at the stars and set off for home feeling happier than she had in a long time. It had been a relief to tell someone her story, and now her conscience was clear. Mr Richards, or Dave as she must try to think of him, was a good and kind man. It was comforting to know that she had a friend. There was a spring in her step as she walked back to the house.

Next day, which she always set aside for baking, she made an extra batch of scones, and as it was her afternoon off, she planned to take them to the cycle shop together with a pot of last year's blackberry jam. Mrs Kemp had taken to her bed with a headache and heartburn, which was hardly surprising as she had consumed a bowl of vegetable soup and several hot bread rolls at lunch time, washed down with a glass of stout. All this was followed by a slice of sponge cake that Susan had of necessity made with liquid paraffin instead of margarine or butter, and it had barely had time to cool before Mrs Kemp demanded a slice.

Virginia had departed for the golf course and would be out for the rest of the day, and Pamela was at work, leaving Susan free to do as she pleased. She decided to smuggle Charlie out of the house and take him for his first daylight walk. After all, Mr Richards knew all about him, and it would get the puppy used to traffic and socialising with people and other dogs. With her basket in one hand and her gasmask case slung over her shoulder, Susan looped Charlie's lead over her wrist and set off for Swiss Cottage.

Dave Richards greeted them both with equal enthusiasm. He put the *Closed* sign on the shop door and ushered them upstairs to the flat. 'I'm due for a tea break,' he said cheerfully. 'Had a sudden rush of work this morning, but I finished it just now, so I can relax. Come into the kitchen and I'll put the kettle on.'

Susan unclipped Charlie's lead and he scurried off to investigate his new surroundings. She followed Dave down a narrow corridor to a small kitchen overlooking the back yard. It was a little bigger than the one in the shop below, but not much cleaner. Dave might be good at mending bicycles but he did not seem to have much of an idea when it came to housekeeping. She noted a mouse hole in the skirting board with a rusty mousetrap set up in front of it, which had been sprung but was empty. A rather ancient gas cooker stood against the far wall next to a chest of drawers that had also seen better days. The oilcloth on the top was littered with packets of tea and sugar, a bill hook crammed with dog-eared papers and half a loaf sitting in a sea of crumbs on a bread board. No wonder the mice thought it was heaven on earth, she thought, trying not to laugh. A gas geyser rumbled away above the sink and the wooden draining board was piled high with crockery, some clean and some in need of a good wash. The white wall tiles were streaked with condensation and the linoleum on the floor needed a good scrub. As Dave put a match to the gas the air was filled with the smell of sulphur, town gas and hot grease. He glanced at her with an apologetic smile. 'I'm afraid it's a bit of a mess.'

That was the understatement of the year, Susan thought, but she merely smiled and made a space on the pine table for her basket. 'I've brought some scones and homemade jam,' she said shyly. 'I baked them myself.'

He filled the kettle at the sink and placed it on the gas ring. 'My, my,' he said, whistling between his teeth as he picked up the jam jar. 'Did you make this too? What a clever girl you are.'

There was nothing remotely patronising in his manner, and unused to praise she felt the ready blush rise to her cheeks. 'It's not difficult.'

'It would be to me. I'm not much of a cook. I live mostly on fish and chips or beans on toast when Tony's away, although I make a bit of an effort when the boy comes home.' He replaced the jar on the table and turned his head to peer at the flame beneath the kettle. He sighed. 'The gas pressure is low today so it will take a bit of time for the kettle to boil. I'll give you the conducted tour of the flat while we wait for our tea. It's very small so it won't take long.' He led the way into a long, rather dark corridor.

To Susan's surprise there were three bedrooms, or rather two reasonable sized rooms that would take a double bed and one much smaller which could only be described as a boxroom. It contained a narrow divan and a single chest of drawers but it was clean and tidy, which was more than could be said for the master bedroom. Mr Richards held the door open briefly, closing it again with an apologetic smile. 'Haven't had time to make the bed. It may look like a jumble sale but I know exactly where to put my hand on things.' He led the way to his son's room a little further along the narrow hallway. 'On the other hand, Tony is always tidy. He takes after his mum, thank goodness.'

After the chaotic scene she had just witnessed, Susan was pleasantly surprised by the neatness and order in Tony's bedroom. The walls were hung with framed photographs of military aircraft. Susan recognised the Spitfire and a Wellington, but she could not identify the others. It was a definitely masculine space with a double bed, and an oak wardrobe with a matching dressing table. On it was a set of hairbrushes, a leather cufflink case, and a photograph of a young woman with a small child on her lap. On closer examination Susan could only guess that the pretty lady with blonde hair and a nice smile was Tony's mother. The round-faced little boy with fair curls like Bubbles and an angelic expression must be Tony himself.

Dave cleared his throat. 'He was four then, Susan. He was the apple of her eye. My Christine was a wonderful mother and the best wife a man could wish for.' He ushered her from the room, moving quickly as if he wanted to shut away unhappy memories. He closed the door and appeared to relax just a little. 'That just leaves the living room.'

Situated at the front of the building with two small windows overlooking the busy street, the sitting rom was untidy, but there were definite feminine touches, which must have been put there by Tony's mother and left undisturbed for years. The pink fringed shade on the standard lamp exactly matched the one on a table lamp by the window. The walls were papered in floral designs and hung with prints of idealised Victorian rural landscapes with thatched cottages and rosy-cheeked children, playing with kittens. A green onyx clock was set in the centre of the cream tiled mantelpiece, flanked by figurines of shepherdesses and cherubs clutching lyres and trumpets. Susan noticed that there was a film of dust on all the surfaces and cobwebs festooned the ceiling. The carpet was threadbare in front of the settee and the hearthrug might have once been white and furry, but was now matted and scarred by singe marks. The coffee table was littered with newspapers, trade magazines and empty mugs that had left scorch rings on the polished tabletop. In one corner of the room was a large wireless, and two saggy armchairs faced each other on either side of the hearth.

'Take a seat, love,' Dave said, shifting a pile of magazines onto the floor with a sweep of his hand. 'I'll bring the tea and scones.'

'Can I help?' Susan asked, keeping a wary eye on Charlie who had found something interesting beneath one of the chairs and was trying to dig it out.

'No. You're the guest of honour today. I'll wait on you.'

It was such a novel experience that Susan sat back

on the sofa, avoiding a spring that was attempting to poke its way through the uncut moquette. She looked round the room with a critical eye. There was nothing here that could not be shifted by an inordinate amount of elbow grease, and the judicious application of Vim or Mansion polish. A wash with vinegar diluted in warm water would clean the mirror above the fireplace and the windows, and the old newspapers would bring them up to a crystal clear shine. She had not thought of housework as anything but a dreary chore, and yet for all its faults this was a much-loved home. She would have loved to get to work and bring it back to its former glory. Another photograph of Christine smiled at her from the sideboard where it had pride of place. She sensed that Tony's mum would have approved of anything that was done to make her men happy. For the first time in her life Susan felt that she was close to finding out what it was like to be part of a real family. She hardly accredited the Kemps with that honour. Virginia and Pamela were barely civil to each other and always squabbling, and their mother seemed to have little interest in anything or anyone other than herself.

Dave returned with the tea and scones. He had found some plates, although they did not match, and two bone-handled knives, but he had forgotten a spoon for the jam, and they used the teaspoon, which they had had to share anyway as the others were in the sink waiting to be washed.

'These are really good,' he said with his mouth full. 'Pity I haven't got any butter or better still a dollop of cream to go on the scones, but they're still delicious, Susan.'

She wiped her lips on her hanky. It would be useless to ask if Mr Richards had such a thing as a table napkin. Mrs Kemp would be shocked to the core if she could see the way they were seated round the coffee table, using newspaper as a cloth and dipping the hot teaspoon into the jam jar. Susan licked her fingers, enjoying the freedom and the feeling of rebellion against middle-class etiquette. 'I'll bring you some more when I do the next lot of baking. Maybe I could smuggle out a bit of cake too.'

Dave shook his head. 'No, love. I don't want you taking things from your employer. That wouldn't be right. Just this once is a real treat, but you'd be in trouble if the old lady caught you.'

'I'm always in trouble anyway,' Susan said, sighing. 'But as long as she doesn't find out about Charlie I can take it.'

'He's going to be a big dog. You won't be able to keep him a secret when he learns how to bark, and he'll need proper food as he grows. Have you thought of that?'

'I'll manage somehow,' she said stoutly. 'Whatever happens, I'm not giving Charlie up. I don't care if I have to live rough. He's mine. He stays with me.'

Dave frowned. 'Good luck then, love. That's all I can say. You can bring him here any time. I'll always be pleased to see you both. Anyway, how about another cup of tea?'

'Yes, please. But then I'd better think about getting back. Mrs Kemp will probably stay in bed all afternoon, but I don't want to bump into Virginia when I've got Charlie with me.'

'And I'd better open up the shop or I'll be losing trade, but you will come again soon, won't you, Susan?'

'I'd love to.' She glanced round the room trying to think of a tactful way to suggest that she might be able to help tidy up, but decided against saying anything. She did not want to hurt his feelings, but her fingers itched to start on the kitchen, even if it was just to do the washing-up.

She left the shop half an hour later. It was mid-afternoon and the light was fading as dark clouds obscured the sky, threatening rain or maybe even a dusting of snow. Soon it would be Christmas, but there was little sign of anything festive in the shop windows. As she trudged homewards she remembered the lines from a poem she had learnt at school: *No sun – no moon. No morn – no noon.* She could not remember the middle bit, and no doubt the poet, Thomas Hood, would be turning in his grave, but she recalled the last line: *No fruits, no flowers, no leaves, no birds – November.* That was just how it felt on this dreary day even though it was now

December. When she arrived home she thought how drab and unfriendly the house appeared in the dusk. She had an inexplicable sinking feeling as she let herself in through the side gate, but as she turned the corner of the building and came face to face with Dudley, she felt even more apprehensive. He was standing outside the kitchen door smoking a cigarette. He stared at Charlie. 'Well, well, well. What's this, Susan? Is there something you've been hiding from us all?'

She stopped, holding Charlie back with difficulty as he bounded forward to greet a prospective friend. 'It's not what it looks like.'

Dudley flicked his cigarette butt into the air and it landed in the flowerbed, the tip glowing on the naked soil. 'It looks to me as if you've got a secret, young lady.' He took a step towards her, laying his hand on her shoulder. 'Now what, I wonder, would it take to make me keep my mouth shut about your little friend?'

Chapter Four

Susan brushed his hand away. 'He's not mine. I was walking him for a neighbour.'

Dudley bared his teeth in a smile. 'Now we both know that's not true, don't we, my dear?'

Suddenly he reminded her of the Big Bad Wolf and she was little Red Riding Hood. She glared at him, meeting his unflinching gaze with a defiant toss of her head. 'I've told you – he's not mine.'

'All right, Susan. Let's take him home where he belongs.' He was still smiling but there was a cold, calculating look in his eyes that sent shivers down her spine.

'Why don't you mind your own business? It's got nothing to do with you, anyway.'

He grabbed her by the shoulders. 'Don't speak to me in that tone of voice, you little skivvy. Show some respect for your elders and betters.'

She made an attempt to break free but he tightened his grip, and the anger died from his eyes, but was replaced by something infinitely more frightening. She had never seen naked lust, but it did not take a genius to recognise it now. 'You'll be nice to me, Susan,' he said, emphasising his words by shaking her until her teeth rattled. 'I promise not to tell, if you'll cooperate.' Despite her struggles, he managed to undo her coat, and with mounting excitement he tugged at the neck of her brown uniform, sending a shower of buttons flying onto the gravel path.

'Let me go. I'll tell Miss Virginia.'

'And you'll lose your job as well as the mutt.' He aimed a savage kick at Charlie, who was chewing his shoelaces. 'Get him away from me or I'll knock the little blighter into next week.'

Susan seized her chance. 'Let me go, then. I'll take him indoors out of the way.'

He hesitated, but Charlie was determinedly attacking his other shoe. 'All right, but no tricks.' He released her, standing aside while she fumbled in her handbag for the key.

'Wait here,' Susan said as she opened the door.

'Don't tell me what to do, miss.' He pushed her aside and stepped into the kitchen ahead of her. 'Give me credit for some brains, you little idiot. You'd have locked me out, given half a chance.'

She forced herself to remain calm. 'You're not so green as you're cabbage-looking.'

'My dear, I love it when you talk like a common shop girl.' He took a step towards her but Charlie jumped up at him, obviously considering that this was a new game. Dudley caught him with the toe of his highly polished leather shoe, sending him slithering across the floor and somersaulting onto an astonished Binkie-Boo. The cat leapt up, arching his back with his fur standing on end like a woolly-bear caterpillar. He let fly at Charlie with claws unsheathed, catching him on the nose and making him yelp.

Susan raised her hand and struck Dudley across the face. 'That's for Charlie, you big brute.'

He caught her by the wrist, dragging her into his arms. She tried to fend him off, but despite his sedentary job at the bank Dudley Chapman was a big man and it was well known in the family that he had followed Charles Atlas' course in body building in order to impress Virginia. Holding her in an iron grip he covered her mouth with his in a wet and slobbery kiss that made her feel physically sick. She struck out with her fists but he seemed to take pleasure in violence. He was sweating profusely and murmuring obscenities in her ear as he thrust his hand beneath her skirt. He tugged at her knicker elastic and his fingers sought the private place between her thighs. Part of her brain told her to fight, but another small voice warned her that it would be useless. He forced her lips open with his tongue, but he recoiled violently as she seized her one chance of escape and closed her teeth on it. 'You little bitch.' He grabbed her by the hair, forcing her backwards over the kitchen table and sending the basket flying. The plate she had used for the scones hit the tiles, shattering into shards.

Susan opened her mouth and screamed, just as the door opened and Virginia strode into the room.

'Dudley. What the hell is going on?'

He pushed Susan away roughly, causing her to fall to the floor. 'She threw herself at me, Ginnie. Honestly.'

Virginia stared at the telltale bulge in his tight-fitting trousers and her lip curled. 'Don't lie to me, you bastard. I know what you're like when you get overexcited, and it's not a pretty sight.' She stepped forward and slapped him hard across the face. 'Get out of here. I never want to see you again.'

Pale and patently shocked, Dudley held his hand to his face. 'Darling, please.'

'Don't darling me.' Virginia marched to the back door and flung it open. 'Get out.'

'Why all the shouting?' Mrs Kemp had entered the kitchen unnoticed, and she leaned on her cane, staring from one to the other. 'What's going on?'

Virginia drew herself up to her full height, pointing a shaking finger at Dudley. 'That brute was all over her. They were about to copulate on the kitchen table. I'll never eat in this house again.'

'Dudley, what have you got to say for yourself?' Mrs Kemp demanded in a calm voice that astonished Susan. She would have expected hysterics at least.

He positively cringed. 'It wasn't me, Mrs Kemp. It was her.' He turned to Susan who had struggled to her feet and was trying to conceal Charlie under her coat, but he was apparently under the impression that life was one long playtime, and had managed

66

to escape. He bounded up to Mrs Kemp, wagging his short tail.

She could not have looked more horrified if Susan had brought a Burmese python into the house. She pointed her stick at Charlie who immediately leapt upon it and attempted to wrestle it from her hand. 'What is that?' she demanded. 'Banks. This is all your doing.'

'No, madam,' Susan cried angrily. 'It was him. He attacked me, the dirty devil.'

'Watch your tongue, young lady,' Mrs Kemp hissed. 'You can't make accusations against a man of Mr Thomson's standing and get away with it.'

'You saw him, Miss Virginia,' Susan said, turning to Virginia. 'You saw what he did to me.'

Pale-faced and trembling, Virginia shook her head. 'You're nothing but trouble, Banks. Dudley is a man and he's led by his male member, but you must have encouraged him. He hasn't the guts to try something like that unless someone led him on.'

'I say, old girl.' Dudley straightened his tie and hastily buttoned his double-breasted pin-stripe jacket. 'That's a bit harsh.' He held both hands up as Virginia rounded on him, eyes blazing. 'But completely justified in the circumstances.'

'Get that beastly creature out of here.' Mrs Kemp took a swipe at Charlie, who had left teeth marks on the end of her walking stick. 'You're at the bottom of this, Banks. Of that I'm certain.'

Susan made a grab for Charlie, sweeping him

up in her arms. 'Leave him alone. He's just a puppy.'

'And you brought him into my house without my consent.' Mrs Kemp spat the words at her. 'I was a fool to rescue you from the orphanage. I should have let you stay there and end up on the counter at Woolworth's or waiting on tables in a Lyons teashop.'

'You did it out of the goodness of your heart,' Dudley said, twisting his lips into a smile. 'You're a good woman, Jane Kemp. She doesn't deserve to live in a house like this.'

'That's not fair. It was him. He tried to rape me.' Susan was shaking with rage, but she was determined to have the last word. 'He's the villain, not me.'

Virginia gave her a shove that sent her tottering across the room. 'Dudley is a fool, but you're a little Jezebel. He'd never have behaved that way unless you gave him some encouragement.'

Dudley nodded his head, but a look from Virginia made him cower and drop his gaze. Mrs Kemp stared at the broken plate, and the telltale scatter of crumbs around the upturned basket. 'That's one of my best plates, Banks. You've been taking the food from our mouths. Call the police, Virginia.'

'It was just a few scones,' Susan said defiantly.

Dudley cleared his throat, running his finger round the inside of his stiff collar. 'Do you think that's strictly necessary, Mrs Kemp? I mean, wouldn't it be simpler to sack the girl? She's obviously up to no good, but you wouldn't want any of this to become public knowledge, I'm sure.'

Virginia slipped her hand through her mother's arm. 'Yes, Mummy. I hate to admit it, but Dudley is right. We don't want anyone else involved in this sordid mess.'

'Brandy,' Mrs Kemp said faintly. 'I feel quite faint.'

Virginia turned her head to shoot a scornful look at Dudley. 'Don't stand there gawping, you fool. Take Mummy to the drawing room and give her some brandy. I'll deal with this.'

'Yes, darling. Of course.' With an ingratiating smile he proffered his arm to Mrs Kemp. She accepted his help with obvious reluctance, and was still insisting that it was a police matter as they left the room.

Susan waited until the door closed on them before putting a wriggling Charlie down on the floor. She opened the cupboard beneath the sink and took out a dustpan and brush.

Virginia stared at her, arms akimbo. 'What do you think you're doing?'

'Clearing up the mess. I don't want Charlie or the beastly cat to cut their paws.'

Virginia snatched the cleaning tools from her. 'It's not your problem now. You heard what my mother said. You're to pack your things and leave this house immediately. Do you understand, or do I have to throw you and that flea-bitten cur out?'

'But I haven't anywhere to go and it's nearly Christmas.'

'You should have thought of that before you tried to seduce my fiancé.'

'I didn't do anything of the sort. I wouldn't touch him with a bargepole.'

Virginia's eyes narrowed to slits. 'You're a liar as well as a thief. Just thank your lucky stars that we're not pressing charges. Now get out, and don't come near this house again.' She stormed out of the kitchen, leaving Susan standing in the middle of the room staring after her.

She remained motionless for a full minute as the full impact of Virginia's words sank into her confused brain. Charlie seemed to sense her distress and he jumped up in an attempt to nuzzle her hand. Binkie-Boo curled up on his bed and closed his eyes, wrapping his tail around his body as if to indicate that the matter, as far as he was concerned, was closed. As the clock struck six Susan came back to life. It was time to start getting the dinner ready – except that she was not going to do that ever again in this house. All she could think of was that the Kemps would go hungry this evening, and for the foreseeable future unless either Pamela or Virginia could find their way around the kitchen. The odd thing was that it was no longer her responsibility. After four long years she was free from their constant demands and their complaining ways. But freedom came at a price. She had no money and nowhere to go. She should have been given at least a week's wages in lieu of notice, but that seemed highly unlikely in the circumstances, and there was no one to whom she could turn for advice.

She went to her room and took the small cardboard suitcase from beneath her bed. It was the same one that she had brought from the orphanage, and had contained her few belongings. She would be leaving with little more. She took off her brown dress and folded it neatly, laying it on the bed together with the black uniform, aprons and caps. She wondered if anyone would notice that there were buttons missing on the dress that Dudley had ripped. Would they bother to look outside and find them on the gravel? She already knew the answer to that question. Virginia might have railed at the man she intended to marry, and she obviously knew his weaknesses, but she was not the sort of woman to allow them to stand in the way of her marriage to a man with prospects. Dudley, with his smarmy, toadying manner, was well on the way to fulfilling his ambition to become one of the youngest branch managers at the Westminster Bank. With Virginia behind him he would probably end up in their head office, and she would bask in his reflected glory. She would breeze through life without ever having to lift a finger to earn her own living, and if her husband had his little flings with girls from the typing pool or waitresses from the staff canteen, she would turn a blind eye.

Susan selected a tweed skirt that Pamela had passed down to her when it became too tight to fit her chocolate-fed frame, and a woollen jumper that she had purchased in a church jumble sale for sixpence. It did not take long to pack the rest of her wardrobe, all of which had been bought second-hand. Apart from her black lace-up work shoes, she possessed only one other pair, which she put on, despite the fact that they were sandals and it was bitterly cold outside. She left the much-hated lace-ups on the floor by the chest of drawers, not wanting to be accused of taking something that did not belong to her. If Mrs Kemp had been prepared to summon the police over some missing scones, she would not hesitate to prosecute if footwear went missing. Buoyed up by anger and indignation, it was not until she was outside the house with Charlie straining on the leash that the full impact of what had just happened hit her. She was homeless and alone. The wailing of the air raid siren was just another addition to her parlous state.

She walked slowly, head down against the north wind that flung dead leaves in her face and tugged at the scarf that she had tied around her head. It was dark without the benefit of street lamps or moonlight, and she almost bumped into an ARP warden coming from the opposite direction. 'You ought to be in a shelter, miss. They don't put out a warning for fun, you know.'

'Yes, I'm sorry. I'll go now.'

'You shouldn't be out at all, if you ask me. A young girl alone in the blackout is asking for trouble.'

Susan could not make out his features clearly, but he sounded quite old. He was probably someone's husband, father and maybe even grandfather. He must have a home of his own to go to when he came off duty, and someone waiting for him with his slippers warming by the fire and a nice hot cup of tea brewing in the pot. At this moment that seemed like the best thing in the world.

'Are you all right, miss?' He sounded anxious.

'Yes. I'm fine. I know where the nearest shelter is. I'm going there now. Thanks.' She pushed past him and hurried off in the direction of the tube station. She would spend the night on the platform amongst the other hundreds or maybe thousands of Londoners who went underground at night.

'Hurry along then, and think twice before you venture out after dark.' The warden walked off on his round, leaving Susan standing on the pavement with Charlie tugging at the lead. She toyed with the idea of going up on the hill and sleeping under a tree, but it was too cold and damp. Perhaps it was not the best idea she had ever had. She quickened her pace, trying to ignore the cannonade of crumps, thuds and the constant drone of aeroplane engines. Her thin raincoat and sandals offered very little protection against the chill of night, and she was shivering by the time she reached the parade of shops.

She hesitated outside the one owned by Mr Richards, wondering what he would say if she knocked on his door and asked if she could stay, just for one night. Tomorrow she would think of something, but her mind was as numb as her feet and she was both tired and hungry. She glanced up at the living-room window, but the blackout curtains were drawn and she had no way of telling whether he had decided to take refuge in the air raid shelter, or had gone for his nightly walk on Primrose Hill in order to commune with his late wife. He must have loved her with all his heart, she thought wistfully. How romantic and how touching that was. She wondered if anyone would ever care that much for her. No one had in the past, not even her mother and father. If they had loved her they would not have abandoned her so carelessly. She was still deliberating, but sleety rain had begun to tumble from the sky and Charlie was whimpering at her feet. 'He did say we could come and see him any time, didn't he, Charlie?'

Taking his tail-wagging as an answer in the affirmative, she hurried down the passageway and rang the doorbell at the side entrance. After what seemed like an eternity the door opened and Dave peered out into the darkness. 'Who's there?'

'It's me, Susan.'

'Good heavens. This is a surprise. Come in.'

'I'm sorry to turn up like this, Mr Richards.' She stepped into the welcome warmth of the narrow stairway. The smell of hot toast wafted down from the flat above and her stomach rumbled.

He closed the door and switched on the light. 'What's up, love?' He angled his head, studying her face with a worried frown. 'No. Never mind the explanations for now. Come upstairs and get warm. You look perished.'

'Charlie's a bit wet and his paws are muddy,' Susan said warily.

Dave threw back his head and laughed. 'You've seen my flat. I don't think a few paw prints are going to make much difference.' He led the way up the steep staircase. 'Mind how you go, Susan. The lino's a bit worn. I keep meaning to do something about it, but I never seem to get the time.'

Minutes later, she was seated by the fire in the living room sipping a cup of hot, sweet tea with Charlie curled up on the tatty hearthrug, oblivious to anything but his own comfort.

'Now then,' Dave said, settling himself on the settee. 'Tell me all about it.'

She had been dreading this moment, but once she got started she found it surprisingly easy to talk to him. She told him about her life in the Kemp household, although she only made vague references to the daily humiliation she had been forced to undergo at their hands. She made light of the drudgery she had endured since she was little more than a child, and she spoke highly of Mrs Wilson, without whom her early years with the Kemps would have been almost impossible to bear. But she left nothing to his imagination when she came to the subject of Dudley and his wandering hands. She was trembling by the time she finished relating the sickening events that had led to her eviction from the house and the loss of her job.

Dave listened quietly without comment, but as she came to a faltering halt he jumped to his feet and paced the room, puffing hard on a cigarette. She wondered if he was angry with her, or whether he blamed her as Virginia had done for leading Dudley on. She gulped the remainder of her tea, which was now tepid. The sound of the all clear echoed round the room, breaking the silence. She leaned over to stroke Charlie's head. 'We'll go now, if it's all right with you, Mr Richards. Thanks for the tea.'

He came to an abrupt halt and turned slowly to face her, taking the cigarette from his lips. 'I won't hear of it, Susan. I've a mind to go round to the house and punch that bastard on the nose, if you'll forgive my language. It makes my blood boil to think of a young girl like you having to put up with such treatment. That Kemp woman should be shot and her daughters too. I never heard such a sorry tale in all my born days.'

'You won't do anything rash, will you?' Susan had visions of him riding one of his bikes round to Elsworthy Road like a middle-aged knight on a rusty charger.

'No. I'm not that daft, but I am very angry.' He tossed the dog-end into the fire. 'Not with you, love. I'm seething at the thought of what you've been through since you were little more than a kiddie. But never mind all that now. You're safe here. You and young Charlie can stay as long as you like. To tell the truth I'd welcome the company.'

Susan blinked back tears. Such unwarranted kindness was as overwhelming as it was unexpected. The best she could have hoped for was a bed for the night, but Mr Richards had offered her what felt like sanctuary. She nodded silently, not knowing how to respond, but miraculously he seemed to understand. He cleared his throat and picked up her empty cup. 'I think this calls for another cuppa,' he said, smiling. 'And I don't suppose you've eaten.'

She shook her head, not trusting herself to speak.

He made for the door. 'I'm afraid it'll have to be beans on toast. I don't suppose it's what you're used to up in poshville.'

His description of the Kemps' Edwardian terraced house made Susan giggle. 'Beans on toast would be lovely, Mr Richards.'

'Dave,' he said cheerfully. 'I told you before, love. We don't stand on ceremony here.'

'Can I help?'

He grinned. 'You're the guest tonight, but tomorrow you can heat the beans and make the toast for tea. How about that?'

'I'd like that very much. Thank you, Dave.'

Next morning Susan set to work with a will. Surprisingly, she had slept well in the tiny boxroom, and had been kept warm by Charlie who snuggled up against her back, barely moving all night. She had awakened refreshed and with a renewed spirit of optimism. The now familiar smell of burnt toast and cigarette smoke wafted along the corridor from the kitchen, and she found Dave in his shirtsleeves staring at a pile of washing-up in the sink. He turned his head and gave her a beaming smile as she entered the room. 'I dunno where it all comes from,' he said, scratching his bald head. 'It just sort of gets away from me.'

'I'll soon get it sorted,' Susan said confidently. 'But if you don't mind I'll take Charlie down to the back yard. I'll clear up any mess he makes.'

'I know you will. We won't worry about small details like that.' Dave stared down at her flimsy sandals, frowning. 'It's very wet and slushy out there. Haven't you got anything more substantial to put on your feet?'

'I had to leave my uniform and that included the shoes. These are all I've got.'

He shook his head. 'I'm not a vindictive man, Susan. But it would serve that woman right if an incendiary bomb landed on the roof of her house, and burnt it to the ground. Not that I wish anyone to be killed, you understand. I'd just like to see how she and her witch daughters would like it if they were left in the clothes they stood up in and no money to buy new.'

'They'd have a pot of gold buried in the back garden and claim on the insurance. But don't worry about me. I'm fine with sandals.'

Susan was about to take Charlie downstairs when Dave called her back. He cleared his throat, which she was beginning to recognise as a sign that he was embarrassed. 'I don't want to offend you, love,' he said, eyeing her warily. 'But I've got a wardrobe full of Christine's things. I never had the heart to throw anything of hers away, but I know she'd be more than happy if you could find a use for any of them.' He took out his hanky and mopped his brow. 'There now, I bet I've put my foot in it good and proper. I know you young ones don't care for old-fashioned or second-hand things.'

Susan laid her hand on his sleeve. 'I'm not like that, and it's a really kind offer, but . . .'

He took his glasses off and began polishing the lenses. He looked surprisingly youthful and defenceless without them, and Susan longed to give him a reassuring hug, but she was too well trained to show her feelings.

He gave her a reassuring smile. 'But you don't want them. I understand.'

'No, that's not it either. Just about everything I have is second-hand or came from jumble sales. I was just worried that it might be hard for you to see them worn by someone else.'

'It's time to move on, love. I'll never forget my Christine, but the memories I carry are in here.' He tapped his chest in the area of his heart. 'She was a good, kind woman, and I know she would want you to have her things. She hadn't got a mean bone in her whole body, and more to the point she was tiny, just like you. So while I'm downstairs in the shop, you can go into my room and take anything you need, but I suggest you start with a stout pair of shoes.' Taking a packet of Kensitas from his breast pocket, he selected a cigarette and lit it by bending his head over the lighted gas jet beneath the simmering kettle. Susan held her breath, half expecting him to lose his eyebrows as well as his hair, but he came up smiling and puffing smoke as he left the room.

Susan was hesitant about wearing a dead woman's clothes and shoes, but her sandals were still damp from her walk in the rain, and one of the buckles had come off. Her first foray into the chaos that was Dave's bedroom produced a pair of brogues that fitted as if they had been made for her. They were virtually brand new and could only have been worn once or maybe twice. She put them on and said, 'Thank you,' to Christine's photograph on the dressing table. Despite her reservations, she could not resist a cable-knit cardigan that felt snug and warm, and would keep out the bitter cold of a December morning. The rest of the garments were of good quality, but dated, and she closed the wardrobe, shutting away Dave's memories for a while longer at least.

She took Charlie out into the yard and he snuffled happily amongst the drifts of dead leaves that had been blown in from the adjoining back yards. She clutched the cardigan around her and was standing with her back to the building when she heard the door open.

'Chris! Christine, is that you?'

She spun round to see Dave standing in the doorway staring at her as if he had literally seen a ghost. The colour drained from his face and his hand flew to his mouth. 'Oh, my God.'

Chapter Five

Susan walked slowly towards him. 'Dave. Mr Richards, it's me. Susan.'

He dragged a hanky from his pocket and took off his glasses, mopping his eyes and making strangled gulping sounds as he made an effort to regain his self-control. 'I – I'm sorry, love. It was just for a moment . . .' He broke off, blowing his nose. 'I'd forgotten what I said and, by God, from a distance you were the spitting image of her.'

'I'm so sorry. I was afraid something like this might happen.' She slipped off the cardigan, holding it behind her back. 'I won't ever wear it again, or the shoes.'

He shook his head. 'No, please. Don't take any notice of me, Susan. I hadn't realised that you were so like her in looks, and even then it was just for a moment. It might have been the way the light was shining on your hair. Christine's was a bit lighter than yours, and more golden than ash blonde, but she was a real stunner. All the blokes were after her. They couldn't understand why she picked me.'

'I can see why she did,' Susan said gently. 'I'm really, really sorry that I've upset you.'

He replaced his spectacles, crumpled up the hanky and put it back in his pocket. 'And I'm sorry that I've embarrassed you, love. Please keep the cardigan and take anything else you want. It's a crying shame to leave her things for the moths to destroy.' He turned on his heel and disappeared into the shop.

Susan did not take anything else from Christine's wardrobe, but she did find an apron in one of the kitchen drawers, and she fastened it around her waist before starting on the epic job of cleaning the kitchen. She emptied the cupboards and scrubbed the stains off the oilcloth that lined the shelves. She washed and dried the dishes, pots and pans and stacked them away tidily. She cleaned the cooker and wiped the wall tiles, ending her task by mopping the floor. The strong smell of caustic oven cleaner, Vim and bleach lingered, and she opened the window to allow the fresh air to ventilate the stuffy room.

Armed with the carpet sweeper, a tin of Mansion polish that she had unearthed from the back of a cupboard and a handful of dusters, she set about the rest of the flat, starting in the lounge. Charlie was obviously enjoying his new-found freedom and he chased the ancient Ewbank round the room. Tiring of this game, he ran off with the hearth brush, and when that was wrested from him he grabbed the end of Susan's duster in an energetic tug of war. It was the first time that she had been able to play with him while she worked, and the sense of release was almost overpowering. Any minute she thought she might turn round and find Mrs Kemp breathing down her neck, or Virginia standing in the doorway with a sarcastic smirk on her lean features. It was almost impossible to believe that they were now part of her past. The future might be uncertain but she was content to live in the present, for the time being at least.

Dave took a mid-morning break and invited her to join him for elevenses. In the warm fug of the scruffy little kitchen at the back of the shop they drank tea and ate the sticky buns that Dave had popped out to buy from the bakery on the corner. 'My favourite,' he said, taking a bite. 'The girl in the shop puts two by for me every morning, and I fix her punctures for free.' He swallowed and sipped his tea. 'I'll tell her to put four aside tomorrow.'

Susan licked her fingers. 'Thanks. I love them too, but Mrs Kemp didn't believe in shop-bought cakes. I had to make them.'

Dave's eyes sparkled. 'You can bake a cake?'

'Yes. Providing I can buy the ingredients, but it's getting harder all the time.'

Plucking a ration book from the shelf, he handed it to her. 'I'm sure I've got points to spare. Perhaps you'd like to go shopping and get whatever we need. My old mum used to make a fantastic seed cake.' He went through to the shop and she could see him at the till. He returned with a ten shilling note. 'This should be enough to get a few necessities.'

Susan tucked it into the ration book. 'I'll go right away.' She hesitated, eyeing Charlie doubtfully. At the moment he was curled up on the linoleum but he was too boisterous to take to the shops.

'Don't worry about him,' Dave said, apparently reading her thoughts. 'He can stay with me. We'll be fine, won't we, boy?'

Charlie opened one eye and wagged his tail.

'I'll just go upstairs and get my handbag and gasmask.' She collected the empty cups. 'I'll give these a good wash.' She stopped, biting her lip. 'I'm sorry, Dave. I don't mean to take over, but I can see you don't have much time for . . .' she looked round, desperately seeking the right word, 'housework.'

'I know, love. Don't worry; I'm not offended by the truth. I'm really grateful for anything you do in the way of tidying up, but don't feel it's obligatory.'

'I'm glad to be able to do something in return, but I'll have to start looking for a job. I can't sponge off you, and I must find a place to stay.' She bent down and patted Charlie on the head. 'You be good for Dave. I won't be long.'

At one o'clock Dave closed the shop for lunch and entered the kitchen sniffing the air like a Bisto kid. 'What's cooking? The smell has been tickling my taste buds and making my customers hungry.'

'It's only liver with onion gravy and mash,' Susan said apologetically. 'The butcher had sold out of everything else.'

He gazed round the kitchen and his eyes widened in amazement. 'You've worked wonders, and liver is another of my favourites.'

'Good,' Susan said, smiling with relief. 'Mrs Kemp said that it was peasant food, but I like it.'

Dave took a seat at the table, staring at the place setting complete with a neatly folded napkin. 'It's like dining at the Ritz.' He watched Susan dish up, licking his lips in anticipation. 'I haven't had a meal like this since last Christmas when my sister Maida came to stay.'

Susan set the heaped plateful of food in front of him. 'Does she live locally?'

'No. Maida lives in Hackney. She teaches maths at a girls' grammar school, and she thinks she can boss me about because she's a couple of years my senior. I love her dearly, but a little of her goes a long way.' He took a mouthful of mashed potato and smiled. 'Lovely grub, Susan. You're a star.'

'Will she be coming this year?' Susan asked tentatively.

'No. She's decided to spend Christmas with our cousin Phyllis in Esher. She's a widow and her son is in the Navy, so she's on her own and not managing very well according to my sister.' He grinned, spearing a piece of liver with a decisive stab of his fork. 'There's nothing that Maida likes better than to organise people, so she'll have a field day with poor Phyllis.'

Susan could not think of anything to say to this

and they ate mostly in silence, interspersed occasionally by murmurs of appreciation from Dave. 'I'd lick the plate if it wasn't bad manners,' he said as he swallowed the last mouthful.

Susan had already finished her more modest portion and she rose to her feet. 'It's only tinned pears and custard for dessert,' she said apologetically. 'I usually make a pie or a suet pudding but I didn't have time today.'

Dave leaned back in his chair. 'I wouldn't have scoffed the last of the mashed potato if I'd known we were going to have custard. You didn't tell me you were a cordon bleu cook.'

Susan laughed, but his open admiration made her feel warm inside. 'I'm not. Anyone can follow the instructions on the side of the tin. Mrs Wilson taught me how to make proper custard with eggs, but that was before rationing. I'm not sure it would work with dried ones.'

'That Mrs Wilson sounds like a good woman. I'd like to meet her and shake her hand.'

Susan took the saucepan from the stove and poured warm custard onto the pears. 'She was very kind to me. I don't know how she put up with Mrs Kemp for all those years.' She put the plate down in front of Dave. He sat staring at the food and she was suddenly anxious. 'Is there anything wrong?'

He looked up, meeting her gaze with a worried frown. 'Not with the grub. It's all this.' He waved his hand to encompass the whole room. 'You shouldn't be slaving away for me. It's not right.'

'But I don't mind,' Susan protested. 'I like cooking and it's nice to see everything clean and tidy. It's my way of repaying you for your kindness.'

'It's not fair on you, Susan. Even if it is wartime, you should be mixing with people your own age.'

She pushed her plate away, her appetite deserting her. 'I know it was a cheek coming here last night, but I was desperate.'

He eyed her thoughtfully. 'You're still very young, Susan, and I'm a sad old widower who's set in his ways and no company for a girl of your age.'

'I'll be nineteen next August. I'm not a kid.' Susan had to bite her lip to prevent it from trembling. 'Do you want me to leave?'

'No. Of course not, love. That's not what I'm saying. I'd be happy for you to stay here until you've decided what you want to do next, but I don't want to take advantage of your situation.'

'You aren't, and I never expected to stay here for long. I'll find myself another place as soon as possible. Maybe I could get a job in a shop and rent a room somewhere round here.'

'Haven't you got anyone of your own, Susan?'

She shook her head. 'No one. But that's not your problem. I'll move on as soon as I can.' She was about to leave the room but he jumped up, pushing his chair back so that it scraped on the linoleum.

'No, wait. I'm just thinking of what's best for you,

but it's too close to Christmas. You won't find a decent job until the New Year.' He scratched his head, frowning. 'Perhaps we could come to some mutually agreeable arrangement.'

She hesitated in the doorway. 'Like what?'

'Maybe you could work for me until you find something that really suits you. I could pay you a wage every week.'

'You mean like Mrs Kemp did?'

'Yes. Although it wouldn't be very much, and you'd probably earn a lot more working in a factory, but it will tide you over until you decide what you really want to do.'

'I'd like to stay here with you. That's if you don't mind me keeping Charlie.'

At the mention of his name, the puppy leapt up, wagging his tail.

Dave reached down to pat his head. 'Of course not. Charlie's a fine fellow, even if he did rip one of my slippers to bits while you were out.'

'He didn't.' Susan frowned at Charlie, shaking her head. 'Bad dog.'

'Don't scold him. He doesn't know what he's done. Anyway, all puppies chew things. We'll be good mates and I can help train him. I could take him with me when I go out at night and you can stay in the warm and toast your toes by the fire, or read a book, or whatever young ladies of your age do.'

Susan smiled. 'You make it all sound so easy.'

'Where's the difficulty? If we're both happy with the arrangement I can't see why it shouldn't work perfectly well.'

During the next few days Susan worked hard, cooking, cleaning and generally tidying up after Dave, who had grown used to living in total chaos. Having sorted out the flat she made a start on the shop kitchen and she even tackled the unsanitary conditions in the outside lavatory. With Dave's blessing, she had already sorted out the jumble behind the counter. His idea of keeping accounts was to simply toss receipts, bills and order forms into a wicker filing basket until it overflowed onto the floor. When he was knee deep in papers he would attempt to make sense of the books, and this was how he spent his Sundays.

Susan had been forced to answer for every penny she spent in the Kemp household, and she volunteered, somewhat shyly, to relieve Dave of this onerous task. It had taken her several evenings to complete the bookwork, sitting by the fire in the lounge after supper while Dave undertook his nightly pilgrimage to Primrose Hill accompanied by Charlie. Several times she had to pack up the papers and hurry down to the air raid shelter, where she continued to work in the light of an old bicycle lamp. She worried about Dave, but she knew that he needed the quiet time alone with his memories, and she did not offer to go with him. When the raids ended she returned to the flat and made cocoa, which she reheated when he returned from his walk, cold and emotionally exhausted.

She felt comfortable with Dave. He made her feel needed, and was grateful for everything she did in the flat. Even though she had only been with him for a short time, it was almost as though they were family, but not quite. She could not conquer the fear that one day all this would end, and she and Charlie would have to leave. With the constant threat from the air, and the dire news broadcast by the BBC of cities as far north as Liverpool being devastated by the Luftwaffe, it was altogether a frightening time. Southampton had received a pasting in November and a number of incendiary bombs had fallen on the airfield. With this constantly on his mind Dave was a bundle of nerves until a phone call from Tony put his fears at rest. Susan also breathed a sigh of relief. Her memories of Tony were vivid and growing more romantic by the day. He was her idea of a perfect man, although she dreaded to think how he would react when he found out how she had deceived him.

'He'll be home on Tuesday,' Dave said beaming as he replaced the receiver after a telephone conversation with Tony in the run-up to Christmas. 'He's been saving up his leave and he hopes to get a thirty-six hour pass.'

Memories of her last meeting with Tony came flooding back and with them the inevitable feelings of guilt and embarrassment. 'What will he think when he comes home and finds me living here?'

Dave eyed her curiously. 'What's up, love? You and he got on like a house on fire. Why should be mind?'

'I lied to him, Dave. I told him I was Susan Kemp and that I lived in the big house. He'll think I'm awful.'

'He won't, and he doesn't.' He patted her on the shoulder. 'I put him in the picture from the start. We don't keep secrets from each other, love. He won't hold it against you. My Tony's not like that.'

'You mean he doesn't mind me being here?'

'Not at all. In fact I think he's glad that I'm being looked after. It means he doesn't have to worry about his old man. So don't you fret. We'll be one happy family.'

Susan swallowed a lump in her throat that was threatening to make her cry from sheer relief. What she felt for him was probably just a childish crush, and Tony would be like a brother to her. She hoped that there would be no ill-feelings or embarrassment. She forced her lips into a smile. 'We'll have the best Christmas ever. Even with rationing, I'm sure I can make a few treats.'

'That's right, love. We'll have a turkey and all the trimmings. Do you think you could make a Christmas pudding? Maida served up a shop bought one last year, but it wasn't the same.'

Susan nodded emphatically. 'Mrs Wilson showed

me what to do. If I can get the sultanas and currants it would be lovely, but if not I've read in a magazine that you can make the dried fruit go further by adding grated carrot.'

Dave scratched his head. 'Carrot pudding? Well, I'm blowed. What will they think of next? Anyway, love. Do your best. I know whatever you cook will be smashing.'

With the prospect of Tony coming home for Christmas, Susan put an extra effort into making preparations for the festive season. She made a pudding, adding grated carrot to the mixture, more in hope than certainty that the recipe was going to work. She managed to eke the ingredients out far enough to make a cake using dried eggs and liquid paraffin, and supplementing the currants, raisins and sultanas with the ubiquitous carrot and grated apple. It smelt all right when it came out of the oven, and it looked appetising enough. She could only cross her fingers and hope that the taste and texture did not let her down.

She decorated the lounge with paper chains and sprigs of holly, and she bought a small Christmas tree from a street vendor, which she dressed with baubles and slightly tarnished tinsel she had found in a box at the bottom of Christine's wardrobe.

Dave kept telling her to help herself to his late wife's things, but Susan had not touched the clothes hanging there since the episode with the cardigan. However, with Tony's visit in mind she had blown her first week's wages on a cherry-red woollen dress from a second-hand shop further along the street. In the same shop she had found an almost new woollen scarf which she bought for twopence, intending it as a present for Dave. He had insisted on paying her an extra half a crown for sorting out his feeble attempt at bookkeeping, and this she put aside to buy a special present for Tony.

She had thought long and hard about a suitable gift for him, and with only a few days to go before Christmas she stopped to look in the window of the bookshop where Pamela worked. Until now she had always hurried past, but a book that she would love to own herself had caught her eye. Her imagination had always been fired by aircraft and this edition of Jane's *All the World's Aircraft* was apparently second-hand, but in mint condition. She knew instinctively that it would be something that Tony would appreciate and cherish. There was no sign of Pamela in the shop, but even so Susan had to pluck up all her courage to open the door. The bell jingled on its spring and the girl behind the counter glanced up briefly before going back to writing something in a ledger. She seemed so preoccupied that Susan did not like to interrupt her, and she wandered around studying the titles on the shelves. The telephone rang and the assistant answered it with a resigned sigh. The conversation was brief and monosyllabic and she replaced the receiver shaking her head and muttering something beneath her breath. Susan was about to claim her attention and ask for the book in the window when the door opened, and to her horror she saw Pamela breeze into the shop.

'Did I leave my glasses case here, Sandra?' She leaned over the counter, peering at the shelf beneath. 'I can't find them anywhere at home.'

Sandra rummaged beneath the counter and produced a leather case. 'You'd lose your head if it wasn't screwed on, Pam.'

'Oh, goody,' Pamela cried, snatching it from her. 'I really must take better care of them.'

'You shouldn't be so vain.' Sandra moved swiftly from behind the counter. 'Anyway, while you're here, I'll slip out the back to the little girl's room. I was going to go but we've got a customer. Not that she looks as though she'll spend much.'

Susan had been hovering behind a stand of books in the hope that Pamela would not spot her, but as her colleague disappeared through the door at the back of the premises Pamela put on her glasses. 'Susan! What on earth are you doing here?'

There was nothing for it but to brazen it out. 'I came here to make a purchase, and that girl was quite rude.'

Pamela recoiled slightly, but made a quick recovery. 'So are you going to buy anything, or did you just come in to get out of the cold?'

'The book in the window,' Susan said, pointing. 'Jane's book on aircraft. I'd like to see it, please.'

Pamela stared at her for a moment as if weighing up whether she was serious or merely being a nuisance, but the desire to make a sale obviously won as she moved to the window and picked up the book. 'It's expensive,' she said curtly. 'And not the sort of thing I'd expect a girl like you to read.'

Susan took it from her, handling it reverently. She loved books, and had spent many happy hours in the public library. This one was something special, and it still had a little of the delicious new book smell lingering between the pages. 'I'll take it.'

'Oh.' Pamela could not have looked more surprised if she had produced a rabbit out of a hat. 'Well, I can't wrap it. We have to save paper.'

'That's all right. I've got a basket.' Susan slipped the book into her shopping basket. She could see that Pamela was dying to find out where she had been since she left the house, but she had no intention of satisfying her curiosity. She took her purse from her handbag and counted out the coins. 'I think that's right. Please check. I don't want to be accused of dishonesty.'

Pamela made a show of counting it before ringing up the sale on the till. 'You always had too much to say for yourself, Banks.'

'I'm not your servant now,' Susan said calmly. 'I'm a customer and I don't think Mr Margoles would take kindly to his staff being discourteous to someone who was prepared to spend money in his establishment. For all your airs and graces, Pamela, you're just a shop assistant.'

'You bitch.' Pamela spat the words at her.

Susan walked to the door. 'Your mother wouldn't like you using that kind of language. By the way, how is your sister? Is she still engaged to that dreadful fellow?'

'Yes. No thanks to you. Dudley told her that you'd led him on.' She curled her lip. 'As if a man like him would want anything to do with a slut like you.'

'He'll go for anything in a skirt, as I'm sure you know very well. I bet he tried it on with you a few times.' Susan could tell by the dull flush that spread from Pamela's neck to her plump cheeks that her suspicions were justified. 'You too? Does that make you a slut like me, Pamela?' She let herself out into the street and smiled as she heard a book hit the glass door and fall with a thud onto the mat. For the first time she had had the last word as far as the Kemps were concerned. It was a small victory, but it made her feel good. She walked homewards, still smiling.

She spent the rest of the day in a fever of antici-pation. Would Tony still find her attractive? Or despite what his father said would he think she was just a silly girl who had lied to him? She was excited and nervous in equal parts. She had risen early and cleaned the flat from top to bottom, paying special attention to Tony's somewhat Spartan bedroom. She had polished the furniture and swept the carpet, reaching under the bed to remove the dust bunnies. This accomplished, she had set about making up the bed with sheets that had been washed and hung on the line to dry. She smoothed them in place, inhaling the scent of frosty winter air and Oxydol soap powder that had permeated the starched cotton. She folded the material into crisp hospital corners as she had been taught in the orphanage, and finished by shaking up the satin-covered eiderdown. She stood back to admire her handiwork. She wanted above all things to make Tony's homecoming special.

By mid-morning on Monday Susan had almost completed her preparations for the big day. The lounge was aired and warm with a log fire crackling in the grate. She had filled a vase with spice-scented chrysanthemums, and placed it on the sideboard next to a bowl of walnuts and almonds. She had found a nutcracker and a corkscrew in one of the drawers, and Dave had been to the off licence the previous evening and bought a bottle of sweet sherry and one of port to add to the festive spread. The decorated tree stood in the corner opposite the wireless, and a small sprig of mistletoe hung off the light shade in the centre of the room.

Susan was in the kitchen stirring batter for the toad-in-the-hole she was preparing for their midday meal, when she heard footsteps on the stairs. 'Lunch won't be ready for at least half an hour, Dave,' she called, thinking that he must have mistaken the time.

He entered the kitchen looking distinctly harassed. 'Susan, love. We've got a visitor.'

Pushing past him, a tall, broad-shouldered woman walked into the room. She wore an expensively tailored tweed suit and a hat modelled on a man's trilby with a feather stuck in the brim. She stopped, staring hard at Susan. 'So you're the girl that my brother has taken in. He's just been telling me about you.'

'My sister, Maida,' Dave said apologetically. 'She's come for Christmas after all.'

'I'm afraid my stay will be a lot longer than that.' Maida set her suitcase down on the floor, taking off her hat and balancing it on top of the baggage. 'A gentleman would have carried this up all those stairs, but what can you expect of a younger brother?' She pulled out a chair and sat down, peeling off her leather gloves. 'I've been bombed out. Luckily for me I was working late at the school, marking exam papers, when the wretched thing hit my block of flats. It went down like a pack of cards. Nothing left.'

'Oh, dear. How awful,' Susan murmured. 'Was anybody killed?'

'Best not to dwell on it, I'd say. Dreadful things happening every day. Damn war.' Maida turned to her brother. 'Don't just hover there like an idiot. Fetch me a drop of brandy. It's been a gruelling couple of days. I slept in the staffroom at the school last night. After all, we have to keep calm and carry on.'

Dave hesitated in the doorway. 'But what about Phyllis? Won't she be disappointed that you're not going to stay with her?'

Maida pursed her lips. 'She's taken up with an ARP warden chap. Apparently he knocked at the door to tell her off for not drawing the blackout curtains together properly, and now they're practically inseparable. Stupid woman, you'd think she'd had enough of men the first time round. Stanley was a drinker,' she said, shaking her head. 'I wouldn't have put up with him for five minutes.'

'I'll get the brandy,' Dave said, heading off in the direction of the lounge.

'So how long do you intend to take advantage of my brother's good nature?' Maida demanded, glaring fiercely at Susan.

Taken aback, Susan was temporarily bereft of speech.

'Well, speak up, girl. You've got a tongue in your head, haven't you?'

'Yes, miss.'

'My name is Miss Richards, and I can tell you now that I don't approve of a girl your age living under the same roof as a widower.'

'He's been very kind to me, Miss Richards. It's a purely business arrangement. I earn my keep.'

Maida looked around the kitchen and nodded her

head. 'I can see that, but people will talk. It's not on, Susan.'

'What isn't on?' Dave demanded, as he entered the room with the brandy bottle clutched in his hand. 'What have you been saying to her, Maida?'

Automatically, Susan reached into the cupboard for a wine glass. She placed it on the table in front of Maida. 'Miss Richards thinks that people will get the wrong impression, Dave.'

'Dave!' Maida's dark eyebrows shot up to meet her hairline. 'A girl of your age should address my brother as Mr Richards.' She snatched the bottle from his hand and pulled out the cork. 'I'm surprised at you, David Richards. How could you allow a situation such as this to develop?' She poured a generous tot into the glass and downed it in one gulp.

'No. Really, Maida. It's not what you think. If you'll just calm down we'll fill you in on all the details, and when you hear Susan's story I'm sure you'll be more than sympathetic.'

'You always were a soft touch, David. Don't forget I teach sixth-formers. I'm used to sorting out the fact from the fiction.' Maida rose from the chair and picked up her gloves and handbag. 'I'll use Tony's room. I'm sure he won't mind sleeping in the boxroom.'

'But that's Susan's room,' Dave said uneasily, 'and Tony's coming home for Christmas.'

'That's not my problem.' Maida marched out of the kitchen. 'You can't expect me to sleep on that lumpy settee, not with my bad back and sciatica.

Bring my suitcase, David, there's a good chap.'

He turned to Susan with his hands held palms upward in a helpless gesture. 'She's a strong-minded woman, is Maida. But don't worry, dear. I'll have a word with her when she's calmed down and recovered from the shock of the bombing and everything. She's not a bad sort when you get to know her.'

Susan opened her mouth to tell him that she would look for another job as soon as Christmas was over, but he looked so upset and sheepish that she had not the heart to add to his problems. 'We'll manage, Dave,' she said softly.

A shriek from the bedroom made them both jump. Dave rushed out of the room. 'What's the matter, Maida? What is it?'

Susan hurried after him and was almost bowled over by Charlie, who raced out of Tony's room as if the devil himself was after him. He tore along the narrow passageway with his ears flattened to his head, and came to a halt, cringing at her feet and gazing up at her with limpid brown eyes. A piece of mangled felt and a feather hung from his mouth. 'Oh, Charlie,' she whispered, 'what have you done?'

Maida emerged from the room holding up the tattered remnants of her trilby. 'That evil brute has ruined my one and only remaining hat. This cost me a fortune in Penberthy's and he has ripped it to pieces. I want you both out of here now. This moment. Right away.'

Chapter Six

'I'll buy you another hat, Maida.' Dave had his back to Susan but she could see his shoulders shaking and when he turned to look at her he was grinning from ear to ear.

'I'm so sorry,' Susan said, keeping a straight face with difficulty. The enormity of what Charlie had done was not lost on her, but she could see the funny side of things and Dave was not helping.

'This was a model hat.' Maida tossed the soggy mass onto the floor so that it landed at her brother's feet. 'It cost me a week's wages and now it's ruined, thanks to that creature from hell. I've always disliked dogs and that one is a little beast.'

Charlie looked up at Susan and wagged his tail. She bent down and seized him by the collar. 'I'll shut him in my room.'

'It won't be yours when my nephew arrives home,' Maida said angrily. 'You can't expect him to sleep on the settee.'

'Now, now, Maida.' Dave advanced on her as warily as a lion tamer facing an angry big cat in the circus ring. 'Don't get in a state. Tony won't mind where he lays his head, so that's not a problem, and

I said I'll stump up for another titfer. I suggest you take it easy until lunch is ready. It won't be long, will it, Susan?'

'It will be ready at one o'clock, as usual.'

Dave shot her a grateful smile. 'There you are, Maida. This girl's got me organised and eating regular as clockwork. She's a smashing little cook and she makes a scrummy suet pud.'

'Spare me the schoolboy slang,' Maida said, sighing. 'I suppose a bath is out of the question?'

Dave nodded. 'Sorry, love. We had our five inches of hot water last night.' He flushed from his collar to the top of his bald pate. 'Separately, of course.'

'Don't be smutty, David.' Maida turned her back on him. 'I suppose a strip wash will have to do. Call me when lunch is ready.' She retreated into the bedroom and closed the door.

Dave looked so embarrassed that Susan felt sorry for him. 'I'll have to find another place to live soon,' she said softly. 'Your sister doesn't approve of me, and Charlie hasn't made a good impression. I'm really sorry about the hat.' She was still holding Charlie by the collar, but on hearing his name he decided to lie down and waggle his short legs in the air, offering his tummy for a tickle. She released him and he leapt up totally unabashed and unaware of the trouble he had caused.

Dave bent down to pick up the mangled hat. 'She'll get over it, and I won't hear talk about you leaving. This is your home, Susan. Maida will just have to get used to the idea.'

'I don't want to cause a rift in your family, and I don't want to ruin Tony's leave. He should have my room when he comes home.'

'Don't worry about him. I'm sure he'll be okay on the sofa for a couple of nights, and Maida will find a place of her own before the start of the spring term. She won't want to commute every day from here to Hackney.' With an attempt at a reassuring smile, he turned on his heel and headed for the staircase.

Susan was not convinced by his reasoning, but to prevent any further upsets she took Charlie to her room. She was relieved that Maida had turned her nose up at the boxroom, but she worried about what Tony would say when he arrived home. It was one thing to be ousted from his bed by his aunt, but he might not be so happy when he discovered that the girl who had pretended to live in the posh house in Elsworthy Road was now occupying the spare room. In all fairness, she decided, if anyone should sleep on the sofa it ought to be her. The thought of Tony occupying her bed was acceptable, if not slightly erotic. She felt herself blushing at the thought, and with a final pat on Charlie's head she left him, feeling extremely mean when he tried to follow her and she was forced to shut the door on him. His soulful expression haunted her as she finished preparing lunch.

It was an uncomfortable meal. Dave was unusually silent but Maida talked incessantly, pausing briefly while she ate and then continuing a monologue that went on uninterrupted through the main course followed by the dessert of stewed apple and custard. Having consumed everything with gusto, she dabbed her lips with a napkin. 'You must have used up half your weekly milk ration in one meal. Don't you think that was a bit extravagant?'

She was looking at her brother but the criticism was obviously aimed at Susan. She stood up and began clearing the table. 'I balance it out carefully,' she said, forcing herself to remain calm. 'And I used half milk and half water for the batter.'

Dave cleared his throat nervously. 'Susan knows what she's doing when it comes to cooking. I've never eaten so well in years.'

'Well, Christine was an excellent cook,' Maida said, seemingly determined to have the last word. 'She may have been a scatterbrain, but she was good in the kitchen.'

'I've got to get back to the shop.' Dave leapt to his feet, pushing his chair back so that it scraped across the linoleum. 'I'll see you girls later.' He hurried off without giving his sister a chance to comment.

Maida rose more slowly. 'I'll take my coffee in the lounge. Unless it's that bottled stuff, in which case I'll have a cup of tea. Milk. No sugar.' She swept out of the kitchen leaving Susan to do the washing-up. It was, she thought, just like old times, only now it was Maida who was calling the shots and not Mrs Kemp.

She had just finished washing the cutlery when Dave slipped back into the room with an apologetic grin. He picked up a tea towel but Susan took it from him, shaking her head. 'It's all right,' she said, smiling. 'I can manage. Maybe it would be best if you went and sat with your sister for a while before you go down to the shop. She must feel a bit down after being bombed out.'

'You're right, of course. But I don't want you to feel that you have to wait on her hand and foot. You're not a servant here, Susan. I hope you know that.'

She patted his hand, leaving a slippery trail of soap suds on his fingers. 'Of course I do. You've been like a dad to me, and I'll always be grateful.'

'I hope you didn't take any notice of what Maida said just now. I mean, I never thought about you in that way.' A telltale flush suffused his face and he pulled a hanky out of his pocket and began polishing his glasses. 'If I had a daughter, Susan, I'd want her to be just like you.' He replaced his spectacles and moved towards the doorway. 'I'll take Charlie for a walk when I close the shop this evening. Poor little chap; he must think he's in prison.'

Susan smiled. 'It serves him right for destroying your sister's hat. He's got to learn.'

'You're a hard woman, Susan Banks.' Dave tempered his words with a wink and a brief salute. 'I'll go and keep Maida company for a while. You will join us when you've finished, won't you?'

'Of course.' She plunged her hands into the rapidly cooling water and began scrubbing away at the baking tin. She could hear Dave's footsteps retreating towards the lounge, followed by the sound of a military band emanating from the wireless, which ceased as he closed the door. She sighed. Her visions of a peaceful Christmas had faded and she was left with a heavy feeling in her stomach. She had been happier living in the tiny flat than she had ever been in the big house with the Kemps, but she had known deep down that it could not last, and now her fears had been proved right. She knew that Maida was an adversary to be reckoned with, and her overt disapproval of their living arrangements had made Susan feel uncomfortable. There had never been anything remotely sexual in Dave's attitude towards her, but she had seen the way he reacted when she had likened him to a father figure. She had never thought of him in any other way, but Maida's reaction had turned what seemed natural and easy into something completely different. She tipped the dirty water down the sink and picked up the tea towel. Perhaps Tony could put things straight when he came home. She had a feeling that he could wrap his irascible aunt around his little finger. If anyone could sort out the tangled web of emotions created by her appearance on the scene, she was certain it was Tony.

When he did not put in appearance that afternoon Dave was beginning to fret and Susan was also worried. Dave had attempted to telephone the airfield but had not been able to get through to anyone who could give him any information, and there was nothing they could do other than sit and wait for him to turn up.

Next morning Susan was up early, taking Charlie for a walk on Primrose Hill before getting breakfast for Dave. Maida rose much later and spent a good half an hour in the bathroom before demanding tea and toast, which she ate in the lounge listening to the BBC news. Susan spent the morning in the kitchen, preparing lunch and making mince pies. Preserves had not yet been rationed and she had bought the last jar of mincemeat in the grocer's shop. Although he would not admit it, she knew that Dave had a sweet tooth and she was pleased to be able to make something that he would enjoy eating even more than the turkey that was sitting in the meat safe outside the back door waiting to be cooked next day.

In the middle of the morning Dave had just sneaked into the kitchen for a cup of tea and a mince pie when the doorbell rang.

'Tony! He's here at last.' His glum expression melted into a huge smile and he headed for the stairs. 'I'll let him in. Put the kettle on again, Susan.'

Maida reappeared at the sound of the doorbell like a genie from Aladdin's lamp, and she stood at the top of the stairs steady as a rock and just about as immovable. Susan remained in the kitchen, and her hands were shaking as she relit the gas beneath the kettle. She spooned tea into the warmed pot and waited.

Maida's reaction was the first hint she had that all was not well.

'Who's this, Dave? Where's Tony? Has something happened to him?'

Maida's large body filled the doorway and Susan had to stand on tiptoe in order to catch a glimpse of their visitor, but all she could see was the top of a peaked cap, which was quickly removed to reveal a head of wavy auburn hair.

'This is Tony's friend, Colin Forbes. My sister, Maida.' Dave sounded cheerful enough, but Susan was quick to hear the note of disappointment in his voice.

Maida held out her hand. 'How do you do, Flight Lieutenant?'

'Colin, please.' He shook her hand. 'Actually it translates as First Officer in the Air Transport Auxiliary, ma'am. I'm delighted to meet you, Miss Richards. Tony has told me all about you.'

Susan could have sworn that Maida blushed, but she soon recovered herself. 'Where is my nephew? Why isn't he here?'

Dave shook his head. 'That's the devil of it, Maida. Tony's leave has been cancelled thanks to the Luftwaffe.'

'The bombing raids on Southampton and Hamble have left a bit of a mess,' Colin added hastily, 'and I'm afraid Tony drew the short straw. He asked me to come and see his father and tell him in person.'

'That was kind of you,' Dave said gruffly. 'But where are my manners? Won't you stay and have something to eat? You must be hungry after your journey, and I'm sure that Susan can rustle up something tasty.' He beckoned to her. 'Come and say hello, love.'

Somewhat reluctantly, Susan edged past Maida and squeezed into the narrow hallway. 'Hello, Colin.'

'Susan,' he said, shaking her hand. 'You're even prettier than Tony said. He told me all about how you met and he was really sorry that he couldn't get home for Christmas.'

She met his smiling gaze shyly. 'I've made some mince pies and they're still quite warm.' She tried not to stare, but he could have stepped from the pages of one of the movie magazines like *Picturegoer*, which Pamela had read avidly and concealed beneath the pillows on her bed together with bars of Cadbury's chocolate. His green eyes were fringed with thick, dark lashes and his hair waved back from a high forehead.

'That sounds fantastic, Susan.' He glanced at

Dave. 'Is that all right with you, sir? I mean, I don't want to take your rations.'

'Go on, old chap. Any friend of Tony's is welcome here.' Dave backed towards the stairs. 'Got some work to finish in the shop but make yourself at home, Colin. I'll see you later. I hope you'll stay for supper.'

'I've really got to go and find a hotel, sir. But thanks all the same.'

Maida eyed him curiously. 'Haven't you got a home to go to?'

'Not within easy reach, Miss Richards. My father died a long time ago and my mother remarried. They emigrated to Canada in 1938, and my grandparents live in Scotland, which is a bit far to travel on a forty-eight hour pass, so I thought I'd spend Christmas in London.'

Dave paused at the top of the staircase. 'You must stay here, son. No question about it. I'm afraid you'll have to sleep on the sofa, but we'd love to have your company for Christmas. Wouldn't we, girls?'

Maida pursed her lips. 'If you say so, David. I'll leave Susan to sort the bedding out. I think I'll go for a lie-down before lunch, if you'll excuse me.' Without waiting for a response she headed for her room.

'I wouldn't want to put anyone out,' Colin said anxiously.

'Take no notice of my sister. She's been bombed out and hasn't quite recovered from the shock.' Dave started down the stairs. 'Look after him, Susan.' He disappeared into the gloom below, leaving Susan standing awkwardly on the landing with Colin. She retreated into the kitchen.

'Would you like a sandwich, Colin? Lunch won't be ready for another couple of hours at least. The gas pressure is pretty low today.'

'Actually I had something to eat at Waterloo.' He took a seat at the kitchen table. 'But a cuppa would be most welcome.'

Susan busied herself making the tea. 'You ought to have my room, but that would mean Charlie would be running loose in the flat.' She paused, realising what she had just said. 'Charlie's a puppy. I'm afraid I let Tony think he was my boyfriend.'

'Yes, he told me about your little joke,' Colin said, laughing. 'Don't look so worried, Susan. His father explained everything, and Tony's a very understanding bloke.'

She almost dropped the milk jug. 'I didn't mean it to happen like that. I was embarrassed, and I said the first thing that came into my head.'

'He saw the funny side of things. Anyway, he's a big boy; he can take a knock back or two. There are plenty of girls who fall for the uniform, so it probably did him good when you didn't collapse at his feet.'

The image this conjured up in her mind made her giggle. 'Has he got many girl friends?'

'One or two, but nothing serious.'

Susan digested this in silence while she made the

tea. She had been longing to see Tony again, but she was faced with this handsome stranger who was looking at her with a twinkle in his eyes and a charming smile that made her head spin. She poured his tea and placed it in front of him. 'If you don't want a sandwich, would you like a mince pie?' It seemed a bit feeble as far as conversation went, but she could not think of anything else to say. He must think she was a complete idiot.

He smiled. 'I'd love one. I could smell them as I came upstairs, and it took me back to my childhood. Mum was a wonderful cook and her pastry just melted in the mouth.' He took one from the plate she passed to him.

'It's not easy to make pastry with so little fat,' she murmured, watching anxiously while he took a bite.

'Then you're a magician,' he said, licking crumbs from his lips. 'These are just as good as Mum's. Maybe even better.'

Basking in the warmth of his enthusiasm, Susan could not feel completely at ease until she was certain that he knew the truth about her. 'Tony did tell you everything about me, I suppose?'

He sipped his tea. 'If you mean that business about the family you worked for, then yes, he did. Forget it, Susan. We all do and say things on the spur of the moment and regret them later.'

'It was a stupid thing to do.'

'If I had a pound for every idiotic thing I'd done in the past, I'd be a rich man.'

A huge weight seemed to have been lifted from her shoulders and she smiled with relief. 'Have another mince pie, Colin.'

'No, thanks. That would be sheer greed, but I would like another cup of tea.' He pushed his empty cup towards her. 'Would it put you out if I stayed here for a couple of nights?'

Startled by the question, and unused to being asked for her opinion, she poured the tea, adding a dash of milk. 'It has nothing to do with me. If Dave says it's all right, then it is.'

'But you live here too, and you're the one who will have all the extra work. I can't imagine Miss Richards setting to and washing dishes or peeling potatoes. She doesn't look the domesticated type.'

This made her laugh outright. 'She is a bit fierce, but then it's not my place to say so.'

Colin frowned. 'Stop it, Susan.'

'Stop what? What did I say?'

'Tony told me how that family treated you and it's left its mark. Don't take this the wrong way, because I know we've only just met, but your opinion is as good as anyone's. As to everyone knowing their place, I think that old-fashioned nonsense will be as dead as the dinosaurs when this war is over.'

She stared at him in amazement. 'Mrs Kemp would have you shot at dawn for saying things like that.'

It was his turn to laugh. 'Well, the Mrs Kemps of this world will soon be history too. Now, I've got a suggestion to make. What do you say to a night out in town?'

'With you?'

He looked round the kitchen with an expansive gesture. 'I don't see anyone else. Yes, with me. It's Christmas Eve and I was planning to go somewhere nice this evening for a meal and perhaps some dancing; that is if I could find a girl who didn't mind her feet being trodden on occasionally.'

'I can't dance,' Susan said hastily. 'I wouldn't know how.'

'Then it's high time you learned. I'll take that as a "yes", shall I?'

'I can't. I've got to make supper for Dave and Miss Richards.'

'I'm sure they could manage with fish and chips for one night. I'll go out and get it myself.'

She was tempted. She had never been to a restaurant, let alone a posh one up West where they had a dance floor, although she had seen them at the pictures. But then reality struck and she shook her head. 'I haven't got anything to wear.'

'You're pretty enough to get away with wearing a sack, not that I'd suggest it was the latest fashion, but I'd be proud to have you on my arm no matter what.'

'You would?'

He nodded emphatically. 'And Tony will be green with envy when I tell him I've taken you out for the evening.'

'Will he really?'

Colin's lips twitched but his expression remained serious. 'Of course. He couldn't stop talking about you when he came back from his last leave.'

'What did he say?'

'Now that would be telling.' Colin drained his teacup and stood up. 'Shall I go and ask Mr Richards if he'll allow you to have an evening off?'

Susan nodded wordlessly.

In her red woollen dress with her hair swept up at the sides and hanging in a loose pageboy at the back, Susan felt like a different person. She could only see herself in sections using the hand mirror in her room, but even so, the result was startling. The schoolgirl image had given way to that of a young woman with style. She might not be the best dressed female in the restaurant of Colin's choice, but she would not disgrace him. She sat down on the bed to put on her tan leather sandals and was dismayed to see that they looked completely wrong. Her brogues were even more unsuitable. She was on the brink of tears when there was a knock on her door. Charlie leapt off the bed and scratched at the paintwork.

'Come in,' Susan murmured, dabbing her eyes with a hanky.

Dave put his head round the door. 'Are you ready, Susan?' He frowned. 'What's up, love? Why the long face? You look smashing.'

She wiggled her bare toes. 'I can't go out, Dave.

I haven't got any stockings and my shoes are all wrong.'

He thought for a moment. 'There are Christine's things. I know you don't like the idea, but if she was here now I know she'd be only too pleased to kit you out.'

'I don't know. It doesn't seem right.'

He bent down to pat Charlie on the head. 'I came to collect this little fellow for his walk, but he can wait for a bit. Come with me, love.' He left without waiting for her answer and Charlie followed him, wagging his tail, leaving Susan no alternative but to go after them.

In his room Dave had opened the wardrobe door and was rifling through the box of shoes. 'There are all sorts here, some of them hardly worn. Have a look through and see if there's any you fancy.' He stood aside and went to sit on the bed.

It was too tempting an offer to refuse and Susan went down on her knees to pick over the pairs of shoes packed neatly in paper bags.

'What's going on?' Maida marched into the room, standing arms akimbo and frowning at Susan, who had a pair of high-heeled black court shoes in her hand.

'None of your beeswax, Maida,' Dave said cheerfully.

'Don't tell me that you're still hoarding Christine's things.'

'I know it's time to let them go. I've been living

on memories far too long.' Dave nodded to Susan. 'Take what you like, love. I should have got rid of them years ago.'

'I've been telling you that for ages.' Maida went to the wardrobe and sorted through the clothes. She pulled out a short fur jacket. 'You can start by throwing out this moth-eaten old thing. I don't suppose the girl has a warm coat.'

'The girl has ears, Maida.' Dave grabbed Charlie by the collar as he lunged at a shoe. 'But you're a genius, old girl. That little coat will be just the thing on a cold night and it will suit her down to the ground. You take it, Susan. You'll knock 'em dead in the Ritz or wherever young Colin takes you.'

Maida sniffed. 'I hope he realises that this is a respectable household.' She tossed the fur jacket at Susan. 'And you're to be back at a decent time, young lady. No gallivanting until the early hours. I've already warned Colin that there's to be no funny business. You've taken responsibility for a minor, David. It's up to you to see that she doesn't come to any harm. Heaven knows I don't approve, but there's no fool like an old fool.'

'Please don't speak to Mr Richards like that.' Susan leapt to her feet with the shoes still clutched tightly in her hands. 'And I'm not stupid. I was brought up to know right from wrong in the orphanage and I'm certain that Colin is a gentleman, or I wouldn't have agreed to go out with him. You're insulting both of us if you think we'd do anything we shouldn't.'

'Well said, love.' Dave clapped his hands but in doing so he let go of Charlie's collar and he made a dive for the fur jacket. It took the combined efforts of Susan and Dave to wrestle it from him without damaging the lining.

'He has to go,' Maida said icily. 'And I'm shocked that you allow a slip of a girl to speak to me in that tone of voice.' She eyed Susan with a disdainful toss of her head. 'You'd better watch your tongue, or you'll be out on your ear before you can say Merry Christmas.' She stalked out of the room, slamming the door behind her.

Susan wiped the dog spittle off the gleaming brown fur. It smelt decidedly of mothballs and there were worn patches under the sleeves, but it was still the most glamorous garment she had ever held in her hands. 'It's not going to work,' she said sadly. 'Your sister is never going to approve of me, no matter what I do.'

Dave rescued another shoe from Charlie and put it back in the box. 'Give her time, love. She's not a bad old stick when you get used to her.'

Susan slipped her feet into the court shoes. They fitted exactly but she could feel the indentations of the dead woman's toes and it sent a shiver down her spine. 'I can't take your wife's things, Dave. It doesn't feel right.'

He moved to the door and opened it. 'Don't let it spoil your evening, love. Go with Colin and have a lovely time. It's Christmas Eve and you're both young. You should be out enjoying yourself.'

She glanced at Christine's photograph on the dressing table, and she seemed to be smiling directly at her. 'Thanks for everything. I won't let you down.'

'I know you won't.' He took a key from his waistcoat pocket and pressed it into her hand. 'Let yourself in, and I'll keep Charlie with me tonight so he won't give the game away by making a noise. Have fun, love.'

She kissed him on the cheek and slipping the fur jacket round her shoulders she left the room. Colin was waiting for her at the top of the stairs. He whistled as she approached him. 'You look terrific, Susan. An absolute peach.'

He was every girl's dream; handsome, dashing and sophisticated. Susan's stomach lurched and she felt sick. Panic seized her. Virginia Kemp would have known how to behave in company, and Pamela might not be the most glamorous female in London but she was well read and could hold an intelligent conversation with her escort. 'I've got to get my handbag and gasmask,' Susan said, making for her room. She closed the door behind her, leaning against it while her heartbeats returned to normal. She hesitated for a moment, taking deep breaths. It was all too good to be true and she had the horrible feeling that it was not going to last. She was excited and terrified at the same time. Colin might find her attractive but he would soon see through her. She was still a girl from the orphanage, and nothing that she was wearing was new. Everything apart from her undies had belonged to another woman. She had no true identity. Everyone, including Colin, would see through her and realise that she was a complete and utter fraud. She could not go with him. It was certain to be a complete disaster. She would have to make an excuse. A sudden headache. A fainting fit. Anything.

'Come on, Susan.' Colin knocked on her door. 'We'll never get a table at the Trocadero if we leave it too late.'

Chapter Seven

She knew she was being a coward. Amy Johnson, her heroine, had flown solo to Australia and from London to Cape Town; she would not have behaved in such a weak-kneed fashion.

'Are you ready, Susan? It's getting late.'

She took a deep breath. 'Coming.' She hitched her gasmask case over her shoulder and tucked her handbag under her arm. This was an evening of firsts. The first time she had worn anything remotely glamorous; the first time she had been asked out on a date by a handsome young man, and the first time she had been taken to a restaurant anywhere, let alone up West. She would put the past behind her and enjoy herself.

The Trocadero restaurant in Shaftesbury Avenue had been built at the end of the last century and it was the most impressive place that Susan had ever seen. The murals on the walls of the grand staircase depicted dramatic Arthurian scenes and the interior was decorated in the opera baroque style, which quite took her breath away.

A rather pompous and intimidating maître d'hôtel demanded to know if they had booked a table, but

Colin seemed in complete control of the situation. Susan watched in awe as he slipped something into the man's hand. It was obviously money, and it must have been quite a generous tip, as the man's demeanour changed quite suddenly and he summoned a waiter who led them to a table close to the dance floor. Lost in the splendour of the setting and intoxicated by the exciting atmosphere, she forgot the war, the dangers and the hardships of the past year. The patrons were mostly young, and many of the men were in uniform. The girls were done up to the nines and everyone seemed to be enjoying themselves. There was music and laughter and if the food was not up to the standard that people like Colin expected, Susan remained uncritical, savouring every mouthful.

Colin ordered a bottle of Graves and he sipped his, watching her with a smile hovering on his lips. 'I thought you might prefer white wine rather than red. This was a good year, and it's not too dry.'

To oblige him she tasted it and nodded. 'It's nice, but I don't think Dave would approve.'

'One glass won't do you any harm. Anyway, would you like to dance?'

Her worst fears were realised as she gazed at the couples gyrating round the floor as if they were glued together. 'I really don't know how, Colin.'

He rose to his feet, holding out his hand. 'There isn't much room to manoeuvre, so no one will notice if we miss a beat or two. I'll promise not to tread on your toes, if you'll promise not to tread on mine.'

She reached for her glass and took a large mouthful of wine. Unused to alcohol in any form, she felt the effects almost immediately, but it gave her the courage to get up and allow him to lead her onto the dance floor. With his arms around her she found herself seduced by the rhythm of the music, and to her surprise it was easy to follow his sinuous movements. At first she concentrated hard, trying not to totter in the unaccustomed high heels, but as she began to relax she discovered to her astonishment that it came quite naturally to her. She could have danced all night, but eventually the music stopped and he led her back to their table.

'That wasn't too hard, was it?'

She smiled, shaking her head. 'No. It was lovely, Colin. Thank you.'

He reached across the table to lay his hand on hers. 'No. Thank you, Susan. You're a delightful partner and a charming companion. I'm sorry for Tony, but I'm glad his bad luck gave me the chance of meeting you.'

She knew she was blushing. Her heart was beating faster than normal and she felt deliciously light-headed. It might have been the wine, or the excitement of the dance, or perhaps it was being the object of someone's admiration and receiving his undivided attention.

The waiter materialised at their table, offering a

leather-bound menu to Susan. 'Would Madame care for a dessert?'

She glanced anxiously at Colin but he smiled his assent. 'Of course.'

'Could I have ice cream?' she murmured. 'Chocolate ice cream.'

'Of course, madame.' The waiter passed the menu to Colin.

He waved it away. 'I'll have the same.'

'Very well, sir.' The waiter glided off in the direction of the swing doors leading to the kitchens.

'Do you like ice cream too?' Susan asked eagerly. 'I thought you might think it was a bit childish.'

'I love ice cream, but I have to be honest. I'd much rather have one of your mince pies.'

This made Susan giggle and she glanced round to see if there were any other waiters hovering nearby. 'They would be most offended if they heard you say that.'

He refilled their glasses. 'I meant it, Susan. If your pastry is anything to go by I'd say that you're an excellent cook. If only they would employ someone half as good as you in our canteen at the aerodrome, we'd be in seventh heaven.'

'What's it like flying an aeroplane?' Susan angled her head, longing to hear first hand how it felt to be free as a bird.

'There's nothing to it.' His eyes sparkled with enthusiasm. 'You just climb into the cockpit and twiddle a few knobs and the thing takes off. Still I'd rather be flying a Hurricane or a Spit than trying to teach bone-headed civilian pilots who only yesterday were working in a bank or an office.'

'So you're an instructor like Tony.'

'I am now, but I flew Hurricanes from the outset. I survived a good many tours of duty, and then my luck ran out over the Channel. I was picked up pretty quickly, but I caught pneumonia and after a bout of pleurisy I was told I wasn't fit for active service. I was given the chance to become a flying instructor and I took it. I reckoned that if I was a cat I'd have used up eight of my nine lives, and I thought I'd hang on to the last one.'

'But you're still doing a splendid job,' Susan said enthusiastically. 'I wish I could go up in a plane. I love the sound of their engines droning like giant bees on a summer's day, and I've followed everything that Amy Johnson has done, either in the newspapers or on the Pathé news at the cinema.'

He sat back in his seat, regarding her with a cynical smile. 'You really are an enthusiast, aren't you, my pet? Maybe one day I'll take you for a joy ride and show you what it feels like to soar in the wild blue yonder.'

She caught her breath on a gasp of delight. 'Would you, Colin? Would you really?'

He smiled lazily. 'It's a promise.' He rose to his feet. 'Come on, this is a waltz. Let's make the most of this evening.'

The inference that this might be their one and

only chance to be together was not lost on Susan, and this time she went willingly onto the dance floor. She felt lighter than thistledown as they moved in time to the romantic strains of a Viennese waltz. Their ice cream was melting on the plates by the time they returned to the table, but Susan did not care. If the world ended this minute, she could not have been happier. In the gilt and plush surroundings and in the company of couples savouring their brief time together, it was like wonderland to a girl more used to scrubbing floors and clearing up other people's mess than living the high life.

All too soon it was over and they emerged into the cold night air to find themselves in bright moonlight. Frost sparkled on the pavements and for once there was no sound of anti-aircraft guns, sirens or the drone of aeroplanes. Colin pulled her into his arms and kissed her. 'Merry Christmas, Susan.'

She gasped as the cold air filled her lungs, but his lips were warm and his breath tasted of chocolate ice cream and wine. Her head was spinning with the thrill of it all. He linked her hand through the crook of his arm. 'Let's get you home before you catch your death of cold.'

There was no danger of that: she was afire with excitement. The thrilling ambience of the restaurant, the music and dancing, together with the magical feeling of Christmas Eve, made her feel ready for anything. She could have walked all the way to Swiss Cottage without her feet having touched the ground.

In the end they caught the last bus and when they got off at their stop they strolled, arm in arm, to the cycle shop. He kissed her again when they reached the side door, and she returned the embrace enthusiastically. His kisses were quite unlike those forced on her by Dudley, and she relaxed against him with a sigh of contentment. 'Thank you for tonight, Colin,' she whispered. 'I'll remember it always.'

He released her with a flattering degree of reluctance. 'You're a sweet girl, Susan. We must do it again some time.'

Her heart swelled inside her breast, making it hard to breathe. She fumbled in her handbag for the door key, and her hand was shaking as she placed it in the lock. She opened the door and went inside, pausing in the pitch dark at the foot of the stairs. She could feel Colin's warm breath on the back of her neck and she turned to him, raising her face in anticipation of his kiss, which was more intoxicating than all the wine in France, but he merely brushed her lips with his. He held her for a second or two and then released her, giving her a gentle push in the direction of the stairs. 'It's late, Susan. High time you were tucked up in bed.'

She paused with one foot on the bottom tread. 'It's Christmas Day.'

'So it is.'

Even in the dark she could feel him smiling. 'I haven't got a present for you, Colin.'

He moved onto the step beside her. 'You've already given me a night to remember, my sweet.' He gave her a hug. 'We'd best keep the noise down. I don't fancy being berated by Miss Richards at one o'clock in the morning.'

She felt a tug of disappointment. So it was over. Their wonderful night had ended in the narrow stairway with the smell of the cycle shop in her nostrils and an ache in her heart. She made her way up the staircase, but she stopped outside her bedroom door, turning to him with a smile. A stray moonbeam filtered through the skylight on the landing, and she could see his eyes lustrous and dark with desire. She felt drunk with power and filled with a need that she could not quite define. 'Shall we have a cup of cocoa?' she whispered in the hope of keeping him to herself for a little while longer.

His answer was a kiss that took her breath away and made her go weak at the knees, but he released her suddenly and placed his finger on her lips. 'It's bedtime for you, kid. I'll see you in the morning.'

She could not speak. Her heart was too full and the magic of the night held her in its thrall. Wordlessly, she entered her room and closed the door. Charlie threw himself at her and she lifted him in her arms, cuddling him as she leaned against the door. Dave must have decided he was better off shut in her room after all. She wondered if Colin was still standing outside, and she was tempted to open it and lure him into her bed, but she knew that would be as foolish as it would be wrong. She had only a rough idea of what transpired between men and women in the privacy of their bedrooms, but her information had been garnered from the whispered conversations of the girls in the orphanage dormitory. Until now it had seemed rather ridiculous, if not slightly unpleasant, and Dudley's attempted violation of her person had confirmed that impression, but suddenly she was seeing things in a different light. The emotions that Tony had stirred in her had simply been heightened by a romantic evening with a man who she suspected was well practised in the art of seduction, and now her heart was beating nineteen to the dozen.

She put her ear to the door and was disappointed to hear Colin's footsteps fading into the distance as he went to the lounge. She had left a pillow and some blankets on one of the chairs before they went out, in the full knowledge that Maida would not stoop to do anything as menial, and Dave would forget.

She did not bother to put the light on as this would have necessitated closing the blackout curtains and shutting out the star-spangled sky. She put Charlie down on the bed and undressed slowly, caressing her bare body with the flat of her hand and pretending that it was Colin who was making love to her. A feeling of guilt washed over her and she shivered. It had been love at first sight when she fell off her bicycle and Tony had come to her aid.

He had been her Sir Lancelot, a knight of old, just like the ones she had read about. How could she be so fickle?

It was bitterly cold in her room and her skin was soon covered in goose pimples. She pulled her serviceable flannelette nightgown over her head. What sort of person fell in love with someone and allowed his best friend to turn her silly head? She climbed into bed and lay gazing up at the stars, but she was exhausted and her eyelids were heavy. She fell asleep to the strains of a Viennese waltz repeating over and over again in her head.

Next morning she was up before dawn and busying herself in the kitchen. It really was Christmas Day now, and she was as excited as a small child. The staff in the orphanage had always made a huge effort during the festive season. Well-wishers had donated toys and games and there was always plenty of food to go round. Christmas had been a special time even then, although she had always tried to imagine what it must be like to have a real home with loving parents and brothers and sisters. Now she had a family, of sorts. Dave was, she thought, the nearest that she would get to having a real father. She would cook a really special Christmas dinner for him, and as it was the season of goodwill she would include Maida, even though she was not her most favourite person in the world.

It went without saying that she wanted to impress Colin. She could never forget Tony, but last night had been magical and Colin's kisses had been more than a casual peck on the cheek. As for herself, surely she could not have longed for intimacy with a man unless she loved him just a little bit? That was how it worked in all the romantic novels she had borrowed from the library. Perhaps she had mistaken her feelings for Tony after all. Colin might whisk her away to Gretna Green and they would be married. Susan Forbes. Mrs Colin Forbes. She chuckled at the thought and raked the ashes in the boiler until they glowed red. She tipped in just enough coke to keep it going in order to heat the water and warm the flat. Two hundredweights a week did not allow for extravagant use of either coal or coke, but today was special. She wanted the best for Colin, and that did not include washing and shaving in cold water.

She had prepared the turkey for the oven, filling the crop with homemade stuffing and covering the legs with the greaseproof paper that came wrapped around butter and lard. Mrs Kemp had been parsimonious when it came to housekeeping, and Susan had learned to be thrifty and never to waste a thing. She set the turkey aside to go in the oven a bit later, and turned her attention to peeling potatoes. She was humming snatches of the *Blue Danube* waltz when the door opened and Colin entered the kitchen. Her breath caught in her throat at the sight of him. His hair was tousled and he needed a shave. In his shirtsleeves with the top buttons undone to reveal a little of his bare chest he looked younger and endearingly vulnerable. She wanted to throw her arms around his neck and hug him, but she was still clutching a potato in one hand and the peeler in the other.

'Is there any hot water, Susan?' he said, grinning ruefully and rubbing the stubble on his chin. 'I'm in desperate need of a wash and shave.'

Her feeling of euphoria plummeted like a stone. She had not expected him to sweep her off her feet and ravish her at this hour of the morning, but she had thought he might have said something a little more romantic.

'I've got the boiler going. The water should be warm enough by now.'

'Thanks.' He made to leave the room, but he hesitated in the doorway. 'I know I said it before, but merry Christmas, Susan. I really enjoyed last night.'

'So did I. Do you think you might come to London next time you get some leave?'

He shook his head. 'I doubt it. I usually travel to Scotland. My grandparents are getting on a bit and I like to spend as much time as I can with them. They virtually brought me up after Mum remarried, and I've got quite a few friends living up there too.'

Her heart sank so far that she felt she was treading on it. 'Anyone special?'

'There is, actually, but she's still living in the

Highlands. Morag and I have had an understanding for a long time. I can only hope she doesn't get fed up with waiting for me.'

I would, Susan thought sadly. I'd wait forever and a day if you were sweet on me. She managed a smile. 'I see. Well, she's a lucky girl.'

'And the chap who steals your heart will be a fortunate fellow. Now I'd better grab the bathroom before Miss Richards gets up.' He blew her a kiss as he left the room.

The door closed on him and Susan stabbed the point of the peeler into the potato. What an innocent little fool I must be, she thought, giving it another savage jab. He was just amusing himself. She brushed angry tears from her eyes, looking up expectantly as the door opened again, but this time it was Dave who burst into the kitchen.

'Merry Christmas, love,' Dave said, smiling. 'Did you have a good time last night? I didn't hear you come in.'

She dropped the potato and the peeler into the water and bent down to make a fuss of Charlie. 'Yes, thank you, Dave. It was lovely.'

'You must tell us all about it at breakfast.' Dave moved to the stove and picked up the kettle. 'I'll make us a pot of tea and cut the bread for toast while you finish peeling the spuds. Young Colin's in the bathroom and Maida's still sound asleep, but we won't wait for her to wake up.'

'I'll take her breakfast on a tray,' Susan said,

picking up the abandoned potato. 'It is Christmas, after all.'

After breakfast, and when Maida had eventually finished her ablutions and had put the finishing touches to her toilette, Dave gathered them all together in the lounge. He had lit the fire but the room was still chilly. Maida sat on the settee, muffled in a thick cardigan. Colin took a seat by the hearth and Susan sat as far away from him as was possible in a relatively small room. She was attempting to maintain a cheerful manner, but she was far from happy. She felt foolish in the extreme and utterly naïve. She could not in all honesty put all the blame on Colin. He had assumed that she was much more worldly wise than she was; it was as simple as that. Just as he was now oblivious to the turmoil he had wrought in her emotions.

Dave had positioned himself by the Christmas tree. 'Now we're all here, I thought we could open our presents. Christine and I always did it this way when Tony was a nipper.' He bent down to retrieve a parcel wrapped in brown paper, which he handed to his sister. 'This is a little something for you, Maida.' He delved beneath the spiky green branches and pulled out another, much smaller parcel, and gave it to Susan. 'This is for you, love. I hope you like it.'

She took it with a grateful smile. 'I'm sure I will.'

Maida had already unwrapped hers and pulled out a Cossack-style fur hat. 'Thank you, Dave. All we want now is ten feet of snow and a troika and I'll be in the latest fashion.'

He grinned. 'Can't arrange that, old girl. But you never know.' He turned to Colin, handing him a bottle encased in a brown paper bag. 'I got this at the off licence last night. It's not very original, but I thought you might need something warming when you travel back to Southampton tomorrow.'

'You're going so soon?' The words had slipped from Susan's lips before she had time to stop herself. 'I mean, I'd forgotten that you had such a short leave.'

'Yes. More's the pity,' Colin said with a rueful smile. He peered inside the bag. 'Brandy. That's super, sir. You shouldn't have, but thanks anyway.'

Susan wished that she had thought to buy him something yesterday, however small, but everything had happened so quickly.

'Aren't you going to open yours, Susan?'

Dave's voice broke into her thoughts and she jumped. 'Yes, of course.' Beneath the layer of paper was a cardboard box and inside it was a silver filigree brooch in the shape of a butterfly. She held it up for all to see. 'Thank you, Dave. It's really beautiful.'

'It's the nearest thing I could find to wings, and I thought you were more like a pretty little butterfly than an eagle or a seagull.' Dave glanced warily at his sister, but she merely raised her eyebrows and had the grace to remain silent. 'I know you'd love to fly, but maybe one day, Susan.'

She jumped up to fling her arms around him and kissed his leathery cheek. 'You're the kindest man I ever met. Thank you so much.' She sat down again, realising that Maida was scowling at her. Once again she seemed to have overstepped the invisible mark. She pinned the brooch to her jumper. 'I love it.'

'Tony sent some gifts for you all,' Colin said, delving into a carrier bag that he had placed strategically beside his chair. He took out three packages, handing the largest one to Dave. 'This is for you, Mr Richards. I think I can guess what it is.'

Dave's eyes lit up behind the thick lenses of his spectacles as he fingered the parcel. 'Cigarettes.'

'Filthy habit,' Maida said, holding out her hand to take her present from Colin. 'Dear Tony. He always remembers his auntie.' She ripped it open and beamed as she held up a leather-bound diary. 'Just what I need. The dear boy might almost have known that I'd lost virtually everything I possess in that beastly air raid.'

'At least you have your life,' Dave said seriously. 'Thousands weren't so lucky.'

Colin turned to Susan. He was smiling but there was a guarded look in his eyes as they met hers. 'And this is for you.'

Tearing off the flimsy wrapping paper Susan gave a gasp of delight. 'A Tiger Moth manual. I can't believe that he took me seriously.'

Colin shrugged his shoulders. 'Tony's a flying

instructor. He's a teacher through and through. He can't resist an eager pupil.'

Was there a hint of sarcasm in his voice? She shot him a curious glance, but his expression was bland. 'I'd give anything to learn to fly,' she murmured, flipping through the pages. 'It's funny, but I bought him a book on planes too.'

'There are two more parcels under the tree,' Dave said quietly. 'Do you know what they might be, Susan?'

'Oh, my goodness. I almost forgot.' Somewhat reluctantly she put the manual down, and went to retrieve the presents for Dave and for Maida. The Roger and Gallet soap had been an inspiration. She had often bought it for Mrs Kemp, who was very fussy when it came to toiletries, and it had been the last box on the chemist's shelf when she had rushed out to the shop on Monday. She handed it to Maida. 'I hope you like carnation perfume,' she said warily. 'I didn't know what else to get you.'

Maida held the box to her nose and sniffed. 'Thank you, Susan. Actually this is my favourite, and much nicer than that awful Lifebuoy rubbish that my brother uses.'

'There's nothing wrong with my soap. You're just fussy.' Dave's frown melted into a smile as he opened Susan's present. 'What a splendid scarf.' He wrapped it around his neck.

'I'd have knitted it myself if I'd had the time, but

I'm afraid it's not exactly new. I got it in the second-hand shop.'

He fingered the warm material, smiling. 'It's the thought that counts, love.'

'It will keep you warm when you go for your evening walk.'

His eyes twinkled. 'It certainly will. It's the best present I ever had.'

Maida cleared her throat. 'Then you won't want the Burberry scarf that I bought for you at enormous expense and great personal inconvenience.'

Susan met Dave's horrified glance with a grimace. He unwound the scarf and looped it over his arm, making a quick recovery. 'Of course I will, Maida. How could anyone refuse such a magnificent gift? I'll wear them on alternate days and be proud to think that two people went to so much trouble for me.'

Maida's gifts were duly passed round and opened; a pair of 15 denier silk stockings for Susan, a box of handkerchiefs for Colin that Maida had somehow managed to procure on Christmas Eve, and of course the Burberry scarf for Dave. Then it was Colin's turn and he tipped the contents of the carrier bag onto his lap. 'Fortunately I was forewarned by Tony,' he said as he handed a package to Maida.

She was flushed and patently flustered as she opened it and took out a silver picture frame. It was small enough to fit in the palm of her hand and oval in shape. She stared at it, her cheeks flushed with embarrassment. 'I don't know what to say, but thank you, Colin. It's very pretty.'

Dave's present was a briar pipe, which he gripped between his teeth, smiling broadly. 'First class. Thank you, my boy.'

Susan was next. The delicious aroma of expensive chocolates filtered through the wrappings and she tore them off to find a large box of Black Magic. 'Oh, thank you, Colin. How did you know that they're my favourite?' She did not add that the only time she had tasted them was when she had pilfered one or two from Pamela's secret stash.

He shrugged his shoulders. 'A lucky guess.'

She opened the lid. 'Would anyone like one?'

Maida frowned. 'Isn't it a bit early in the day to start eating sweets?'

'Leave the girl alone, Maida.' Dave rose from his chair and went to the sideboard. 'Susan can eat the whole box before lunch if she likes, and I'm going to start the festivities with a glass of beer. Will anyone join me?'

Colin opened his mouth to reply but Maida spoke first. 'Thank you, David. I'll have a small sherry.'

Susan popped an orange cream into her mouth and savoured the delicious taste. 'I think I'd better go and baste the turkey.' Leaving them to sort out their drinks, she went to the kitchen, taking the chocolates with her. She was just about to put the potatoes in to roast when Colin entered the kitchen carrying two glasses. He put one on the table. 'Sherry for the cook,' he said, smiling. 'Can I do anything to help?' He sipped his beer. 'I mean it, Susan. I can peel carrots or do the sprouts for you.'

She closed the oven door, wiping her hands on her apron. 'No, it's all done. Thanks anyway. And thank you for the chocolates. They're lovely.'

'But a manual on flying a Tiger Moth is better.'

'Both are good.' She tasted the sherry and wrinkled her nose. 'It doesn't go well with chocolate.' She had to squeeze past him to get to the sink, and quite suddenly she felt shy in his company. The nearness of him made her long for the intimacy they had shared last evening, but the knowledge that it had meant little or nothing to him made her feel small and inadequate. Suddenly she wanted him to leave. She wished that he would go back to Hamble and fly his beastly planes, no doubt showing off to the rich and glamorous women of the ATA. He must think I'm a gullible child, she thought miserably. 'Excuse me. I need to get to the sink to wash the cabbage. I couldn't get sprouts. They'd sold out.'

He took her by the shoulders, turning her so that she was forced to meet his gaze, which was serious for once. 'Have I done something to upset you, Susan? I thought we were getting along so well.'

She stared at the knot in his tie. 'No. I'm just busy.'

He released her, moving aside. 'If I went too far then I apologise. I keep forgetting that you're just a kid.'

She turned on him angrily. 'I am not a kid, and I wasn't upset. You make me sound like a silly schoolgirl.'

His brow creased in a frown. 'I certainly never intended it to look that way. I think you're lovely. You're unspoiled and charming. I wouldn't hurt you for anything.'

'Well, you haven't. I'm all right. There's just a lot to do, and poor Charlie is locked in my room because of her.' She wiped her eyes on the back of her hand, realising that they were unaccountably wet with tears. 'Miss Richards hates him, and he's been shut away for ages. Not much of a Christmas for him.'

Colin threw back his head and laughed. 'Is that all that's worrying you?' He held up his hands. 'No offence meant, but that's easily remedied. We'll take him out for a long walk after lunch.' He stripped off his uniform jacket and hung it on a hook behind the door. 'And now I'm going to help. Give me something to do and we'll get the party started. Charlie's turn will come later.'

The meal was a great success. Susan's cooking was praised by everyone, even Maida. Dave and Colin did the washing up while Maida dozed on the settee. She awakened with a start at three o'clock when Dave switched on the wireless and they sat round listening intently to the King's Christmas message. When it was over Colin rose to his feet. 'Come on, Susan. Let's take that hound for a walk.'

*

Charlie bounded across the grassy hump of Primrose Hill uttering delighted barks and wagging his tail so that his whole body swayed from side to side. Heavy clouds caressed the spire of the distant St Paul's Cathedral and a light powdering of snow fluttered down from the featherbed sky. The light was fading fast and Colin reached out to hold Susan's hand. 'You are all right, aren't you? About last night, I mean.'

She managed a tight little smile. 'Of course. It was fun.'

He leaned over to kiss her on the cheek, but at that moment three figures appeared out of the gathering gloom. Susan recognised them instantly and her first instinct was to turn and run away.

Chapter Eight

Muffled in a fox fur coat and matching hat, Virginia was leaning on Dudley's arm as she approached them. Dressed in a more modest camel coat and a headscarf, Pamela was following several paces behind them. Susan hoped that they would merely walk past, but Virginia obviously had other ideas. She stopped, glaring at her with a malicious twist to her lips. 'Look at you, Banks. All dolled up in a fur jacket. No need to ask how you came by it, as I see that you've found another man. It didn't take long, did it?'

'I've nothing to say to you, Virginia.' Susan attempted to sidestep her but Virginia barred her way.

'But I've got plenty to say to you, miss. Pamela told me that you were still in the area and obviously doing very well for yourself.' Virginia looked Colin up and down. 'I suppose he's keeping you. Nice work.'

Colin squeezed Susan's fingers. 'That was as uncalled for as it is untrue. I don't know who you are, but I think you should apologise to Miss Banks.'

Dudley cleared his throat nervously. 'Come on, Virginia. Don't stoop to her level.'

'My level?' Susan wrenched her hand free from Colin's grasp as he attempted to pull her away. 'You're the one who behaved like an animal. You forced yourself on me.' She turned to Virginia. 'You saw what he was trying to do, and yet you blamed me. What does that make you?'

Virginia's eyes narrowed. 'Take that back, you liar.'

'I will not, and if you don't believe me, ask your sister. Pamela could tell you a thing or two about your precious fiancé.'

'Leave me out of it,' Pamela said, flapping her hands at Charlie who was sniffing her coat.

Colin bent down and snapped the lead onto Charlie's collar. 'Come along, Susan. I've had enough of this.' He tipped his cap to Virginia. 'I can't say it was a pleasure to meet you, but I think it's time we were going on our way.'

'He's right,' Dudley said, catching Virginia by the sleeve. 'Don't demean yourself, my dear. She was always a little tart, and nothing has changed.'

Colin took a step towards him, his chin outthrust and his eyes blazing. 'Do you want me to flatten the fellow, Susan? For two pins I'd do it anyway.'

'He's threatened me with violence. I want you both to witness that. Come one step nearer, my man, and I'll report you to the authorities.' Dudley grabbed both sisters by their hands and headed off in the opposite direction.

Susan shook her head. 'Let him go. He's not worth

bothering with.' She set off walking briskly towards home and Colin had to quicken his pace in order to catch up with her.

'So what's the story there? Tony told me a bit about the Kemps, but he didn't mention the idiot with the Ronald Colman moustache.'

Susan shivered, despite the fact that she was wearing Christine's fur jacket. 'I don't want to talk about it.'

'All right. I think I can guess most of it anyway. I wish I had smacked the blighter.'

'It's just as well you didn't. He's the type who would take great pleasure in making trouble for you.'

He hooked his arm around her shoulders. 'I'm not scared of him, but I wouldn't want to make things any more difficult for you than they are. You've had quite a time of it, haven't you?'

She nodded her head. His sympathy was almost harder to take than Dudley's preposterous lies.

'Well, if things get too tough here I want you to come to Hamble. It looks as though I'm going to be there for the duration and so is Tony.'

'But I'm happy looking after Dave. He's like a dad to me and it's all above board. He pays me a wage.'

'I don't want to sound like a Job's comforter, Susan, but living above a cycle shop and keeping house for Dave isn't going to get you very far. Anyway, it's on the cards that they'll bring in conscription for young women before too long. You'll either have to enlist in the services or you'll end up doing some kind of war work. Somehow I can't imagine you in a munitions factory or slaving away on a farm.'

'I hadn't thought that far ahead, but Dave needs someone to look after him.'

'He's got Maida, and you never know, he might marry again some day.' He gave her a gentle hug. 'I think that his big sister is under the impression that you've got ideas along those lines.'

Susan looked up at him in horror. 'No! How could she imagine that I'd want to marry a man old enough to be my father?'

He shrugged. 'It happens.'

'You don't think that Dave . . .?' She broke off, feeling the blood rush to her cheeks even though it was bitterly cold. 'No, that's impossible.'

'He's a decent bloke, but he's a man and you're a very pretty girl.' He chuckled. 'And a good cook too. I'd marry you myself if it wasn't for Morag.'

'I might not want to marry anyone,' Susan said firmly. 'If I had a chance to join the ATA I'd devote my life to flying. But as that is as impossible as walking to the moon, I'll just have to keep washing Dave's sock and cooking his dinners. Maybe I'll join the ARP. I'd considered that when I was working for the Kemps.'

'Well, if you change your mind and make your way to Hamble, I promise to do my best to give you at least one lesson in a Tiger Moth. Study the manual that Tony gave you and we'll see what we can do.'

She smiled tiredly. The intense cold had penetrated the soles of her brogues, numbing her feet, and her fingertips were tingling inside her woollen gloves. 'At least it will give me something to do in the air raid shelter, and I can but dream.'

Colin left early next morning, having promised to pass on a string of messages to Tony. The Christmas truce apparently over, air raids recommenced and Susan, Dave and Maida celebrated Boxing Day eating cold turkey sandwiches in the shelter, washed down with the last of the beer and sherry.

Despite the fact that she had mistaken his attentions for something more serious, Susan missed having Colin around. It had been a relief to talk to someone closer to her own age. When she was alone with Dave she was always mindful of his seniority and Maida was the headmistress figure of her childhood. With Colin gone she felt lonely and unsettled. He had made her think that perhaps her dreams were not as impossible as she had thought. He had given her hope where there had been resignation and he had shown her a glimpse into another world. He might have been amusing himself at her expense, but she realised now that there was more to life than mere drudgery, and it had left her wanting more.

Dave opened the shop on Friday morning, but

Maida showed no sign of wanting to move out and find a home of her own. Instead she began dictating what went on in the confines of the flat. She decided that the Christmas tree was shedding too many needles and ought to be disposed of before Twelfth Night. Susan saw to this immediately, as she was tired of pushing the carpet sweeper round the floor twice a day in order to satisfy Maida's demands. The next day it was the turn of the paper chains and the holly, both of which had to be consigned to a bonfire in the back yard. Dave said nothing. He was obviously used to being ordered about by his elder sister and he would do anything for a quiet life.

Maida was now completely in charge. She chose what programmes they were allowed to listen to on the wireless, and she would have banished Charlie to an outside kennel if she had had things completely her own way. It was only when she suggested this that Dave actually stood up to her, and all her attempts to browbeat him into submission failed. A compromise of sorts was reached and Charlie was banned from the lounge. He was allowed in the air raid shelter, and then only because Dave threatened to remain in the flat if Maida refused to have the dog with them during the bombing raids. Dave's nightly walks with Charlie were also under question. Maida nagged and bullied, threatened and sulked until on Sunday night Dave agreed to stay at home.

It was the worst night of the Blitz so far. They were forced to remain in the small, dank space until morning, although Dave kept going outside for a cigarette. It was not until they listened to the BBC news that they realised the true extent of the air raids. At least 10,000 parachute fire bombs had been dropped on the city, and the resultant devastation was beyond belief. The raid had been planned to coincide with low tide, making it difficult for the fire brigades to pump enough water from the Thames to put out the fires. It was terrible news, and Maida decided that nothing would tempt her to move back to the East End. She said that she would fill out the necessary forms for compensation from the government, but when the new term began she would commute daily to Hackney. Dave and Susan exchanged meaningful glances and said nothing.

Their life was organised from the moment they got up in the morning until they retired to their rooms at night. Maida even drew up a set of menus for each day of the week, together with a detailed shopping list. The only problem with this was that it was impossible to guess the availability of food-stuffs, especially meat and fish. Susan spent hours standing in long queues at the various shops, often coming away without anything that was on Maida's list. The system fell apart after the first few days and Susan went back to her former routine of buying what was on offer and making do. She prayed for the term to start and for Maida to return to work.

The news that Amy Johnson had been reported missing after her plane crashed into the Thames estuary came as a terrible blow to Susan. She could hardly believe that her heroine had come to grief whilst on a routine flight delivering an aeroplane from a factory to an RAF base. Dave was sympathetic, but Maida merely shrugged and said something about the fortunes of war, and perhaps it would stop Susan daydreaming about learning to fly. It was high time she grew out of such childish fantasies. Susan retired to her bedroom to cuddle Charlie and have a good cry.

Matters improved slightly when the spring term began and Maida returned to her job at the school, which had so far miraculously escaped the Luftwaffe's attempts to raze the whole of the East End to the ground. With the flat to herself in the daytime Susan was able to let Charlie out of her room and allow him to roam freely, but one fateful day he managed to get into Maida's bedroom. Susan was busy doing the washing and she did not notice that he was missing until it was too late. She found him in the lounge playing with what remained of a leather shoe. It was beyond repair but Charlie was unrepentant. He wagged his tail and tossed the damaged article into the air, pouncing on it and then dropping it at Susan's feet. She would have laughed had it not been such a serious matter. She knew that Maida would go berserk.

*

'That animal has to go,' Maida stormed, clutching the ruined shoe to her bosom. 'Have you any idea how much this pair cost, Susan?' She turned to Dave, who was nervously lighting a cigarette. 'I blame you as much as her. You should have put your foot down from the start, David. And go outside if you want to smoke. I can't bear the smell, and I don't want to go to school tomorrow reeking of second-hand tobacco smoke.'

Dave cupped the cigarette in his hand, holding it behind his back. 'With all the smoke from the burning buildings, not to mention the factories in that area, I wouldn't have thought anyone would notice.'

'Out!' Maida pointed a shaking finger to the doorway. 'Not you,' she added as Susan made to follow Dave from the room. 'I haven't finished with you, young lady.'

Susan hesitated in the doorway. She had apologised most sincerely but her words had fallen on deaf ears. She tried again. 'I am truly sorry about the shoe, Miss Richards. I'll buy you a new pair.'

'They were Italian leather,' Maida hissed. 'And we won't be importing anything from that country while we're fighting them in North Africa and beyond. It's only a matter of time before the government rations shoes and clothing as well as food, and you stand there telling me you're sorry. What was that animal doing roaming the flat anyway? I told you to keep him locked in your room.'

This was too much for Susan. 'It's not your flat,' she cried angrily. 'It's Dave's home and he never made a fuss about Charlie before you came here.'

Maida drew herself up to her full height. Her bosom heaved and a dull flush stained her cheeks. 'You should remember your place, Susan Banks. You might get round my soft-hearted brother but you're just a live-in servant.'

'And you're a mean bully. You make Dave miserable in his own home. If he wants to smoke it's up to him, not you. And if he doesn't mind Charlie being here then that's none of your business either.'

'That's it,' Maida screamed. 'You've gone too far this time. You're sacked. I want you out of this flat by the end of the week. That gives you time to find another place to live and a job, although don't expect to get a reference from me.'

Susan stared at her aghast. 'You can't do that. I work for Dave, not you.'

'And don't think I haven't seen what you're up to, miss. I thought that you were after my nephew in the first instance, and you were quick enough to make up to Colin, but now that didn't work you've set your sights on my poor brother.'

'That's just not true. I'm not like that.'

Maida advanced on her like a battleship with all guns primed and ready to fire. 'I know exactly what you are, and don't go running to my brother because it won't work. You've been given notice, which in the circumstances is very generous of me. Now go to your room and stay there until I give you permission to come out.'

'You can't treat me like a naughty child. I've done nothing wrong, and anyway I'm in the middle of preparing supper. Perhaps you'd like to take over the cooking and the washing-up.'

Maida raised her hand and slapped Susan across the left cheek. The sound echoed round the room. 'Now do as you're told.' Maida's voice shook and her eyes narrowed to slits. 'Get out of my sight.'

'What's going on?' Dave rushed into the room, glancing anxiously from one to the other. He recoiled at the sight of Susan's reddened cheek. 'Did you hit her, Maida?'

'I did, and with good reason too. I've told her to pack her bags and leave at the end of the week.' Maida brandished the shoe in his face. 'This was the last straw. She has to go and that animal too.'

'But Maida, love . . .' Dave held his hands out to her, 'be reasonable. You're upset now but you'll have a laugh at all this tomorrow.'

'Italian leather, David.' Maida slapped the damaged shoe into his hands. 'Expensive and almost impossible to come by these days, and that hound chewed it to bits. I daresay she gave it to him and pretended that he got into my room. She's a trouble-maker and a scheming hussy to boot. Either she goes or I do.' She glared at him, folding her arms across her chest. 'Well?'

'Don't do this to me, Maida,' Dave said, sighing. 'Can't we all live in peace and harmony? It's bad enough having Jerry trying to annihilate us, but we should be able to get on as a family.'

'That's just it, though. She's not part of our family, even though I suspect she'd jump at the chance to change her name to Richards.'

'That's a lie.' Susan plucked at Dave's sleeve. 'Don't listen to her. She's been saying awful things. I think she's gone mad.'

He frowned, shaking his head. 'I wish you ladies could make an effort to get on with each other. You're making my life a misery.' He turned away, his voice breaking with barely suppressed emotion.

'Pull yourself together, David.' Maida raised her voice to the pitch of a sergeant major on a parade ground. 'Make a decision for once in your life. It's her or me. Make your choice. Are you going to turn your only sister out into the cold, or are you going to let that little gold-digger wrap you round her little finger?'

Susan noticed that the tips of Dave's ears had turned bright red. She could sense the inner turmoil that was tearing him in two, and she could bear it no longer. 'All right, Miss Richards. You win. I'm going and I won't stay until the end of the week. I'll go first thing in the morning.'

Dave spun round to face her. He was now deathly pale and he seemed to have aged suddenly. 'Don't go like this, Susan. We've been the best of mates, haven't we?'

She hardened her heart. He could have stood up to his sister but he had allowed himself to be browbeaten by her. 'I'm sorry,' she said gently. 'You've been so good to me and I'll miss you, but it's for the best.'

'It certainly is.' Maida linked her hand through her brother's arm. 'We'll do very well without you.'

'But where will you go?' Dave's eyes reddened and he turned to his sister with a beseeching look. 'Maida, have a heart. She's just a kid and there's a war on. You can't simply turn her out on the streets.'

'Shut up, David. You're too soft by half. Her sort always land on their feet. Look how you were taken in by her.'

'That's not fair, Maida,' he protested, taking off his glasses and rubbing his eyes. 'Why do you always have the last say?'

Susan knew then that Maida had won. She was suddenly drained of anger and left feeling nothing but a deep sadness. She had wanted Dave to be like a father but he had failed her, just as everyone in the past had failed her. 'I'll finish making supper,' she said dully. 'I'll eat in my room and I'll leave in the morning.' She left the room without giving either of them a chance to reply.

Supper was an uncomfortable meal. Neither Dave nor Susan had much appetite although Maida ate her toad-in-the-hole and mashed potato with relish.

No one spoke, and Susan was glad when the pudding of stewed pears and condensed milk was eaten and she was left alone to do the washing-up. When she had finished clearing everything away and the kitchen was once again spotless, she took Charlie for a long walk, despite the fact that it was raining. She went to her room on her return and spent the rest of the evening packing her things in the old cardboard suitcase. She would have loved to take the fur jacket but she decided against it in case Maida accused her of stealing. She hung it over the back of the bentwood chair and left the brogues on the seat. She would take only what she had come with or had bought with her own money.

She waited until all was quiet in the flat before tiptoeing to the bathroom to get ready for bed. When she returned to her room she took her purse from her handbag and counted out the money that she had managed to save from her wages. Having spent most of what she had earned on Christmas presents, she realised with a pang of anxiety that there was precious little left to keep her going until she found another job. She could not afford London rents and the first person she thought of who might help her was Tony. He had told her to look him up if ever she was in the area, and that was exactly what she intended to do. She might have just enough money to get her to Southampton and on to Hamble if it was not too far away. She would find the pub that Tony had mentioned and ask them to direct her to the aerodrome. It was a wild plan but she was desperate.

Charlie seemed to sense her distress and he pushed his wet nose into her hand, gazing up at her with adoring eyes. She smiled down at him. 'I suppose you realise that this is all your fault?'

He wagged his tail, grinning at her, and she bent down to rub her cheek against his silky head. 'You're the best friend I ever had,' she murmured. 'We'll be okay together, Charlie. We won't let them beat us.'

She switched off the light and drew back the curtains so that she could see the stars. *Per ardua ad astra.* That was the motto of the Royal Air Force. If it was good enough for them it must surely be good enough for her. She curled up with Charlie nestling against her back and was drifting off to sleep when she heard the door open. She snapped into a sitting position as Dave approached the bed, putting his finger to his lips. 'I'm sorry, love. I didn't mean to startle you.'

'What is it? I didn't hear the air raid siren.'

'It's not that.' He perched on the edge of the bed. Even in the dim light she could see that he was tense and uncomfortable. He clasped his hands in his lap, staring down at them as if they were the most interesting thing in the world.

'What's the matter then? What can't wait until morning?' She hugged Charlie as he wriggled into her arms and licked her face. He too seemed to feel the tension in the room.

Dave twiddled his fingers nervously. He did not look at her. 'I'm sorry that Maida lost her rag,' he said slowly. 'She was upset about her shoes.'

'I know that, and I apologised over and over again. I even offered to give her my week's wages to pay for a new pair.'

'She's lost everything. You have to make allowances for her. Perhaps if you speak to her in the morning and tell her again how sorry you are, it might make her change her mind.'

'You know that won't work,' Susan said gently. 'She doesn't want me here and she hates Charlie. There's no way I'm getting rid of him, so we'll have to leave.'

He turned his head to look at her. His eyes were in shadow but she could see his mouth working soundlessly for a few seconds before he spoke. His distress was obvious. 'I don't want you to go, Susan. Having you here has made all the difference. I was a sad, lonely old man until you walked into my life. You've made me feel young again.'

Alarm bells were beginning to sound in Susan's head. She was feeling distinctly uncomfortable. 'Don't you think you ought to go to bed? We can talk about it in the morning.'

'But that will be too late, won't it?' He glanced at her suitcase which lay open on the floor, waiting for the last of her belongings to be packed. 'You'll be off before I can stop you. Anyway, I don't want Maida to hear what I've got to say to you.

She'll only get angry and tell me I'm an old fool.'

Susan was now really anxious. She shifted Charlie to the side and brought her knees up to her chest, wrapping her arms around them. 'Then don't say it, Dave. Let's part like friends. I'll always be grateful to you for what you've done for me.'

'I don't want gratitude, Susan.' He slid off the bed and went down on one knee. She heard his joints creak, and she smelled the telltale whiff of brandy on his breath.

'Please, Dave. Don't say something you'll regret in the morning.'

'No. I must say what's in my heart. I'm a lot older than you, but I've got plenty of good years left in me. You'll never want for anything again and you'll be secure for the rest of your life. I'm not a rich man, but I've got a nice little nest egg stashed away in the bank. I make a good living from the cycle shop, but if you don't want to live in the flat I could sell up and buy a little place in the country. We could start a tearoom or something like that. I'd treat you like a queen, Susan.'

She shook her head vehemently. 'Please don't say any more.'

'I can't stop now. I've been rehearsing this in my head all evening. Susan, I'm asking you to marry me.'

Chapter Nine

The train rumbled through the English countryside, the iron wheels beating out a monotonous clickety-clack rhythm as they passed over the points. It was bitterly cold in the guard's van, which was the only place where Susan had been able to find a space for herself and Charlie. The train was packed with servicemen and civilians, and the corridors were crammed with people standing or perching on their suitcases. Sitting on a wooden crate with Charlie at her feet Susan stared out of the window at the wintry landscape of ploughed fields and bare hedgerows. Skeleton trees wedge-shaped by the prevailing winds stood out against a gunmetal sky. Heavy cumulus clouds promised rain. Small stations flashed past and were immediately lost in clouds of steam as the train travelled on at speed. She was tired and hungry and her thoughts inevitably turned to the events that had led her to leave London.

She had slept very little after Dave's astonishing proposal of marriage, and she had risen early hoping to leave the flat before anyone was about. She had been making tea and toast in the kitchen when Dave stumbled into the room, bleary-eyed with sleep and what little hair he had left standing up on his head like the fluff on a dandelion clock. He had mumbled his apologies for upsetting her, but had been at pains to convince her that his offer had been sincerely meant and still stood. 'Any time you change your mind you can come home, Susan,' he said earnestly. 'There'll always be a place for you here, no matter what my sister says.'

She had murmured her thanks, but she found she had no appetite for food, and she left as soon as she had gathered her things together. Dave had insisted that she kept the fur jacket and the sturdy brogues, for which she was truly grateful as she set off in a chill wind that would have sliced through her old cloth coat. When she reached Waterloo she bought a cup of tea in the station buffet, but the thought of food still made her feel nauseous. She had had to wait until late morning for the train, and even then the journey was slow. The weather broke just before the train pulled into Southampton station, where Susan had been told she had to change for Hamble.

She climbed down onto the platform, stiff and suffering from cramp. Charlie shook himself and looked up at her with shining eyes and his tongue lolling out of his mouth. It was all a game to him. Not so for Susan. She had attempted to put a call through to the aerodrome at Hamble when she arrived at Waterloo with the vague hope of contacting Tony, but she had been told that he was not available and advised to ring back later. Now, with nowhere to go and panic beginning to set in, she decided to try again. She went in search of a public telephone box, but when she found one she had to wait while a soldier talked at length, feeding coins into the slot one after the other. Eventually he finished and pushed the heavy door open. 'Sorry, ducks,' he said, grinning. 'It's all yours now.'

She stepped inside, wrinkling her nose at the smell of stale tobacco and disinfectant. She tried the number again but was told that First Officer Richards was not available, and advised yet again to try later. Someone tapped on the glass and she saw a young Wren waiting impatiently, stamping her feet and rubbing her hands together as if to emphasise that it was cold outside. Susan left the phone box and went to retrieve Charlie from the fence post over which she had looped his lead. It was mid-afternoon and she had not eaten all day. She had reached the stage when she felt as though her knees had turned to jelly and she realised that she was starving. She found a WVS mobile canteen and spent some of her dwindling resources on a cup of tea and a sticky bun, which she shared with Charlie while they stood on the windswept platform for the train to Hamble. Eventually, after she had been waiting for what seemed like an interminable time, a tank engine chugged into the station pulling a couple of wagons. She found an empty compartment, which was the height of luxury after the uncomfortable journey from Waterloo, and she settled down, wondering what she was going to do when she reached her destination.

She had just about enough money for a week's bed and board in a cheap lodging house. Dave had pressed a ten bob note into her hands as she left the flat. She had been reluctant to take it, but he insisted that it was in lieu of wages. It would have been undignified to argue and she did not want to hurt him any more than she had already done by refusing his offer of marriage. Even thinking about it now made the blush rise to her cheeks. She had never for a moment thought of him in that way, and it shocked her to imagine that he had wanted her as anything other than a daughter. She stared out of the window. The light was already fading and soon it would be dark. Her first priority now was to find a bed for the night. She fumbled in her handbag and pulled out her purse. In the back pocket she found the scrap of paper on which Tony had written the telephone number of a pub called the Victorious. She remembered him saying that the landlord was a friend of his. Perhaps she was being unrealistic in thinking that Tony would help her, but she had lost faith in Colin since he admitted that he had a fiancée in the Highlands. She wondered if poor Morag knew that he flirted shamelessly with other women when he was far from home. In any event, she had decided that he was too charming by half, and he was well aware of his power over women.

'Right, Charlie,' she said out loud as they alighted

from the train at Hamble station. 'Will we be victors at the Victorious?' She pulled a face at the dreadful pun. 'There's only one way to find out, old boy.' With his lead held in one hand and her suitcase in the other, she set off for the village. The wind whipped across open countryside to snatch strands of hair from beneath her woollen cap. She was footsore and exhausted by the time she arrived in the High Street. Even though the dusk was rapidly swallowing up the ancient buildings she was struck by the timeless beauty of the place. It was like walking into the pages of one of the expensive magazines illustrated with picture-perfect English villages that Mrs Kemp kept on her coffee table to impress Mrs Girton-Chase. She found the pub easily enough but the doors were closed. Opening time was not for another hour, and it had started to rain. She huddled in the doorway with Charlie sitting obediently at her feet until he spotted a cat crossing the road and heading in a leisurely manner towards them. Charlie uttered a yelp of delight and bounded forward, pulling the lead from Susan's nerveless fingers. Clutching the handle of her suitcase, which contained all her worldly possessions, she raced after him. The cat had decided to make a run for it, and Charlie was now in full chase. The sleek ginger tom leapt over the wall into the pub garden with Charlie in hot pursuit. Susan called him back but he affected not to hear her. Peering over the top of the wall, she could see him attempting to clamber up the leg of a rustic table on which the cat had taken refuge and was hissing loudly as it swiped at Charlie's nose with unsheathed claws.

'Charlie. Heel,' Susan cried in desperation. 'Come here, you bad dog.'

He ignored her as he bounced up and down barking excitedly. Susan was just wondering whether to go and knock on the pub door when she saw a slight figure appear from somewhere at the back of the building. A woman emerged from the shadows and hurried across the paved yard to the beer garden. 'Here, boy.'

Charlie stopped prancing and ran to her, wagging his tail. Susan stood on tiptoe, waving madly. 'Hello. That's my dog, I'm afraid. He jumped the wall.'

The woman walked slowly towards her. 'We don't get too many strangers here these days.'

'I'm sorry. I didn't mean to disturb you. I was waiting for the pub to open. I'm looking for lodgings and I wondered if you had any vacancies.'

'Go round to the front door and I'll let you in.'

Susan needed no second bidding. Her teeth were chattering and she had lost all feeling in her fingertips and toes. She went to the door and waited. Moments later she heard the rasp of a key in the lock and she felt a blast of warm air as the door opened.

'Come in. You must be frozen.'

It was dark in the bar but as she closed the door the woman flicked the light switch, revealing a welcoming bar room with a low beamed ceiling and a log fire burning in the ingle nook. Horse brasses decorated the oak beams and there were copper jugs filled with bronze and wine-red chrysanthemums on the polished wooden tables. Their spicy scent mingled with the resinous aroma of the pine logs burning on the fire and the overlying smells of ale and tobacco smoke. Charlie rushed over to Susan and jumped up at her.

'You bad boy,' she murmured, but she could not help smiling. It was impossible to be cross with a creature so full of exuberance and love of life. She glanced at her hostess, who was much younger than she had first thought. 'I really am sorry. He wouldn't have hurt your cat.'

'That's all right. Orlando can look after himself.' The girl held out her hand. 'I'm Rosemary Fuller, but everyone calls me Roz. My dad is the landlord.'

Susan shook her hand. 'Susan Banks. You've already met Charlie.'

'So you're looking for somewhere to stay. Have you got a job locally?'

'No. It's a long story, but I can pay my way.'

'Never mind that now. You look done in. Why don't you take a seat by the fire and I'll get you something to drink.'

'I suppose a cup of tea is out of the question?'

'Not at all. I was just making one for myself when I heard the rumpus in the garden. I thought a fox might have got in and fancied Orlando for his dinner.'

'Why Orlando? It's a very grand name for a cat.'

Roz grinned sheepishly. 'I know, but I called him after *Orlando the Marmalade Cat*. It's a book I bought for Alice before the war when she had measles and needed cheering up. I just thought it suited my moggy.'

At that moment, as if on cue, Orlando himself marched into the bar. Greeted enthusiastically by Charlie the offended animal arched his back, hissed and leapt gracefully onto the settle next to Susan. She stroked his head and he curled up beside her. Charlie sat down, staring warily at the cat as if memories of Binkie-Boo had come back to haunt him.

'That's right, Charlie,' Roz said, patting him. 'Don't mess with Orlando. He's a tough street fighter and he won't stand for any nonsense.' She headed for the door at the back of the bar. 'I won't be two ticks. Make yourself comfortable, Susan. There's almost an hour before we open up.'

She returned minutes later carrying a tray of tea. Susan's mouth watered as she spotted a plate of sandwiches.

'Help yourself,' Roz said, setting the tray down in front of her. 'I'd only just made these for my tea, but I can soon cut another couple of rounds. You look as though you could do with something to eat.'

Susan took a sandwich and bit into it. She chewed and swallowed, savouring the taste of the roast chicken. 'Thank you so much. This is a real treat.'

'We have a deal with one of the local farmers,' Roz said, pouring tea into two mugs. 'We've got a bit of land at the bottom of the beer garden. Dad's talking about getting our own hens and a pig as well, but I'm not sure if I could raise one and then send it to the abattoir, never mind eating the meat. On the other hand we have to feed our customers or they'll go elsewhere.' She sat down on a chair opposite Susan. 'When you're ready I'm dying to hear your story.' She tossed a biscuit to Charlie and settled back, sipping her tea as she waited for Susan to finish her food. 'Okay then. Now you can talk.'

The clock on the wall behind the bar was ticking on relentlessly. Susan made haste to explain her circumstances to Roz as briefly and succinctly as possible. At the mention of Tony's name, Roz chuckled. 'Oh, him. Yes, I know Tony Richards. He's a great guy, full of fun and a real gentleman. Some of them aren't, you know.' She winked at Susan. 'You've got to watch some of the glamour boys, like Colin Forbes. They think they're God's gift to women, and to be truthful some of them are quite dreamy, including Colin, but Tony's not like that.'

'He told me to get in touch if I was in the neighbourhood.'

Roz angled her head. 'And you're here now. What d'you think you'll do?'

'I don't know. I'll have to find work soon.'

'Well, first you'll need to find some digs.' Roz frowned. 'We don't have any letting rooms, because it's just Dad and me running the place.' She met Susan's questioning look and smiled. 'My mother died giving birth to me, so it's always been just the two of us.'

'I'm sorry. But at least you've got your dad.'

'And he's a poppet. I love him dearly, but he needs looking after. Heaven knows what he'd do if I ever left home. More tea, Susan?'

'No, thank you.' She shook her head, placing her empty mug on the tray. 'You've been very kind, but we'd best leave now and start looking in earnest. Are there any boarding houses or pubs that take in paying guests?'

'I'm sure there are, but it's a bit late to go wandering around on your own. I've been thinking, Susan. We do have a spare room. It's in a bit of a muddle but you could stay here tonight, and start again in the morning.'

'Oh, I don't know. I don't want to put you to any bother. And then there's Charlie. He's used to sleeping with me.'

Roz reached out to stroke his head. 'That's okay, and I'm sure that Dad won't mind. He's having his afternoon nap, but I'll introduce you to him later.' She rose to her feet. 'Perhaps Tony or Colin will pop in for a pint this evening, and then you can collar one of them. We'll see if they meant what they said, or if it was just man talk. I'll show you the room and then you can decide whether or not you want to stay.'

'I'm sure it will be fine.' Susan heaved her tired body from the settle. She could have fallen asleep sitting where she was, and the thought of going out in the cold and knocking on doors was daunting. She picked up her case and followed Roz out of the bar and up a narrow, creaking staircase to the first floor.

The spare room was at the front of the building. In the faint glimmer of light from the landing Susan could see that Roz had not been exaggerating about the mess. In order to reach the window and draw the curtains Roz had to clamber over cardboard boxes and a selection of odd items, including a standard lamp without a shade and a mock Tudor doll's house perched on top of a metal-studded steamer trunk. She felt her way back in almost complete darkness and reached for the light switch. 'As you can see it needs a bit of a tidy up, but the bed is quite comfortable, and the bathroom is just along the landing.'

'Can I help? It doesn't seem fair that you do all the work.'

'It's no trouble, and I think that Charlie can smell something that we can't.' Susan said, chuckling as he rooted around like a truffle hound. 'My friend's daughter, Alice, was the last person to sleep in here when I babysat for her. It's quite possible that there's a packet of biscuits stashed away somewhere. Perhaps it would be best if you take Charlie to my room, which is just across the landing.'

Susan called to Charlie and was surprised and delighted when he obeyed instantly. She waited while Roz went into her room, glancing round as if to make certain that everything was in order. 'Come in, Susan. Make yourself at home, and feel free to use the bathroom. Dad won't stir for a while yet. I always open up at five thirty, which I don't mind because he's very good about giving me time off if I have a date.'

'Are you going out with anyone special?' Susan was curious. She was certain that someone as attractive as Roz, with her shoulder-length dark hair and large lustrous eyes fringed with thick lashes, would have admirers queuing at the door for the chance to take her out.

'Oh, you know how it is,' Roz said vaguely. She left the room, closing the door hastily as Charlie made an attempt to follow her.

'That was odd,' Susan said to Charlie, who cocked his head on one side as if waiting for her to explain her remark. 'I hope I didn't put my foot in it.' She slipped off her coat and laid it neatly on a chair by the door, but she paused for a moment, looking round the room with a touch of envy. Judging by the contents and the relics of childhood, Roz had occupied this space since she was a child. It was not a large room, and the ceiling sloped down to a dormer window with a wide sill covered in patch-work cushions. A kidney-shaped dressing table with a frilled floral skirt had pride of place in the alcove next to the chimney breast. It was cluttered with pots and jars, bottles of nail polish and a matching mirror, brush and comb set.

The mantelpiece was crowded with china ornaments in the shape of baby animals and chubby-cheeked nursery rhyme characters that would appeal to any child. An old-fashioned clothes press filled the space on the other side of the chimney breast, adding a note of period charm to the eclectic mix of furnishings. A double bed took up most of the opposite wall, its end legs propped up on two piles of books to accommodate the eccentrically sloping floor. Reclining on the pink satin eiderdown was a nightdress case in the shape of an elegant French doll, and a fluffy white rug was placed strategically on the pink and green linoleum at the side of the bed.

Nothing in the room matched, and yet the result was both welcoming and homely. It was very much a girl's room, and it seemed that Roz had been given everything she could possibly want to make her happy. Even if she had lost her mother, she was lucky to have a doting father. Susan thought of Dave and shivered. She had been genuinely fond of him, but his proposal with all it entailed had somehow tarnished a relationship that, in her mind at least, had no sexual connotations.

Silence engulfed her for the first time that day. She sat down on the edge of the bed and Charlie leapt up beside her. She checked his paws and was relieved to find that they were clean and dry. It would be awful to leave muddy prints on the pristine pink satin. She could have lain down and gone to sleep there and then, but consideration for her hostess, and a degree of nervousness, made her get up and open her case. She took her spongebag to the bathroom and had what was known as a lick and a promise in the children's home. She would have loved to fill the bathtub with hot water and luxuriate in its depths, but she resisted the temptation and made her way back to the bedroom. She picked up her hairbrush and took a seat at the dressing table. She had never worn makeup, but she had noticed that Roz's maquillage was perfect. The array of pots and potions in front of her was amazing, and a furtive glance in each of the drawers beneath the floral skirt revealed sets of combs, curlers, iron curling tongs and a box filled with lipsticks. Susan was tempted to try one, but she overcame the urge, and was brushing her hair when the door burst open.

Roz beckoned to her. 'I've fixed the room up for you. Come and see.'

Susan stood up, shaking the creases from her skirt, and followed her out onto the landing.

'There,' Roz said, flinging the door open. 'I've stowed all the rubbish away in the boxroom. I can't think why I didn't do it sooner, only with the pub open seven days a week there's very little time for housekeeping.' She smiled and a dimple appeared in her cheek. 'That's my excuse anyway. Actually we do have a charlady who comes in every day. She's the proverbial treasure. You'll meet her in the morning.'

'But I have to be on my way first thing,' Susan said pointedly. 'I've got to find work as well as somewhere to live.'

Roz shrugged her shoulders. 'Let's worry about that tomorrow, shall we? In the meantime I'm going downstairs to open up. Why don't you put your things in here and come down and keep me company? There'll only be a couple of locals to start with. They're old chaps who work on the land and they come in on their way home every evening for a pint of mild and a chat. It will be nice to have someone closer to my own age to talk to.' She nodded her head in Charlie's direction. 'He can come too, if he promises to behave himself and leave poor Orlando alone. Dad loves dogs, although I can't say the same for my cat.'

Roz had not exaggerated. The bar was quiet for the first hour with the two locals sitting in the snug smoking roll-ups and sipping their ale.

Bob Fuller made an appearance just as they were starting to get busy. He greeted Susan without surprise, as if his daughter made a habit of taking in waifs and strays. His dark eyes twinkled beneath thick black eyebrows and he exuded bonhomie, although Susan thought she would not like to get on the wrong side of him. Despite his pleasant demeanour, he looked tough with his hair cropped close to his head, and his sleeves rolled up to the elbows to reveal muscular forearms. Taking account of his square jaw and a nose that deviated slightly to the left, he had the appearance of a prize fighter. When he caught Susan staring at him he gave a throaty chuckle. 'You're wondering where I got this fine physique, aren't you, Susan?'

Murmuring an apology, she looked away, but he took her by the hand and led her into the snug. The walls were hung with photographs of himself in the days when he was a successful middle-weight, and his trophies were locked in a glass-fronted corner cupboard for all to see. 'That was me in my heyday,' he said proudly.

'Stop boasting, Dad,' Roz said, tossing a tea towel at him. 'I could do with a hand, if you're not too busy.'

Bob grinned. 'See how she bullies me, Susan? Anyone would think that she's the boss round here, not me.' He picked up the cloth and went behind the bar to help Roz and chat to the customers.

Susan watched them as they worked side by side. Bob clearly adored his daughter, and Susan could see that the feeling was mutual. Once again she felt the slight tug of envy and the sensation of being forever an outsider. She settled down in the corner of the ingle nook as a mere onlooker, but it was Charlie who was the star of the evening. Virtually all the customers made a fuss of him, particularly the women, and he made the most of his newfound popularity. He was shameless in his antics, giving paws and greeting each new person as if they were his lifelong friends. Susan sat on her own, sipping a glass of ginger beer shandy. The warmth of the log fire combined with the small amount of alcohol in the drink made her feel pleasantly sleepy. She watched Roz doing her job with growing admiration. She was good with people without being over-familiar, and she obviously knew how to handle the men who attempted to flirt with her. As the evening went on there was no sign of either Tony or Colin.

Susan was fighting off sleep when Bob came over to collect some empty glasses from a nearby table. He stopped, looking at her with a frown puckering his brow. 'You look done in, young lady. Roz can have the rest of the evening off. She'll look after you.'

Somewhat shakily, Susan rose to her feet. 'I am a bit tired, Mr Fuller.'

'Bob,' he said, grinning. 'Now get along with you before you fall asleep and I have to carry you upstairs to bed. That would give the locals something to talk about.' He signalled to Roz. 'You can finish for tonight, love. Take care of Susan. I can manage on my own.'

Roz lifted the flap in the counter but she hesitated as the door opened to admit a man whose undeniable good looks and air of authority would have made him stand out in any crowd. His tweed hacking jacket and cavalry twill trousers were obviously bespoke, and extremely expensive. He took off his cap to reveal a head of wavy blond hair that refused to lie flat and flopped over his brow only to be pushed back as if he was quite unaware that all the females in the bar were gazing at him. He greeted everyone as if he knew each one individually, and Bob strolled over to meet him with a cheerful quip.

Susan hesitated. She had been watching Roz's face and she had been quick to note the delicate blush that tinted her cheeks and the sudden alertness of her expression. Unless she was very much mistaken, this man was more than just another customer. She wondered if he was the reason for her reticence when she had asked Roz about boyfriends.

'I'll be with you in two ticks, Patrick.' Bob took the glasses to the bar. 'I'll take over now, Roz.'

'It's all right, Dad,' she said, reaching for a pint mug. 'The usual, Patrick?'

He moved swiftly to take a seat on a bar stool. 'Yes. Thanks, Roz.'

Susan could only see their profiles but she could tell by the way Roz was smiling at him that he was definitely someone special, and he seemed to have eyes for her alone. Susan had read enough romantic novels to know the signs. She stood in the middle of the bar, momentarily forgotten, watching the tableau as if she was at the pictures. It was Charlie who decided to break things up and he bounded over to the newcomer and jumped up at him.

The spell was broken and Susan moved forward to grab him by the collar. 'I'm so sorry,' she said apologetically. 'I thought I'd managed to stop him doing that.'

Patrick turned his head to look at her and he smiled. Susan could see why Roz had fallen for him. He was not classically handsome, but his blue eyes shone with humour and his generous mouth curved into a ready smile. His skin was tanned, giving him the look of a man who spent a good deal of his time out of doors, and he seemed to know exactly how to handle a frisky young dog.

'Down, boy.'

Charlie obeyed instantly.

'You're obviously used to handling animals,' Susan said unnecessarily.

'He should be,' Roz said, drawing a pint of bitter from the beer engine and passing it to him. 'Patrick is our local vet. Patrick, this is Susan Banks, she's looking for work in the neighbourhood. Do you know of any jobs going?'

He held out his hand. 'How do you do, Susan?'

Suddenly shy, she felt herself blushing. 'How do you do?' At least she had learned something from Mrs Kemp, she thought vaguely. Her former employer had been a stickler for manners and etiquette, and even if she had not directed her teachings at Susan personally it would have been impossible to spend four years in her home without absorbing some of her high standards.

'What sort of work are you seeking?' Patrick took a handful of coins from his trouser pocket. 'Would you like a drink, Susan?'

She shook her head. 'No, thank you. And as to jobs, I don't mind. I'll mop floors and clean windows if necessary.'

'Well, if I hear of anything I'll let you know. Where are you staying?'

'Roz has been very kind and offered me a bed for the night.'

Patrick smiled. 'That's just like her, but she'll probably make you work for your keep. Don't tell her I said so, but she's a real slave driver when she gets going.'

Roz pulled a face at him. 'Thanks for that, Patrick. I know who to come to if I ever need a reference.'

'Let me buy you a drink to make amends, Roz.' He pushed some coins towards her, his gaze fixed on her face. 'How about a gin and It?'

She reached out to take the money and for a second their fingers touched. Susan could almost feel the electricity that crackled in the air between them. Then the expression on Roz's face changed subtly as she glanced over his shoulder. Susan felt a gust of cold air and turned her head to see a young woman stride into the bar. She was tall and slender with glossy auburn hair confined in a snood at the back of her head. She wore a fur coat that simply had to be genuine mink and she carried a crocodile-skin handbag. 'So there you are, Patrick.' Her voice was as icy as the winter air that she had brought in from the street. 'I thought I might find my husband lurking in the bar of the Victorious.'

Chapter Ten

Patrick stood up, offering her his seat. 'Hello, Elspeth.'

She slipped off her mink and draped it over the stool. 'I'll have a gin and tonic. A double.'

'A large G and T for my wife, please, Roz,' Patrick said with an attempt at a smile.

Watching from the sidelines, Susan felt quite sorry for him. It was obvious that his wife, beautiful though she was, had quite a temper when roused. She was obviously seething now and ready to erupt like Vesuvius.

'Good evening, Elspeth.' Roz took a goblet from the shelf and held it under the optic.

'Is it? I wouldn't know. I've been waiting for my husband to come home for dinner for the last two hours, and he didn't even have the good manners to telephone and let me know that he was going to be late.'

'I was called out to Tanner's farm,' Patrick said in a low voice. 'I asked Sally to let you know.'

'Well quite obviously she had better things to do, or else you simply forgot. We all know where your priorities lie, darling.' Elspeth snatched up her glass and took a mouthful. She glared at Roz. 'I suppose it's no use asking you how long my husband has been propping up the bar.'

Roz shrugged her shoulders. 'Don't drag me into this. I just serve the drinks.'

Bob strolled over to deposit several empty glasses on the counter. 'Hello, Elspeth. You're always a sight for sore eyes, and you look particularly lovely this evening.' He lifted the hatch and took his place beside his daughter.

Elspeth eyed him suspiciously. 'Don't try and flannel me, Bob Fuller. You men always stick together.'

Patrick downed the last of his pint. 'This isn't the time or the place, Elspeth. Let's go home.'

She tossed her head. 'Why? I think it's my turn to relax and enjoy myself.' She finished her drink in one gulp and pushed the glass towards Roz. 'I'll have similar. I do hate it when people say "the same again", which is absolute nonsense and appalling misuse of the English language.'

Bob picked up her glass. 'I'll serve Mrs Peterson, Roz. You go on up and take young Susan with you. She looks fit to drop.'

'Thanks, Dad.' Roz ducked under the hatch. 'By the way, Elspeth, your husband came in about ten minutes before you arrived.' She walked away without giving either of them a chance to respond.

Susan was about to follow when Charlie decided

that the mink coat was fair game and attempted to drag it from the stool.

Elspeth let out a loud scream. 'Patrick, do something. My beautiful coat.'

He uttered a sharp command and Charlie let go, backing away with his tail between his legs. 'No harm done,' Patrick said, smoothing the pelts and replacing the coat on the stool.

'No harm?' Elspeth raised her voice to the pitch that would shatter glass. 'My gorgeous mink is covered in dog spit. Another minute and the brute would have ripped it to shreds.'

Bob took her glass and held it under the optic. He pushed it across the bar. 'On the house, Elspeth.'

Susan grabbed Charlie's collar. 'Sorry,' she murmured, hurrying him out of the room. She almost bumped into Roz who was standing in the narrow hallway with her hand clamped over her mouth in an attempt to stifle her giggles. Susan closed the door before releasing the unrepentant Charlie. 'That could have been nasty,' she said, trying not to laugh. 'That wretched fur coat must be worth a fortune.'

'That was the funniest thing I've seen in years. Elspeth's face was a picture.' Roz made her way to the kitchen.

'You don't like her, do you?'

'Would you like some cocoa?' Roz went into the larder and emerged seconds later with a bottle of milk in one hand and a tin of cocoa in the other. 'I'm going to have some.'

'Yes, please.' Susan watched while she measured two cupfuls of milk into a saucepan and put it on the hob. 'Is it all right if I let Charlie out into the garden? Where's Orlando, though? I don't want a repeat of this afternoon's performance.'

'I expect he's asleep on my bed by now. Yes, let him out by all means, and give him a biscuit for annoying Elspeth. She's a real bitch to poor Patrick.'

Susan let Charlie out into the darkness. She waited by the back door, hoping that he did not decide to jump the garden wall for a second time that day. She need not have worried as he returned almost immediately. He explored the kitchen with his nose to the ground as if hoping to find a morsel of food that someone had dropped on the floor. Susan took a seat at the table. She was tired, but she was also curious. 'Why does Elspeth treat her husband like that? He seems such a nice chap.'

'He is,' Roz said, spooning cocoa into two cups. 'But she's got heaps of money and he's building up his practice. She never lets him forget who holds the purse strings.' She lifted the pan from the stove, adding the milk to the cocoa powder and stirring.

'Then why on earth did he marry her?'

Roz passed a cup to Susan. She sat down at the table adding a spoonful of sugar to her cocoa. 'She was pregnant, so he did the right thing. Then she had a miscarriage, so it was all a waste of time.'

'That's awful.'

'Awful for him.'

Susan stared at her in surprise. She was shocked that someone as nice as Roz could be so unfeeling when it came to another woman's tragedy. 'I'd say losing their baby must have been a terrible blow for both of them.'

Roz looked up, fixing her with a hard stare. 'Who said it was his? Elspeth was engaged to Patrick's elder brother, Martin. The wedding was going to be a grand affair at Colby Grange three years ago, but Martin's appendix flared up and although they operated almost immediately he died of septicaemia. The she-wolf was already pregnant and Patrick stepped up, like a gentleman, to save the family name.'

'That's quite sad.'

Roz sipped her cocoa. 'Bloody tragic, if you ask me. It's not as if the Colbys were gentry or anything like that. Old man Colby made his money in munitions during the Great War. Now they're coining it in for the second time and Elspeth is filthy rich.'

Susan's head had begun to ache. The intensity of Roz's outburst together with her own desperate situation had suddenly become too much for her. She pushed back her chair and stood up. 'Would you mind if I take the cocoa to my room? I'm really tired.'

'No, of course not. Take no notice of me, Susan. I'm being bitchy because I hate to see a nice man dragged down by a predatory female.' Roz managed a tight little smile. 'Night night. Don't let the bed bugs bite.'

Susan went up to her room, and having washed and changed into her nightgown she climbed into bed. Charlie flopped down on the floor and closed his eyes with a deep sigh. 'I agree,' Susan said, sipping her rapidly cooling drink. 'It's been quite a day.' She placed the empty mug on the bedside cabinet and switched off the lamp. Enveloped in darkness she could hear the muffled drone of voices from the bar below, and the faint soughing of the wind. Exhausted both physically and mentally, she drifted off into a deep sleep.

She was awakened next morning by the steady plod of horse's hooves and the rumbling of cart-wheels, followed by the clunk of milk bottles being deposited on doorsteps. She sat up and stretched. Charlie opened one eye and yawned. 'It's all right for you,' she said softly. 'You haven't got a care in the world. I have to find work and a place to live today. We were lucky to get a bed for the night but we can't impose on the Fullers.' She rose from the warm cocoon of blankets and shivered as her bare feet touched the cold linoleum. Bracing herself, she went to draw back the curtains. It was still dark outside but she could just make out the irregular line of the rooftops across the street. A faint glimmer of dawn lightened the sky to the east, and she could see shadowy figures on the pavement below as people made their way to work. Inside the pub all was silent with no sign of anyone stirring. She took advantage of the fact that Roz and her father were not early risers and made her way to the bathroom.

Washed, dressed and feeling suddenly ravenous, she tiptoed downstairs to the kitchen with Charlie padding along behind her. He made a dash for Orlando as they entered the kitchen and was met with an arched back, flailing claws and a hissing mouth opened wide to expose a set of sharp white teeth. Charlie sat down, staring at the cat, obviously bewildered by this show of aggression. Ignoring them both, Susan made a pot of tea. Driven by hunger, she took a loaf from the bread bin and cut a slice. She found a block of margarine on a marble slab in the larder and spread some thinly on the bread. She was sitting at the table and about to take a bite when Roz walked into the kitchen. She was wrapped in a candlewick dressing gown and her hair was hanging loose around her shoulders. She blinked, rubbing her eyes. 'I thought I heard some-one moving about.'

'I'm sorry. I didn't mean to wake you. I was hungry so I helped myself. I hope you don't mind.'

Roz yawned and reached down to pat Charlie on the head. 'Mind what?' She stared at her bleary-eyed. 'Oh, the bread. Heavens no. Take all you want. Is there any tea left in the pot?' She slumped down on a chair, running her hand through her tousled mop of hair.

Susan jumped up to fetch another cup and saucer.

She poured the tea and passed the cup to Roz. 'I'll go out as soon as it's light and start looking for work. Perhaps there might be something at the aerodrome.'

Roz reached for the sugar bowl. 'It's a pity that none of the boys came in last night, but they'll turn up sometime.' She swallowed a mouthful of tea. 'You're welcome to stay until you get fixed up.'

'Thanks, I'm really grateful, but I've got to start somewhere.'

'Talking of making a start . . .' Roz glanced at the clock on the wall, pulling a face. 'I should have got up earlier to make the soup. It's quite popular at lunchtime with a freshly baked roll. That's if the boy from Hookers delivers the bread in time. He's a lazy little scamp and I'll swear he eats half of the order before he gets here.'

'I could make the soup,' Susan said eagerly. 'I'd be glad to do something to help.'

Roz brightened visibly. 'You can cook? How marvellous. I can, after a fashion, but it's not something I like doing.' She drained her cup, and stood up. 'I'd best get dressed. Mrs Delaney will be here soon. She's our charlady and she's a real treasure. I don't know what we'd do without her.' She was halfway out of the room when someone knocked on the back door. She hesitated, wrapping her dressing gown more tightly around her slim figure. 'Answer that for me, Susan, there's a dear. It might be Mrs D.'

Susan went to open the door with Charlie on her heels. He bounded outside and jumped up at a small boy wearing school uniform, almost knocking him over in his excitement. 'I'm so sorry,' Susan said, grabbing Charlie by the collar. 'Are you all right?'

The boy squared his shoulders. 'I'm fine. Who are you?'

'Is that you, Terry?' Roz called from the kitchen. 'Is anything wrong?'

He craned his neck in an attempt to see her. 'It's me mum, miss. She took a tumble on the icy pavement last night and broke her ankle. She had to go to hospital in an ambulance and they put her leg in a plaster. She says she's very sorry but she can't come to work today.'

Roz came to the door. In the early morning light and without the benefit of makeup, she looked pale and vulnerable. Her eyes widened with concern. 'I'm sorry to hear that, Terry. But she mustn't even try to come back until the doctor says it's all right. Tell her we'll manage somehow and I'll pop in and see her when I've got a moment.'

He tipped his cap. 'I will, miss. Got to go or I'll be late for school.' He bounded off through the back yard and disappeared into the garden with Charlie hot on his heels.

'Come back, you bad dog.' Susan made to follow them but Roz caught her by the sleeve.

'Don't worry. Terry's a smart kid. He won't let Charlie out of the garden.' Shivering, she retreated into the comparative warmth of the kitchen. 'God alone knows how we'll manage without Mrs D. I can't do the cleaning as well as the cooking and serving in the bar.' She paused, turning to Susan with a sudden smile. 'It's a sign. It was meant to be.'

Susan frowned. 'I don't know what you're talking about.'

'Don't you see? Poor Mrs D's accident is terrible for her, but you know what they say about an ill wind. Well, it blew you here and there's a job vacancy, if you're willing to take over the cleaning until she's back on both feet. You say you can cook too.' Roz threw up her hands. 'Alleluia! Problem solved. You can stay here rent free and I'll pay you a wage. It's perfect.' She hesitated, staring anxiously at Susan. 'You will do it, won't you? I mean I wouldn't stop you looking for other more suitable employment, but it would help both of us in the short term.'

Susan's head was spinning. It seemed too good to be true. She was sorry for Mrs Delaney, but thanks to the poor woman's misfortune her most pressing worries had been relieved, if only temporarily. 'I'd be glad to help out,' she said, smiling. 'Where shall I start? With the soup or with a mop and bucket?'

Roz pointed to the larder. 'There's a pile of veggies in the rack and a couple of beef bones in the meat safe outside the back door. I'll leave the rest to you. And the bar opens at ten thirty, so it will have to be cleaned and ready. Do you think you can manage?'

Thinking back to the long hours she had spent working to Mrs Kemp's exacting standards, Susan smiled and nodded. 'Don't worry. Leave it all to me.'

'How often I've longed to hear those words.' Roz blew her a kiss. 'Now I'm going to take my five inches of water and wallow in it, if that's possible.' She danced out of the kitchen, leaving Susan to face what seemed to be an uphill task, but she was ready for anything. The relief of having a roof over her head for the foreseeable future gave her all the encouragement she needed to roll up her sleeves and start work.

After a quick exploration of the kitchen cupboards and the meat safe hanging on the outside wall, she found everything she needed to begin preparing the soup. With the bones simmering on the stove, she set about cleaning, peeling and chopping the vegetables. Suddenly she felt at home. It was good to be needed, and to find a way of repaying Roz and her father for their kindness. She worked with a will, and when she had tidied the kitchen she set out to clean and tidy the bar. There were glasses left from the night before and ashtrays spilling over on the tables, but she went about her task with enthusiasm.

Bob put in an appearance just before opening time and was suitably impressed. 'Roz has just told me that you're willing to help out,' he said, looking round with an approving nod. 'I really appreciate this, Susan. I always feel slightly guilty for putting so much on her. She never complains, but sometimes I think this is not the best environment for a young woman.'

Susan picked up the tin of polish and tucked the dusters in her apron pocket. 'I'm sure she doesn't think that.'

He shrugged his shoulders. 'I hope not, but she doesn't meet the right sort of bloke. I'm beginning to think that it might be a good thing if you girls have to do war work or join the forces. It would get you out of the village and let you see a bit of the world before you settle down.' He glanced at the clock as someone rattled the door. 'Opening time. Thanks for stepping up, Susan. I'm truly grateful.' He crossed the floor, moving swiftly for a large man, and opened the door.

Susan picked up the mop and bucket and was about to retreat to the kitchen when she heard the now familiar cut-glass tones of Elspeth Peterson.

'It's too annoying, Bob,' she said, stepping over the threshold. 'I've lost an earring. I thought it might have fallen onto the floor in the bar.'

Bob glanced over his shoulder. 'Did you find anything this morning, Susan?'

'I didn't find any jewellery when I swept the floor,' Susan said, shaking her head. 'But if I come across it I'll put it somewhere safe.'

'So this is your new charwoman?' Elspeth said thoughtfully.

'You've heard about Mrs Delaney's accident, I suppose.' Bob took his position behind the bar. 'Susan's kindly stepped into the breach.'

'Yes, I did. It's a frightful nuisance. She cleans for me in the afternoons, and goodness knows how long she'll be laid up.' Elspeth cast a speculative glance in Susan's direction. 'I don't suppose you'd like to do another two or three hours a day, would you? You look young and strong, and my house is teensy-weensy compared to the Grange, so it wouldn't take you long to get around. Besides which, there's only the two of us, and my darling husband is hardly ever at home.' She shot a glance at Bob beneath her long lashes. 'He finds his barfly cronies much more interesting than his long-suffering wife.'

'I'm sure that's not true, Elspeth.'

She turned her lambent gaze on Susan. Her red lips pouted prettily and she smiled. 'You will help me out, won't you?'

'I – er – I'm not certain how much work there is for me here, Mrs Peterson.'

Bob gave her a reassuring smile. 'It's entirely up to you, Susan. If you think you can cope with the work then it's all right by me. Anyway, I'm sure that Elspeth is a much more generous employer than me.'

'Chars are like gold dust. I'll double whatever Bob is paying you.' Elspeth opened her handbag and took out a bulging purse. She thrust a pound note into the pocket of Susan's apron. 'Think of that as a retainer, my dear. I'll see you at two o'clock this afternoon. Bob will point you in the right direction.' She snapped her bag shut and swept out of the bar without giving Susan a chance to argue.

Bob shook his head. 'I've known Elspeth since she was a gangly schoolgirl, and I've never known her fail to get what she wants.' He paused, frowning. 'Except perhaps the husband she thinks she deserves. But that's none of my business.' He opened the till and began counting the coins. 'You don't have to do as she says, Susan. But it might be a stepping stone to a more permanent position. The Colbys are very influential round here.'

Roz was not so sanguine when she heard Susan's news. Her eyes narrowed and she tossed her head. 'You'd have to be desperate to work for that bitch.'

Susan recoiled at her tone. 'Isn't that a bit unfair? Just because she isn't happy in her marriage doesn't make her a bad person.'

Roz turned away to fill a bowl with soup. 'Don't take any notice of me, Susan. It's a personal thing and it shouldn't prevent you from taking the job, particularly if it means you can save a bit of money. Who knows what's going to happen in this beastly war? Anyway, if she likes you she might take you for a spin in her Tiger Moth. That wretched plane is the real love of her life.'

'She's got an aeroplane?' Suddenly Susan felt weak at the knees. She could not imagine anyone, let alone a spoilt beauty like Elspeth, having enough money to purchase their own aircraft.

Roz put the bowl on the tray and proceeded to fill another. 'Pass me a couple of bread rolls, please. There are two hungry factory workers waiting for their lunch.' She ladled the soup. 'Yes, Elspeth got her pilot's licence after she met Martin. They were both members of the same flying club. It's all right for some. That cow has never done a day's work in her whole life, and never likely to either.' She piled the plates onto a tray. 'By the way, the soup smells delicious. I'll have some for my lunch if the gannets in the bar don't finish it up.'

Susan automatically wiped the table with a damp dishcloth, scooping the breadcrumbs into the sink. The thought of knowing someone who actually owned an aeroplane was stunning. She could barely wait for two o'clock when she was due at the Petersons' house.

Riding Roz's bicycle through the picture postcard village streets, Susan followed the map that Bob had sketched on the back of a beer mat. The Petersons' house was about three miles from Hamble, set amongst a stand of oak trees on the banks of the river. From Elspeth's description, Susan had been expecting to find a suburban villa or a modest cottage, but as she approached the double wrought-iron gates and the long drive leading up to a seventeenth-century mansion, she realised that she had been misled.

She dismounted and opened the gates, which

swung effortlessly on well-oiled hinges. Closing them again, she pushed the bike slowly towards the house, taking in every detail of the Jacobean frontage with mullioned windows and a studded oak front door set beneath a stone arch. If this was Elspeth's idea of a modest dwelling, Susan could only hazard a guess as to the grandeur of Colby Grange. She propped the bike up against the wall and rang the doorbell. She waited, shifting nervously from one foot to the other for what seemed like ages, but eventually, just as she was about to ring again, she heard approaching footsteps. The door opened and Elspeth greeted her with a frown. 'It's customary for staff to use the tradesmen's entrance,' she said crossly.

'I'm sorry. I didn't know.'

'Well, you do now.' Elspeth held the door open. 'Come in anyway, but remember what I said the next time you come.' She turned her back on Susan and tip-tapped across the flagstone floor on her high heels.

Stepping over the threshold Susan found herself in a spacious wainscoted entrance hall with a polished oak staircase leading up to a galleried landing. She half expected to see suits of armour standing to attention at the foot of the stairs, with crossed halberds and broadswords decorating the walls, but it seemed that Elspeth's taste ran to slightly more modern furnishings. Even so, it was obvious even to a layman that the chairs, side table and monk's bench were genuine antiques. She led the way through a maze of narrow passages to a large kitchen at the back of the building. Despite the quarry-tiled floor and oak beams there was a modern range and an electric cooker. The walls were lined with glass-fronted cupboards and sturdy floor units.

A Belfast sink, large enough to act as a bath for a small child, sat beneath a lattice window over-looking a courtyard and a stable block.

'This is Mrs Harper's domain,' Elspeth said with a vague wave of her hand. 'She lives in a flat above the stable block and she has every afternoon off between two and five, so you can start work in the kitchen and scullery.' She indicated a side door. 'You'll find all the cleaning materials in the broom cupboard, and there's a vacuum cleaner which you'll use for the carpets in the reception rooms and bed-rooms. Mrs Delaney has her own routine, although I haven't the faintest idea as to how she goes about her tasks. Anyway, I'll leave you to work it out for yourself.'

Susan looked round the large room in dismay. 'Am I supposed to clean the whole house in one afternoon?'

Elspeth raised a pencilled eyebrow. 'Mrs Delaney manages and you're a good twenty years her junior. Obviously most of the bedrooms are unused unless we're entertaining, so they just need dusting and vacuuming, but I've no doubt you'll manage.'

'Do you mind telling me how many bedrooms there are?'

'Six and two bathrooms. I told you this is not a large house.' Elspeth glanced at her watch. 'It's ten past two. I'll expect you to work until ten past five to make up for lost time. I may be generous, Susan, but I expect to get my money's worth.' She walked towards the door, pausing to glance over her shoulder. 'I'm going to my room to change and then I'll be in the hangar with the Moth. Should anyone telephone, you'll find me there.'

In the hangar with the Moth. Susan's heart missed a beat. She had not doubted Roz when she had told her about the aeroplane, but to be this close to a real flying machine had made her pulses race. 'You have your own aeroplane.'

'Yes, and I like to do my own maintenance.' Elspeth threw back her head and laughed. 'Don't look so surprised. I'm a qualified pilot and I know enough about engines to keep mine tuned and in good order.'

Susan stared at her in amazement. It was almost impossible to imagine Elspeth getting her hands dirty, but now the subject of the aeroplane had been broached it gave her a chance to ask the question that had been on her lips from the moment Elspeth had offered her the job. 'Could I – I mean, would you let me see your aeroplane one day? I've read everything I can about Tiger Moths, but I've never been close to one.'

'Really?' Elspeth was suddenly alert. 'You're not just saying that?'

'No, honestly, I'd give anything to go up in a plane. My ambition has always been to fly one, but I know it's impossible.'

'I suppose that's true for a girl like you.' Elspeth frowned thoughtfully. 'However, if you work well for me who knows what might happen? There is one thing I must make clear: I expect complete loyalty from my staff, and the utmost discretion at all times.'

Susan had been too well schooled by Mrs Kemp to show any surprise. 'I understand.'

Elspeth's tawny eyes narrowed, giving her the look of a big cat on the prowl. 'You're obviously getting on well with Roz Fuller.'

'She's been very good to me.'

'You're much of an age, and no doubt share girlish secrets.'

'I wouldn't say that. We only met yesterday.'

'Yes, of course. I was forgetting that. You looked so at home in the bar when I came looking for my errant husband. But apparently he'd arrived just minutes before I did.' Elspeth's smile did not quite reach her eyes and her mouth hardened into a painted line.

'That's right,' Susan said, making a move towards the broom cupboard. 'Perhaps I'd better make a start.'

Elspeth's hand shot out to catch her by the sleeve. 'I'm very good to those who serve me well. But I'm not a person to cross. Do you understand what I'm saying, Susan?'

Chapter Eleven

If the house in Elsworthy Road had seemed large, the Petersons' establishment was enormous. Dave's flat would have easily fitted into the drawing room. By the time she had finished cleaning the upstairs Susan was beginning to think that Mrs Delaney was a miracle worker, a sentiment obviously shared by Mrs Harper, who had begun preparing the evening meal when Susan returned briefly to fetch a clean duster. She looked Susan up and down, shaking her head. 'You won't last long, young lady. The mistress is a perfectionist.'

'I'll do my best,' Susan said, backing towards the doorway.

'Mrs Delaney was due for a rest. Fair wore out, she was.' Mrs Harper sighed heavily. 'It's a pity she had to break her ankle in order to stay at home and put her feet up.'

Faced with such a lugubrious personality, Susan took what she needed from the cupboard and retreated to the peace and quiet of the first floor.

When she returned to the kitchen she was relieved to find that Mrs Harper, the antithesis of the rotund, smiling cook as portrayed in books and films, was now in the scullery peeling vegetables. Her rendition of 'For those in peril on the sea', slightly off key and very much out of tune, was enough to put anyone off a life on the ocean wave. At a quarter to six, long after she was supposed to have finished, Susan was just putting the vacuum cleaner away when Mrs Harper stopped singing to greet Elspeth as she strolled in from the stable yard. Susan could see her through the open door and she was impressed. Elspeth might be wearing a standard navy-blue boiler suit but she still looked as though she had stepped straight from the pages of *Vogue* or *Harper*'s. There was an artistic streak of engine oil on one cheek, but she looked surprisingly immaculate for someone who had been tinkering with an aircraft engine all afternoon. She stopped, staring pointedly at the wall clock.

'I thought you'd finished, Susan. Don't expect me to pay you overtime.'

'I don't,' Susan said, closing the cupboard door with a sigh of relief. 'I'll get into my stride tomorrow.'

Elspeth patted a stray hair into place, shrugging her slender shoulders. 'It's time you went home anyway. I'm going upstairs to take a bath.' She paused in the doorway. 'If my husband stops off at the pub, tell him that dinner is at seven thirty sharp.' She disappeared from view leaving a trail of Arpège and engine oil in her wake.

Susan found the bicycle where she had left it and

started out for home, but she was tired and it was dark, cold and starting to rain. She did not hear the car until it was almost upon her and she saw the slatted beam of the dipped headlights as it rounded the bend in the narrow lane. She flung herself into the hedge and the vehicle's brakes squealed as it came to a halt a few yards along the road. A man leapt out and ran to her assistance.

'Oh my God. I'm so sorry. I didn't see you until it was too late. Are you hurt?'

She struggled to her feet. 'I'm okay. I think.' She thought she recognised the voice. 'Mr Peterson?'

He steadied her, placing his hand beneath her elbow. 'Yes. I'm sorry. Do I know you?'

She grimaced as she flexed a scraped knee. 'Not really. I was in the bar last night when . . .' She hesitated. 'I'm staying with the Fullers.'

'I remember now, you're the girl with the yellow Lab. I'm afraid I've forgotten your name. Sorry.'

'It's Susan Banks, and I'm helping out at your house while Mrs Delaney is laid up. I've just come from there now.'

'I heard about poor Mrs D.' He bent down to retrieve the bicycle. 'Let me give you a lift back to the pub, Susan. The bike will go on the back seat.'

'I don't want to put you to any trouble.'

'It's the least I can do in the circumstances.' He wheeled the bicycle towards the large and expensive-looking cabriolet and propped it against the wing. Having put the top down he lifted it onto the back seat despite Susan's protests that it might make the leather upholstery muddy. 'It will brush off,' he said cheerfully. 'Hop in. I'll have you home in no time at all.'

'I was supposed to give you a message,' she said, climbing into the passenger seat.

'Don't tell me. Dinner's at seven thirty sharp and I'm not to be late. My darling Elspeth is a stickler for punctuality, and I'm forever upsetting her by turning up at all hours. It's the nature of my job, I'm afraid.' He leapt into the driver's seat and started the engine. He negotiated the tight bends with ease and when they reached a straight piece of road he shot a curious glance at Susan. 'Have you known Roz long? I don't think I've ever heard her mention your name.'

'We only met by accident yesterday. Charlie chased Orlando into the pub garden.'

'It's none of my business, of course, but you seem awfully young to be wandering the countryside on your own.'

'I had Charlie with me.'

'I was forgetting the faithful hound.'

'I couldn't keep him in London. It's all a bit complicated.'

'I'm a good listener.'

By the time they pulled up outside the pub Susan had told him her life story. He was surprisingly easy to talk to and she could understand why Roz enjoyed his company. He was, as he had said, a good listener, and he laughed appreciatively at her deliberately whimsical descriptions of life in the Kemp household. She decided that he was wasted on Elspeth. 'Thanks for the lift,' she said as he turned off the ignition.

'Don't mention it.' He was already on the pavement, lifting the bicycle from the back of the car. 'I don't think there's any damage,' he said cheerfully, 'but of course I'll pay for any necessary repairs.'

She eased herself off the seat. Her knee was painful and stiff, but she did not want to upset him by admitting she was in pain. 'It wasn't your fault.'

'You're a very generous girl, Susan. You must allow me to buy you a drink.'

'I'm under age and you'll be late for dinner if you're not careful.' She took hold of the handlebars. 'I can manage. I'll take it round to the garage.'

'I'll be in the bar if you fancy a glass of ginger beer. And don't worry, I won't stay long.'

She wheeled the cycle to the back entrance and stowed it away for the night. Charlie greeted her with ecstatic yelps as she entered the kitchen and she made a fuss of him, stroking his head and tickling his ears which always sent him into paroxysms of bliss. When he finally settled down she realised that she was hungry. She had not eaten since lunchtime but the worktops were bare and there was no evidence that Roz had started to make supper. Susan had not intended to venture into the bar. Last night's episode with Charlie attempting to ravage Elspeth's mink coat had made her wary of letting him loose on the drinking population of Hamble. She had no intention of accepting Patrick's offer of a drink, but she needed to speak to Roz.

She found her deep in conversation with Patrick. The bar was empty apart from the usual couple of regulars who sat in the snug nursing their pint mugs of brown ale. Neither Roz nor Patrick seemed to be aware of her presence and Susan felt an apprehensive shiver run down her spine. Their heads were close together and although there was the whole width of the bar counter between them it did little to keep them apart. Their elbows were touching as they leaned on the polished surface and their voices were low and intimate. In that instant Susan knew for certain that Elspeth's suspicions were justified, but now she was beginning to think that there might be an ulterior motive behind Elspeth's offer to take her on while Mrs Delaney was incapacitated. There must be dozens of local women who would have been glad of the work. Suddenly it all made sense: the lecture on loyalty, the generous wages and the vague promise of a joyride in the Moth. Elspeth had set her up to spy on the star-crossed couple. It would have been obvious to anyone observing them now that they were on the verge of an affair, if not already deeply involved. Susan's heart contracted with sympathy for both of them. She knew instinctively that Roz was not the sort of girl who would set out to break up a marriage, and Patrick did not seem like a womaniser. It appeared that fate had dealt all three of them a rotten hand. Susan was about to retreat when the pub door opened and two men in RAF uniform walked into the bar.

'Tony!' She would have known him anywhere. Her fleeting attraction to Colin was as nothing compared to the way her heart leapt at the sight of Tony Richards. She took a tentative step towards him. 'Tony. It's me, Susan.'

He stared at her blankly for a moment and she held her breath. He did not recognise her – so much for the romantic notions that she had built up since their last meeting. She had been chasing rainbows. Charlie chose this moment to wriggle free from her restraining hand on his collar and he bounded over to Tony, jumping up at him as if he were a long lost friend.

'Charlie. Come here this minute.' Covered in confusion and wishing the floor would open up and send her hurtling down to the cellar below, Susan clicked her fingers at her errant puppy.

At the sound of her voice, Tony's expression changed. 'Susan. It really is you. I thought for a moment that my eyes were deceiving me. What on earth are you doing here?'

Her mind had gone completely blank. 'I thought a change of scene would do me good,' she murmured in desperation. She had imagined the moment when they met again a hundred times or more, but now they were face to face the reality of the situation hit her forcibly. She had fled from London in the childish hope that Tony would welcome her with open arms. It was only now she realised that she had not thought it through. She had come running to ask help from a man she had come to know through the stories his father told about him and the photographs proudly displayed around the tiny flat. She had dusted them every day, small black and white images of Tony as a chubby-cheeked baby, a tousle-haired schoolboy, a slightly sulky-looking teenager and a proud new recruit in RAF uniform. She had fallen in love with him by proxy. But what did he know of her apart from the fact that she had lied to him from the outset? She felt her cheeks burning with embarrassment, and she was acutely aware that both Roz and Patrick were staring at her. She turned to them with an attempt at a smile. 'I told you about Tony and his dad. They were very good to me when I needed a helping hand.' She knew that she was stating the obvious, and that they probably knew Tony better than she did. She wished the floor would open up and swallow her.

'It's good to see you again, Susan,' Tony said with his easy smile. He turned to his companion. 'This is my very good friend, Danny Gillespie. Danny, this is Susan Banks, who by some amazing twist of fate has turned up in Hamble.'

Danny grinned and shook her hand. 'Pleased to meet you, Susan.'

'How do you do?' She managed a weak smile.

Roz took a pint mug from the shelf beneath the bar. 'The usual, boys?'

Tony nodded emphatically. 'Yes, please, Roz.' He was about to place a handful of coins on the counter, but Patrick forestalled him.

'This one's on me, chaps.' He turned to give Susan a friendly grin. 'I still owe you that drink.'

She was trapped. Tony was standing close by her side and Danny was making a fuss of Charlie. She would have liked to flee to her room and lock herself in, but that would have made her look even sillier. 'Lemonade, please.'

'Lemonade it is, and two pints of best bitter for the boys, if you please, Roz.' Patrick glanced at his watch. 'I'll have one for the road and then I really must be off.'

'Yes. You don't want to upset Elspeth again.' Roz was smiling but she could not quite disguise the hint of bitterness in her voice.

'Thanks, Patrick,' Tony said with an appreciative nod. He turned to Susan. 'Let's go and sit by the fire. Danny will bring the drinks.'

She followed him to the ingle nook. He waited until she was seated and then sat down beside her. 'What's this all about, Susan? I'm delighted to see you, but I thought you were settled in the flat with Dad. I thought you two were getting on well.'

She gazed into the orange flames as they licked around the logs. The sap hissed and sizzled, sending plumes of aromatic smoke up the chimney. 'We were, but it was a bit difficult when your aunt came to stay.'

'Colin told me that things were a bit tense, but the old girl's not too bad when you get to know her.'

'He gave me your Christmas present.' Susan looked him in the eyes for the first time and she smiled shyly. 'I love the book and I've been studying it.'

'And the one you gave me was an inspiration on your part, and probably much too expensive.' He laid his hand on hers as they rested in her lap. His expression was suddenly serious. 'What went wrong? I really thought you were settled in the flat with my dad. Colin said that he thought the world of you. He also said that you're a wonderful cook and he had the best Christmas dinner ever.'

Still she could not bring herself to tell him the truth. 'Your aunt didn't like me, and she couldn't stand Charlie. I tried my best to get on with her, but you know what they say about two women in the kitchen. It doesn't work.'

'I didn't know that Aunt Maida could boil an egg, let alone cook a proper meal. But I'm sorry it didn't work out, more for Dad's sake than anything. He won't admit it, but I know he's been really lonely since Mum died.' He gave her a searching look. 'I'm still not certain you're telling me everything. Did you come here because of Colin? I know he's a charmer, but if he's led you on . . .'

'No,' Susan said hastily. 'He didn't. He took me to a lovely place called the Trocadero on Christmas Eve and bought me dinner. He told me about Morag, his childhood sweetheart in Scotland.'

'Ah, yes, Morag. The faithful Highland lassie.' He frowned thoughtfully. 'But that still doesn't explain why you decided to come here. Was it something I said? I mean, I wouldn't want to have given you the impression that life was easy here, or any safer than in London. We had a huge bomb drop slap in the middle of the airfield a couple of weeks ago.'

'I didn't know where else to go. I haven't any friends or family and you did tell me to look you up if I was in the area.'

He squeezed her fingers. 'Well, I'm glad you did, and I'm really pleased to see you again. ' He looked up as Danny brought their drinks to the table. 'Thanks, old man.'

'Thank you, Danny.' Susan made room for him on the settle but he shook his head.

'It's nice to meet you, Susan, but I can see you two have some catching up to do. I'll be at the bar, chatting to Patrick.' He strolled off, leaving them with just Charlie for company.

Susan glanced over her shoulder but Patrick showed no sign of getting ready to leave, and a quick look at the clock on the shelf between the optics told her that he would never make it by seven thirty.

'He'll cop it when he gets home,' Tony said as if

reading her thoughts. 'Poor old Patrick. He has a hell of a life with Elspeth, but you'll find that out if you stay round here for long.'

Susan had only been in Hamble for just over twenty-four hours. She was an innocent bystander and yet she found herself becoming entangled in the complicated lives of the inhabitants. She bent over to pat Charlie as he settled on the hearth, stretching out in front of the fire. His coat was smooth and warm and his presence was comforting. At least she had one good friend on whom she could rely. She looked up to find Tony regarding her with a thoughtful expression.

'What are you going to do about a job, Susan?'

'It's all sorted, at least for now. I'm working here until Mrs Delaney's broken ankle mends, and I'm helping out at the Petersons' house in the afternoons.'

'Good luck with that.' Tony pulled a face. 'I don't think I'd like to work for Elspeth.'

'You don't like her?'

'I didn't say that, but she's not the easiest person to get on with, and she leads poor Patrick a bit of a dance.'

'She owns a Tiger Moth. She's got a pilot's licence. I really admire her for that.'

'You really have been bitten by the flying bug, haven't you, Susan?'

'Now you're laughing at me.'

His smile faded. 'No, honestly, I'm not. I think

it's super. Most of the girls I know are only interested in the pilots, not their machines.'

'Maybe I like both.' She could not resist flirting with him, just a little. He was just as good-looking as she remembered, and he had kind eyes. She found herself falling in love with him all over again.

He laughed. 'Now you're flannelling me, Susan.'

'Maybe, just a little, but one day I'll get to fly a plane. Elspeth's sort of promised to take me up in her Moth.'

'Then I hope she keeps her word. Did she tell you that she's a friend of Pauline Gower?'

Susan shook her head. 'Should I know who she is?'

'She's the commanding officer of the women's section of the Air Transport Auxiliary, and I shouldn't really tell you this, but rumour has it that they're going to be transferred here from White Waltham later this year.'

Susan could hardly believe her ears. 'Really? That's wonderful. I'd give anything to meet the women pilots and hear first hand about their exploits. They're so incredibly brave.'

'Well, you never know. I might be able to swing it for you.'

'Would you? I'd be in your debt forever.' Forgetting decorum, she flung her arms around his neck and planted a kiss on his cheek, but the realisation that everyone was staring at them made her pull away instantly. She reached for her glass and took a mouthful of lemonade. 'I'm sorry. I didn't mean to embarrass you.'

Tony chuckled. 'I can take that sort of humiliation a hundred times over. It's not every day that a pretty girl kisses me so enthusiastically.'

'You did mean it, didn't you? You wouldn't tease me about anything so important.'

He crossed his heart. 'I'll see what I can do.'

'I was hoping I might get a job at the aerodrome,' Susan said wistfully. 'But I don't know what I could do.'

'If I hear of anything I'll let you know.' He looked up as Danny came to join them. 'Susan is looking for work on the base. Is there anything going in your department?'

Danny pulled up a chair and sat down. 'Not unless she's good at riveting and welding bits of smashed up machines back together again.' His smile was genuine and his snub nose and freckled face made him look like an overgrown schoolboy.

Susan took an instant liking to him. 'I'll do anything within reason.'

'I don't suppose you've got any engineering experience?'

'No, but I could learn.'

Tony drained his mug and stood up. 'I'm getting this round. Won't you have something a bit stronger, Susan? A shandy or a port and lemon, perhaps?'

She glanced at the bar and saw Patrick still deep in conversation with Roz. Reluctantly she rose to her feet. 'No thanks. I'd better get back to the kitchen and make supper. I think that's part of my job here, although we haven't had a chance to talk it through properly.' She turned to Danny, smiling. 'It was nice to meet you.'

'Likewise, Susan. I expect we'll be seeing a lot more of you.' He handed his empty glass to Tony. 'Thanks, mate.'

Susan called to Charlie who was sound asleep and twitching as if in the middle of an exciting dream. He opened one eye and yawned, but as Susan followed Tony to the bar Charlie leapt up, shook himself, and lolloped after them.

The pub was filling up and Tony had to wait to be served. Susan hesitated; she felt she still owed him an explanation as to why she left London in such a hurry. 'I don't want you to think that I let your dad down by leaving.'

He set the empty glasses on the bar. 'But you weren't unhappy in London with Dad and Aunt Maida, were you? I'd hate to think you felt you had to leave.'

'Your dad did everything he could to make me feel at home, but it was cramped in the flat and your aunt objected to Charlie. He chewed up one of her best shoes and she was furious. She wanted me to get rid of him but I wouldn't do that. Anyway, I would have had to leave sooner or later and find a more permanent home for both of us.'

Tony looked down at Charlie, shaking his head.

'I wonder if you know what a lucky chap you are to have someone who loves you enough to give up everything for you?'

Charlie wagged his tail and offered a paw. Tony bent down and shook it solemnly. 'You look after your mistress, old boy. She's one in a million.'

Susan glanced anxiously at the people standing at the bar. 'Patrick is still here,' she whispered. 'He's going to be in terrible trouble at home.'

'That's his problem. He's a big boy and he knows what he's doing.' Tony frowned as Roz laughed at something that Patrick had said. 'It's Roz I feel sorry for. I think he's leading her on and she's worth more than that.'

Susan's heart sank. It had not occurred to her that Tony might have someone else in mind, and the idea that he might harbour feelings for Roz was unexpectedly and unbelievably painful. She knew now why she had travelled this far in war-torn England, and it was not simply to satisfy her ambition to fly an aeroplane. Suddenly she needed time to think. Murmuring an excuse she left him waiting in line to be served and edged her way towards the door which led to the Fullers' private quarters.

She was not certain how much was expected of her in order to earn her keep, but she realised that if she did not make an effort to cook something they would have to exist on bread and cheese. She met Bob at the foot of the stairs.

'Sounds as though it's getting busy in the bar,' he said cheerfully. 'I'm going to play mine host now and relieve Roz. By the way, how did you get on with the dragon lady?'

Susan stifled a giggle. 'It was fine. She was okay with me.'

'Then you're honoured. Elspeth has been known to reduce the toughest women to tears on their first day working for her. Luckily Mrs D is made of sterner stuff and I think Elspeth is a bit scared of her.' He was about to head for the bar but Susan called him back.

'Mr Fuller, wait.'

He turned with a grin. 'Call me Bob, everyone does.'

'I was wondering if it would be all right to make something for supper. Unless you've already eaten, that is.'

'That's a capital idea, young Susan. We usually grab a sandwich at the end of the evening, but if you can rustle up something hot and tasty I might have to adopt you as my second daughter.' Chuckling, Bob opened the door to the bar and was met with a wave of sound and a waft of tobacco smoke.

Susan smiled to herself. 'They say the way to a man's heart is through his stomach, Charlie, and it certainly seems to work.'

Happily oblivious to human problems, he pranced on ahead of her, pushing the kitchen door open with

218

his nose and making a half-hearted dive at Orlando, who met his enthusiastic greeting with an arched back and a warning hiss.

Susan set to work exploring the shelves in the larder, which was well stocked with tins of baked beans, soup and condensed milk, but very little else. There was however a large packet of macaroni and a slab of cheese, which was a luxury considering the strict rationing of dairy products. Susan could only suppose that there must be fewer restrictions on catering establishments, or else Bob did a bit of black market trading on the side. Milk did not seem to be a problem either and she was able to make a rich cheese sauce to pour over the cooked pasta.

She put the dish in the oven to brown and busied herself by tidying the kitchen and washing the teacups and side plates that Roz and Bob had abandoned on the draining board. She had just finished and was taking the dish from the oven when Roz entered the kitchen. She was flushed and her dark eyes glowed with an inner light. She looked, Susan thought, like a woman in love. Her heart ached for her, and also for Tony who did not stand a chance while Patrick was around, but most of all the pain was her own. She forced a smile. 'I hope you're hungry, Roz.'

Roz went to the sink and filled a tumbler with water. She drained it in two thirsty gulps. 'It gets so stuffy in the bar with everyone smoking.' She turned to Susan with a bright smile. 'Dad said you were making something nice for supper. I could smell it in the bar.'

'It's just macaroni cheese. Sit down and have some while it's hot.'

Roz pulled out a chair and took a seat, resting her elbows on the table. 'Have you ever been in love, Susan?'

She almost dropped the serving spoon. 'Nothing serious.'

'You're damn lucky in that case.' Roz took the plate from her and sat looking at the steaming pasta covered in bubbling cheese sauce. 'Love isn't all it's cracked up to be.'

Susan took her plate to the table and sat down. 'Especially when the man is married.' She bit her lip. She had not meant to blurt it out in such a blunt manner.

Roz paused with the fork halfway to her mouth. 'Pardon?'

'Oh, Roz, it's so obvious. You and Patrick, I mean.'

'You didn't say anything to Elspeth, did you?' Roz glared at her, visibly shaken.

'Of course not. What do you take me for?'

'I don't know, but you turn up on our doorstep like a stray cat and all of a sudden she offers you a job. Why would she do that unless she had an ulterior motive? Or did she send you here in the first place? I wouldn't put it past the bitch.'

Susan stared at her in dismay. 'That's ridiculous. I'd never met the woman until yesterday.'

'But you were pretty quick in taking the job with her, and then you come back here making ridiculous accusations.'

'I'm sorry if I upset you. I wish I hadn't said anything.'

Roz pushed her plate away, rising to her feet. 'I don't need you spying on me.'

'That's not true and it's not fair.'

'Who asked you to stick your nose into my business anyway?'

'I didn't. I mean, I was just telling you how it must seem to everyone who sees you and Patrick together.'

'You don't know what you're talking about, and I obviously can't trust you to keep your mouth shut. I think you'd better pack your bags and leave here first thing tomorrow morning.' Roz stormed out of the room, slamming the door behind her.

Chapter Twelve

Susan went to bed early. She was exhausted, upset and furious with Roz for believing that she would betray her secret to anyone, least of all Elspeth. She slid beneath the covers but she could not get warm. She was shivering and her teeth were chattering more from distress than actual cold. It was not very warm in her room and even with Charlie lying across her feet they remained like blocks of ice. She closed her eyes, but she could still see Roz's angry face and hear her bitter accusations.

A few well-meant words spoken in sympathy had made an enemy of someone who until that moment had been her friend, and now she and Charlie would be on the move once again. She turned on her side, listening to the babble of voices coming from the bar. The smell of tobacco smoke and beer wafted up through the cracks between the ancient floorboards, and she could hear the pub door opening and closing as the customers left for home. Then all was quiet, except for Charlie's gentle snoring.

She was just drifting off to sleep when she heard the click of the latch and her door opened. She snapped upright, pulling the sheet up to her chin.

'Susan, it's me.' Roz slipped into the room, closing the door behind her. She switched on the light.

'What d'you want, Roz? I think you said it all downstairs.'

Roz perched on the edge of the bed, stroking Charlie in an abstracted way. She had removed her makeup and her dark hair hung loose around her shoulders. She wrapped her dressing gown around her, folding her arms across her chest. 'I came to apologise,' she said softly. 'I shouldn't have gone for you like that. It really wasn't fair.'

Susan leaned back against the headboard, blinking as her eyes grew accustomed to the light. 'I wouldn't dream of saying anything to anyone, least of all Elspeth.'

'I know, and I'm really sorry. It was just a shock to hear it put into words.'

'You're making it pretty obvious,' Susan said gently. 'Both of you.'

Roz ran her hand through her tumbled locks. 'Oh, God. What a mess. Elspeth is already suspicious, and if Dad finds out there'll be hell to pay.'

'I don't know what to say.'

'The obvious thing would be to put a stop to it, but it's not that easy. It's gone too far.'

'You mean you're . . .' Susan stopped herself just in time. A dull flush coloured Roz's cheeks and she averted her gaze. 'I'm sorry. It's really nothing to do with me.'

'Yes. That's what makes it such a terrible mess,

but I love him. We never intended it to happen, but things went too far.' Roz threw back her head and laughed, but it was a humourless sound. 'I never thought I'd lose my virginity in the back of someone's car, even if it was an expensive model like the Triumph Gloria. That sort of thing is for sluts like Connie Makepeace, the village floozy, not for Roz Fuller whose dad sent her to an expensive boarding school and expected her to grow up to be a young lady.' She flicked angry tears from her eyes. 'I'm just terrified I'll get pregnant like bloody Elspeth, but there won't be a younger brother willing to step up to save my reputation, such as it is.'

'You told me that was why Patrick had married Elspeth, but I don't understand why he felt it necessary to make an honest woman of her. It sounds like something out of a Jane Austen novel.'

Roz sniffed and wiped her eyes on the sleeve of her dressing gown. 'It does, doesn't it? The fact is that the Petersons are what you'd call genteelly poor. Patrick's elder brother, Martin, worked for old man Colby and he made a play for Elspeth. I don't know if his reasons were mercenary or if he really loved her, but anyway, as I told you, they were engaged to be married and just weeks before the wedding Martin died. Elspeth was left pregnant and unmarried.'

'But it's not as if she was poor and would have had to struggle on alone. She had a wealthy family to support her.'

'Yes, but her father is the old-fashioned type. Elspeth is an only child and Mr Colby didn't want to pass his business on to a bastard. He made Patrick an offer he couldn't refuse.'

Susan stared at her in disbelief. 'Why did he go along with such an outrageous plan? He could have said no.'

'He could, but his parents are tenant farmers on land owned by Colby. They've been there for generations and Mr Colby bought the estate some years ago when the landowner died and his heirs wanted the cash. Patrick says that Colby threatened to evict his mum and dad if he didn't marry Elspeth. It was straightforward blackmail, but Patrick had only just qualified and he didn't have a bean.'

'What about Elspeth? Didn't she have any say in the matter?'

'Not much, but I think she was happy to go along with it. She always had a soft spot for Patrick, even when she was going out with Martin. Anyway, she knew she would be damaged goods and her dad would have his work cut out to find another mug to marry her, even with all the cash incentives he could offer.'

'So Patrick did the honourable thing.'

'You could say that, although I didn't really know him then. I'd only just left school when they got married. I'd seen him around the village, of course, but he was several years my senior and anyway he'd been away at university, so our paths had rarely crossed.'

'How did you get to know him?'

A reminiscent smile curved Roz's generous lips. 'It was his stag night. He held it here and he came in with several of his old friends. They were buying the drinks and he was standing quietly on the other side of the bar. I was helping out by washing glasses and I looked at him and he looked at me.'

Susan breathed a sigh. 'And you fell in love as your eyes met?'

'No. Not then. Actually I felt a bit sorry for him. I'd never seen anyone look so hunted, but I didn't think much of it until later.'

'So how did you two get together?'

'It was through Orlando. He got run over in the High Street and I took him to Patrick's surgery. He was so kind and gentle with the poor cat. I was in floods of tears and I thought he was going to die, but Patrick told me not to worry and he'd fix Orlando up so that he was as good as new. And he did.'

'And you had to see him quite often then, I suppose.'

'I did, and then he started calling in for a drink after work. I began to look forward to seeing him, and then I couldn't wait for him for walk through the door. My day wasn't complete unless I'd seen him and spoken to him.'

'And he obviously felt the same.'

'Yes.' Roz stared dreamily into space. 'Then one day I realised that Orlando had fleas.' She giggled. 'I know it doesn't sound very romantic but I was horrified and I took him to Patrick, practically knocking down the surgery door in my haste to get something done about the little perishers. Or perhaps I just wanted to be alone with Patrick. I don't know, but somehow we ended up kissing, and it went on from there.'

'I'm so sorry, Roz.'

'Don't be. It's the most wonderful and yet the most terrible thing that's ever happened to me. I live for the moments we're together and I suffer the torments of hell when he goes back to his wife. I hate Elspeth with a passion, and yet I'm the scarlet woman, and she's the wronged wife. Does that make any sense to you?'

'I think so. But I've never felt that strongly about anyone.'

Roz sighed and rose to her feet. 'If you ever do, I hope it's in happier circumstances. Being the other woman is agony, and I can't see it ending in anything but disaster for both of us.'

Susan drew her knees up to her chest, wrapping her arms around them. 'But your dad will stand by you, won't he?'

'Dad's old-fashioned like Mr Colby. He's put so much store by me that it's frightening. He thinks that because he gave me a private education I'm going to marry a doctor or a lawyer and make him proud.' She moved slowly towards the door. 'I'm sorry for before, and I apologise for dumping my problems on you, Susan. You will stay on, won't you? I need a friend right now.'

'Of course I will, and I'll tell Elspeth I can't cope with two jobs. I won't go back there after tomorrow.'

Roz paused with her fingers curled round the doorknob. 'Don't do that. If you can bear to work for the witch I'd rather you kept going there. I think she'll try to persuade you to spy on us, and you must tell me what she says. I'm putting all my trust in you, Susan. I hope that you won't let me down.' She switched off the light as she left the room.

Susan uncurled herself and stretched out in the bed with Charlie snuggling up against her. She could not help envying Roz, who had a nice home and a loving parent; everything in fact that Susan had always longed for. Even though Roz's love affair seemed doomed, at least she had a man who adored her and would risk everything just to be with her. Susan lay staring into the darkness until eventually her eyelids grew heavy and she fell asleep.

Next day Susan returned to the Petersons' mansion. Her knee was stiff and sore, which made riding the bicycle painful, but she was determined to keep her job. She knew instinctively that Elspeth would have no qualms about sacking her if she proved to be unpunctual, and she would not be interested in excuses however valid. She did her work, following

Elspeth's previous instructions to the letter, but the only time she saw her that day was when she happened to be shaking a duster out of an upstairs window and Elspeth was strolling across the stable yard. She was wearing overalls and her hair was confined in a turban. Susan could only suppose that she was going to the hangar to play at being an engineer. Somehow she could not believe that Elspeth knew one end of a spanner from the other, and her manicured hands with their long, painted fingernails were hardly suited to manual labour.

She closed the window and went back to dusting the dressing table. She had to work quickly and efficiently in order to get round the whole house in the short space of an afternoon and it was dark by the time she had finished cleaning the first floor. She went downstairs to stow away the cleaning materials, murmuring a greeting to Mrs Harper in passing.

'It's all right for some,' Mrs Harper said, chopping onions with vicious cuts of a surgically sharp blade. 'You can go home now and put your feet up. I've got dinner to prepare and now Madam wants tea in the drawing room. I've only got one pair of hands since young Connie upped and left to work in a factory for three times what she earned here.'

Susan wondered if this was the infamous slut Connie Makepeace, but she did not like to ask. 'Um, I could help if you like,' she said cautiously. 'What needs doing?'

'You?' Mrs Harper stared at her, red-eyed and sniffing back tears as the strong odour of the onions made her cry. 'Are you a parlour maid? Have you had any training?'

Memories of Mrs Kemp's strict regime flashed through Susan's mind. She nodded. 'Actually I spent some time in service. I know what's what.'

'Well, now. Life is full of surprises.' Mrs Harper dashed her hand across her eyes. 'Go on then. It'll be tea for two. Make some sandwiches and butter some scones. Luckily I made a batch before I had my afternoon rest. And make sure you cut the crusts off the sandwiches. Madam doesn't like them left on.' She jerked her head in the direction of the larder. 'You'll find everything in there. She'll have to put up with salmon paste today. That's all I could get sent from Spakes.'

'Right you are,' Susan said cheerfully. 'Tea for two it is.' She set about her task, exploring the depths of the walk-in larder with its well-stocked shelves. Obviously the Petersons had no intention of going hungry. Despite rationing there were always going to be people who could afford luxuries. She took what she needed and with the expertise of long practice she made a plate of dainty sandwiches and buttered some scones. She filled a cut-glass dish with homemade strawberry jam and put it on the tray. 'Where do you keep the table napkins, Mrs Harper?'

'In the dresser. Left hand drawer.' Mrs Harper threw the chopped onions into a pan on the stove.

'So you do know how things are done, young lady.'

'I should hope I do.' Susan found the napkins, folded them neatly and put them on the tray with two small knives. 'Shall I take this in, or will you?'

'Can't you see I'm busy? If I burn the onions it'll ruin the dish.' She poured boiling water onto the tea leaves in the warmed pot. 'Here, don't forget the tea, silly girl.'

Susan carried the tray carefully to the drawing room, pushing the door open with her foot. It would have been physically impossible to knock and she went straight in, but she came to a sudden halt at the sight of Elspeth in the arms of a man in uniform. She hesitated, not knowing quite what to do, but the sound of the teacups rattling on their saucers and the teaspoons clinking against bone china caused the couple to break apart.

Elspeth flushed angrily. 'You should knock before entering a room, you stupid girl.'

The young officer turned round and his smile froze. His eyes widened in surprise. 'Susan.'

'Colin.' She almost dropped the heavy tray.

He hurried forward to take it from her. 'What on earth are you doing here?'

'You know each other?' For once Elspeth sounded unsure of herself. 'Colin?'

He placed the tray on a Georgian-style coffee table. 'We met in London at Christmas,' he said, apparently unabashed. 'Susan was staying with my friend's family in Swiss Cottage.'

'Really?' Elspeth raised a delicate eyebrow. 'And now she's living at the pub and working for me. How did that come about? I don't suppose you had anything to do with her moving down here, Colin?'

He blew her a kiss. 'Jealous, darling?'

Ignoring him, Elspeth glared at Susan. 'Well? Perhaps you'd like to enlighten me?'

Susan clasped her hands tightly behind her back. She felt as though she had entered a strange world, like Alice when she had tumbled down the rabbit hole. She half expected the Mad Hatter to rush into the room and pop the dormouse into the teapot. She gazed helplessly at Colin. 'It's complicated,' she murmured.

'Never mind the details,' he said, giving her his most charming smile. 'It's super to see you again, Susan. We must catch up soon. Does Tony know you're here?'

'Yes, I saw him last night at the pub.'

'Which pub would that be? There are plenty to choose from in Hamble.'

'She's staying with the Fullers at the Victorious,' Elspeth said impatiently. 'And now she's working for me. That will be all for now, Susan. I think it's time you went home.'

'Yes, Mrs Peterson.' Susan hurried from the room. She was more shocked by what she had just witnessed than she could have imagined. Elspeth was pretending outraged innocence because she suspected her husband of infidelity when in fact she was behaving just as badly with Colin. Susan could not even begin to imagine what poor Morag, the faithful Highland lassie, would say if she ever found out that Colin was two-timing her. She was halfway to the kitchen when he caught up with her.

'Susan, wait.'

She stopped, rounding on him angrily. 'What do you want?'

'It's not how it seems.'

'It's none of my business.'

He caught her by the hand. 'Look, Susan. We're all grown-ups. You know how it is.'

'No,' she said coldly. 'I'm afraid I don't. You made up to me on Christmas Eve, and then you told me that you've got a sweetheart in Scotland. Now I find you messing about with a married woman.'

'Charmingly put.' He squeezed her fingers. 'Come on, love. It was just a bit of fun. I've been helping Elspeth tune up the engine on the Moth, and things got a bit out of hand. There's nothing going on between us.'

Suddenly it all made sense. 'And you were here yesterday too.'

His smile faltered for a moment but he made a quick recovery. 'Yes, I was. But I can assure you that we're just friends. Surely you can understand that.'

'I'm not certain that I do.'

'Well, you're just a kid. You haven't seen much of the world, but let me tell you that a kiss or two means nothing.'

'Not to you anyway. I'm just beginning to realise that.'

'Our evening out was just a bit of fun, I thought you understood that. If you didn't then I obviously gave you credit for being more of an adult than you really are.'

'Colin. Where are you?'

At the sound of Elspeth's voice Colin released Susan and backed away. 'I'm sure I can trust you to be discreet. Forget what you just saw, and I won't tell Tony that you were up for it at Christmas.'

'You rotter.' Susan clenched her fists. 'If I were a man I'd knock your blooming block off.'

His laughter echoed round the entrance hall as he strolled back towards the drawing room. Susan rushed into the flower room and ran the tap, dousing her hot cheeks with cold water at the butler's sink. She felt sullied by his coarse remark. In his eyes she was no better than Connie Makepeace. She experienced a sudden rush of sympathy for the girl with the dubious reputation. It only took a man like Colin to make scurrilous remarks and a young woman could be ruined. She dried her hands and face and went to retrieve her jacket from the cloakroom. She had taken to wearing her old school mac and leaving the fur that Dave had given her in the wardrobe, and she was glad now that she had chosen to brave the cold rather than be seen in a garment that she could never have afforded to buy for herself. In her former sheltered existence she could never have imagined that people could be as judgemental or as cruel to someone less well off than themselves. She set out for home, pedalling hard as the wind whipped across the flat land surrounding the Hamble estuary.

She did not mention the incident to Roz. Somehow she could not bring herself to admit that Colin was a heartless charmer, or that he and Elspeth were on the brink of an affair. It might make Roz feel a bit better about her relationship with Patrick but it had occurred to Susan during the chilly bike ride that perhaps the Petersons had what might be called an open marriage. She had read about such arrangements, particularly amongst the smart set. It was just possible that Patrick and Elspeth were amusing themselves, and if their peccadilloes became common knowledge they would abandon their lovers. Susan did not think that Colin would suffer too much but she knew that Roz would be broken-hearted as well as publicly humiliated. She decided to say nothing.

There was an air raid that night and everyone, including Charlie, hurried to the shelter in the pub garden. Luckily it happened fairly early on and the bar was quiet, otherwise they would have been packed into the small space like sardines. Always the generous host, Bob had been prepared for such eventualities and had thoughtfully provided a keg of bitter and a crate of lemonade, and soon a party atmosphere prevailed. To Susan's intense relief there was no sign of Patrick, and Roz seemed to be in an exceptionally good mood, leading the singing in 'Run Rabbit Run' and 'Kiss Me Goodnight Sergeant Major'. When the all clear sounded everyone trooped back into the building.

'What's the matter?' Roz demanded, catching Susan by the sleeve as she was about to retire to the peace and quiet of the kitchen. 'You look down in the mouth.'

'I'm just tired,' Susan said truthfully. 'But you look like the cat that's got the cream.'

Roz drew her aside, lowering her voice. 'This is strictly between you and me, but I've had the most wonderful afternoon ever.'

'You've been with him?'

'Shh!' Roz placed her finger on her lips, glancing round anxiously. 'A certain someone has got the keys to a darling little cottage on the river bank not far from here. Apparently it's hers, but she never uses it. It was sheer heaven, Susan.'

'You will be careful, won't you, Roz?'

She tossed her head, chuckling. 'Careful is my middle name. By the way, I'm starving. Do you think you could rustle up something tasty again tonight?'

'Yes, of course.' Susan managed to smile but her heart was heavy as she made her way to the kitchen.

The next day she had just arrived at the Petersons' house and was taking off her hat and coat when Elspeth appeared at her elbow, smiling broadly.

Susan wondered if it was the smile on the face of the tiger before it ate its victim.

'Susan. Just the person I wanted to see.'

Now for it, Susan thought, holding her breath. She's going to sack me. In some ways it would be a blessed relief to be free from the Petersons' complicated lives, but on the other hand she needed the money. She exhaled sharply. 'Yes, Mrs Peterson.'

Elspeth beamed at her. 'I always keep my promises, Susan. Come with me.' Without waiting for an answer she led the way out of the house, walking quickly through the stable yard and across a lawned area leading to a paddock, on the far side of which Susan could just make out what looked like a hangar-sized barn situated next to a wooden chalet. Above them the sky was winter blue with barely a cloud in sight. It was cool rather than cold and there was a tang of salt in the air mingled with the resinous scent of pine from the distant woods. Elspeth took a key from the pocket of her dungarees and opened the door. 'This is my hideaway,' she said proudly. 'Come in.'

Baffled and still a little nervous, Susan followed her into the room. The slatted wooden walls were covered in framed photographs of aeroplanes and pictures of Elspeth wearing a variety of outfits from a pilot's Sidcot flying suit to a glamorous ball gown. 'This is my little Swiss chalet,' she said with a girlish giggle. 'This is where I change into my flying gear.' She waved her hand at a pile of garments laid out on a low couch. 'I've got a spare, thanks to my connections with the gallant boys in the RAF. Try one on for size, Susan.'

'You're joking.'

'No, dear. As I said, I keep my promises and you undoubtedly will keep yours.' Elspeth's expression changed. 'You know when to keep that pretty mouth shut, don't you, Susan?'

'I'm not sure about this. Perhaps I ought to get back to the house and start work.'

'Nonsense. I said I'd take you up in the Moth, so stop prevaricating and put on the damned Sidcot. I don't want you to freeze to death up there.'

Half an hour later they were soaring above the Hamble estuary with Elspeth at the controls and Susan seated behind her in a rapturous daze. Suddenly her dream of flying had come true. Her reservations had vanished the moment she climbed into the fragile-looking aeroplane, and her heart had lifted the moment they took off. She felt like a bird; she felt free. Elspeth was a surprisingly good pilot. She had dropped the airs and graces and become a true professional. Susan could not help but be impressed. Flying was everything that she had imagined it to be and more. As they soared upwards in the vast expanse of blue sky she felt that she was close to heaven. Down below was a patchwork of fields, farms and wooded areas. The River Hamble twisted like a silver ribbon and the buildings below them looked like doll's houses. In the distance she could see the grey expanse of the city and as they turned back towards home she could see Southampton Water and the outline of the Isle of Wight.

All too soon Elspeth indicated that they were going to land, but suddenly the engine began to cough and splutter like a bronchitic old man, and they were losing height rapidly. Susan held on, too terrified even to cry out as the land rushed closer and closer. She could see people below them, cattle in the fields, a horse pulling a farm cart, and then they scraped over a stand of trees. They were so close that she could have reached out and picked a bare twig. She closed her eyes.

'Hold on, Susan,' Elspeth screamed. 'I'm going to crash land.'

There was a rush of air, the engine screamed – or was it herself who had let out that animal-like howl? Susan had read enough in the aircraft manual to know how to assume the crash position. This is it, she thought as the air was sucked from her lungs. This is the end of my flying career. I'm going to die.

Chapter Thirteen

'My God, it's Susan.'

Dimly she heard a familiar voice, but the darkness still held her firmly in its grasp.

'Susan, can you hear me? Susan.'

It was warm and safe where she was. If she opened her eyes she would have to acknowledge the pain in her legs, in her back, in her head.

'Carefully, man. She might have broken bones.'

'Shut up, Danny. I've got to get her out. Where are the bloody medics?'

She could hear a bell ringing. She was being lifted bodily from the plane. She opened her eyes. 'Elspeth?'

'She's okay, which is a downright miracle.' Tony had his arms around her and someone else was holding her legs as they eased her from the damaged Tiger Moth.

Gradually, bit by bit like the pieces in a jigsaw puzzle, she was beginning to remember what had happened. 'We crashed,' she murmured. 'Is the Moth all right?'

'Trust you to think of the plane first,' Tony said grimly as they laid her on the ground. 'It's nothing that can't be fixed. Luckily for you, Elspeth had the sense to head for the airfield. She made a pretty good shot at a crash landing, or else you two would have bought it.'

Susan attempted to sit up but Tony shook his head. 'Wait until the medics have checked you over. You've got a lump the size of an egg on your forehead, but I don't think anything's broken.' He glanced up at Danny. 'How's Elspeth?'

'Colin's with her. He's playing Florence Nightingale, after a fashion.' Danny pulled a face. 'He doesn't need an excuse to lay his hands on an attractive female.' He winked at Susan. 'Glad to see that you're still with us, Susan. You gave us a hell of a fright just now.'

Tony rose to his feet as a medical orderly rushed from the ambulance.

'I'll take over now, chaps.' The medic knelt down beside her. 'Got any pain, love?'

She shook her head. 'I ache everywhere but I don't think I've broken any bones.'

'We'll just give you a quick check over.' After a brief examination he helped her to a sitting position. 'We'll let the doctor give you a once over seeing as how you've had a nasty bang on the head, but I'd say you and the other lady have been very lucky.' He beckoned to Tony. 'Give us a hand, sir. We'll get the young lady into the ambulance and take her to the medical centre. I'd be happier if the doctor took a look at her because of the head injury. Otherwise, she seems fine.'

Between them Tony and the orderly helped Susan to her feet. She was dazed and a bit shaky but she managed to walk to the ambulance. Elspeth had arrived ahead of them and was seated next to Colin with a blanket wrapped around her shoulders. She was pale and there was a cut on her chin, but she seemed none the worse for the accident. She gave Susan a calculating glance. 'Are you okay?'

'Yes, Mrs Peterson. I'm fine.'

'We'll let the medical officer be the judge of that, miss,' the orderly said, helping Susan into the ambulance.

'You two girls were very lucky,' Colin said, frowning.

'It was not luck,' Elspeth said sharply. 'It was excellent piloting. I made a textbook crash landing, and you know it.'

His expression softened. 'Do you want me to telephone Patrick and tell him to collect you?'

'No, don't do that.' Elspeth treated him to a smile. 'I expect there'll be a lot of paperwork to fill out. You know what I mean, darling. A civilian plane crashing onto a military airfield and all that. I suppose we're lucky we weren't suspected of being spies and arrested.'

'All right then, Elspeth, you win.' Colin was about to climb from the vehicle but Elspeth linked her hand through his arm.

'Help me down, darling. I've got to make sure they're handling the Moth properly.'

'Don't be silly, Elspeth. You're more important than a bloody plane.'

Her delicately pencilled eyebrows drew together in a menacing frown. 'Help me down now or I'll jump.'

'Really, ma'am,' the orderly said anxiously, 'the First Officer is only thinking of your own good.'

She shot him a withering look. 'I'm not a child, corporal.' Slowly and with obvious pain she slithered off the seat, and still clinging to Colin's arm she managed to get out of the ambulance. She drew her hand free, shaking her head when he protested. 'Stop fussing. I'm absolutely fine.' Squaring her shoulders she marched off towards the damaged aircraft.

'Hell's bells,' Colin muttered beneath his breath. 'Bloody woman.' He strode off after her.

Susan made an almost involuntary movement to rise but Tony pushed her back onto the seat. 'Don't even think about it. Let them take you to the medical centre. I'll come over later and make sure you're okay. Then we'll see about getting you home.'

'I'm supposed to be working at the Petersons',' Susan said anxiously. 'I should get back there straight away.'

'You won't be doing anything of the sort today, and maybe not tomorrow either. We'll see what the doc says.' Tony backed away as the orderly climbed in beside Susan and closed the doors.

'You'll be fine, miss. Don't worry.'

An hour later, having had a thorough examination and a cup of hot sweet tea in the medical centre, Susan was given the all clear by the doctor but told to rest and take things easy for a day or two. Tony had left her sitting in the outer office while he went off to arrange transport to take her home. She had not seen Elspeth since she stormed off to inspect the damage, and she was wondering whether she ought to go looking for her when the door opened and Elspeth strode in, followed by a harassed-looking warrant officer.

'Don't tell me what I can and can't do,' she said angrily. 'My father is a personal friend of Gerard d'Erlanger and Sir Francis Shelmerdine. I want my aeroplane repaired and I want it done now.'

'But, ma'am, there's a war on. This is a military airfield now. We don't handle civilian aircraft.'

'Don't you?' Elspeth snatched the receiver off the telephone. 'We'll see about that. Hello. Give me an outside line.' She listened to the operator's response with growing impatience. 'Then put me through to Cyril Colby at Colby Enterprises. Blasted red tape.' She waited for the connection, tapping her foot and drumming her long, scarlet fingernails on the desktop. 'Daddy. Hello, it's me. Look, darling, I'm having a bit of bother with a little man at the airfield.'

Susan recovered quickly and her enthusiasm for flying was even greater after the accident than it had been before. She had had a taste of aviation and it had left her hungry for more. Her desire to conquer the air had won Elspeth's approval. So much so that when the Moth was repaired and restored to its owner, thanks to Cyril Colby's intervention and the possible pulling of a few strings at the Air Ministry, Elspeth offered to take her up again. Perhaps it was a test of her nerve, but Susan leapt at the chance, and when Elspeth allowed her to take over the controls she was at once terrified and elated. She had studied the manual that Tony had given her until she knew it word for word, and she discovered to her delight that she was a natural pilot, even earning praise from Elspeth. In spite of all her obvious faults, Susan found that she was beginning to admire her employer. At times she almost liked her, but then Elspeth would have a tantrum or make a catty remark that destroyed her credibility as a nice person. She was also quite ruthless in her pursuit of Colin.

At first, Susan had thought that it was Colin who was chasing Elspeth, but as the year progressed and spring evolved into summer, she began to realise that it was Elspeth who dictated the running in the affair. She alternately charmed, wheedled and bullied the men in her life, and that also included her father and Patrick. Elspeth was spoilt, selfish and arrogant, but Susan had a sneaking admiration for the single-minded way she went about getting what she wanted. Added to that, Elspeth was fear-less in the air and Susan suspected that she was only truly happy when she was flying her aeroplane.

The chalet next to the hangar where the Moth was kept was Elspeth's hideaway. It was where she went when she wanted to be alone or when she decided that she would allow Colin to come and spend an afternoon with her. He telephoned almost every day and sometimes she would speak to him and at other times she refused, instructing Susan to say that she was otherwise engaged. She seemed to be playing a cat and mouse game with him, but occasionally he arrived unexpectedly and demanded to see her. The ensuing row could be heard throughout the house and probably outside too. Mrs Harper seemed used to such goings-on and merely shrugged her shoulders. Susan was upset and worried at first, especially when she had to clear up the china figurines and glass ashtrays that Elspeth had hurled at her lover's head. Gradually as the summer wore on it became part of her job and she was able to ignore the screams and shouts, often followed by the sound of enthusiastic love-making that shook the ancient floorboards.

That summer Susan divided her time almost equally between the pub and the Petersons' house. She had become close to Roz, listening to her confidences with growing anxiety as the affair with Patrick became more intense and their feelings for each other were ever more difficult to conceal. Almost every afternoon, if he could get away from the surgery, Patrick met Roz at the riverside cottage. On these occasions Roz shimmered with happiness like a diamond sparkling in the sunlight, but on the days when they were apart, for whatever reason, she found it hard to raise a smile. At first her father seemed to think that she was sickening for something, and at other times he quizzed Susan anxiously, asking if anyone in the bar had upset his beloved daughter. She found herself caught up in the middle, and it was not a comfortable place to be.

Susan grew to rely more and more on Tony's cheerful company as an antidote to the intrigue and deception that surrounded her. She suspected that he visited the pub with the intention of seeing Roz rather than herself, but she had long given up all ideas of romance. She had seen first hand how complicated life could be when someone fell in love with the wrong person, and she had no intention of becoming a victim. She managed to convince herself that Tony was the big brother that she had always longed for. Sometimes, on the long summer evenings when she had finished her chores, she joined Tony and Danny in the beer garden. She drank shandy and laughed at their jokes. It had been a poor summer generally, but there were occasional warm nights when the air was scented with roses and honeysuckle, and it was good to be alive, despite the threat of air raids and the grim stories in the newspapers and on the wireless.

Despite the terrible bombing that London had sustained during the winter and spring the shop in Swiss Cottage had been spared. Susan had written to Dave soon after she settled in with the Fullers. She had thanked him sincerely for everything that he had done for her and apologised for leaving in such a hurry. He had written back to say that he understood perfectly and was relieved to know that she was safe and well, and to keep in touch. It had been a huge weight off her mind, and she never revealed the true reason for leaving London to Tony. She kept quiet about Colin's involvement with Elspeth, although she suspected that he already knew or at least suspected that his fellow officer was having an affair with Patrick's wife. Everything was so complicated, and Susan had to continually watch what she said in case she let something slip. The only time she could completely relax was when she took Charlie for long walks by the river, although there was the ever present threat of air raids on Southampton or the airfield. Danger was always lurking just around the corner.

The only place she felt completely safe was in the air, and she had Elspeth to thank for that. Somehow, and probably thanks to her rich and influential father, Elspeth had enough fuel to take the Moth up whenever she felt so inclined. It was probably highly illegal but it was not Susan's problem, and she always jumped at the chance when Elspeth offered to give her a flying lesson. It seemed to please her that Susan was so enthusiastic and was proving to be a good student.

At the end of a particularly enjoyable flight

Elspeth had allowed Susan to take the controls for the landing. Her heart was hammering away inside her chest and the blood racing through her veins as she concentrated on the task in hand, but she managed to land the Moth with barely a jolt. As they climbed out of the cockpits Elspeth took off her helmet. 'That was well done. You're a quick learner, Susan,' she said, smiling. 'An apt pupil.'

'I've had a good teacher, Mrs Peterson.'

'Yes. I'm the best. You're a lucky girl.' Elspeth headed for the chalet. 'I'm going away for a couple of weeks, Susan. I want you to check on the Moth every day, and make sure that everything is okay.'

'Of course.' Susan hurried after her. 'Are you going somewhere nice?'

'White Waltham.' Elspeth glanced at her over her shoulder. 'You know what that is, don't you?'

'Yes,' Susan said breathlessly. 'The women's branch of the ATA is stationed there.'

'Keep this under your hat, but I'm going to join up. My friend Pauline suggested it ages ago. I only hesitated because Patrick and my father were dead against it.' She let herself into the chalet, tossing her helmet and gloves onto the sofa. 'However, I've decided to do what I want for a change.' She went to the side table and poured herself a stiff gin, adding a splash of tonic water. 'I won't offer you one, since you're under age. How old are you exactly, Susan?'

'I'm nearly nineteen, Mrs Peterson. My birthday is next month.'

'August. So you're a Leo.'

'No. I'm a Virgo.'

Elspeth threw back her head and laughed. 'A little virgin. Of course, I should have guessed.'

Susan stared at her, baffled. 'Sorry?'

'Take no notice of me, my dear. Astrology is one of my interests. I believe that our lives are ruled by the stars. I know mine is.' She gulped her drink. 'It's a short life, make every second count. That's my motto.'

Susan slipped off her borrowed Sidcot suit. 'Will there be anything else today, ma'am?'

Elspeth downed the last of her drink and poured another. 'No. That will be all. I'm leaving first thing in the morning, so I'll see you in a couple of weeks' time.' She turned away, and Susan found herself dismissed. As she walked slowly back to the house she realised that now she had another secret to keep. She had promised not to tell anyone of Elspeth's plans, and that must include Roz. Although they were now more like sisters than mere friends, Susan knew that Roz would be unable to keep anything from Patrick, especially if it concerned his wife. Whether it was born of jealousy or resentment, Roz made it obvious that she hated Elspeth with a passion. Susan was fairly certain that the feeling was mutual, although she sometimes doubted whether Elspeth felt anything deeply, other than her love of flying and her adoration of the Moth. It might be a structure made largely of wood, glue and canvas, but to Elspeth it was a living, breathing entity. The Moth was the true love of her life and flying her obsession.

With Elspeth away, having informed everyone that she was going to stay with an old school friend in Gloucestershire for a fortnight, Susan had little to do in the big house. Mrs Harper was taking a well-earned rest as Patrick used the excuse of his wife's absence to eat at the pub every day. Roz could not have been happier as she made preparations for the party to celebrate her twentieth birthday. When she realised that she and Susan had been born on the same day and only a year apart, she doubled her efforts to make it a day to remember.

Susan was delighted but also a little nervous. Birthdays had been low key affairs at the children's home, marked by a single present from the house mother, and greetings cards made by her special friends. There had been a cake of sorts with the requisite number of candles and a special tea, consisting mainly of jam sandwiches, sticky buns and jelly, which was a great treat. Susan was not prepared for the sort of party that Roz had in mind, although her efforts were hampered greatly by rationing which was becoming stricter with each passing month.

However, nothing was going to stop Roz from putting up bunting in the pub garden and persuading her father to provide free beer and sandwiches for their guests. Finding enough ingredients for a birthday cake was quite a problem, but Susan remembered a pudding that she had enjoyed in the orphanage, and although she did not have a recipe, she made what they used to laughingly call navvies' wedding cake. As far as she could work out, this had consisted mainly of stale bread, soaked in milk, to which was added cinnamon, mixed spices, sugar, dried fruit, and beaten egg. The aromatic mixture was baked in a roasting tin, and at the home it would have been cut into squares and served warm with custard. It was a stodgy but filling favourite amongst the children. She could not afford to experiment and so she crossed her fingers, hoping that the improvised recipe would work. The end result smelt appetising, and when decorated with some of the tapers used to light the gas stove cut down and used as candles it looked suitably festive, even if it was heavy enough to sink the proverbial battleship. Susan finished it off with a red ribbon tied in a bow.

Roz had spent a couple of hours getting ready for the big event and she left it until the bar was packed with guests and customers before making a grand entrance. She wafted into the bar wearing a low-cut crimson satin gown that flattered her curvaceous figure and made all the men stare at her open-mouthed. She tugged at the décolletage, turning to Susan with a worried frown. 'Is my neckline too low?'

Susan smiled. 'Don't worry about it. You look super.'

Roz tugged at her bodice again. 'I seem to have put on weight up top.' She indicated the swell of her breasts. 'I can't think why.'

Susan was about to reassure her when she remembered Flossie Boxer, a girl at the children's home who was not the brightest soul in the world, and had a habit of showing her knickers to the boys. One day when the girls were taking their daily shower someone had pointed to the fact that Flossie's boobies were getting bigger, and her tummy looked as though she had swallowed a football. The house mother had overheard the conversation and Flossie had been whipped off to the sanatorium. The shocking news had flown around the establishment in a series of Chinese whispers that had poor Flossie blown up like a barrage balloon and finally popped with a pin. The truth had come out later that Flossie had given birth to a bouncing baby boy in a home for unmarried mothers. What happened to her after that had been pure conjecture.

'I'm talking to you, Susan,' Roz said impatiently. 'You were miles away.'

She came back to the present with a start. It must have been making the wretched cake that had stirred up childhood memories. 'Sorry. What did you say?'

'Do you think I should go upstairs and change into something less – revealing?'

Susan was about to answer when the pub door opened and Patrick breezed in. His face lit up when he saw Roz. 'Wow. You look beautiful tonight, Miss

Fuller. Happy birthday.' He fished in his jacket pocket and took out an oblong jeweller's box. He presented it to her with a flourish. 'For you.'

Susan was uncomfortably aware that they were being watched. She had heard whispers in the village shops concerning Roz and Patrick, but the conversations had always ceased abruptly when her presence was noted. She knew it was only a matter of time before the rumours reached Elspeth. She glanced anxiously at Roz, who was beaming with delight as she unwrapped the gift. Her long, dark lashes fluttered and her generous mouth widened in a smile as she took a gold locket from its velvet bed. She held it by the slender golden chain and her eyes shone as she leaned across the bar to kiss Patrick on the cheek.

Susan heard a gasp ripple round the women guests and saw the knowing nods and winks exchanged by their partners. 'Roz,' she said in a low voice. 'Everybody's looking at you.'

Roz tossed her head and her shining hair swung about her shoulders in a dark cloud. She looked like a film star, there was no denying it. Love and happiness had made her beautiful and Patrick was her slave. His expression was one of open adoration and Susan half expected him to leap across the bar and take her in his arms. She nudged Roz in the ribs. 'Your dad's coming.'

She slipped the pendant back in its box and thrust it into Susan's hand. 'I love it, Patrick,' she murmured. 'But I'd best keep it out of sight for a bit.'

He nodded, still keeping his eyes fixed on her face as if he could not bear to look away. 'I understand.' He mouthed the word 'darling' before turning to greet Bob who had walked into the bar. 'Good evening, squire. What will you have to drink? I gather we're celebrating two birthdays today.' He winked at Susan. 'Happy birthday, Mrs Mopp.'

'Thank you, Patrick.' She smiled. It was impossible to be cross with him for long. He was obviously head over heels in love with Roz and she with him, but it seemed as though they had no idea of the trouble they would be in if her suspicions were confirmed and Roz was indeed pregnant. She slipped the gift box into the pocket of her apron. She had not yet had time to change into her one and only good frock, but she was well aware that she would look like a sparrow compared to Roz's bird of paradise plumage, but she did not care. They might share a birthday but this was Roz's night.

'I'm here now, Susan,' Bob said, lifting the hatch and joining them behind the counter. 'Go upstairs and put your glad rags on, love. It's your party too. No work for you tonight. You've done enough today.' He held the hatch, giving her a means of escape.

'Thanks, Bob.' She flashed him a grateful smile and was about to head to the kitchen when Tony and Danny burst in through the pub door.

'Happy birthday, Susan.' Tony caught her round the waist and kissed her on her lips. He held her rather longer than was necessary, looking deeply into her eyes until Danny pushed him aside.

'My turn, if we're in the kissing game.' He planted a kiss on Susan's mouth.

She drew back wrinkling her nose. Danny was a smoker and his kiss tasted of stale tobacco. Susan's heart had quickened a beat when Tony embraced her, but she drew away from Danny, embarrassed by the sudden physical contact. With Tony there was still that indescribable tug of attraction that she had felt the first time they met. She mumbled an excuse and hurried from the room to the quiet of the kitchen where Charlie, now fully grown, lay curled up with his good friend Orlando. She smiled at the sight of the marmalade cat and the yellow dog, matched like cushions on a sofa, with all their animosities forgotten. She did not think that would have happened with Binkie-Boo; never in a million years.

She picked up the large platter of Spam sandwiches and with it still wrapped in a damp tea towel to prevent the crusts from curling up, she carried it carefully into the bar. She arrived just as Elspeth walked into the pub looking cool and elegant in a slim-fitting white linen dress with a scarlet belt that emphasised her tiny waist. Her hair was brushed up into a sleek victory roll and she looked like a fashion plate. Susan hesitated, watching in some trepidation as Elspeth walked slowly towards the bar. The crowd parted to let her through. She might, Susan thought, have been the Queen of Sheba processing through a gathering of devoted subjects. There was complete silence apart from the tip-tapping of her high-heeled sandals on the quarry tiles as she sashayed towards her husband.

'Elspeth,' Patrick said, making an obvious effort to sound pleased. 'I wasn't expecting you back tonight.'

'Obviously, darling,' Elspeth drawled, fixing her gaze on Roz. 'I can see why you wouldn't want your wife cramping your style.'

'Elspeth, this isn't the time or place . . .'

She held up a gloved hand. 'I realise that, darling.' She turned her limpid gaze on her audience. 'What man would want his wife present at the birthday party of his mistress?'

A gasp rippled round the room. Men and women alike seemed frozen to the spot, gaping at Elspeth in horror. She turned slowly to face Roz. 'His pregnant mistress, unless I'm very much mistaken.'

Chapter Fourteen

The colour drained from Roz's face and she clutched the bar counter for support. 'It's not true. She's just come to make trouble. Get her out of here, Patrick.'

Elspeth threw back her head and her laughter echoed off the nicotine-stained ceiling. 'That's rich. Throw out the woman who's been away doing her patriotic duty by joining the Air Transport Auxiliary in favour of a whore who's been sleeping with the husband.'

Patrick took her by the elbow. 'That's enough, Elspeth.'

She wrenched her arm away, glaring up into his angry face with a curl of her lips. 'Yes, Patrick. You've done quite enough to give me grounds for a divorce.' She turned to her startled audience. 'You're all witnesses to the fact that my husband doesn't deny the fact that he's been having an affair with this woman.' She paused, taking a deep breath. 'I don't have to remind you all that I lost my baby. Shame on you both.' She marched out of the bar, leaving the door to swing on its hinges.

All heads turned to Roz. She seemed to be frozen to the spot. Her eyes were huge in her pale face and her lips worked soundlessly. Bob was the first to recover. He put his arm around her shoulders, giving her a hug. 'I think we can all sympathise with Mrs Peterson's loss,' he said in a loud, clear voice. 'But this is a party, folks. Drinks are on the house.'

Patrick stood up. 'I'd best go after her,' he muttered, making a move to follow Elspeth, but Susan barred his way, thrusting the platter of sandwiches into his hands.

'I'll go, Patrick. I think Roz needs you more.' She was too angry to give him a chance to refuse, and she raced after Elspeth. Flying lessons aside, she had taken as much as she was going to from Mrs Patrick Peterson. She caught up with her just as she was about to climb into her yellow and black roadster. 'No you don't. You're not getting away with it that easily. That was cruel and uncalled for.'

'Uncalled for?' Elspeth's eyes narrowed. 'That cheap little tart has been having it off with my husband. Have you any idea how that makes me feel?'

In the normal run of things Susan would have backed down in deference to her employer, but she was furious with Elspeth for her hypocrisy as well as her cruelty in denouncing Roz in such a public manner. The resulting scene would be the talk of the village for months, if not years. 'You've been having an affair with Colin for goodness knows how long,' she cried angrily. 'You don't give a damn about Patrick. You just wanted to make trouble for him and Roz because they love each other. I don't think you know the meaning of the word.'

'You ungrateful little bitch.' Elspeth slapped her hard across the face. 'After all I've done for you.'

Susan's hand flew automatically to her bruised cheek, but she hardly felt the pain. 'You didn't teach me to fly out of the kindness of your heart. Personally speaking I don't think you have one, and if you do then it's a lump of ice.'

If looks truly could kill Susan knew that she would have been struck down in a second, but Elspeth's retort was lost in the roar of an approaching motorbike engine. Colin drew up, stopping a little further down the road. He dismounted and came strolling towards them, but almost immediately his smile turned into a look of concern.

'What's going on, Elspeth?' He glanced at Susan's reddened cheek. 'Who did that to you?'

'Ask her.' Susan's voice trembled as anger evaporated, leaving her feeling drained and exhausted. She was about to walk away when he caught her by the hand.

'No. Wait.' He turned to Elspeth. 'Did you hit her?'

She tossed her head. 'She asked for it, darling. I won't be spoken to in that manner.'

'Don't worry,' Susan said coldly. 'I won't be coming back to work for you ever again. Not after what you've done today.'

Elspeth stared at her in what seemed to be genuine

astonishment. 'You're giving notice? You're leaving me in a spot?'

'Come on, girls. Let's sort this out like grownups,' Colin said, making an obvious attempt to lighten the atmosphere. 'What caused this bust-up?'

'I may have said a few things,' Elspeth admitted, pouting. 'But I caught Patrick making up to that common tart of a barmaid.' She looked away, her lips trembling.

'What are you talking about? For God's sake someone tell me what's bloody well going on.' Colin threw up his hands. 'Susan, you're a sensible girl normally. Can you give me a straight answer?'

She took a deep breath, controlling her voice with difficulty. 'Elspeth barged in on the birthday party and told everyone that Roz was having an affair with Patrick and that she's pregnant. Now it's common knowledge.'

'My God, you know how to throw a spanner into the works, don't you, darling?' Despite his attempt to be serious, Colin chuckled. 'I'm sorry, Susan. I know that Roz is your friend, but surely you can see it from Elspeth's point of view?'

'She didn't have to humiliate Roz so publicly, especially today of all days.'

'Take me home, darling,' Elspeth said, leaning her head against Colin's shoulder. 'I'm too upset to drive myself. You can pick up your motorcycle later.'

'Of course, sweetheart. Anything you say.' Colin opened the car door and helped her into the passenger seat. 'You can tell me all about your holiday with Lucy in Gloucester.'

'Later, darling,' Elspeth said, casting a warning glance at Susan.

So she hadn't even told Colin about her intention to join the ATA, Susan thought wearily. Elspeth was playing a dangerous game and one day she would go too far.

'I'll see you tomorrow afternoon then, Susan,' Elspeth said with an attempt at a smile as Colin climbed into the driver's seat and started the engine.

'I've just told you that I won't be working for you any more.'

'I know you didn't mean it, my dear. Good jobs are hard to come by these days. There is a war on, you know. Two thirty, sharp. We'll have a chat about a pay rise then.' She looked straight ahead, avoiding eye contact with Susan. 'Take me home, Colin. I've missed you so much, darling.'

Susan watched them drive off in a cloud of dust. She rubbed her sore cheek. That woman is impossible, she thought with a resigned sigh, but she knew that she would go back to work next day. She needed the money, and the lure of the Moth was something that she could not ignore, no matter how much she disapproved of Elspeth. She took several deep breaths and opened the pub door. Despite the dramatic scene so recently played out, the party appeared to be in full swing. No doubt Bob's free drinks had something to do with the quick recovery of the guests, but there was no sign of Roz or Patrick.

Bob himself looked grim as he served behind the bar. He met Susan's questioning look with a frown. 'I've sent him packing,' he said, giving the beer pump a savage jerk. 'He's barred from my pub for life, the bastard. I don't know where Roz is.'

'Don't worry. I'll go and find her,' Susan murmured, making a quick exit through the door to the living quarters. She found Roz and Patrick in the garden, standing beneath a pergola dripping with late roses. They had their arms around each other and Roz's face was tear-stained as she laid her head on his shoulder.

'You mustn't upset yourself, sweetheart,' Patrick said softly. 'Elspeth was saying anything she could think of to embarrass us. If she agrees to a divorce I'll be only too happy to walk away with nothing.'

'You don't understand,' Roz said, raising her head to look him in the eyes. 'She was only guessing, but she was right about one thing.'

Susan cleared her throat. 'I'm sorry,' she said, backing away. 'I didn't mean to intrude. I'll be in the kitchen if you need me.'

'No, don't go, Susan.' Roz beckoned to her with an attempt at a smile. 'I'll need all the help I can get.'

Patrick's face clouded with anxiety. 'If you're worried about the village gossips, don't be. I'll marry you like a shot once I'm a free man.'

'It's not just us now,' Roz whispered. 'Elspeth was right. I'm pregnant, Patrick. I've only just found out for certain. We're having a baby.'

His reaction was not what Susan would have hoped for had she been in Roz's position. He looked dumbstruck, as if the possible result of their love-making had never occurred to him. 'You're pregnant. But we were so careful . . .'

'Not careful enough,' Roz said slowly. 'Don't look at me like that. I didn't conceive on purpose.'

He shook his head. 'I know. I'm sorry, darling. It's just a bit of a shock and something I hadn't bargained for. Not while I was tied to Elspeth, anyway.'

Susan shifted uncomfortably from one foot to the other. 'I really should leave you two to sort it out between you.'

Roz broke away from Patrick with a strangled sob. 'It looks as though I'm on my own with this. Thanks a lot. Now I know where I stand.' She hurried off in the direction of the kitchen. He made to follow her, but Susan caught him by the sleeve.

'Don't you think you've done enough already? Why the hell couldn't you have given her a hug and told her that it was the best thing that had ever happened to you?'

He stared at her as if he had not understood a word she said. 'It was a shock. I love her, but it's complicated.'

'Of course, it would be. So you were just having a good time at her expense, were you?'

He shook his head vehemently. 'No, of course not. I want to marry her and have kids, but it's not that simple.'

Susan stood arms akimbo. 'Tell me then.'

'Elspeth holds the purse strings, or rather her old man does. He set me up in business, but everything is in Elspeth's name. If we divorce I'll be virtually penniless and have to start all over again.'

'Would that be so bad? I'm sure that Roz wouldn't care.'

'I didn't want it to turn out like this,' he said, sighing. 'It's such a bloody mess.'

Susan glanced over his shoulder. The party was about to spill into the garden, and she could see Tony and Danny standing by the gate. Behind them was a crowd of tipsy partygoers. 'You're the only one who can sort it out,' she said urgently. 'Talk to her now, while you've got the chance. It won't be easy to see her now that Bob's barred you from the pub. I'm sure he'll come round in time, but you've got to go in there and tell Roz how you feel about her. For God's sake, Patrick. Are you a man or a bloody mouse?'

He gave her a dazed look. 'At this moment I really don't know. Elspeth is good at emasculating men. She's like the black widow spider that gobbles up her partner when she's got what she wants from him.'

'Stop feeling sorry for yourself. You've got two other people to think of now.' Susan jerked her head in the direction of the kitchen. 'Go after her before it's too late. Bob will be busy in the bar and you might just catch her before she goes upstairs and locks herself in her room. This was supposed to be her special day.'

As if on cue the air raid siren started up its dirge-like wail. Galvanised into action, Patrick ran towards the building leaving Susan alone under the pergola. A sudden breeze sent a shower of rose petals falling all round her just as Tony arrived at her side, breathless and smiling. He plucked a pink petal from her hair. 'Poor Susan. It hasn't been much of a birthday for you so far.'

She shrugged her shoulders. 'I think Hitler's put paid to the celebrations. We'd best go into the shelter with everyone else.'

He slipped his arm around her waist. 'We'll continue the party in there. Danny's bringing the drinks, and I haven't given you your present yet.'

'A present? How did you know it was my birthday, anyway? I didn't mention it.'

'No, but Roz did, and we've all clubbed together to give you something special, but I'm afraid you'll have to wait for the all clear.' Taking her by the hand he led her to the shelter where the party was still in full swing.

Bob was already there serving pints and was too busy to notice that his daughter was not amongst the revellers. There was wine and cider for those who did not drink bitter and someone had had the forethought to bring the Spam sandwiches and cheese rolls. No one went hungry. It was cramped and stuffy in the shelter but the party mood persisted, and when Danny started singing 'As Time Goes By' everyone joined in. The singsong went from strength to strength and although there was hardly room to move, some people paired off and began dancing. The hubbub was so loud that they barely heard the all clear.

Everyone trooped out into the gathering dusk with bats zooming overhead like miniature fighter planes in a dog fight, and most people returned to the bar to continue partying, but Tony took Susan by the hand and led her to the garage with Danny following close on their heels. 'Roz should be here as well,' he said, turning a key in the padlock and opening the double doors, 'but in the circumstances I guess she'll have to miss the presentation.'

Susan started to giggle. 'I can't believe you're giving me a car.'

'Not quite, love, but close.' Tony disappeared into the darkness and came out moments later pushing a brand new bicycle. 'Happy birthday, Susan. It's from all of us, including Elspeth and Patrick. The old bike was a danger to life and limb, and seeing as how my dad isn't here to fix it, we got the next best thing.' He pushed it towards her. 'Try it for size.'

Danny nodded his head. 'Get on, then. Let's see you riding it.'

She took the handlebars, staring at the gleaming machine in amazement. 'It's wonderful. I've never owned anything new in my life.'

Tony and Danny exchanged meaningful glances.

'Well now you do,' Tony said softly. 'You've worked like a Trojan since you came to Hamble, Sue. You deserve something special.'

'And he got it trade price through his dad,' Danny said, grinning. 'Mr Richards put it on the train at Waterloo and I picked it up yesterday. We've all done our bit, Susan.' He leaned over and kissed her on the cheek. 'Go on. Take it for a spin.'

Susan was overcome with emotion. It was a magnificent gift. She had a lump in her throat as she thought of the trouble her friends had gone to on her behalf, and she covered her confusion by mounting the bike and riding it down the path to the garden gate. Tony and Danny followed her, standing on the pavement and waving as she pedalled off along the High Street. She was on the return lap when she almost ran into Patrick, who crossed the road without looking as he made his way to his car. 'You idiot,' she cried, steadying herself with one foot on the ground. 'I almost ran you over.'

As he turned his head she was shocked to see the bleak expression on his face. Even allowing for the deepening shadows, she could see despair written all over his features. 'It's over,' he said with a break in his voice. 'She doesn't want to see me again.'

'What do you mean? What on earth did you say to her?'

'I tried to explain my difficulties. I told her I wanted her and the baby, but I couldn't do anything until I was divorced. That's reasonable, isn't it? I mean, I can't marry her until I'm free, and Elspeth is a law unto herself. She changes her mind all the time.'

'But she said in front of a whole pub full of people that she wanted a divorce.'

'She'll say anything for attention, but when it comes to it she'll do what she wants, and if she thinks I'd be happier with Roz she'll hang on like grim death. I tried to explain it to her, but she couldn't or wouldn't understand.'

'She's upset and emotional. She needs you to stand by her, Patrick.'

'I will, of course. I'll look after her financially as long as I'm able to continue in the practice, and I'll do my best to make Elspeth keep her word.'

Susan stared at him in dismay. 'Do you know how weak-kneed that makes you sound? You're the man, you should tell Elspeth to go to hell. If you lose Roz you'll regret it for the rest of your life.'

He climbed wearily into the driver's seat of the Triumph. 'This will go first if the old man gets wind of the situation. I'll be begging Roz for the loan of the old bike that you used to ride.'

'No chance. If that happens you'll be using Shanks's pony, probably for the first time in your pampered existence. I thought better of you, Patrick, but now I can see you're just a puppet controlled by your wife and her rich dad. Roz will be better off without you.' She could just make out Tony and Danny waving to her from the garden gate, and she rode off to join them.

'What did Patrick have to say?' Tony held the bike while she dismounted. 'I hope he's proud of himself.'

'Poor Roz,' Danny said sadly. 'She's a lovely girl. I'd marry her tomorrow if she'd have me.'

Tony nudged him in the ribs. 'No you wouldn't. You're just saying that because Patrick's been such a bastard.'

'I'm not so sure about that . . .'

Susan wheeled the bike into the garden. 'She's in more trouble than either of you could imagine.'

'What do you mean by that?' Tony hurried after her as she headed for the garage. 'She's not really up the spout, is she? I thought that was just Elspeth being bitchy and over-dramatic.'

'Unfortunately it's true, and it's bound to be common knowledge by the morning, and Patrick isn't facing up to his responsibilities. I'm really disappointed in him.'

'So the blighter isn't going to do the right thing by her.' Tony shook his head. 'I've a good mind to punch him on the nose.'

'Me too,' Danny added angrily. 'What a bastard.'

'Neither of you must say anything.' Susan stowed

the bike in the garage and secured the padlock. 'Thanks for the wonderful present, boys. I'll be able to ride to work in style now.'

'You're not thinking of going back to the Petersons'?' Tony stared at her in amazement. 'Not after tonight.'

'I can't afford to lose my job. I don't earn much here, and I'll need to have some money saved up before I go looking for a more permanent job and a place of my own.'

Tony gave her a searching look. 'I suppose your decision wouldn't have anything to do with Elspeth's Tiger Moth, would it?'

'It might, I suppose. But I can't afford to be proud and Elspeth lets me fly it occasionally. I could get a pilot's licence if I had more practice. Just think of that, Tony.' She clasped her hands together, smiling at the thought, but was instantly sobered by the expression on his face. 'I wish you could be the one to teach me, but I know that's impossible.'

'Maybe one day. You never know, Susan, if the war goes on for long enough you might even be able to join the ATA like dear Elspeth, although you'd still need the right qualifications.'

'You mean a pilot's licence?'

'Yes, that too, but it seems to me that the famous eight are all society beauties with rich daddies. You don't qualify there.' He gave her a hug. 'Well, you do in the looks department. You're a peach, Susan Banks.'

'I'll second that,' Danny said earnestly. 'But we're missing the party, and it'll be closing time soon. I could do with a pint, especially if the drinks are still on the house.'

'You go on,' Tony said, moving closer to Susan. 'We won't be far behind.'

Danny gave him a mock salute and a knowing wink. 'Okay, squire. I'll get the drinks in.'

It was almost dark and growing chilly. Susan shivered and Tony wrapped his arms around her. 'Are you all right? I know you're close to Roz. You must be worried about her.'

'I'm okay.' She raised her eyes to meet his and the warmth of his gaze made her heart give a funny little jiggle against her ribs, but there was something she had to know. 'You're very fond of her, aren't you?'

He recoiled slightly. 'I wouldn't put it quite so strongly. I like her a lot and she's a damned attractive girl, but I don't fancy her, if that's what you mean.'

She looked away. 'I thought you did.'

'Let's get one thing straight. I admire Roz, and I think any man would be lucky to have someone like her, but there's this girl I met last year. I can't get her out of my mind.'

'Oh.' A suffocating cloud of disappointment threatened to overwhelm her. 'She must be something special.'

'Yes, she is.' Tony lifted her chin with the tips of his fingers, looking deeply into her eyes. 'I thought she was just a kid when she came off her bike in front of me. I imagined that I was too old for the little girl lost with the big sorrowful blue eyes, and then she told me she had a boyfriend called Charlie.' His lips twitched and he dropped a kiss on her forehead.

Her heart was beating so fast that she could hardly breathe and an involuntary gasp escaped from her lips as she attempted to push him away. 'You're teasing me. That's not fair.'

He drew her closer, caressing her lips with his, gently at first but with growing desire until she relaxed against him, sliding her arms around his neck and returning the kiss. Her experience with Colin had made her wary, but she realised now that there had been no genuine feeling behind his practised embrace. He had been toying with her emotions expertly but coldly and without emotion. Kissing Tony was like coming home. She could feel the heat of his body penetrating the thin cotton of her summer frock. She was melting against him like a candle set too close to the fire, moulding to him so that they fitted together in a perfect match.

He released her lips, holding her close with his face buried in her hair which had somehow come loose from the snood at the back of her neck. He drew back slightly, brushing a long golden strand back from her forehead. 'Now do you believe me?'

Her legs threatened to give way beneath her and she clung to him, scarcely able to believe her ears. It was difficult to breathe and yet she was overwhelmed with a sense of completeness and deep joy. 'I'm not sure. What did you want to tell me?'

His lips curved in a smile and his eyes glowed with inner fire. 'That I fell in love with you the first moment I saw you, but I didn't think I stood a chance. Then Colin told me about Christmas, and . . .'

She stiffened. 'What did he say?'

'That you two had got it together on the sofa in my dad's flat.'

Horrified, she pushed him away. 'That's a wicked lie. He kissed me but that's all. How could he tell such awful whoppers?'

He laid his hands on her shoulders, giving her a gentle shake. 'I didn't believe him, sweetheart. Colin's always fancied himself as a ladies' man, and I was pretty certain he was just saying those things to get me going.'

'Elspeth's welcome to him,' Susan said bitterly. 'They deserve each other.'

He studied her face as if he were trying to read her thoughts. 'There's something else that he said which concerns you and my dad. I need to get it out in the open before it drives a wedge between us.'

Suddenly she was ice cold. The cool breeze had turned into a chill winter wind. She dropped her gaze. She could guess what was coming next.

'Colin was drunk at the time and I think he was having a bad time with Elspeth, but he said that you'd made a play for my father. He said that Aunt

Maida had warned Dad not to fall for a girl half his age, but he was besotted with you. I shut him up, of course, but not before he'd accused you of being a gold digger.'

'And you believed him.' She stared at him in horror. 'How dare you say you love me when you're prepared to believe anything that anyone says about me? What sort of girl d'you think I am, Tony Richards?'

He took a step backwards, recoiling as if she had struck him. 'I didn't mean it to come out like that, Susan. Of course I didn't believe you were capable of such a thing.'

'Then why say it? Why bring it up.'

'Because I want everything to be open and above board between us. I do love you . . .'

'Then you've got a funny way of showing it.'

He ran his hand through his hair. 'It wasn't just what Colin said. Aunt Maida wrote to me saying much the same thing. She said that Dad had given you some of my mother's things and you were trying to take her place. I just wanted to hear your side of the story, Susan. I'm not accusing you of anything.'

'Yes, you are. You're doing just that, and whatever I say you're always going to have a niggling suspicion that what they said was true.' She turned away, unable to bear the stricken look on his face but too hurt and angry to make concessions.

'Please, Susan, be reasonable.'

'You don't love me. There can't be love if there

isn't any trust. I'm beginning to wish that I'd never met you or your dad.'

He stood with his hands clenched, his face pale in the gathering dusk. 'You don't mean that, darling.'

'I was a fool to come here, and even more stupid to think that there could ever be anything between us.'

'You really wanted to see me again? It wasn't just because I promised to help you find a job?'

'Not entirely.' She clenched her fists at her sides. 'You wanted the truth so here it is. I ran away from London because your dad asked me to marry him. He did give me a couple of things that had belonged to your mum because I came away from the Kemps with little more than what I stood up in. I tried to give them back but he wouldn't hear of it. I was genuinely fond of him, but not in that way. For God's sake, he was old enough to be my father.' She glared at Tony, silently daring him to speak, but his face was now in deep shadow and he said nothing. She choked on a sob. 'There. It's all out in the open now. We know where we stand, thanks to your aunt and your friend Colin. He's wrecked Roz's life and mine too.'

'Susan. Please don't be like this.' He took a step towards her but she backed away.

'Don't speak to me. Don't saying anything, Tony. Keep away from me. I don't want anything to do with a man who thinks so little of me.' She fled in the direction of the kitchen.

Chapter Fifteen

Susan would have left the pub there and then had it not been for the fact that Roz begged her to stay. She said that she needed a friend now more than ever. They had both been betrayed by the men they loved, and they could support each other through the coming difficult months. Susan could see the sense of this, and anyway she had nowhere else to go. Her half-hearted enquiries into renting rooms had met with a firm rebuff when the landlords discovered that she owned a large, bouncy Labrador. Leaving him behind or giving him away was unthinkable, and the Victorious had become their home. The Fullers were the nearest thing to a family that Susan had ever had and she made a solemn pact with Roz to stand together no matter what, but it was obvious that life from now on was going to be anything but easy.

Despite the fact that Susan refused to see him, Tony came to the pub every evening. Roz tried to act as mediator but Susan was still hurt and angry. The fact that he had suspected her, even for a moment, of encouraging his father's advances made her feel physically sick. She knew she was being irrational, but she was terrified by the depth of feeling he aroused in her. Deep down what she feared most was rejection. Only someone who had been abandoned at birth could understand the need to be loved unconditionally. She dared not let Tony back into her life. It was easier to be alone than to be with someone who doubted her integrity. She tried to explain her feelings to Roz, but although Roz was sympathetic she was preoccupied with problems of her own. On her twentieth birthday she had received notification that it was compulsory for women her age to register for war work. This did not apply to married women with young children, but Roz did not fit into that category. When she looked into it further she discovered that her options were limited. She was adamant that she did not want to work in an armaments factory or as a nursing auxiliary. She was, she said, too young to join the Women's Voluntary Service, as the old tabbies would treat her like a fallen woman, which she supposed she was since there was no likelihood of her getting married before the baby was born. Patrick had begged her to see him, sending messages through Susan as he was still barred from the pub, but Roz's reply was always the same. She would not have anything to do with him until he could assure her that he had filed for divorce.

In the end it was Tony who came up with a suggestion that appealed to Roz. He told her that there was a vacancy at the Armstrong Whitworth factory at the airfield. He was not certain whether the job in the workshop would suit her, but he suggested she might like to apply. Despite her father's protests that it was unsuitable and she could do better, Roz sent in her application and received a reply by return.

Tony took her to the interview. She rode pillion on his motorbike, and when Susan protested that it might harm the baby, Roz replied shortly that she did not care. Life had to go on, even if hers was a ruin. She returned home later that day with a triumphant smile on her face. Connie Makepeace had gone for the same job but had been rejected, mainly because she was six months pregnant and beginning to waddle. Roz patted her gently rounded belly with a satisfied sigh. 'I won't show for ages, especially wearing one of those dreadful overalls. At least that slut didn't beat me. That would have been the ultimate humiliation.'

Susan returned to work at the Petersons' and she continued to cook and clean for the Fullers, but her life seemed to be on hold. She could think of nothing but the pain that Tony had caused her, and she could barely force herself to be civil to Colin on the occasions when she saw him with Elspeth. Their affair alone seemed to be going on as before. The two people who had wrecked the lives of others had got off scot free. There seemed to be one law for ordinary people like herself and Roz and a completely different set of rules for those like Elspeth, who had been born with a silver spoon in their mouth. She was either oblivious to the suffering she had caused, or else she simply dismissed it as a trivial matter. She treated Susan in exactly the same way as she had before the disastrous birthday party, but her offers of a ride in the Moth had grown more frequent. Perhaps, Susan thought, Elspeth had felt a tiny pang of guilt, or maybe she simply liked showing off her flying skills to an audience. Whatever the reason for the invitations, Susan was not going to turn down the chance to fly. In that she was as single-minded as Elspeth, and her enthusiasm paid off. She was allowed to take the controls more often and Elspeth was as generous with her praise as she was hard on Susan when she made mistakes.

The countryside basked in a golden haze of September sunshine. Susan had just made a perfect landing and she climbed out of the cockpit feeling very pleased with herself. Elspeth was smiling as she took off her helmet and goggles. She slapped Susan on the back. 'We'll make a pilot of you yet. That was textbook perfect, my dear.'

'Thank you.' Susan tucked her helmet under her arm as she followed Elspeth out of the hangar and helped her close the huge doors. 'When are you going off to join the ATA, Mrs Peterson?'

Elspeth smiled. 'Darling, they're coming to join me, would you believe? It's hush-hush, of course, but number 15 ferry pool is moving to Hamble on the twenty-first of September, next week in fact. I might have told you that my friend, Margot Gore, is the commanding officer, and I met most of the other girls when I visited White Waltham. I went to boarding school with a couple of them, so it was like an old girls' reunion. It's going to be such fun. I can't wait to get my hands on the controls of a Spitfire or a Hurricane. We'll show the Brylcreem Boys what the female of the species can do.'

'I really envy you,' Susan said sincerely. 'I'd give anything to do what you're doing.'

Elspeth angled her head. 'Would you, darling? Well, stranger things have happened. Anyway, I've got a special job for you, Susan.' She walked slowly towards the chalet. 'I'm moving into the cottage on the riverside. It will be nearer to the aerodrome and much more convenient. I expect the place is in a bit of a mess and I know all about Patrick using it as a love nest with that trollop, so don't look at me like that. I want you to clean it from top to bottom. Strip the beds and send everything to the laundry. I want it spick and span by next week.'

'Yes, Mrs Peterson. Will I still be needed here?'

Elspeth shrugged her shoulders. 'I suppose so. I'm allowing Patrick to stay on with Mrs Harper to look after him. I don't want to give the authorities the opportunity to billet evacuees here or even worse the army. So, yes, you will be needed, but probably not quite so often.'

'And will you want me to clean the cottage too?'

'Of course. You don't think I'm going to soil my lily-white hands doing housework, do you, Susan?' She laughed as if the idea was too hilarious to even consider. 'I'll pay you double, and that will ensure your silence as well. I don't want any of my affairs made public. Do you understand what I'm saying?'

'Of course, ma'am. ' Susan waited while Elspeth searched her pockets for the door key.

'Come to the cottage at nine o'clock sharp tomorrow morning. If you don't know where it is just ask the tart. She's spent enough time there, as is evidenced by her thickening waistline.' She paused with the key clutched in her hand. 'Does he see her very often?'

'Your husband is barred from the pub, ma'am.'

'That's not what I asked. Are they still seeing each other?'

Susan shook her head. 'Not that I know of, and I'd rather not talk about it, if you don't mind. Roz is my friend.'

'Loyal to the last.' Elspeth turned the key in the lock. 'I hope you're as stalwart when it comes to fending off gossip about me. Come inside and change out of the Sidcot. You won't be needing it after next week.'

Susan's heart sank. 'I suppose not. What will happen to the Moth?'

Elspeth went to help herself to her customary gin and tonic. 'She'll be quite safe in the hangar. I might take the old girl out on the odd occasion but she'll be there waiting for me when the war's over, which is more than I can say for my husband. I'm not even sure that Colin will be around for long when all the glamour girls descend upon Hamble. Poor darling, he'll be spoilt for choice with all the rich society beauties on his doorstep.'

Susan changed out of her flying suit in silence. For a moment she almost felt sorry for Elspeth, but she put the thought out of her mind. Elspeth was no victim. She was quite capable of standing up for herself, and if she allowed Colin to stray it would be because she had tired of him. She was like a spoilt child in a toyshop, snatching up things that amused her and casting them aside when the novelty wore off. She would almost certainly end up with nothing and no one.

Having put on her day clothes, Susan folded the Sidcot suit neatly and left it in a pile with her helmet, goggles, gloves and boots. Elspeth had put a record on the gramophone and she lit a cigarette. Standing with her back to Susan she swayed to the music of Joe Loss and his band with her drink in one hand and a cigarette in the other. Finding herself forgotten, Susan let herself out of the chalet and returned to the house.

'She's told you, I suppose,' Mrs Harper said in her usual lugubrious tone as Susan walked into the kitchen. 'At least I'll only have to cater for Mr Peterson, and he's no trouble.'

'Yes. Mrs Peterson said she's moving to the cottage.'

'Well, just so long as she doesn't expect me to make up food parcels or go over there and cook for her, I don't mind. It'll make my job easier. Although, to tell the truth, I've been thinking about giving up here and going to live with my sister in Cornwall, except that she's a bit of a misery, always complaining. I don't know where she gets it from. We was always a cheerful lot at home.'

'Yes, I'm sure.' Susan could not begin to imagine what Mrs Harper's sister must be like, but she did not want to get drawn into a lengthy discussion. 'I'm off then, Mrs Harper. I'll see you when I see you.'

'So you've drawn the short straw then?' Mrs Harper dropped a peeled potato into a saucepan filled with water. 'She'll get her money's worth out of you, young Susan. Beware, that's all I can say. She's sweetened you up with flying lessons and then she'll come down on you for what she's really after. I know her sort.'

'I don't know what you mean.'

'She'll have you at her beck and call. You'll be lady's maid, cook-general and charwoman, all rolled into one, and paid very little for your pains. Take my advice and don't stand for any of her nonsense.'

Susan stared at her in astonishment. 'If you dislike her so much, why do you stay on here?'

'What sort of question is that? I've got a lovely little flat, I'm well paid and I don't have to kowtow to a snooty housekeeper or a stuck-up butler as I did when I was first in service. I know when I'm well off, dear. Now get along home. I think it's going to rain.'

'Goodbye, Mrs Harper.' Susan made her way to the stable yard where she had left her bicycle. It was a pleasure to ride it and she knew she had Tony to thank for the generous birthday present. She could not help thinking about him as she pedalled through the green country lanes. The clouds might be gathering from the west but the sun was still shining and the first signs of autumn were evident in the hedgerows. Shiny red hawthorn berries vied for position with orange rosehips. She would have liked to stop and pick blackberries but she pedalled harder, hoping to get home before the rain set in.

She arrived at the pub just as Tony was helping Roz off his motorcycle. He had taken to giving her a lift home after work, which also gave him an excuse to stop for a drink before returning to the airfield. There was no avoiding him now. Susan drew to a halt and dismounted. She had not seen him face to face since their row after the party, but she realised that her anger had evaporated. She was suddenly nervous, dreading a rebuff if she spoke to him, but he greeted her with a broad smile.

'Hello, Susan. I see you've mastered the new machine.'

The ice was broken. It was impossible to be cross with someone who looked so pleased to see her. 'Yes, it's marvellous. I love it.'

'I'm going in for a lie-down,' Roz said, opening

the pub door. 'I've been on my feet since stupid o'clock this morning. It was barely light when I left for work, and that damn bus jolts so much it's like riding a bucking bronco. God knows what Spud thinks of it all.' She disappeared into the bar, leaving the door wide open.

Tony grinned. 'Spud?'

'It's her name for the baby,' Susan said with a nervous giggle.

He took a step towards her. 'It's good to see you smile again. I've wanted to see you to apologise properly for what I said at the party, Susan. I was an idiot.'

'I won't argue with that.'

'You were right to be angry. I should have known better.' He held out his hand. 'Can we start again?'

She met his earnest gaze with a doubtful smile. 'I don't know. I'd like to, but I'm not sure it would work.'

'That's a start. At least you're speaking to me now.' He took her hand and raised it to his lips.

The warmth of his breath on her skin and the whisper of a kiss made her tremble with pleasure, but a small voice in her head warned her to hold something back. She did not want to fall headlong into a relationship only to have her heart broken. 'I landed the Moth today,' she said, changing the subject. It came out in a rush, but she had to share her triumph with someone and she knew that Tony would understand.

'Did you now? That's fantastic. Well done, sweetheart.'

She frowned, pulling her hand away. 'Don't call me that. I mean, not yet. Let's get to know each other as friends, Tony. If we'd had a chance to talk about things in the first place we wouldn't have got ourselves into such a tangle.'

He nodded. 'You're right. We'll play it any way you like, but I'm not giving up on us, Susan. I've missed you like hell these past few weeks and I don't want to go through that again.'

'Really?' She smiled shyly. 'I missed you too.

'Just friends,' he said, smiling. 'For now, anyway.'

'Thanks for understanding. It means a lot to me.'

He linked her hand through his arm. 'Come on. I'll buy you a drink. That's if we can get any service in the bar. Bob isn't used to opening up.'

'That would be nice. I've got lots to tell you.'

As they entered the pub Susan was almost knocked over by an exuberant Charlie. He greeted her with yelps and excited barks, forgetting his training and jumping up at her until Tony grabbed him by the collar and made him sit. Charlie obeyed, but Susan was convinced that he was smiling as he gazed lovingly up at her. She stroked his head and told him he was a good boy, even though he had broken the non-jumping up rule that she had attempted to instil into his doggy brain. He followed her as she went over to the fireplace where Bob was working the bellows and cursing softly beneath his breath. He glanced over his shoulder. 'Damn fire won't light. The logs are damp.'

'Let me,' Susan said, kneeling down beside him. 'There's a knack to it.'

He struggled to his feet, thrusting the bellows into her outstretched hand. 'Get it going and I'll stand you a port and lemon.' He held up his hand. 'I know you're under age, but it's high time you started getting in practice, girl. One day you'll go out with a young chap like him,' he jerked his head in Tony's direction, 'and you'll only have to sniff a wine cork and you'll be paralytic.'

Susan covered her confusion by working the bellows energetically until the kindling burst into flames.

Bob retired to his usual position behind the bar and served Tony. 'On me,' he said when Tony attempted to pay. 'You've been good to my girl, giving her a lift home every evening, but she's not going to be able to ride pillion much longer, if you get my drift.'

'I do, of course. Maybe she ought to share a room with one of the other girls who work in the factory.'

Bob shook his head. 'I can't see that happening. Roz isn't used to slumming it.'

'No, perhaps not.' Tony picked up the drinks and carried them over to the ingle nook, placing them on a table. He sat down, stroking Charlie's head as he flopped onto the floor beside him. 'I'm sorry for Roz,' he said in a low voice, 'but I don't see what anyone can do to help her, other than Patrick that is.'

Susan sat back on her haunches, watching the orange and scarlet flames licking around the logs. 'He can't do anything if Elspeth won't agree to a divorce.' Rising to her feet she went to sit beside him. 'She's moving to the cottage by the river.'

'Who, Roz?'

Susan chuckled and slapped him on the knee. 'No, silly. Elspeth. I've got to go there tomorrow and get it ready for her. Patrick will be left all by himself in the big house.'

Tony handed her the glass of port and lemon. 'Here, try this. You don't have to drink it if you don't like it. I'm not one of those blokes who'll get you tipsy for my own wicked ends.'

She sipped the drink and smiled. 'It's nice and warming.'

'Go easy on it, or you'll be tiddley.' He covered her hand with his and his smile faded. 'Seriously though, I couldn't bear the thought of losing you again, Susan.'

'You do believe that I did nothing to lead your dad on, don't you?'

'Of course I do, and I always did. I shouldn't have told you what Colin and Maida said. I ought to have known it would upset you.' He slipped his arm around her waist and gave her a hug. 'Am I forgiven?'

She answered him with a kiss on the cheek, but

she broke away as Bob came over to draw the blackout curtains.

'Carry on,' he said grinning. 'Don't mind me.' He strolled back to the bar to serve the two regulars who had wandered into the pub, heading straight for their usual positions in the snug.

'I want to know everything about you, Susan,' Tony said softly. 'I only gathered snippets of your past during that brief visit to London, and I simply can't imagine what it must have been like to be brought up in a children's home, or what you went through when you were working for that woman Kemp.'

'It wasn't all bad in the orphanage. The house mother tried hard to make us feel as though we were a real family, but I think all of us knew that there was something missing.' In the flickering firelight with the scent of burning apple wood mingling with the heady fumes from the port, Susan leaned against Tony feeling warm and safe. He listened quietly without comment until she began to describe the insults she had suffered at the hands of the Kemps, and she felt him stiffen as she recounted the humiliating experience when Dudley had attempted to force himself upon her.

'You're safe now, sweetheart,' he murmured. 'I won't let anyone hurt you ever again. The past is over and done with. This is the beginning for us. I'm never going to mess things up again, Susan. I promise you that, on my honour.'

Susan went to bed that night feeling happier than she had in a long time. With the misunderstandings put firmly behind them the future looked rosy, and it was almost possible to forget the war that raged around them. She drifted off to sleep with Charlie snoring gently on the rug beside her bed.

She was up early next morning and arrived at the cottage on time. Elspeth was already there, wrapped in her mink coat, and obviously had no intention of getting her hands dirty. Her car was piled high with suitcases and bandboxes and the only thing she carried into the building was a mauve leather vanity case, which she dumped unceremoniously on the Welsh dresser. She glanced around the living room with an expressive shudder. 'I can smell her cheap perfume, Susan. I want every inch of this place scrubbed, and all traces of their occupation removed before I move in tonight.'

Susan stared at her aghast. 'I'm not sure I can get everything done by then.'

'You'll have to manage, because I'm not spending another night under the same roof as that rat. I've told him he's to find accommodation elsewhere, but I'm not an unreasonable woman. I've given him a month, which I think is more than fair. You're to go there twice a week only from now on. I need you here first thing each morning, weekends included.'

'But I have work to do at the pub.'

Elspeth shrugged her shoulders. 'Not any more,

darling. Now you're working permanently for me. I have no idea how to light that black monstrosity in the kitchen, the thing that one is supposed to cook on. Anyway, I can't cook. I've never needed to and I don't intend to start now. A little bird tells me that you're a dab hand in the kitchen, so you can start today. I want a hot meal for two at about seven thirty.' She raised her hand as if expecting Susan to argue. 'And you can make yourself scarce as soon as you've served the food. I'm not a hard taskmaster. You'll be paid for your trouble. Have I made myself clear?'

Susan nodded. She was too stunned to think of a plausible reason for refusing. She knew that Bob would not raise any objections as long as she did her work at the pub, but she was far from happy with the new arrangements.

Elspeth picked up her handbag and gloves. 'Now, unload my car, Susan, and I'll be off. I'm meeting some of my flying chums at the aerodrome, and then we're going out to lunch. I can't wait to start work at the ferry pool. It will be terrific fun.' She stood in the doorway, watching as Susan hefted the luggage out of the car and carried it into the cottage. When the last suitcase was deposited on the pile, Elspeth climbed into her car and drove off in a cloud of dust, leaving Susan with a task that would have made Sisyphus blench.

It was dark by the time Elspeth returned, and her supper for two had turned into a party that included three other young women, all frighteningly glamorous, good-looking and patently used to the good things in life. They erupted into the sitting room like a flock of colourful parakeets, laughing and chattering, and exclaiming in delight at the doll's house proportions of the cottage. Susan retired to the kitchen and made up a batch of dumplings seasoned with some rather withered thyme that she had found in the garden. She dropped them one by one into the onion soup she had made earlier, and hastily grated the rest of Elspeth's cheese ration to sprinkle on top of each serving when the ladies had finished their drinks. Elspeth might not have thought to buy food but it seemed as though she had brought almost the entire contents of her cocktail cabinet with her.

It was almost nine o'clock when Susan arrived back at the pub. She put her bike away and entered through the kitchen where she found Roz seated at the table in floods of tears. Charlie was sympathetically nuzzling her hand, but she was too distressed to take any notice. He abandoned her to give Susan his customary enthusiastic greeting. She patted him absently on the head. 'What's the matter, Roz?' she asked anxiously. 'Are you ill? It's not the baby, is it?'

Chapter Sixteen

Roz shook her head. 'No. It's Patrick.'

Pushing Charlie gently out of the way, Susan pulled up a chair and sat down beside her. 'What's happened? Has he had an accident or something?'

'No. It's worse. He's volunteered. He's joined the Royal Army Veterinary Corps.'

Susan stared at her in dismay. 'Being a vet is a reserved occupation, isn't it?'

'It is, and the stupid blighter didn't have to join up. It's all her fault.' A fresh bout of sobbing rendered Roz speechless. She buried her head in her hands and her shoulders heaved.

'But it may not be too bad. Surely the army doesn't need vets abroad. I mean they don't use horses any more, do they?'

'Apparently they do. The cavalry are still in Palestine, so he told me, although they're being mechanised, but he could be sent to Italy or even worse India or Burma. She did that to him, Susan. She told her father about us, and he's got his solicitor to look into the lease of the surgery. It's due to be renewed, and old man Colby isn't going to pay any more. Patrick doesn't earn enough to cover the rent, let alone the renewal of the lease. He's lost his job and she wants him out of the house within a month. He's going away and he might be killed. My baby will be an orphan.'

Susan placed her arm around Roz's shoulders. 'I don't suppose he'll be in the front line. He probably won't see any fighting at all.'

Roz fumbled in her pocket and produced a rather soggy hanky. She mopped her streaming eyes and blew her nose. 'But he'll be thousands of miles away when the baby is born. He won't see his own child.'

'But that's happening all over the country, and you're not alone, Roz. You've got your dad and me.' Susan smiled as Charlie licked her hand. 'And Charlie, of course. We all love you and we'll adore the baby. It will be something for Patrick to look forward to when he gets home.'

'If he doesn't get himself killed.'

'You mustn't think like that.' Susan rose to her feet and went to the stove where the kettle was simmering on the hob. 'A nice hot cuppa will make you feel better, and then you can go for a lie-down. You've got to think of the baby, Roz. It's not good for you to get in such a state.'

Roz wiped her eyes and sniffed. 'I know. I realise that I must seem pathetic to you, but what really upset me was the fact that he didn't talk it over with me first.'

Susan warmed the teapot, tipping the water into the sink. 'It can't have been easy for him since your dad barred him from the pub. I haven't seen him at the house either.'

'No. He's been up in London making arrangements. He's going tomorrow, Susan. He'll be leaving first thing in the morning.'

Susan paused with the heaped caddy spoon held mid-air. 'So this will be his last night of freedom.'

'Don't say things like that.' Roz glared at her with reddened eyes.

'I've got an idea. Sit tight. Don't move a muscle until I get back.' Susan went out into the hallway, closing the door behind her. She picked up the telephone receiver and dialled the Petersons' number, hoping that it would be Patrick who answered it and not Mrs Harper. She breathed a sigh of relief at the sound of his voice. 'Hello, Patrick. It's Susan.'

'If it's a message from Elspeth I—'

She cut him off short. 'No. It's nothing to do with her. It's Roz.'

'Oh, God. What's happened?'

'Don't panic. She's fine, just very upset.'

'I know, and I feel terrible, but there's nothing I can do about it, Susan. I want you to understand that.'

She bit back a sharp retort. 'You're alone in the house tonight, aren't you?'

'Yes, well there's Mrs Harper, of course. Why do you ask?'

'Mrs H doesn't count. Look, if you're really serious about Roz, get in your car and come to the pub. I'll make sure she's ready and waiting by the garage. You can pull in there and no one will see you.'

'What are you suggesting? I'm leaving first thing in the morning.'

'That's just it. Don't you think you both deserve one night when you can be alone together? You need to talk to her, Patrick.'

'You're right. Of course, you're absolutely right. Tell her I'll be there in twenty minutes. You're a genius, Susan. A bloody genius.'

The line went dead and Susan replaced the receiver, smiling grimly. It had taken a swift metaphorical kick to get him moving, but at least they would be able to sort things out between them. She hurried back to the kitchen. 'Patrick is picking you up in twenty minutes. You've got one night together to sort things out, so don't waste time, go and make yourself beautiful.' Despite her protests, Susan sent Roz upstairs to wash her tear-stained face. Following more slowly, Susan went to the bedroom and threw a few necessities into a large handbag.

Shiny-faced and red-eyed, Roz burst into the room and flung herself down on the stool in front of her dressing table. She began brushing her hair with long frantic strokes. 'I look awful,' she said miserably.

'You're fine. Powder your nose and put on a dab of lipstick if you must, but he'll be here soon, so hurry up.'

Minutes later they were waiting by the garage. It

had started to rain but Roz was now in high spirits. 'I can't believe I'm doing this,' she whispered excitedly. 'It feels so – naughty.'

Susan smothered a giggle. 'Well, be naughty then. Enjoy yourself and forget about the war and Elspeth and everything.' She cocked her head on one side. 'I can hear a car coming.'

'I'm nervous,' Roz said, clutching her arm. 'I haven't ever been in their house. What if Elspeth turns up?'

Susan gave her hand a squeeze. 'She won't. Judging by the amount of cocktails those women drank and the bottles of wine they opened to have with their meal, I don't think any of them will be in a fit state to go anywhere tonight.' She gave Roz a gentle push towards the car as it drew to a halt.

Patrick leapt from the driver's seat and hurried round to open the passenger door. He embraced Roz tenderly before helping her into the car, closing the door reverently as if he carried a precious cargo. He turned to Susan, giving her a peck on the cheek. 'Thanks for this. I'd never have dared suggest it myself, but I'll always be grateful to you for this chance to set things right with Roz. I do love her, Susan. I'm only sorry that I'll be leaving her to go through the birth on her own.'

'I've already told her that she's not alone. We'll look after her and the baby, and when the war is over you'll be together again, if that's what you really want.'

'It is, and perhaps now I can convince Roz that I meant every word I said. Bless you, Susan.'

She stood aside, watching the car until it was out of sight. She shivered. It was not particularly cold, but she was exhausted and emotionally drained. She went back to the kitchen and finished making the tea, but before she sat down to have her supper she took a mug into the bar for Bob. He never drank alcohol, which had always seemed a bit odd to her considering his occupation, but he was addicted to tea. As long as he was kept constantly supplied with hot, sweet Darjeeling, he declared that he was a happy man. He gave her a beaming smile as she put the mug on the counter. The bar was full and the air thick with tobacco smoke. 'I could do with a hand,' he said as she was about to return to the kitchen. 'Would you give Roz a shout, love? The last hour is going to be a bit hectic.'

She was tired and hungry, but she was prepared to cover for Roz. 'She's got a bit of a headache, and she's gone to bed early. I said I'd help out if you needed me.'

His dark eyebrows met in a frown. 'Is she okay? Should I send for the doctor?'

'She's absolutely fine, and she'll be right as rain in the morning.' Susan turned to face the queue of eager customers. 'Who's next?'

She was up early next morning. It was still a good hour until dawn, but she needed to be there to unlock the door when Patrick dropped Roz off, and she had to finish her work at the pub before she went to the cottage. She started by clearing the ash from the grate in the ingle nook where the logs had burned away to almost nothing. She laid the fire ready to light later in the day before turning her attention to the coke boiler in the kitchen. She had banked it up with cinders, and it only needed a little encouragement to glow back into life. She returned to the bar and was busy emptying the ashtrays when she heard a car approaching. There were few enough vehicles on the roads, and as it drew up outside she was certain it must be Patrick's Triumph Gloria. She turned off the lights and opened the outer door. In the faint greenish glow of dawn she could see Patrick and Roz wrapped in a last lingering embrace. With the greatest reluctance they drew apart and Roz stood at the kerb, waving. She turned and walked slowly towards Susan.

'Are you all right, Roz?' She had been expecting floods of tears, but to her relief Roz was smiling and her cheeks were delicately flushed. She looked positively glowing.

'Thank you, Susan,' she said simply. 'Thanks for giving me the most wonderful night of my life. We talked about so many things and I know he really loves me, and he wants this baby as much as I do. I can put up with everything now.'

Susan led the way to the kitchen. 'I knew that you would sort it out if you just had time together. I'm so happy for you, Roz.' She busied herself making tea and toast while Roz took off her coat and settled down at the table. She spread her hands flat on the scrubbed pine surface just as Susan put the teapot on its stand.

'That's an engagement ring,' Susan said, staring in amazement at Roz's left hand.

'It was his mother's. Elspeth refused to accept it and insisted on having one made especially for her, as if she was blooming royalty.'

'It's lovely, but you can't wear it.'

'Why not? Patrick gave it to me. It's mine.'

'Because your dad will want to know how you came by it when he had forbidden you to see Patrick. If it gets round the village, and it will, then Elspeth will hear about it and she'll be mad as fire. If you want her to divorce her husband you're going the wrong way about it.'

Roz stared at her hand and then nodded slowly. 'I hadn't thought it through, but I suppose you're right.' She slipped the ring off her finger and put it in her pocket. 'I'll put it on a chain and wear it round my neck, close to my heart.' She gave a self-conscious giggle. 'I never thought I'd do soppy romantic things like that.'

Susan poured the tea. 'It's called being in love.'

'And you would know, wouldn't you?'

'What d'you mean?' Susan's hand shook and she slopped tea into the saucer.

'Come off it, Susie. I've seen the way Tony looks

at you and it's obvious that the feeling is mutual. Admit it.'

Susan smiled. 'Well, yes. But we're taking things slowly. I've got to be absolutely certain that he feels the same way about me as I do about him. I can't bear the thought that it might all go wrong.'

'All I can say is don't leave it too late. The war has turned everything upside down, and it makes you realise just how short life is.' She laid her hand on her stomach. 'Oh.'

'What is it? Are you in pain?'

'No. It moved, Susan. It felt like a butterfly in my tummy. It's a real little person in there. Oh, my God. I wish Patrick was here.'

Susan arrived at the cottage expecting to find Elspeth sleeping off the excesses of the previous evening, but instead she found her looking immaculate in her navy worsted uniform. She was standing in front of the empty grate, studying her reflection in the mirror while she put on her forage cap, adjusting it several times to set it at the most flattering angle. Despite Elspeth's many failings, Susan could not help but admire her. 'You look very smart, ma'am.'

'I do, don't I?' Elspeth patted her hair in place. 'I think I look the part.' She picked up her shoulder bag and gasmask case. 'I didn't have time to unpack my cases, so you had better do that first. I won't be in for supper, so you can go when you've finished.' She opened the door, pausing on the threshold. 'I'm off then. I'm afraid there's a bit of a mess to clear up, but I'm sure you'll cope magnificently.' She left with a wave of her hand, closing the door against a sudden gust of wind and rain.

Susan glanced round with a sigh. Elspeth had not been exaggerating. There were overflowing ashtrays and empty glasses scattered all round the room. The remnants of last night's meal had been left to congeal on the table, and the white linen napkins were stained with lipstick and lay crumpled on the floor. The kitchen was in an even worse state of chaos. Susan had washed and dried the saucepans before she went home, but later in the evening someone had been making sandwiches. There were crusts and breadcrumbs spilling onto the floor and a half-empty jar of meat paste had been left without its cap so that what was left inside looked grey and unappetising. Empty bottles littered the table top and an attempt to grind coffee beans had obviously ended in disaster as most of it had ended up on the quarry tiles. It was obvious that Elspeth's elegant friends were unused to looking after themselves. Susan rolled up her sleeves and set to work.

It took her all morning to get the ground floor back into shape, and having treated herself to a cup of tea and toasted the last of the stale bread she went upstairs. She had been dreading what she might find, but she was pleasantly surprised. There were only two bedrooms and once she had made the beds there was little to do other than sort out the jumble of clothes that Elspeth had left piled on a chair. After an hour of putting gowns on hangers and sorting lingerie from knitwear, Susan had stowed every-thing neatly away apart from the two Sidcot flying suits, helmets and gloves. She laid them on the bed in the spare room intending to ask Elspeth whether she needed them or wanted them packed away.

Having satisfied herself that she could do no more in the bedrooms, Susan turned her attention to the bathroom. Apart from looking as though there had been a snowstorm in the night, it was simply a matter of wiping up the liberal amounts of talcum powder scattered over the linoleum. She had just cleaned the bath when she heard someone banging on the cottage door, and she hurried down the steep staircase which led directly into the living room. 'Hold on,' she called out when the visitor knocked again. 'I'm coming.' She opened the door to find Tony standing on the step. 'Hello. What brings you here?'

He took off his cap, grinning. 'I've had warmer welcomes.'

'I'm sorry. I was surprised to see you.'

He stepped inside, looking round at the now spick and span room with an admiring nod. 'Very cosy, but I'd have thought it was a bit bijou for Elspeth's tastes.'

'She seems to like it, but you haven't answered my question. Is there anything wrong? I mean, shouldn't you be at work?'

'One of my trainees is off sick,' Tony said cheerfully. 'I've got a couple of hours free so I thought I'd give you a treat.'

'Really?' She stared at him in surprise. 'What sort of treat?'

'Did Elspeth bring the flying suits with her?'

'Of course. She wouldn't leave them behind.'

'Go and put one on. I'm taking you up in a Mosquito.'

'No! You're teasing me.'

He crossed his heart solemnly. 'Hope to die.'

'Don't say that, even joking.'

'So you're superstitious, Sue. That's another thing I've learned about you.' He touched her cheek with his fingertips and his eyes glowed with tenderness. 'Go upstairs and change. We haven't got all day.'

Sitting in the cockpit of the Mosquito was quite literally a dream come true for Susan. She could barely begin to imagine how it must feel to fly such a beautiful machine. Giving her the thumbs up signal, Tony started the engine and taxied onto the airfield.

Susan held her breath as they took off. Used as she was to the Tiger Moth, this was a new and thrilling experience. She fell in love all over again, but this time with a flying machine. She closed her eyes, visualising the instrument panel and working out in her mind which each one did from the air speed indicator to the artificial horizon. She followed

Tony's actions as closely as she could, imagining that she was in sole charge of the plane as they soared high above the fields, farms and the silver thread of the river. He looped the loop and executed a victory roll. She could hardly catch her breath in between each skilful manoeuvre, but it was over too soon. Even after they had landed she sat in the cockpit, unwilling for the experience to end.

Tony climbed onto the wing. 'Did you enjoy that, Susan?'

'More than you'll ever know. It was just amazing. The most wonderful thing that's ever happened to me.' She smiled up at him but his attention had been diverted and her heart sank as she saw his expression change. She turned her head and saw an officer striding towards them. There was no mistaking his feelings. He looked positively furious.

'Better hop out,' Tony murmured. 'I think I'm in for it.' He leapt off the wing and stood to attention, saluting smartly.

Susan climbed out more slowly and slithered to the ground. She could tell from the superior officer's thunderous expression that Tony had not exaggerated.

'My office, First Officer Richards. Now.'

'Yes, Flight Captain.'

The officer turned on his heel and marched off towards the buildings on the edge of the airfield. Susan laid her hand on Tony's arm. 'Will you be in a lot of trouble?'

'Probably, but don't worry, Susan. It was worth it to see the look on your face.'

'What will they do to you?'

He shrugged his shoulders. 'I'll get my wrist slapped, and a good ticking off. I'm sorry I won't be able to see you home.'

'No, of course not. Go on.'

He leaned over and kissed her on the cheek. 'I'll see you in the pub tonight.'

Susan watched him disappearing into the distance. He had done it for her and she had enjoyed every minute of the flight, but at what cost? She knew nothing about military discipline but judging by the look on the Flight Captain's face he was not going to congratulate Tony on his demonstration of the Mosquito's aerobatic powers. She set off for the cottage, wondering whether the news of her escapade would get back to Elspeth. She had been so eager to go up with Tony that she had not stopped to think of the possible consequences for either of them.

She was anxious for the rest of the day, hoping that he would not get into too much trouble, but that evening when closing time approached and there was still no sign of him, she began to feel extremely anxious. Roz had returned from work earlier that evening looking pale and exhausted, and Susan volunteered to take her shift in the bar. Roz had accepted gladly and had gone to bed early. Susan was also tired, but when she eventually got to bed she was too overwrought to sleep, and she tossed and turned in her bed until the early hours of the morning when she eventually fell into a fitful doze.

She was up early and at the cottage before Elspeth left for the aerodrome. 'Good morning,' she murmured, taking off her jacket. 'Is there anything special you want me to do today, ma'am?'

Elspeth's expression was unreadable and the silence ominous.

'I borrowed the Sidcot suit yesterday,' Susan said awkwardly.

'Yes, I heard about your little escapade. In fact everyone on the airfield knew about it by lunchtime.'

'I'm sorry. I didn't think . . .' Susan broke off miserably. She knew she was going to be fired, and there was nothing she could say in her defence. When Elspeth did not reply Susan glanced up and was shocked to see a slow smile spreading across her face.

'You little devil,' Elspeth said, shaking her head. 'I didn't think you had it in you. Do you realise that you broke all the bloody rules, including unlawful use of a military aircraft? You could have been shot as a spy.'

'No. Could I?'

Elspeth chuckled. 'Well, probably not. But you could have been arrested for being on the aerodrome without a pass. What were you thinking of, Susan?'

'Tony knew that it was my dream to fly in a

military aeroplane and he took me up. What will happen to him? They won't shoot him, will they?'

'No, but he's been sacked. I could wring your neck for losing me the best instructor I could ever have. You might have waited until I completed my training.'

Susan's legs gave way beneath her and she sank down on the sofa. 'I knew he'd get into trouble but I didn't think he'd lose his job. This is all my fault.'

'Don't be silly. Tony knew the score but he quite obviously wanted to make an impression on a pretty girl, only he went too far. He's not the first idiot to do something so utterly stupid because of a woman, and I doubt if he'll be the last.' She picked up her forage cap. 'I'm off to the ferry pool. I'll be dining with some of the girls tonight, so you needn't prepare anything.'

'Aren't you going to fire me?'

'Why should I? I think you were misguided, but I can understand your passion for flying. However, I'd advise you to steer clear of the airfield from now on, or you might end up on jankers, and that would reflect badly on me.' She glanced out of the window. 'Bloody weather. There won't be any flying this morning, so it looks like it will be bridge and gossip, or else someone will be playing songs from 'The Strawberry Blonde' on the gramophone. If I have to listen to 'And the Band Played On' once more I swear I'll smash the wretched record. Too ghastly. Never mind, I suppose it's all in a day's work.'

'I'd give anything to be there,' Susan said, sighing. 'It sounds wonderful.'

Elspeth's lips curved in a cynical smile. 'You're very young. Wait until you're a mature woman of twenty-seven who's had her heart broken more times than she can remember, and then see how wonderful you think life is.'

'Have you had your heart broken?'

'Not me personally, sweetie.' Elspeth flung her mink coat around her shoulders. 'Try not to get into any more trouble today, Susan. I'm the girl with the reputation for breaking all the rules; I don't need competition from you.' She let herself out of the cottage and moments later Susan heard the roar of the roadster as Elspeth drove off, even though it was only a ten minute walk to the aerodrome. She set about her tasks methodically, but her heart was not in her work. Tony was constantly in her thoughts and she was swamped by feelings of guilt. She knew that he would contact her as soon as he was able, but that did not make waiting any easier.

She was outside in the tiny garden sifting the ashes from the fire when she looked up and saw a familiar figure walking down the lane. She dropped the sieve and ran towards him. 'Tony.' She flung her arms around him regardless of the fact that her clothes were powdered with ash. 'I've been so worried about you. I couldn't bear it if anything bad happened to you.'

He held her close, a slow smile spreading across

his face. 'It was worth losing my job if only to hear you say that.' He kissed her and she responded wholeheartedly.

Minutes later they were sitting side by side on Elspeth's sofa. Susan traced the outline of his jaw with the tip of her forefinger. 'I feel dreadful. You'd never have done anything so rash if it hadn't been for me. Elspeth told me that you'd lost your job, so what will happen now?'

'They can't afford to lose a good pilot. I'm being sent to number 3 ferry pool. I'm quite pleased, because flying is what I love to do, but there's a drawback.'

She swallowed convulsively as an ice-cold shiver ran down her spine. 'What? Tell me.'

'That particular ferry pool is at Hawarden, near Chester.'

'They can't send you that far away when we've only just found each other.' Her voice broke on a sob. 'It's not fair.'

He wrapped his arms around her, holding her as if he would never let her go. She could feel his breath warm on her cheek and the now familiar scent of him filled her with longing. She laid her head on his shoulder, savouring the bittersweet moment.

'It won't be forever, darling,' he said softly. 'I might even be sent here to pick up a Spitfire from the factory. I'll write to you every day and I'll come to see you whenever I can.'

'But are you fit enough for that sort of work?

What will your dad say when he finds out that you're flying again and risking your life?'

'Of course I'm fit enough. They'll take pilots with glasses and one arm missing, they're so desperate. As to Dad, he'll understand.'

'Your Aunt Maida will say I led you on, and I can't say I'd blame her. You'd be safe here training ferry pilots if it wasn't for me. Oh, Tony, I'm so sorry.' Fighting back tears, she buried her face in his shoulder.

'Forget them,' he said, stroking her hair. 'Nothing matters except you and me. We belong together, Sue. It'll take more than a war and a couple of hundred miles of air space to separate us now.'

She raised her face, closing her eyes as his eager mouth sought hers. For an achingly short while she was able to blot out the war that was tearing them apart. She knew now that she loved him with all her heart. He was all the family that she needed. They belonged together. When he drew away just far enough to gaze deeply into her eyes, she managed a smile. 'I love you, Tony.'

'And I love you, Susan. I always have. Tell me again, just once before I have to go.'

She froze. 'You're not going already?'

'The Flight Captain didn't give me any option, sweetheart. I'm taking a repaired Spit to Filton aerodrome near Bristol this afternoon. I'll get further orders there.'

Susan swallowed hard. Now she knew how Roz

had felt when Patrick was spirited away so suddenly. Her whole world seemed to be crumbling about her ears. 'We've had such a short time together,' she whispered. 'But I'll write to you. I'll send you all the gossip and let you know what's happening in the village. I'll wait for you forever, if that's what it takes to bring you back to me.'

He answered her with a kiss that sent her senses spiralling into infinity, and then he was gone.

She struggled through the remainder of her working day feeling as though she was stuck inside a huge bubble. Shock and disbelief were replaced by anger and frustration, but if she were to be honest with herself she knew that she was the only person to blame. It was her foolish obsession with flying that had made him risk everything in order to give her what she had longed for. She could understand his passion for flying, but that did not disguise the fact that accidents and fatalities amongst the ferry pilots happened all the time. They flew without navigational aids other than maps and without the benefit of radios. They were unarmed and vulnerable to attack from the Luftwaffe and occasionally mistaken for enemy aircraft. They were at the mercy of the weather and exhaustion, and she had sent him back to the danger zone. She knew that she would never forgive herself should anything happen to him.

After a day of agonising and self-recrimination, Susan rode home with a heavy heart. She had jeopardised the life of the man she loved. She was alone again, and desperately lonely. She was pedalling along the High Street, wrapped in her own dismal thoughts, when she heard the sound of an approaching motor vehicle. She pulled in at the kerb as an ambulance flashed past her with its bell ringing. It had come from the direction of the aerodrome and was obviously answering an emergency call, but accidents were not uncommon in the two factories on the airfield and the workshops. Some poor soul had been unlucky that day. She arrived at the pub to find it parked outside. The doors were open and Bob was about to climb in, but he hesitated when he saw her. 'Look after the bar until I get back, Susan.' He thrust the door key into her hand. 'It's Roz. She's had an accident at the factory. They're taking her to Southampton General.'

Chapter Seventeen

Susan wanted to question Bob further, but the ambulance man barred her way. 'Please let me speak to Mr Fuller,' she said breathlessly. 'I must know what happened.'

He shook his head. 'Best do as the gentleman said, miss. The young lady's in good hands.' He climbed into the vehicle and closed the doors. It sped off, leaving Susan none the wiser and in a state of considerable agitation. Roz's condition must be serious or Bob would have taken the time to put her mind at rest. Fearing the worst, she picked up her bicycle and wheeled it into the pub garden. She left it propped up against the wall regardless of the fact that it had started to rain. Normally she would have put it under lock and key in the garage, but at this moment she had more pressing matters on her mind. She let herself into the pub, acknowledging Charlie's bouncy welcome with an absent-minded pat on the head. Her concern for Roz was uppermost in her mind. An accident at this stage of her pregnancy might cause a miscarriage and she knew how much Roz wanted this baby. She seemed to have come to terms with the fact that her child would bear the stigma of illegitimacy, even though she was suffering at the hands of the village gossips. Sly remarks and covert glances were cast her way whenever she went to the shops. Roz had managed to rise above it so far, but there was only so much a person could take, and Susan suspected that she was teetering on the edge. Losing the baby as well as Patrick might be the last straw.

Susan checked the bar. Bob had obviously been preparing to open up and everything was in readiness for the evening trade. She threw a log on the fire, warming her hands over the heat. She felt chilled to the bone although it was not a particularly cold evening. She wished that she could go to her room and lock herself in with just Charlie for company. The last thing she wanted was to have to put on a brave smile and face the customers that evening, but someone was tapping on the outside door and a quick glance at the clock above the bar showed that it was five minutes past opening time. Somewhat reluctantly, she unlocked the door and the two locals wandered in, touching their caps to her in a silent greeting. She went behind the bar to serve them.

'The usual, is it, Nutty?'

Nutty Slack, a grizzled man in his late fifties, had earned his nickname when he was a coalman. He nodded his head. 'Saw the ambulance. Was it the boss they took?'

'No, it was Roz. She's had an accident at work. I

don't know any of the details.' Susan pulled his pint and passed it over the counter. 'Same for you, Todd?'

Nutty's lifelong friend and drinking partner grunted his assent. 'Bad do. Poor girl. She hasn't had much luck recently.'

Susan gave him his beer, taking their money which they had counted out to the last penny and putting it in the till. There was nothing she could do now other than wait for news from the hospital. Until she knew the extent of Roz's injuries she could only imagine what might have happened to her at the factory. She knew very little about the type of work Roz undertook, although she knew that it had something to do with repairing damaged Spitfires. Roz made no secret of the fact that she hated her job, but Hamble was a small village and her only alternative would have been to travel daily to Southampton. She might have considered it once, but being pregnant had changed her priorities and she had chosen to work closer to home.

She had, to Susan's knowledge, so far only received one letter from Patrick. He had told her that he was about to be sent abroad, although he could not say where. Susan had comforted her as best she could, but only now could she fully empathise with the sense of loss and foreboding that Roz must have been feeling. The future was an uncertain place for everyone in the country, and now Susan had joined the millions of women who lived on hope and waited.

The evening passed slowly with a trickle of customers stopping off for a drink on their way home after work. Nutty and Todd sat at one of the tables playing dominoes and sipping their pints of mild. Susan kept glancing at the clock but it seemed as though the hands barely moved. She emptied ashtrays, washed and polished glasses and waited. It was not until nine o'clock that the bar started to fill up and she was kept busy serving drinks. She looked up expectantly every time the door opened hoping to see Bob returning from the hospital, but it was always just another local eager for warmth and company.

It was almost nine thirty when Danny strolled into the pub. He threaded his way towards the bar with a cheery smile on his face, although Susan was certain that she detected a slight wariness in his eyes as he greeted her. Perhaps he thought she was about to fall apart if he mentioned Tony or Roz.

'The usual, Danny?' She pulled a pint of bitter and put it on the bar in front of him.

'Thanks, Susan.' He drank thirstily. 'That's a good pint.'

'What happened?' Susan asked in a low voice. 'Were you there when Roz had the accident?'

His smiled faded. 'I saw her fall. Is there any news?'

'Not yet. I've been hoping that Bob would telephone from the hospital, but I don't know anything about her injuries. You obviously do.'

Danny took another swig of his drink. 'She fell from the wing of the plane. I don't know whether she had a dizzy spell or why she suddenly toppled over, but she landed awkwardly. We got the medic to her as soon as we could and made her comfortable until the ambulance arrived. I guess she's broken some bones.'

'But she was conscious?'

'Yes. I don't think she hit her head, but of course in her condition it's a hell of a worry.'

Susan frowned. 'I suppose it could be worse, just so long as the baby is all right.'

'We've got to hope. Poor girl, she's had a rotten time recently.' He eyed her over the rim of his glass. 'And how are you?'

'I suppose everyone knows that Tony took me up in a Mosquito?'

'Pretty well. You know what it's like.'

'I blame myself. He only did it for me.'

'Pretty damn dashing, if you ask me. I never had old Tony down for the romantic sort but there you go, he risks everything for the woman he loves. How about that?'

'It's not funny.'

'No, I suppose not. Sorry.' He reached across the bar to pat her hand. 'Chin up, Susan. If I know Tony he'll be counting the days until he sees you again.'

She felt a blush rising to her cheeks and she turned away to serve another customer, but her thoughts were elsewhere and she had to tot up the round all over again. 'That will be two and tenpence half-penny, please.'

The man with the florid complexion handed over the money with a snort of derision. 'Daylight robbery.' He picked up the tray, walking away carefully so as not to spill a drop.

'I added it up twice,' Susan said, turning to Danny who was perched on a bar stool in the corner. 'It's not my fault that beer costs eightpence a pint.'

'Don't let them get to you, love,' Danny said, pushing his glass towards her. 'I'll have another, and one for yourself.'

She pulled his pint but refused the drink as politely as she could without hurting his feelings. He was about to argue when the pub door opened and Bob walked in. There was a sudden hush. Word had got round and expectant faces turned towards him. He raised his hand, a wry smile on his lips. 'She's all right, folks. Broke her ankle and sprained her wrist, which is bad enough, but everything else is fine.' He made his way to the bar. 'Thanks, Susan. I owe you one.' He lifted the hatch and came to stand beside her. 'Don't look so worried. She'll be fine.'

'What about the baby?'

'So far, so good. There are no guarantees but the doctors seem to think everything will be okay.' He took a glass from the shelf and held it beneath the whisky optic, measuring out a double. 'I need this.'

Susan had never seen him drink anything stronger

than tea and she was suddenly anxious. Roz had hinted that her father had had a drink problem after her mother died, adding hastily that he had managed to stay on the wagon for a good many years. Judging by the way he knocked back his drink it looked to Susan as though he had fallen off it with a vengeance. He downed a second large Scotch with equal speed.

'Steady on, Bob,' Danny said softly. 'She's okay, and that's all that matters.'

'I don't need you to tell me what I can or can't do in my own pub, son.' Bob went to refresh his drink but the bottle was empty.

Susan moved swiftly to take it down. 'I'll see to it, Mr Fuller.'

'You've done enough, Susan.' Bob's voice was thick and his speech already slightly slurred. 'I'll finish off here.'

She cast an anguished glance at Danny and he responded immediately by getting off his stool and letting himself into the cramped space behind the bar. 'Tell you what, Bob. Why don't you let me do last orders so that Susan can get you both some supper? The poor girl looks done in.'

Bob recoiled slightly, glaring at Danny with a suspicious gleam in his eyes. 'What do you know about working in a bar, sunshine?'

'My dad runs a pub in Catford. I've helped out there more times than I can remember, and you look as though you could do with a break. Let me help. I'd like to.'

Susan clutched Bob's arm. 'I'll make us something to eat, and I'm dying to know everything the doctor said. It's not very private out here.'

He glanced round, seeming to realise for the first time that people were staring at him. He shrugged his shoulders. 'All right, you win the pair of you.' He turned to Danny with an ominous scowl. 'You can do the bar but I'll cash up.' He ducked under the hatch and moving a little unsteadily made his way out of the bar.

Susan flashed Danny a grateful smile. 'Thanks. Come through to the kitchen when you've locked up and I'll save you some supper.'

'You're on.' Danny leaned on the counter. 'Yes, sir,' he said, grinning at the young airman who was waiting to be served. 'What can I do you for?'

Susan followed Bob to the kitchen. He slumped down in a chair at the table, holding his head in his hands. 'I thought I was going to lose her,' he muttered. 'Her mother died in childbirth, and I thought that Roz was going the same way.'

Susan filled the kettle and put it on the hob. 'She's not going to die. You said that she's got some broken bones and the baby is all right. She'll be home in no time at all.'

'She's not out of the wood yet. Things could still go wrong and I could kill that bloody vet. He had his way with my little girl and then buggered off abroad to look after sick horses. I'd like to put him in front of a firing squad.'

'He loves her,' Susan said gently. 'They love each other.' She took a loaf from the bread bin and cut several thick slices. She found cheese in the larder and cut slivers ready for toasting. 'You did say that she's going to be all right, didn't you? There isn't anything you aren't telling me?'

He shook his head. 'No, that was all. You're a good girl, Susan. Thanks for stepping in this evening.'

'I'm happy to help out. I don't know where I'd be if it wasn't for you and Roz.'

She made the tea and put a liberal helping of sugar in Bob's cup. She served the cheese on toast and they ate in silence. She shot him sidelong glances, hoping that he would not turn to the bottle again once he was out of her sight, but he seemed to have returned to his former good-humoured self, and when he had finished eating he rose from his seat. 'I'll cash up and then I'm going to bed. I'll phone the hospital first thing in the morning to check on Roz.'

'You must try not to worry. Roz needs you now more than ever. She'll always need her dad.' She swallowed hard as a lump in her throat threatened to choke her. She would give anything to have a loving father like Bob. 'She's so lucky to have you,' she added in a whisper.

'Thanks for supper, and don't worry – I'm not going to hit the bottle. I'm okay now. Anyway, I'll send young Danny through to get his grub.' Bob hesitated in the doorway, a ghost of a smile on his lips. 'I thought it was young Tony who was sweet on you. I can't keep up with you young people.' He wandered off in the direction of the bar.

Susan shook her head. He must still be a little bit drunk if he thought that there was anything between her and Danny. She put another two slices of bread under the grill and cut more slivers of Cheddar cheese. She wondered what Tony was doing at this moment. Was he thinking of her too? She hoped so.

For the first time since she had lived in the pub Bob was up before her next morning. She could hear him bellowing down the telephone as she came downstairs. She hurried past him with Charlie running on ahead, and as she opened the kitchen door she heard Bob moderate his tone slightly and the clunk of the receiver as it was replaced in its cradle. She prayed silently that it was good news. She studied his face as he entered the room, and to her intense relief his stern features creased into a wide grin. 'She's doing well. They've set the broken bones and the baby is fine.'

'That's wonderful.' Susan rushed over and gave him a hug, but the smell of whisky on his breath made her draw away quickly.

He shrugged his broad shoulders. 'It was just a tot, Susan. I won't touch another drop.' He walked over to the stove. 'I'm making scrambled eggs for breakfast. I'm seriously thinking of buying a few laying hens and then we can be self-sufficient in eggs. Roz has been on at me for ages to make use of the barren strip of land at the end of the garden.'

Susan left him to prepare their breakfast while she let Charlie and his now best friend Orlando out into the garden. She smiled as she watched them ambling around together, with Charlie sniffing scents undetectable to humans and Orlando looking on in his superior feline manner. Everything seemed wonderfully normal now that Roz was on the mend and she heaved a heartfelt sigh of relief. Roz was the sister that she had always longed for and nothing and no one could take that away from her. She went indoors to have her breakfast and get ready for work.

When she arrived at the cottage there was no one in the living room, although there were empty glasses and wine bottles on the coffee table. The large cut-crystal ashtray was overflowing with cigarette ends ringed with scarlet lipstick and several cigar butts. Susan shrugged off her coat and hat and hung them on the coat stand in the corner. Picking up as many glasses as she could fit between her fingers she used her foot to open the kitchen door.

She had half expected to see Elspeth standing by the table with a cup of coffee in one hand and a slice of toast in the other, but the sight that met her eyes made her stop and stare open-mouthed.

'Hello, Susan.' Naked except for one of Elspeth's pink silk negligees, Colin was seated at the table attacking a week's bacon ration and a slice of fried bread. He flicked a strand of pink marabou away from his face as he forked a piece of bacon into his mouth. 'Cat got your tongue, darling?' He chewed and swallowed, chuckling. 'You should see your face, Susan.'

She covered her confusion by going to the sink and putting the glasses into the washing-up bowl. 'It's none of my business,' she murmured.

'You could have had your share if you'd played your cards right,' he said, wiping the plate with the last of the fried bread and popping it into his mouth. 'If you hadn't been such a shy little virgin we could have made wonderful music together last Christmas.' He dropped his fork on the floor and when she bent down to pick it up he cupped her buttocks in his hands. 'We still could, darling. I won't tell Tony, if you keep it a secret from Elspeth.'

She almost fell over in her attempt to free herself from his grasp. 'You're disgusting, Colin. I wouldn't sleep with you if you were the last man on earth.'

He smiled lazily. 'Sweetheart, you wouldn't get much sleep if you went to bed with me.'

'How can you behave like this when you're engaged to that poor woman in Scotland? Does Elspeth know about Morag?'

'Morag?' He stared at her blankly for a moment and then a slow smile spread across his handsome features. 'Oh, her. Sweetheart, she's a figment of my imagination. I trot dear Morag out when I want to make a swift getaway. She's my insurance against young women like you getting the wrong idea.'

'She doesn't exist?'

'Got it in one. Sorry, darling. Now, if you don't mind I think I'd better go upstairs and retrieve my clothes.' He stood up and the skimpy garment hung loosely, leaving nothing to the imagination.

Susan averted her gaze. She knew that she was blushing and that made her even more embarrassed. She suspected that he was laughing at her but Colin was in between her and the door, and there was no way of escape. 'You'd better hurry,' she said hastily. 'You'll be late for work.'

His response to this was forestalled by the sudden appearance of Elspeth, fully dressed and clutching her forage cap in her hand. She leaned against the doorpost, taking in the scene with raised eyebrows. 'Really, darling. You look like a stallion put out to stud. Cover up, do.'

Colin struck a pose. 'I thought that was why you liked me, my sweet. Come upstairs and we'll make the most of my enthusiasm.'

'Stop it, you naughty boy, you're embarrassing poor little Susan.' Elspeth shooed him out of the room. 'Sorry about that, my dear. He has no finesse, but he's frightfully good in bed.'

Susan began clearing the table. 'It doesn't matter.'

'No. Well, sweetie, you'd better get used to Colin's little ways because he's moving in with me.'

'He's going to live here?'

'That's what I said, Susan.'

'Then I really can't continue working for you, ma'am.'

Elspeth opened her eyes wide, shaking her head as if completely astounded. 'Why not? You didn't seem to mind when we were at the big house. What's the difference?'

Susan had to bite her tongue in order to prevent herself from telling her that Colin was the worst kind of rat and totally untrustworthy. She averted her gaze. 'I don't know, but he makes me feel uncomfortable. I'd rather find work elsewhere.'

'So you're leaving me in the lurch? After everything I've done for you, Susan. What about the free flying lessons? A girl like you would never have had the chance to get airborne if it weren't for me.'

'And I'm truly grateful, but it's getting too complicated. I've just found out something about Colin that makes me think he's not a good person.'

'Darling, don't be so melodramatic. I don't believe that he would say anything to upset a child like you.'

Stung into retaliation, Susan forgot her scruples. 'He made suggestions that were very embarrassing, and he lied about his long-suffering fiancée, Morag. Did he tell you about her?'

Elspeth threw back her head and laughed. 'Darling, you're such a little innocent and a bit of a prude. Of course I know about Morag, his devoted Highland lass. Let me tell you, that Morag is real but she's a bitch. In the true sense of the word, she is a bitch. An Irish wolfhound to be exact and she is the most faithful creature, always pleased to see him when he visits his relations in Scotland.' Elspeth rammed her cap on her head. 'Must go, Susan. We'll talk about this later when you've had time to calm down. You really must grow up, my girl.' She left the room still chuckling.

Susan turned to the sink and ran the hot tap but the water was cold. Colin and Elspeth must have used up the last of it and they had let the fire go out in the boiler. She filled the kettle and while she was waiting for the water to heat up she cleared the breakfast table. Upstairs she could hear footsteps on the bare linoleum followed by a shriek of laughter and the creaking of bedsprings. Elspeth, she decided, was going to be very late for roll call this morning.

She went into the living room and attempted to ignore the sounds of their enthusiastic love-making, but the vision of Colin in pink silk and marabou continued to haunt her. Having plumped up the cushions on the sofa and cleaned the grate, she laid the fire so that all Elspeth would have to do was put a match to the kindling. All was now quiet upstairs and she scooped up the rest of the glasses and took them into the kitchen, closing the door so that she would not have to see the lovers when they eventually set off for the aerodrome. She would have liked to walk out there and then, but she felt she owed it to Elspeth to leave the cottage clean and tidy. Her feelings were mixed as she went through her tasks with the efficiency of an automaton. She had come to like Elspeth in an odd sort of way, despite her tantrums and her single-minded approach to life in which her own comfort was paramount. Elspeth neither knew nor cared what other people thought, and she seemed to breeze through life breaking all the rules and getting away with her outrageous behaviour. The strict discipline in the children's home had left its mark on Susan but sometimes she found herself wishing that she could be just a little bit like Elspeth. Life would be so much simpler if she could go through it riding roughshod over anyone who got in her way.

Eventually both Elspeth and Colin left for the aerodrome and Susan was able to get on with her work. By the end of the morning she had put everything to rights and left a pan of vegetable soup ready for Elspeth to heat up on her return from the flying pool that evening. She locked the door behind her and posted the key through the letterbox. She paused as she was about to unlatch the garden gate, looking back over her shoulder at the thatched cottage, which looked like an illustration from a story book. The last of the late summer roses clung to the porch and a hazy October sun reflected off the lattice windows. Tall hollyhocks laden with seed heads swayed gently in the cool breeze and some rather straggly bronze chrysanthemums made a splash of colour amongst the curling leaf skeletons of the summer bedding plants. Susan closed the gate with a snap. She was allowing her desire for security and continuity to cloud her judgement. Elspeth would soon find another willing slave and no amount of free flying lessons would make up for being at Colin's beck and call, or putting up with his lewd suggestions and groping hands. She set off for the pub, wondering how she was going to tell Bob that she had walked out on a perfectly good job. Whatever Elspeth's faults, parsimony was not one of them.

Bob had been drinking. His face was flushed and he was talking loudly. He greeted Susan like a long lost daughter, giving her a hug and breathing whisky fumes into her face. 'You're home early, love. Got the sack, have you?' He roared with laughter and winked at the customer on the other side of the bar. 'She's a good girl, is Susan. Don't know what we'd do without her.'

She drew him aside. 'Is everything okay? Have you rung the hospital?'

His face darkened. 'They won't discharge her yet. The snooty bloody ward sister said that they were keeping her in for observation, whatever that means. I'm going to see her this evening.'

'But she is all right, isn't she?' Susan was suddenly anxious. Things could still go wrong and it was upsetting to see Bob in such a state.

'I don't know and that's the truth.' Bob patted her

on the shoulder. 'I'll be leaving young Danny to run the bar. He offered and I said you'd give him a hand if need be.'

'Yes, of course. I'll do anything.'

'So what are you doing home at this time of day? If you've given notice to that bitch I wouldn't blame you in the least, but you'll have to find another job pretty damn quickly, Susan. I'm not running a charity here. I can't afford to support you as well as Roz and the baby.'

Chapter Eighteen

Danny passed a half-pint mug of best bitter across the counter to a well-dressed elderly man. 'That'll be fourpence, please, guv.' The customer paid up without a word and took his drink to one of the tables near the ingle nook. Danny tossed the coins into the open till. 'So what's bothering you, Susan? You've hardly said a word all evening.'

She looked up from washing glasses in the small sink beneath the bar counter. 'I lost my job with Elspeth and I really need to find another one quickly.'

He frowned. 'What happened?'

'It was something and nothing. I'd rather not talk about it.'

'Okay, but I wouldn't want to work for that bitch. Not after the way she's treated Roz.'

'It really wasn't Elspeth's fault this time. It was Colin.'

Danny's face darkened and he fisted his hands. 'If that bastard's laid a finger on you, I'll bloody well poleaxe him.'

Susan stared at him open-mouthed. She had never seen this side of him before and it shocked her. 'It really doesn't matter, but I do need to find another job.'

'I might be able to help you find work at the factory, if that's what you want.'

'It is.'

Danny leaned against the counter, eyeing her thoughtfully. 'There's Roz's job. As far as I know they haven't filled it because they think she's coming back as soon as she's well enough.'

'You don't think she will?'

He shook his head. 'They might find her something less strenuous, but everything the girls are doing in the factory would have been done by men in peacetime.'

'I've studied the manual. I reckon I could take a Merlin engine apart if I had to.'

His serious expression melted into a grin. 'I'm sure you could. D'you want me to have a word to the chief engineer in the morning?'

'Would you? I'd be so grateful, Danny.'

'You mustn't worry; I'll sort it out tomorrow.' He turned away to serve Nutty Slack who was thumping his mug rhythmically on the counter. 'Yes, squire. Same again?'

It was almost closing time when Bob finally returned. His expression did not bode well. Susan hardly dare frame the question but she had been anxious all evening and now she was really worried. 'How is Roz? Is she all right?'

He pushed past her to take a glass and raise it to the whisky optic. He helped himself to a double and drank it in one gulp. 'They won't tell me anything, except to say that she's as well as can be expected, whatever that bloody means.' He refilled his glass. 'She's very low. She couldn't even raise a smile for her old dad. It's that damn vet's fault.' He glared at Susan. 'What with him ruining my girl and that bitch of a wife giving you the sack, those two have really rocked the boat.' He downed his drink and was about to take another when Susan laid her hand on his arm.

'I didn't get fired, Bob. I told you before that I left of my own accord. Anyway, I've kept supper for you. It's your favourite shepherd's pie, only there's more carrot and swede in it than mince.'

'It's very tasty, Bob,' Danny said cheerfully. 'I had some earlier. This girl is a dab hand in the kitchen.'

'Not hungry,' Bob growled, unhooking the whisky bottle. 'You can call last orders, Danny my boy. I'm going to bed.' He stumbled out of the bar, ignoring the well-wishers who attempted to speak to him.

Danny cleared his throat. 'Last orders, please, ladies and gentlemen.'

When the pub was empty and Danny had locked the street door, they finished clearing up in silence. Susan put a spark guard round the fire although it had burned away to nothing but ash and a few glowing embers. She turned to find Danny watching her intently. 'I don't know how I would have managed without you the last couple of evenings,' she said, smiling.

He shrugged his shoulders. 'Glad to help out in a crisis.'

'I'm going to make some cocoa. Would you like a hot drink before you go home?'

'I would, but I think it's best if I make tracks now, Susan.' He plucked his jacket from a row of pegs outside the snug and shrugged it on. 'It's getting late, and you know what the village gossips are like. I'd only have to stay on for half an hour after closing time and they'd say we were having a torrid love affair.' He took his cap from his pocket and rammed it on his curly auburn hair.

'But that's ridiculous.'

'I know, but that's what it's like living in a small place.' He leaned over and brushed her cheek with a kiss. 'I'll see what I can do about Roz's job.'

Susan followed him to the door. 'Goodnight, Danny.'

He stepped outside. 'I expect Bob will need me again tomorrow night. See you then.'

'I'll be here.'

'You're a girl in a million, Susan. Tony's a lucky man.' He walked off into the darkness and she closed the door, turning the key in the lock.

Early next morning Susan took Charlie for a walk along the river bank. She watched the dawn breaking in the east, casting a pearly green light on the countryside, and in minutes the horizon was a fiery furnace of scarlet and orange, turning the waters of the Hamble into a stream of molten copper. She strolled past the cottage but the curtains were drawn and there was no sign of life. She wondered how Elspeth would manage without her there to wash and iron her clothes, cook her meals and in general act more like a nanny than a maidservant. She shuddered as she thought of Colin and his two-timing ways. She could only hope that Elspeth was having fun at his expense and would not get her heart broken. She glanced down at Charlie bounding along at her side, his lead held in his mouth and his eyes shining as he gazed adoringly up at her, and she smiled. There were no half measures when it came to canine devotion and unconditional love. Charlie was always pleased to see her, even if she had been out all day. He was never mean or cross, and he was utterly trustworthy. If only men had similar qualities. She quickened her pace as the sky lightened and people began to emerge from their homes, setting off for work.

She let herself into the pub and went straight to the kitchen. Orlando got up and stretched, rubbing himself against her legs as if she was his favourite person in the whole world, but she knew it was cupboard love and all he wanted was a saucer of milk.

Bob did not put in an appearance until after opening time. He was unshaven and bleary-eyed and Susan made him tea and toast whilst keeping an eye on the bar.

'Should I apologise for last night?' he murmured, staring into his cup as if the answer might be floating about amongst the tea leaves.

'Not at all. You've had a lot to worry about. Everyone understands.' She scraped some butter onto a slice of toast and put it on his plate.

'If I lose Roz I lose everything.'

'She'll be home in no time. I'm sure she will.'

'I wish I could be so certain. I heard the nurse muttering something about toxaemia. That's how I lost her mother. They saved Roz but they couldn't do a thing for my poor Jennifer.' He shuddered and tears trickled down his lined cheeks, falling unheeded onto his toast.

Stricken with pity, Susan slipped her arm around his shoulders. 'Roz is fit and healthy. She had a bad fall and broke some bones, that's all. She's fine and so is the baby. You've got to get these morbid ideas out of your head.'

He wiped his eyes on the back of his hand, glancing up at her with a tortured expression. 'Then why won't they send her home? Why won't she buck up and talk to me?'

'I don't know. Maybe I could go and see her this afternoon? Perhaps I could cheer her up.'

He nodded slowly. 'Do what you like. I'm obviously no good for her at the moment.'

'Where are you, Bob Fuller? Postal delivery.'

A voice calling out from the bar saved Susan from thinking of a suitable response. She patted Bob on the shoulder. 'I'll go. You stay there and eat your breakfast.' She hurried into the bar and found the postman standing by the counter, waving an envelope like a flag of truce.

'It's for Roz. It was posted in London but I'd lay bets it's from her boyfriend.' He tapped the side of his nose with his forefinger. 'Say no more.'

'Thanks.' Susan took it from him, resisting the temptation to snatch. 'Anything else?' She was not going to gratify his curiosity by agreeing with him.

His face fell. 'No. But I'm right, aren't I? That there letter's from the vet. I'd know his writing anywhere. Our moggy has been there so many times I could wallpaper the back bedroom with the bills.'

'That's life, Mr Johnson.' She turned away to tuck the letter behind a bottle of ginger wine, and she heard him stomp across the tiled floor, muttering beneath his breath as he left the pub, closing the door with unnecessary violence. No doubt he was angry because she had not given him anything to pass on to the rest of the village. She sighed. Bert Johnson was a notorious gossip, although of course he always denied any such accusation. He said he liked to think of himself as a conscientious public servant who had everyone's best interests at heart. Susan was too polite to tell him what she really thought. Retrieving the envelope she tucked it into her skirt pocket. Some things were best kept secret from an over-anxious father, and this was one of them.

Roz tore the envelope open with trembling fingers. Susan sat on the chair at her bedside, waiting in silence. She had been shocked by Roz's pallor and drawn features, which could not be explained away merely by the pain of a broken ankle and wrist, but now she had the satisfaction of seeing a smile spreading across her face and a flush colouring her pale cheeks. 'Well?' she said when Roz folded the paper and clutched it to her breast. 'What did he say? It's from Patrick, isn't it?'

'Yes.' Roz brushed tears from her eyes but she was smiling. 'He loves me, Susan.'

'Of course he does. I can't think how you ever doubted it.'

'I know, but it all seemed hopeless, and then he went away and I was afraid I'd never see him again.' She spread the sheets of paper on the bedcover, smoothing them almost reverently. 'Anyway, he says he's instructed his solicitor to start divorce proceedings. He's lost the practice as well as his home, so he said that there's nothing more that Elspeth or her father can do to him. He says we'll have to rough it at first, but I don't care. I'd live in a tent with Patrick and be happy.'

'I'm really happy for you. But now you must concentrate on getting well again. Your dad is very worried.'

'He's not drinking again, is he?'

'I won't lie to you, Roz. He's been knocking back whisky as if his life depended on it. You have to make an effort to get better for him as well as the baby. They're both depending on you.'

'You're right. I've been selfish, but I just couldn't bear the thought of life without Patrick.'

Susan nodded. It was no use telling Roz that already there were three war widows in the village and likely to be many more before hostilities ended. She did not bemoan the fact that Tony was also far away, or that she had given up her job with Elspeth. There would be time to bring Roz up to date with the outside world when she was safe at home and strong enough to cope. She could see some of the other visitors getting ready to leave, although it seemed as though she had only been in the ward for ten minutes, but the hour was almost up. She laid her hand on Roz's arm. 'There's something I must ask you before I go.'

Roz stared at her wide-eyed. 'What?'

'Don't look so alarmed. It's about your job at the factory.'

'Oh, that. I really couldn't care less if they sack me. I hated working there anyway.'

'So you wouldn't mind if I applied for it?'

'You? But I thought you were happy working for that cow Elspeth.'

'I wouldn't go so far as that, although she has been good to me in her own way. It's a long story and I won't bore you with the details, but I don't work for her now.'

'What happened? I always said she was a meadow lady of the first order.'

'It all got too much, but now I need to find work. Danny said he'd put in a good word for me at Armstrong Whitworth, but only if you agree. I wouldn't go behind your back, Roz.'

'I'd be delighted if you took the job, Susan,' Roz said eagerly, but then her smile faded and was replaced by a worried frown. 'That doesn't mean you'll be leaving us, does it? I don't think I could cope without you.'

'I'm not going anywhere. Just come home and we'll be one happy family again.'

'I'll be out of here as soon as they let me and I'll sort my dad out, the silly old thing.'

Thanks to Danny's efforts, Susan was taken on in the workshop where they repaired damaged Spitfires and other types of aircraft. At first she seemed to be merely making cups of tea and picking up nuts and bolts that had fallen on the floor, but as she was quick and eager to learn she was taught how to rivet and to do routine maintenance on the engines. She even managed to sneak into a few of the classes on meteorology, map reading and navigation that were compulsory for the ATA trainees, and she memorised the instrument panel which was almost the same as every class of aircraft used by the RAF:

air speed indicator, altimeter, gyro compass, altitude indicator, turn and slip gauge and artificial horizon. On one occasion she was spotted in a classroom by Elspeth and for a horrible moment she thought that she was going to denounce her as an interloper, but Elspeth merely smiled and turned her head away. Susan knew then that she had been forgiven for leaving so suddenly, or perhaps Elspeth had realised that it was Colin who had been at fault. Susan saw him occasionally, strutting about the airfield like the cock of the walk, but she always ignored him and he did not acknowledge her.

She had received several letters from Tony, and at first she did not know whether to be pleased or resentful that he seemed to be enjoying his new job, but then she told herself not to be stupid. Tony loved flying and it must have been awful for him to have been grounded due to his back injury. She tried to be glad that he was completely well again and doing something that made him happy; she just wished that he was not so far away.

She missed him more than she would have thought possible. All the things about him that she had taken for granted had become vivid memories. At night when sleep evaded her she remembered the way his eyes lit up when he smiled, and deepened in colour when his passions were aroused. She loved him for his sense of humour and his innate kindness. Their quarrels now seemed foolish and unimportant. Her heart called out to his, receiving echoes in response. She prayed nightly for his safe deliverance. He was the only person who she would ever love, and only he would understand her over-whelming ambition to join the ATA. She saw them daily, those smart, clever and courageous women. They were her idols and her demons rolled into one. She longed to be one of them, but the fact that she had been abandoned as a baby would always set her apart from the rest of the world. Sometimes she felt like an alien who had come from another planet and found herself amongst a different type of being.

When the blue moods came upon her she did her best to put them aside. She knew that she was lucky to have Roz and Bob, and in April there would be an addition to her adopted family. Roz's injuries were healing and she could walk with the aid of crutches, but the doctor had forbidden her to work outside the home, and she had to content herself with taking over the cooking and helping in the bar. Mrs Delaney returned at the beginning of December to do the cleaning, and that left Susan free to do overtime at the factory or to go into the lecture rooms and study. It was a vain hope that one day she might sit the exams that she must pass before she could get her pilot's licence, but she was determined to seize any opportunity that came her way.

At first the security guard had questioned her, but she was now well known at the aerodrome, and if such behaviour was not countenanced by those in authority, the lesser beings were prepared to turn a blind eye. Each day her ambition to become a qualified pilot grew stronger. It seemed like an impossible dream, and to be accepted into the elite of the ATA was even more unlikely, but Susan had set her sights on her goal and nothing was going to stop her. Her motto was now that of the Air Transport Auxiliary: *Aetheris Avidi*, Eager for the Air, or as the ferry pool pilots said, any aircraft, anywhere.

She was in a lecture room one evening just before Christmas. She had stayed on after work in the hope of doing some quiet studying. Danny had offered to give her a lift home on the pillion of his motorbike but she had said that she was doing overtime. He must have known that it was just an excuse as they worked in the same area, but he had accepted her refusal without comment. He spent most evenings in the pub although he only drank a couple of half-pints of bitter and passed most of the time chatting to Roz or the locals, amongst whom he was something of a favourite. Danny had the happy knack of getting on with almost everyone and he was one of the few people who could make Roz smile. Bob had noticed this and instantly approved. Susan suspected that he was attempting a bit of quiet matchmaking, and she was even more certain when he invited Danny to spend Christmas Day with them.

As for herself, Susan was not looking forward to spending another Christmas without Tony. It had been bad enough last year when she had been living in the flat with his father and Aunt Maida, but her feelings for him then had been little more than a schoolgirl crush. Now she knew it was the real thing, and the prospect of a lengthy separation was almost too hard to hear. She chewed the end of her pencil, staring at the textbook in front of her but she could not concentrate. It was bitterly cold and her fingers were numb. She closed the book and was about to get up when the door opened. She froze, hoping that it was just the security officer who would give her a nod and a wink and leave her to it, but as she turned her head she saw Elspeth standing in the doorway.

'Darling, what a little swot you are.' Elspeth sauntered over to the desk and flipped the textbook open. 'Navigation. So you're still hankering after getting your wings.'

It was a statement rather than a question and Susan nodded wordlessly.

Elspeth pulled up a chair and sat down beside her. 'D'you know, sweetie, you may be a pain in the neck sometimes, but I rather admire you for your guts and persistence.'

'I didn't encourage Colin,' Susan said, averting her gaze. 'I wouldn't do a thing like that, and I'm sorry if I left you in the lurch.'

'It's water under the bridge, darling.' Elspeth closed the book and pushed it towards her. 'You'd better scram. I think the Head Girl is on the prowl.

It really is like being back in the sixth form, but I'm having a frightfully good time. I've qualified for the ferry pool now, you know. I'll be doing my first delivery tomorrow and I simply can't wait.' She rose to her feet. 'Good luck with the studies, Susan. Stick to it and one day you might get your pilot's licence.'

'So you're not going to report me then?' Stowing her textbooks into her handbag, Susan stood up.

'Now would I do such a thing to a fellow aviator?' Elspeth's laughter echoed round the lecture room. She put her arm around Susan's shoulders and gave her a hug. 'Darling, I have a lot to thank you for.'

'You have?' Susan stared at her in amazement.

'Your friend the barmaid is welcome to my husband, and I'll soon be a free woman. Daddy's paying for the divorce and he's acknowledged the fact that my marriage to Patrick was a huge mistake. If the baby had lived things might have been different, but I don't think so. Poor old Pat bored me to death and I can't stand the smell of the stables or the farmyard. I was never cut out to be a vet's wife.'

'So will you marry Colin?'

Elspeth threw up her hands in mock horror. 'Heavens, no. Can you imagine what my life would be like married to a man I couldn't trust for a minute? I adore Colin, but he has to be kept firmly in his place. I like it better that way.' Elspeth cocked her head on one side, listening. 'I know those footsteps. Sit tight for a moment, sweetie, and I'll head her off at the pass. Then you'd better make tracks.' Moving with the stealth of a panther on the prowl, Elspeth left the room.

Susan could hear voices in the corridor and then they faded away. That was a near one. She did not want to get on the wrong side of the head of the ferry pool, and if she was found out it would mean an end to her studies. She grabbed her coat and hat and hurried out of the lecture room. She left the building, still struggling into her outdoor things.

'Here, let me help you.'

She jumped, clutching her hand to her chest as her heart missed a beat. 'Tony.'

'They told me you were working late. God, I've missed you, Susan.'

She was lost in the warmth of his embrace. The buttons on his greatcoat dug into her flesh but she did not care. She gave herself up to the exciting sensations that rippled through her body. 'Tony,' she whispered as he released her lips, giving her a chance to draw breath. 'I can't believe that you're here.'

'I've got a twenty-four hour pass, sweetheart. I can't get leave at Christmas but it's only a week away so this is the next best thing. I couldn't go a day longer without seeing you.' He linked his arm around her waist. 'Let's get you home, it's bloody freezing out here.'

'I don't care. Nothing matters now you're here.' She fished in her pocket for her pass as they reached the perimeter gates, showing it to the guard, who waved them through. Once outside the gates, Susan slowed her pace. 'How did you know where I was?'

'I went to the pub first and Bob told me you were probably working late, then Danny wandered in and said you were still at the factory. I was coming in to look for you when you walked straight into my arms.' He stopped, pulling her close to him and kissing her hungrily. 'You don't know how many times I've imagined this moment, sweetheart. I go to sleep thinking about you and you're in my dreams. I can't get you out of my mind.'

Breathless and dazed by the intensity of his desire, Susan slid her arms around his neck. 'Me neither. It's been awful without you, and I thought you were having such a good time without me.'

He tilted her chin and answered her with a kiss. 'I love flying, but I love you more. If I were to lose you . . .' He broke off, shaking his head.

In the moonlight she could see tears glistening on the tips of his thick lashes. She pulled his head down and caressed his eyelids with her lips. 'You won't lose me, Tony Richards. I'm stuck to you like glue.'

He brushed her cheek with his fingertips. 'Do you mean that?'

'Of course I do. I love you.'

'And I love you too.' He hesitated, looking deeply into her eyes. 'I promised myself that I'd take things slowly and not rush you into anything, but this damned war is turning everything upside down. I want to ask you something, darling . . .' His arms tightened around her as the air raid siren started its dismal wailing sound. 'We'd best take cover.'

'No. Not until you tell me what you were going to say.'

The air around them was suddenly filled with the crump, crump of anti-aircraft guns followed by the whistle of bombs falling and the reverberating thuds of the explosions as they landed on their targets. On the other side of the river the sky over Southampton was lit up by fire and smoke billowed up to form dense clouds above the city. They stood close together, watching in silence. Susan could feel Tony's heart thudding against his ribs as she slipped her hands beneath his greatcoat. They might have been watching a film at the cinema except that this was real and even at this distance the acrid smell of burning filled her nostrils. 'Poor things,' she murmured. 'Is it never going to end?'

'Not yet, but at least the Yanks joined in after Pearl Harbor. Together we stand more of a chance against Jerry.' He hugged her closer. 'Let's get you home. You should be in Bob's shelter, not standing out here in the bitter cold watching Southampton cop it.'

'I'm safe when I'm with you,' she said as they turned their backs on the horrific scene and started walking towards the pub. 'You still haven't told me what it was you were going to say just now.'

He pulled her into a shop doorway. 'I was going to ask you to marry me, Susan.'

'You were?' She could hardly speak. Her head was spinning and her heart pounding with joy such as she had never known. She had imagined him saying these words but not in the middle of an air raid on a bitterly cold night with frost sparkling on the tarmac road surface and icing the roof tiles on the buildings.

He laid his finger on her lips. 'I would have loved to do it over a romantic meal for two with candles and flowers; the lot. But now there won't be time for any of that, because I'm afraid there's something else.'

She was trembling now; shaking from head to foot. Her teeth were chattering as if she was standing naked in the snow. 'What is it? Don't do this to me, Tony.'

'I'm back in the RAF. I passed the medical and they said I was fit for active service.'

'No. You can't be. You were going to be relatively safe at Hawarden, working in the ferry pool. They can't do that to us.'

'They can, and they have, my darling. I'm returning to Bomber Command. I'll be leaving tomorrow lunchtime for a base in East Anglia. I can't tell you more than that.'

She stared at him in disbelief, her world suddenly crumbling about her ears.

Chapter Nineteen

'What are you two doing out here?' Ted Hollis, the local taxi driver and ARP warden, stood arms akimbo, glaring at them. 'You should be in a shelter. Get along with the pair of you.'

Taking Susan by the hand, Tony gave him a brief salute. 'You're right, of course, but I've just proposed and she hasn't had a chance to answer.'

Never known for his sense of humour, Ted tut-tutted and cast his eyes heavenwards. 'You won't be able to marry her if you both get blown to bits. Get going.'

Shocked by Tony's announcement coming on top of a proposal of marriage, and faced with a pompous official, Susan started to giggle.

'You won't find it so funny if a bomb drops out of the sky, miss. Now be sensible and do what I say.' Ted Hollis marched off with an irritated twitch of his shoulders.

'He's right. Come on, Susan.' Tony broke into a run, dragging her towards the pub garden and the relative safety of the shelter. He stopped outside the door to pull her to him, claiming her mouth in an urgent kiss that bruised her lips and sent her pulses racing. She gave herself to the moment, oblivious to the mayhem that was happening all around them.

'I will,' she murmured when she regained her breath. 'I will marry you, Tony. I'll wait forever if I have to.'

The joy in his eyes and the tenderness of his smile was all the answer she needed. He held her as if he would never let her go. 'I'll come home to you, Susie,' he whispered into her hair. 'The next time I get leave we'll tie the knot. I love you with all my heart.' A particularly loud explosion was too close for comfort, and he thrust the shelter door open. They were met with a wave of sound and a thick fog of cigarette smoke.

Danny edged towards them through the crowd of seemingly happy locals. 'You took your time. I was beginning to think you'd bought it.'

'She said yes, old boy,' Tony said with a tremor in his voice. 'Susan and I are engaged.'

She tugged at his arm. 'Don't tell everyone yet.'

'Too late.' He looked round, grinning. 'I think they all heard.'

'Congratulations,' Danny said with a genuine smile. 'You're a lucky dog, Richards.'

'Don't I know it?' Tony slapped him on the back. 'Drinks are on me, folks.'

Suddenly they were surrounded by people wanting to congratulate them. Susan had not realised that she was so popular. Everyone seemed genuinely pleased for them. Roz hugged her and Bob was kept busy refilling pint mugs from the keg he kept in readiness for just such an occasion. When he had satisfied their demands he pushed through the throng to give Susan a glass of cider. 'It should be champagne, but I can't get to the cellar thanks to Jerry.' He kissed her on the cheek. 'I'm happy for you, love. If this fellow is what you want, then I wish you all the luck in the world.'

Susan smiled at Tony and he squeezed her hand. 'He is,' she said simply. 'I love him.'

Bob leaned closer to Tony. 'No funny business tonight, mate. I've got an unmarried daughter who's up the duff and I don't want a repeat with young Susan.'

'Bob!' Susan glanced round anxiously, hoping that no one was listening. 'How can you say such a thing?'

He grinned. 'Very easily. He knows what I mean, don't you, boy?'

'Yes, sir. I do. I love Susan. I wouldn't do anything to hurt her.'

'He can bunk with me tonight,' Danny said, grinning from ear to ear. 'I'll make sure there's no hanky-panky, boss.'

Susan bit back an angry retort. Much as she loved all three of them, they had no right to talk about her as if she was little more than a child and unable to speak for herself. She felt her cheeks burning and she went to sit next to Roz on the uncomfortable wooden bench.

'Don't take any notice of them,' Roz said sympathetically. 'They care about you, Susan, even if they've a funny way of showing it.'

She nodded, too choked with emotion to speak.

'What's up?' Roz peered at her in the dim light. 'You should be dancing for joy. It's not every day a girl gets engaged.'

'Tony passed his medical. He's been accepted back in the RAF and he's going to join Bomber Command tomorrow. It's just not fair.'

Roz gave her a hug. 'None of it's fair. War is horrible, but we've got to get through it the best way we can.'

Susan glanced down at Roz's left hand. 'You're wearing Patrick's ring.'

'Of course. Now that everyone knows about us there's no point in keeping it secret.'

'I'm glad. You deserve to be happy.' She gazed at Tony, who was being congratulated by the occupants of the shelter, and she felt a surge of love for him that made her dizzy, but her joy was tinged with fear. She could not help wishing that he was still ferrying planes from factories to aerodromes. That was hazardous enough, but not nearly as dangerous as bombing missions over Germany. She wished that she could spend these few precious hours alone with him, but it seemed they were fated to be in the midst of a crowd of well-wishers all evening. The celebrations continued even after the all clear had sounded and everyone trooped back into the pub. A party atmosphere prevailed and although Roz helped out for a while she was soon too tired to carry on and Susan had to go behind the bar.

After closing time, Bob and Danny sat in the snug like old-fashioned duennas while Susan and Tony said their goodbyes. It was hardly the most romantic way to end the evening, particularly when Danny complained that he would be locked out of his digs if he did not get back soon. He stood by the door staring pointedly at the clock above the bar, while Bob busied himself collecting dirty glasses and ashtrays.

'I'll have to go, sweetheart.' With a wry smile, Tony took Susan into his arms and kissed her long and hard. 'I'll write when I can. Take care of yourself.'

Panic rose within her. 'But I'll see you again before you go.'

'I've got to get an early train to London. I must see the old man and tell him what's happening. I haven't been home for over a year so I owe him that at least, and I want to break it gently about us. It's not something I can do in a letter, not after all he's been through. You do understand, don't you, Sue?'

She nodded, but she could not frame the words. All she could think of was that he was leaving. Just as they had sorted everything out between them, he was going away and venturing once more into the danger zone. She might never see him again. The realities of war that had so far just been words really hit home now. She felt physically sick and close to tears, but she showed him a brave face. 'Of course I do.'

'You're a wonderful girl, Susan. I can't wait to make you my wife.'

Danny coughed and shuffled his feet. 'I don't want to hurry you, old man. But we'll find ourselves sleeping in a telephone box if we don't get a move on.'

Kissing Susan one last time, Tony backed towards the door.

She stood very still, imprinting the moment in her memory. She would have to live off this for as long as it took for them to be reunited. She would not break down and cry. She would send him off with a smile. That was how she wanted him to remember her.

She was still standing there, statue-like and frozen in time, when Bob came up behind her and pressed a glass into her hand. 'Brandy,' he said, breathing whisky fumes in her face. 'Forget the under age drinking ban. If you're woman enough to send your man off to war, you can take a tot of something to ease the heartache.' He raised his glass. 'Here's to Tony and all those brave men and women who risk their lives for us. I wish to God that I was young enough and fit enough to join up. I reckon the hardest part of all is having to stay at home and bloody wait.' He downed the whisky in a single gulp.

Sometimes it all seemed like a dream and when Susan woke up in the morning she wondered if Tony had really come home a week before Christmas, or if it was a figment of her imagination. Had he really held her in his arms and kissed her with such burning desire that it set all her senses aflame, or was it merely wishful thinking? Was she really engaged to be married, or was that something she had conjured up in her mind to help her get through the difficult days of air raids, food shortages, rationing and dismal winter weather?

Christmas was a busy time in the pub which left Susan little time to brood. She had been cheered considerably by a letter from Dave Richards, which she received on Christmas Eve. In it he apologised for any embarrassment he had caused her by his proposal, and for the delay in putting matters straight. Reading between the lines, Susan thought that Maida was probably at the bottom of that. She had not bothered to disguise her disapproval of Susan's presence in the flat, and she must have been delighted when she found that she had left and taken her dog with her. Dave wrote that his sister had moved back to the East End and that he was coping quite well on his own. He added that he was pleased to hear that Susan was settled in a good job and even happier to know that she was engaged to his son.

The letter was clumsily phrased and had

obviously taken him some time to compose but the sentiments were genuine enough, and Susan was relieved to think that her future father-in-law would welcome her into the family. She had been bitterly disappointed that Tony left early to go to London to see his father, but now she knew that he had done the right thing.

With the festive season over, Susan went to work each day as before, and she spent all her free time studying. She was now familiar with the workings of the Spitfire engine as well as the theory of flying. She would have given almost anything for more lessons, but with Elspeth fully occupied in the ferry pool and her aeroplane mothballed, there was virtually no chance that she would get off the ground again. Still, some stubborn streak in her makeup kept her focused on continuing her studies. Working hard kept her mind off Tony and his dangerous missions. He telephoned as often as he could and for a few precious minutes they were able to talk. It made him seem closer, but then it was all the harder to say goodbye. She was living in limbo and it was no comfort to know that she was one of millions of women left at home doing vital war work but separated from those they loved. She too dreaded the arrival of the telegram with the news that no one wanted to hear. At night she lay awake with only Charlie for company, and his furry body lying on the foot of her bed to keep her warm during the cold winter weather. On particularly bitter nights he slithered up the bed and when she awoke in the morning she would find him snuggled against her back, snoring gently.

Gradually winter began to loosen its icy grip on the countryside and March, true to the old adage, came in like a lion. The wind whipped up the waters in the river, rattled the bare branches of the trees and made taking off and landing even more tricky than usual. Roz was close to term now and growing ever more weary of her burden. She was short-tempered and tearful. Her father was worried and turned to whisky to calm his nerves. It fell to Susan to try to keep the peace between them. She awaited the baby's birth almost as eagerly as Roz. Bob was dreading it and he made no secret of his fear that history would repeat itself, which only added to the tension between the two of them. Even Orlando seemed to sense the atmosphere and he hissed and spat, arching his back with his fur standing on end and his green eyes blazing every time Charlie trotted through the kitchen. A kind of madness had descended upon the pub and Susan was glad to get out every morning and go to work. She was now an accepted part of the engineering team. The men had teased her at first and given her all the dirty jobs to do, but she had won them over by her good humour and her willingness to try anything once.

The month was drawing to an end when the news filtered through of the RAF bombing raid on the Baltic port of Lübeck, and the massive offensive against the German arms factories. Spitfires had escorted the bombers and some of them were damaged and brought to the factory for repair. Susan had heard nothing from Tony for almost a fortnight and she was beginning to worry, but she was kept busy both in her daytime job and at the pub. Roz was no longer able to work in the evenings as her feet and ankles were swollen and the doctor had told her to rest, and Bob was drinking more heavily than ever. By closing time each evening he was just about able to call last orders before he staggered off to bed, leaving Susan and Danny to finish serving and close up.

On a blustery Monday morning, Roz woke up complaining of vague pains. The doctor was called but he told her there was no need to worry, the baby was not ready to come into the world for a few days yet. Susan went to work as usual but when she returned in the early evening Roz was still getting contractions although they were intermittent. Then, almost as if the laws of nature wanted to prove the doctor wrong, Roz went into labour just before closing time. Danny had been about to go back to his digs, and Bob had gone to the kitchen to make a cup of tea over an hour before but had not returned. Susan found him slumped over the kitchen table, dead to the world. She could hear Roz's cries of anguish from the bedroom and she shook him violently, but he merely grunted and told her to go away. She ran upstairs to find Roz white-faced and terrified by the strength of the pains that racked her body.

'Do something, Susan,' she pleaded. 'It bloody hurts.'

Forcing herself to appear calm, Susan tried to remember the midwife's instructions. 'Don't worry; it's going to be fine. Just think of the lovely baby you're going to hold in your arms. After all these months you'll have Patrick's child. I'll go now and ring for the doctor.' She raced downstairs to telephone the doctor's house. She waited, tapping her foot on the floor while the ringing tone went on and on for what seemed like an age. For a moment she felt panic rising in her throat. What would she do if no one was at home? She was just wondering whether she ought to phone for an ambulance when the doctor's wife answered, sounding slightly grumpy and rather sleepy. Susan explained the reason for the call.

'I'm sorry, but my husband is out on an emergency. I'll pass the message on when he comes home.'

'Wait,' Susan cried, sensing that the tired woman was about to replace the receiver. 'Please tell him it's urgent. She's in agony and I don't know what to do.'

'Keep her calm. First babies usually take a long time to come. The doctor will get there as soon as possible. In the meantime I'll see if I can get hold of the midwife. Don't worry, Susan. Babies are being born all the time. Rosemary will be fine.'

The line went dead, leaving Susan staring at the rather hideous wallpaper. She dropped the receiver back on its cradle and went into the bar. Danny was standing in the middle of the floor, looking anxious. 'Is she all right?'

'The doctor is out on a call,' Susan said dully. 'Mrs Snow is going to try and get hold of the midwife.'

He gave her a searching look. 'Are you okay? You're white as a sheet.'

'Have you ever seen a woman in labour?'

'No, can't say I have.'

'Well, she is. Well and truly now, and Bob's out for the count. He's drunk himself into a stupor because he's so terrified that Roz is going to die in childbirth like her mother. I know it's silly but he's got it stuck in his head and he won't listen to sense.'

Danny nodded slowly. 'So that's what started it. I know he had a drink problem some time ago, but everyone thought he'd got over it. If the brewery find out he'll be out on his ear.'

'I can't think about that now. I'd better get back to Roz.' She hesitated. 'Will you stay for a while? I need someone here to let the doctor in, or the midwife, whoever gets here first.'

'Of course I will, honey,' he said, grinning. 'Shall I start boiling kettles of water like they do in the films?'

His attempt at humour was not lost on Susan and it brought a reluctant smile to her lips. 'Maybe you ought to make Bob a cup of coffee. There's a bottle of Camp in the larder. Make it strong and black.' She turned with a start as a loud scream from Roz's bedroom echoed through the building. 'I'd best go and see what I can do.' She hurried from the bar and ran up the stairs, taking two at a time. Charlie bounded after her, but issuing a sharp command to stay she shut him outside on the landing.

Roz glared at her. 'Where the hell have you been? Doesn't anyone care what happens to me?'

Susan smoothed the sheets and plumped the pillows behind her head. 'I've been trying to get hold of Dr Snow or the midwife. Just hold on until they get here, Roz. I'm no Florence Nightingale. I wouldn't know how to deliver a baby. Now if you were a Spitfire engine . . .'

A gurgle of laughter was replaced by a groan. 'Oh God. I'm never having another kid as long as I live. Where's that bloody doctor?'

Susan settled down to do what she could for Roz. She did her best to appear calm, but inwardly she was terrified. She really had no idea what to do if the baby decided to arrive before the doctor or the midwife put in an appearance. She hoped against hope that someone would come soon and take over. Roz was alternately screaming and writhing in agony or falling into a fitful doze. There seemed to be quite a few minutes between contractions, but Susan was now wishing that she had read some books on midwifery instead of poring over manuals on aeroplane engines.

She glanced at the clock on the bedside cabinet. It was almost midnight. She was growing sleepy and found herself nodding off occasionally, but she came to her senses with a start at the distant sound of the telephone. Roz seemed to be asleep and Susan rose to her feet, tiptoeing quietly from the room. She heard Danny's deep tones as he answered the phone. She met him at the foot of the stairs. His expression was carefully controlled but she knew instantly that something was wrong.

'What is it, Danny? Can't the doctor get here?'

'It's Tony's dad on the phone. You'd better speak to him, Susan.'

It could only be bad news. Nobody rang up at this time of night unless it was a dire emergency. She swayed dizzily and had to lean on him for support as her knees threatened to give way beneath her. 'It's Tony, isn't it?'

'He's missing in action. He's not dead, Susan. Speak to Dave; he'll tell you everything he knows.'

Somehow she managed to walk the short distance to the telephone. She picked up the receiver. 'Dave, it's Susan.' She listened only half hearing what he was saying. His voice droned on and on, but all she could hear were the words repeating again and again in her head. 'Missing in action.'

'Are you there, Susan?'

She pulled herself together with an effort. 'Yes, I'm listening.'

'I know it's a terrible shock, love. It was for me

too, but after I had the official telegram I had a phone call from one of the Spitfire pilots who escorted the Wellingtons. He said that they had reached the German coast and when Tony's plane took a hit he saw parachutes. Obviously he didn't know who had managed to escape from the burning fuselage, but one of them could have been Tony. We can only hope and pray.'

'Yes,' she said dully.

'Are you all right, love?'

'Yes,' she said, 'thank you.'

'We've got to be positive, Susan. We've got to keep hoping. It's all that's left to us. I know you love my boy as much as I do.'

'Yes. I – I'm sorry, I can't talk now. Thank you for letting me know.' It was only when she replaced the receiver that she realised Danny was standing close behind her, and Charlie was nuzzling her hand as if he understood her distress.

'Are you okay?'

'Yes. I mean no. I don't know.'

He made an attempt at a smile. 'You know Tony. He'll be fine. He's a survivor if ever there was one.'

'I can't believe it. He couldn't be dead, could he?' Too stunned for tears, she looked to him for confirmation but he shook his head.

'Don't even think about it, Susan.' He went to put his arms around her but a scream from upstairs made him freeze. 'You'd better go to her. She needs you.'

'Yes.' Susan still could not move.

Gently but firmly, Danny guided her to the foot of the stairs. 'Go on. I'll wait for the doctor. I won't leave you.' He grasped Charlie's collar as he attempted to follow her. 'You stay with me, old chap. There's nothing we fellows can do to help in a situation like this.'

Her feet felt like lead weights and every step was an effort but somehow Susan made it to the bedroom. One look at Roz's contorted features and agonised expression was enough to bring her abruptly back to the present. Pushing her worries to the back of her mind Susan concentrated all her efforts on calming and soothing her. She bathed her forehead with cool water and made sympathetic noises, encouraging her to push and hoping that she was doing the right thing. Loud snores emanated from Bob's room and Susan could only wonder that he could sleep through his daughter's agonised screams interspersed with swearing that would have made a trooper blush. But as the night wore on she could only be glad that he was not pacing the floor downstairs, frantic with worry and desperately afraid.

It was almost two o'clock before Dr Snow walked into the bedroom, and by that time Susan's hands were bruised and painful. Roz had gripped them with surprising strength as each wave of pain overtook her. Susan had had to bite her lip in order to prevent herself from crying out as she felt her knuckles crack. She extricated her hands from Roz's frantic grasp and stood up. 'I'm so pleased to see you, Dr Snow.'

His face was grey with fatigue and lines criss-crossed his brow, but he managed a glimmer of a smile. 'You've done well. Now I suggest you go downstairs and make a pot of tea.'

'I don't want bloody tea,' Roz groaned. 'Just get this thing out of me.'

'Now now, Rosemary. That's enough bad language from you, and the tea is for me. I've just delivered a baby at Latchet Farm and he's a fine healthy little boy, so now let's concentrate on you.'

Susan made her escape. She went to the kitchen and was almost knocked over by Charlie's enthu-siastic greeting. Danny was standing at the stove pouring boiling water into the teapot. He turned to her and winked. 'This is why they boil water in the movies. They've got someone making quarts of tea for the actors and camera crew.'

She sank down on the nearest chair. 'Danny, you're a treasure. I don't know what I'd do without you.' She patted Charlie as he laid his head on her knee. 'Good boy.'

'I am a good boy, aren't I?' Danny said, chuckling. He took a seat beside her and his comical expression forced a smile to her lips.

'You are such a fool, Danny. You can always make me laugh.'

He pulled a face. 'Court jester, that's me.'

'No,' she said earnestly. 'You're the best friend a girl could have. I don't know what I'd do without you.'

'What you need is a nice hot cup of tea.' He reached for the pot and poured tea into two mugs, adding a dash of milk and a spoonful of sugar into Susan's despite her protests that the doctor's need was greater than her own. In the end it was Danny who took a cup to Dr Snow and he returned quickly. He was, Susan noted, slightly green around the gills and unusually quiet.

Less than an hour later, although it had seemed much longer, Susan was called upstairs by the doctor. She ran all the way and arrived in Roz's room breathless and panting. Dr Snow thrust a small bundle of humanity into her arms and despite his obvious exhaustion he was smiling. 'It's a girl,' he said proudly. 'I want you to hold her while I look after Rosemary.'

Susan clasped the baby in her arms. 'Is Roz all right?' she asked, looking anxiously at Roz's still form lying beneath the sheet. Her face was drawn and her eyes were closed, the rise and fall of her chest the only indication that she was still breathing.

'She's exhausted but she'll be fine. I'm just going to do the necessary and then I'm sure a cup of tea would be just the thing. I could do with another one if there's any left in the pot.'

Dismissed from the bedroom, Susan carried the baby downstairs as if she were handling a fragile piece of porcelain that was worth a king's ransom. She gave Charlie a curt order to sit as she entered the kitchen, and Danny rushed forward to look at the baby. He drew the shawl back gently from the infant's face. 'Is it a girl or a boy?'

'A girl. She's beautiful, isn't she?'

He studied the baby's face with a critical eye. 'Looks more like a wizened old man or a little monkey, but I'll take your word for it.'

The baby opened her big blue eyes and stared at Susan. She felt a tug at her heartstrings and a protective love for the child even though they were not in any way related. 'She's really beautiful,' she breathed ecstatically. 'She's so tiny. Just look at her little hands and her perfect fingernails.'

Danny put his head on one side. 'Still looks like a monkey to me.'

Susan giggled. 'You have no soul, Danny Gillespie.' She stopped short as she remembered Dave's phone call and the dreadful news that Tony was missing in action. She blinked back tears. 'I'd better take her back to Roz.'

She found Roz propped up on the pillows and Dr Snow making ready to leave. She laid the baby carefully in her mother's arms. 'She's gorgeous, Roz. You are so clever.'

'She is lovely, isn't she?' Roz gazed at her daughter as if seeing a miracle. 'She's so little. I can't believe she's mine.'

Dr Snow cleared his throat. 'You wait until she

wakes you several times a night for a feed, young lady. You won't be so starry-eyed then.'

Roz shrugged and cuddled the baby to her. 'I won't mind. She can do anything she likes. I can't wait to show her to Patrick. He'll be such a proud father.'

Dr Snow made a harrumphing noise and picked up his bag. 'I'll call in tomorrow, my dear. Try to get some rest now.' He patted Susan on the back. 'You did well, Susan. I'll know who to call on if I need help in the midwifery department.'

Roz yawned sleepily. 'There won't be a next time for me, doctor. That damn well hurt.'

'They all say that, Rosemary, but I guarantee she won't be your only child.' He left them, closing the door softly behind him.

'What are you going to call her?' Susan said, moving the Moses basket closer to the bed. 'Have you chosen a name yet?'

'Jennifer Maureen. Jennifer after my mother and Maureen after one of my best friends at school.' She was suddenly alert. 'Where's Dad? Was he pacing the floor all night? I want him to meet his granddaughter.'

Susan was not going to upset Roz by telling her the truth. 'He was worried, of course, but he'll be thrilled. I'll go and tell him it's all over and he's a proud grandfather.'

It took Susan several minutes to awaken Bob. His room smelt like a distillery and when he finally opened his eyes he had the look of a man who had been to hell and back. She suggested tactfully that he had a shave before he went to see Roz and Jennifer and then she went downstairs to make him a cup of strong black coffee. Danny was having a one-sided conversation with Charlie when she entered the kitchen. She paused in the doorway, smiling. 'You've been wonderful, Danny. I don't know how I would have managed without you.'

'It was nothing.' He patted Charlie on the head. 'Look after your mistress, old man. I've got to get back to my digs. My landlady is going to think I'm a dirty stop-out.'

Susan went to draw the blackout curtains. 'It's getting light. I could make us some breakfast and we could go straight to work.'

He stared at her, his eyes wide with astonishment. 'You're going in today? Don't you think it would be better if you got some sleep?'

She shook her head. 'I won't be able to rest. I'll keep thinking about Tony and it'll be torture. I'd rather go to work as usual, and keep myself occupied.'

Halfway through the morning Susan was sent to the canteen with an order for biscuits and cake, if there was any, for the tea break. *Workers' Playtime* was blaring out in the factory and it was a relief to escape to the relative peace and quiet of the aerodrome. She was striding past the ferry pool when she saw

Elspeth standing outside smoking a cigarette. Even at a distance Susan could see that her hand was shaking and her face pale beneath her makeup. She knew Elspeth well enough to realise that there was something seriously wrong. She walked over to her. 'Are you all right?'

Elspeth took a long drag on her cigarette before answering. She exhaled smoke into the air. 'Bad news, I'm afraid, sweetie.'

With her own pain still raw Susan was more than sympathetic. 'I'm so sorry.'

Elspeth stared at her with narrowed eyes. 'It's Patrick. You can tell that tart that he'll never marry her now. I've only just heard the news. He's dead.'

Chapter Twenty

'No.' Susan shook her head. 'It must be a mistake. He's not in the front line.'

'Nothing so heroic. The poor devil was kicked in the head by a horse he was treating. It fractured his skull and there was nothing they could do to save him.'

Susan stared at her in horror mixed with astonishment. There were tears in Elspeth's eyes and her mascara was smudged, giving her a panda-like appearance that might have been comical if it were not so sad. 'I thought you hated him.' She had not meant to blurt the words out, but she was as shocked by the news as she was astounded to realise that Elspeth had feelings for the husband she had been so eager to divorce.

'Love, hate, it's all the same thing, darling.' Elspeth sucked smoke into her lungs and exhaled on a sob. 'It's all my fault. He'd never have enlisted if Daddy hadn't made it impossible for him to keep his practice. I sent the poor devil to his death because I was jealous. I didn't want him but I couldn't stand the thought of him being happy with that woman.'

At a loss as to how to deal with her in this state,

Susan could not help wondering if Elspeth's emotions were genuine or if she was simply acting out the part of tragedy queen. She took her hanky out of her pocket and handed it to her. 'You might want to wipe your eyes.'

'I suppose my mascara has run. It's the last of my expensive spit-black too. I suppose I'll have to resort to soot like the rest of the girls now. I hate this bloody war.' Elspeth snatched the hanky and dabbed ineffectually at her eyes. 'I must look like hell.'

Susan was relieved to see a shadow of the old Elspeth coming to the fore, but she still could not believe that Patrick had met his death in such a way. 'How did you hear about Patrick? I mean, could it be a mistake?'

'His commanding officer telephoned me, darling. He's a golfing pal of Daddy's, so I had it straight from the horse's mouth, you might say.' Elspeth gave a hysterical giggle and buried her face in the handkerchief. 'I was such a bitch to poor old Patrick. Now I'll never be able to tell him I'm sorry.' She burst into a noisy bout of sobbing.

With her own feelings still raw from the news that Tony was missing, Susan did not know whether to sympathise or to walk away and leave Elspeth to wallow in her feelings of guilt. It was Roz and her baby daughter who were uppermost in her thoughts now. How would she break the news that would shatter her friend's dreams of married life with

Patrick? Her heart would be broken, and Jennifer would grow up never knowing her father. That was something Susan understood only too well. At least Jennifer had a loving mother and grandfather. She would know that her parents had loved each other. She jumped as someone hailed her across the tarmac.

'Hey, Sue. Where are those snacks? The chaps have almost finished their tea.'

She glanced over her shoulder and saw one of the mechanics coming towards them. She put her hand in her pocket and took out the money she had collected from her workmates. 'I've got a friend in crisis, Phil.' She thrust the coins into his hand as he came up to her panting and out of breath. 'Be a sport and fetch the stuff from the canteen. I'll get back to work as quickly as I can.'

He tipped his cap, grinning. 'Okay, ma'am. But you'd better get a move on. The foreman is on the prowl. We've got seven Spits in for repair and more to come. We'll be doing overtime tonight.' He strode off in the direction of the canteen.

'I'm all right, sweetie,' Elspeth said, blowing her nose and sniffing. 'I've got to deliver a Mossie today, but I don't think I can do it.'

Was she acting or had her self-confidence taken a near-fatal blow? Susan stared at her, making an effort to understand what made her tick and failing miserably. Torn between the desire to slap her or to put her arms around Elspeth's elegantly slim body and hug her, she did neither. 'That's not like you. I can't believe I'm hearing this sort of talk from one of the stars of the ATA.'

This brought a reluctant smile to Elspeth's lips. 'Star? I don't think so, darling. I'm more like a comet that's lost its tail. I can't fly today. I simply can't.'

'Yes, you can,' Susan said firmly. 'You're fearless when you're airborne. I've been up there with you, so I know.'

'You are a sweetie, Susan. I'm sorry that Colin behaved so badly. I know the bastard has more hands than an octopus, but I can't help myself. I suppose I must love him, although it's come as a bit of a shock. I never thought I had a heart.'

Susan glanced at her watch. The tea break would be over now and if her absence was noticed she would be in trouble, but she could not simply walk away and leave Elspeth in such a state. 'Forget Colin, forget everything other than your job. You'll never forgive yourself if you chicken out now.'

Elspeth sniffed and shook her head. 'You're right, of course, but I don't feel up to it.'

Susan resorted to anger. 'You're not the only one who's lost someone they care about. Tony was shot down over Germany. He's missing in action, and for all I know he might be dead. We'd only just got engaged, so don't pretend you're a special case. You're just feeling guilty and you'd better get over it because if you don't go up today you'll be letting everyone down. I don't think you'll be very popular in the mess if you refuse to fly because your ex-husband has bought it.'

Elspeth recoiled and her eyes widened with shock. 'That's not fair, sweetie. I'm sorry about your man, of course, but it's different for me.'

'Stop acting like a spoilt brat and get on with it.'

Susan's harsh words appeared to have the desired effect. Elspeth bridled. 'How dare you speak to me in that tone of voice?'

'We're all equal now. I'm not your servant, but for some odd reason I care about you, Elspeth. Maybe it's because we both love flying, I don't know. What I do know is that you've got a job to do.'

'I feel ghastly. I really can't do it on my own, but if I don't go I might be chucked out of the ATA. I've broken too many rules latterly to get any second chances.' Elspeth held her hands out to Susan in a helpless gesture. 'Come with me, darling.'

For a moment Susan thought that she was joking. 'I can't do that. I'm not one of you lot.'

'But you're a mechanic of sorts, Susan. I need someone to give me confidence.' Elspeth took off her forage cap and ran her hand through her hair. 'It's not just Patrick's death that's thrown me. Colin walked out this morning. He told me he'd fallen for a cigarette girl who works in a London nightclub. Can you believe that, darling? Me, Elspeth Colby-Peterson, thrown over for a brainless bimbo?'

'All the more reason to show him you don't care.'

'But I do, that's the bugger of it. I've always been

the one in the driving seat, and now I'm not. It's shattering, sweetie. Absolutely, bloody shattering. Please come with me, Susan. I've never begged for anything in my life, but I'm begging you now.'

Susan was torn between loyalty to her fellow workers and the debt of gratitude she felt for Elspeth in that she had given her the opportunity to fly. She knew it was a foolish thing to do and she would get into enormous trouble if she did what Elspeth asked, but with Tony gone there was nothing much left that could hurt her. She nodded her head. 'All right, but I'll need a Sidcot suit and everything.'

'That's not a problem. Come to the girls' changing rooms. The others should have gone their separate ways by now.'

'I must be mad,' Susan muttered as she followed Elspeth into the building. 'Stark staring mad.'

Wearing a flying suit, helmet and goggles, Susan climbed into the cockpit of the Mosquito. It was one thing to go for a joyride in such a giant but quite another to be on a real mission, and it was hard to believe that she was actually sitting in the co-pilot's seat. She had managed to put a quick phone call through to the workshop and had told Danny what she proposed to do, and had asked him to warn Roz that she might be late home, hanging up without giving him the chance to argue.

To her amazement no one on the airfield had questioned her right to accompany Elspeth, who seemed to have recovered some of her old spirit, as she started the engine and checked the instruments before taxiing onto the runway. She performed with such skill and confidence that Susan wondered why she had allowed herself to be talked into accompanying her. But as they took off she knew why she had come and it had nothing to do with Elspeth's attack of the jitters. The truth, if she cared to admit it, was that she simply could not pass up the opportunity to get airborne again.

The sky was colour-washed pale blue and the sun shone down on the peaceful countryside below. She was flying free as a bird and loving it, but with her elation there came bitter-sweet memories, and she was seized with almost uncontrollable feelings of grief. It had been just such a day when Tony had taken her up in the Mosquito. At the time she had not fully appreciated the risk he had taken in order to make her dream come true, and now he was gone. Inside she was numb. She knew that she would never love another man as she loved Tony. The fates had decreed that she would always be alone. From now on there was just her and Charlie. That was how it would always be.

With nothing to lose, she gave herself up to the pleasure of being airborne, but after an hour or so the sun was obscured by a thick blanket of cloud and the weather had deteriorated. It was only then she realised that Elspeth was not piloting the plane as well as she might. Susan's enjoyment turned rapidly into anxiety. Down below she could see the patchwork pattern of the fields divided by dark hedgerows, but visibility was poor and in the distance she could see a line of hills, their tops obscured by the cloud. I did not take a genius to realise that the weather was closing in on them.

They flew on for a while and then quite suddenly the aeroplane nose-dived towards the ground. Elspeth appeared to have lost control. They were plummeting down at a terrifying speed. Scarcely able to breathe, Susan thought she was going to die. She almost welcomed the opportunity to join Tony in heaven, but just as she was resigned to meeting her end, Elspeth pulled back and they descended at a more appropriate speed. As her fear subsided Susan realised that they were coming in to land on a grassy field in the middle of nowhere. Startled cows scattered in all directions.

It was a bumpy landing but somehow Elspeth managed to accomplish it without any damage to the Mosquito. As soon as it was safe to do so, Susan climbed out onto the wing. She found Elspeth slumped over the controls. 'What's the matter? Are you ill?'

It took some time for Elspeth to rally enough to raise her head. 'Migraine attack, darling. Suffered from them for years. Can't see straight and the pain is crippling.' She struggled to get out of the cockpit. 'Move aside. Going to upchuck.'

Susan moved just in time. She waited until the

spasm of vomiting had passed before helping Elspeth out of the cockpit and onto the ground. 'Sit down for a few minutes. Maybe you'll feel better.'

Elspeth held her head in her hands. 'No chance, sweetie. I suppose this was coming on before we left, although I didn't recognise the signs.'

'What can I do? Have you got any aspirins?'

Elspeth's laugh was hollow. 'It would take more than an aspirin to cure this one, sweetie. Hammers and picks inside my head. Frightful.'

Susan glanced round anxiously. There was no sign of habitation and without a radio there was no way they could contact the nearest airfield or get help. 'What shall I do?'

'You'll have to fly the Mossie, darling. It's your big chance. One you've always longed for.'

'But Elspeth, I've only ever flown the Moth. I'm not trained for this.'

'Then we're stuck here until I get better. Could be days, sweetie. Your choice.' Elspeth stuck her head between her knees. 'Going to puke again.'

There was no gainsaying the fact that Elspeth was genuinely unwell. Susan had heard about people suffering from migraine but she had never seen anyone in the throes of an attack. She felt helpless and a little scared. It was almost midday and in a few short hours it would be dark. They could only fly in daylight and she needed to make a quick decision. She knelt on the ground beside Elspeth. 'Where were we headed for?'

'Castle Camps, Cambridgeshire. Map in the cockpit. You can do it, Susan. Get me to civilisation, sweetie. I need a soft pillow and some hot water bottles.' She rested her head in her hands, groaning.

'All right. I'll try, but you've got to help me.' Susan half lifted, half dragged her to her feet. 'We've got to get you into the cockpit, or else you'll have to lie here until a farmer finds you.'

It took a huge amount of effort on both their parts but eventually Elspeth managed to get into the co-pilot's seat. Susan took her place and her hands were shaking as she spread the map out on her knees. She flicked through the instruction manual given to all ferry pilots, and refreshed her memory as to the instrument panel. Panic seized her. Her lips were numb and her throat constricted. She knew it all in theory, but could she carry it out in practice? There was only one way to find out. She started the engine. She could feel the power of the twin Merlin engines throbbing through her whole body. She could do it; she would do it. 'Here we go,' she shouted above the engine noise. 'Fingers crossed.'

Elspeth raised her head. They were perilously closed to a stand of trees. 'For God's sake, pull back on the joystick, you bloody idiot.'

Too terrified to protest at being called names, Susan did as she was told. They skimmed the top of the bare branches, soaring skywards. 'Keep an eye on the artificial horizon,' Elspeth murmured before slumping forward with her head in her hands. 'Well done, you.'

Susan's nerves began to settle. She could scarcely believe that she had got the affectionately termed "wooden wonder" off the ground, but they were actually flying. She kept glancing at Elspeth and hoping that she would recover enough to land the plane when they eventually reached the airfield, but until then she had to rely on the map and landmarks on the ground in order to find her way. The cloud remained low but as long as she kept below it she knew that they would be safe. She spotted the silver ribbon of the Thames and in the distance she could see the tightly packed buildings that marked the beginning of suburbia. They were getting close to London. She wondered what Dave would think if he could see her now. She thought of Tony and her eyes filled with tears. She blinked them away. She must not allow anything to interfere with her concentration.

Elspeth groaned and then was silent. Perhaps she was asleep? Susan hoped that she would wake up refreshed and ready to take the controls when they reached Castle Camps. She could see a forest of barrage balloons and she altered course slightly in order to avoid them. She headed north of London before veering eastwards. She was growing more confident by the minute and she was actually beginning to enjoy herself, but as they neared their destination she became anxious. 'Elspeth, wake up.

I think we're getting close to the airfield. I need your help.'

Elspeth opened her eyes, staring blearily at her. 'You're doing fine, sweetie. Just imagine you're flying the Moth.' She closed them again.

After what seemed like hours, Susan spotted the airfield. 'Elspeth, help me.'

Elspeth lifted her hand and let it drop. She groaned and that was all the response Susan received. She gritted her teeth, going through the landing procedure over and over in her mind. She had come this far. She was not going to fail now.

She had never been so scared in her whole life. She had the responsibility for both their lives, not to mention delivery of an expensive aircraft to 157 squadron at the aerodrome. Death would be preferable to failure. She went through everything in her head before attempting to put theory into practice. In the air she had felt safe but the ground was approaching at an alarming rate. She glanced at Elspeth but she was either asleep or unconscious. Susan knew that she was on her own. She had everything to prove.

The wheels touched the ground, the Mosquito did a rather undignified bunny hop, but Susan regained control and to her surprise and delight she brought the huge twin-engine aeroplane to a slightly undignified halt. Frozen to the seat, she could not move a muscle. She did not know whether to laugh or cry. She saw an aircraftman walking towards the plane and she forced herself into action, opening the cockpit and getting stiffly to the ground.

He looked her up and down. 'Bloody hell, they get younger all the time.' He looked up at the empty pilot's seat as if expecting to see someone sitting there. 'Did you just land this kite, miss?'

Shaking from head to foot, Susan nodded. 'The pilot took sick. I had no choice.'

'Where is he?'

'She's still in the cockpit. I might need a hand to get her out.'

He swore softly. 'Two women flying a Mossie. What's the bleeding world coming to?'

'She really is quite ill,' Susan said urgently. 'I think she ought to see a medic.'

'All in good time, miss. You should report in. I'll see to the rest.'

Walking on legs that felt like jelly, Susan managed to get as far as the control tower. The warrant officer on duty was at first sceptical, apparently deciding that someone was playing a joke on him, and then frankly puzzled as to how a slip of a girl with no official pilot training could fly a military aircraft. She found herself passed on to the squadron leader, who was equally suspicious and then extremely put out. 'You realise of course that this is strictly against all the rules, young lady.'

'I know, sir.' Susan clasped her hands tightly behind her back, staring down at her dusty shoes.

'You should not have been on-board in the first

place, let alone given a chance to wreck an expensive piece of military equipment.' He paced the floor in his office, glaring at her from time to time in a baffled manner. 'Are you telling me the absolute truth? You actually took off from a field and then landed here on your own?'

'Yes, sir.'

He whistled through his teeth. 'I wouldn't have believed it if the pilot had not been taken to the sick bay suffering from a suspected migraine attack. She is recovering, I believe.'

'Yes, sir.'

He sighed heavily. 'I suppose I should congratulate you on an amazing feat, but I don't think you realise how complicated the paperwork will be.'

'No, sir. I'm sorry.'

He sat down behind his desk and shuffled a sheaf of papers, putting them neatly in the out tray. 'Leave this with me, Miss . . . er, what is your name?'

'Susan Banks, sir.'

'And how did you come to be on the airfield at Hamble in the first place, Miss Banks?'

'I work in the Armstrong Whitworth factory, repairing Spitfires. But I have learned to fly a Tiger Moth. I'd do anything to become a pilot, sir.'

He stared at her for a full ten seconds before shaking his head. 'Incredible. How old are you, Susan?'

'Nineteen, sir. But I'll be twenty in August.'

A faint smile curved his lips and his handlebar

moustache quivered. 'Really? That old, eh?' He leaned his elbows on the blotter, steepling his fingers. 'Well, Susan, I think for the sake of my paperwork we'll say that First Officer Peterson piloted the Mosquito but you assisted in the landing when she was taken ill. That will be the official line, but I'll be reporting privately to the appropriate person in the ferry pool. I have to ring them to arrange for your transport back to base anyway.'

'Yes, sir. Thank you, sir.'

He picked up the telephone receiver. 'That will be all. This really is a most irregular occurrence.' He dismissed her with a wave of his hand.

She found Elspeth in the sick bay, lying down on a bed with a cold compress on her forehead. 'How are you feeling?'

Elspeth managed a weak grin. 'Not too bad, darling. I gather you're the talk of the aerodrome. They'll be lining up to shake your hand in the mess.'

'The squadron leader said he was going to hush it up. They'll say that you flew the plane and I just helped.'

'Bastards,' Elspeth groaned. 'I'll confess to the whole thing when we get back to Hamble, darling. I can't steal your thunder.'

'You'll do no such thing. It would mean you'd get the sack. I think we'd best keep to what the squadron leader suggested. After all, it was more luck than judgement that got us through it safely.'

Elspeth raised herself on one elbow. 'Don't talk poppycock, Susan. You're a natural. You should have your wings, you've earned them.'

'Not according to the squadron leader. I'll probably lose my job in the factory because of what I did.'

'There's no chance of that, Susan. You might get a telling off, but I don't think it will go any further. Now be an angel and get me a cup of tea. Two sugars if the blighters will spare it.'

Susan was not convinced. She fully expected to get the sack when they eventually arrived back at Hamble, although there was no possibility of travelling that night. She found the officers' mess and was amazed to discover that she was something of a celebrity. Everyone she met offered to buy her a drink and she was bombarded with questions. She was overwhelmed by all the attention and completely exhausted both mentally and physically. She was desperate for sleep but every time she attempted to leave the table after dinner someone came up with another question and she felt obliged to answer. If only Elspeth had been well enough to join them Susan knew that she would have been able to merge into the background and leave all the talking to her, but Elspeth was tucked up in bed and no doubt sound asleep. Susan had been given a bed in the sick bay too, as there were no other females living on the base. She longed for her bed but the session looked as though it was going to be a long one, until the night fighters were scrambled and the mess emptied in seconds. She made her way to the sick bay, stumbling in the darkness and listening to the roar of engines as the Mosquitoes took off on their mission. She crossed her fingers, silently wishing them a safe return.

Elspeth was pale-faced and dark smudges under-lined her eyes, but after a good night's sleep she was deemed well enough to travel. After a long journey first by military lorry and then by train, they arrived back at Hamble late next day. Elspeth was told to report to the commanding officer. She gave Susan a hug. 'Don't worry, sweetie. I'll put the record straight. You won't lose your job.'

Somewhat doubtful, Susan made her way to the factory and found Danny waiting for her outside the workshop. He grabbed her by the hand. 'Are you okay, Susan? You must have been mad to go with that woman, but at least you're home in one piece.'

'How did you know we'd arrived?'

His serious expression softened into a grin. 'There are such things as telephones, love. It's not the dark ages and everyone's talking about what you did.'

'Am I in big trouble, Danny?'

'You might have been killed and all you're worried about is losing your crummy job.' He dragged her into his arms and hugged her so tightly that she could hardly breathe. 'We thought you were a goner.' He released her almost instantly and his eyes flashed with anger. 'Have you any idea how that affected poor Roz? She'd just heard the news that Patrick had bought it, and then she discovered that you'd gone on a joyride with that crazy woman. If we'd known you were actually piloting the bloody kite it would have been even worse.'

Susan pulled away from him. 'Elspeth's many things but she's a damn good pilot, and she taught me well. I didn't want to take over but she was really ill. It all came right in the end, except that now I've got to face the super. Is he really mad?'

'Hopping,' Danny said bleakly. He opened the door and ushered her into the building. 'Go on. Get it over. He can't kill you.'

She was almost as nervous as she had been when taking off in the Mosquito. Susan made her way to the manager's office and knocked on the door.

'Come in.'

His expression was not welcoming, and when she left a few minutes later her worst fears had been realised. She was considered a security risk in the factory and her services were no longer needed. She would have to sign up for war work elsewhere. There were plenty of munitions factories in need of workers.

'One thing you can be certain of, Miss Banks,' the manager said in icy tones, 'is that you won't be allowed anywhere near aircraft for the duration of the war. Your action could have killed both you and the ATA pilot as well as wrecking a costly aeroplane. You were irresponsible and foolhardy to say the least.' He thrust a pay packet into her hands. 'Goodbye, Miss Banks. I don't expect to see you anywhere near the workshop until the war is over, and hopefully not even then.' He bent his head over his work and she found herself summarily dismissed. Outside she pinched herself to make sure she was not dreaming. She had only done what was absolutely necessary. Now she was to be banished from the aerodrome. Her dream of flying her beloved Spitfire was at an end.

Chapter Twenty-One

Susan walked into the pub kitchen and was almost bowled over by a bundle of golden fur. Forgetting all his training, Charlie leapt up at her licking her face and yelping ecstatically. It took her a minute or two but eventually she managed to calm him down, and was immediately accosted by Roz who flung her arms around her and sobbed on her shoulder. 'Where were you when I needed you, Susan? Why did you go off with that bitch, when you must have known that my heart was breaking?'

Bob had been sitting at the table drinking tea but he rose to his feet and put his arms around both of them. 'Leave the poor kid alone, Roz. It's not her fault. From what Danny said our little Susan's a heroine. She flew a bloody great military plane all by herself.'

Roz drew away, wiping her eyes on her sleeve. 'I know, Dad. But she could have been killed, and I needed her here with me and Jennifer.'

Susan could see from her friend's swollen eyes that she had done her share of weeping over the past twenty-four hours and now she felt even guiltier for her impulsive decision to stand by Elspeth. 'It was a spur of the moment thing. Elspeth was in a state because . . .' She broke off abruptly. 'I'm so sorry about Patrick.'

Bob cleared his throat noisily. 'Susan's back with us now, love,' he said gently. 'That's the main thing. You two mustn't fall out; you've got to support each other.' He dropped his arms to his sides and turned away from them 'It's a terrible time.'

Roz gulped and swallowed. 'I'm sorry, Susan. It's just that everything is so beastly. I don't know how I'm going to manage without Patrick. I can't believe that I'll never see him again. It's too cruel.'

'You've got your baby to think of,' Bob said firmly. 'I know exactly how you're feeling, love. I went through the same thing when I lost my Jennifer, but I had you to live for and that's what I've done for the past twenty years. We'll get through this, Roz. I promise you.'

She dashed her hand across her eyes. 'Promise me you'll stop drinking, Dad.'

He crossed his heart. 'Hope to die, love.'

'I can hear Jennifer crying.' Stifling a sob, Roz fled from the room leaving the door swinging on its hinges.

Bob let out a sigh. 'She's taking it hard, Susan. Thank God you're back; you can talk sense to her.'

'I can't mend a broken heart.'

His cheeks flushed and he dropped his gaze. 'I'm sorry. I know you're mourning for Tony. He was a good bloke.'

'He's not dead,' Susan said with more conviction than she was feeling. 'He was listed as missing. I'm sure I'd feel it in my bones if he hadn't survived.'

'I hope you're right, girl. I really do.' Bob moved towards the door. 'I've got to open up in ten minutes. Make yourself a fresh pot of tea and get something to eat. I expect you're hungry.'

He was about to leave the room but she called him back. 'Bob, I'm afraid I haven't told you every-thing.'

'What's up, Susan?'

'I've lost my job. They gave me the sack for what I did, but I'll start looking for another one first thing in the morning.'

'Bloody idiots,' he said angrily. 'That's all the thanks you get for risking your neck. Don't worry about the housekeeping. We'll manage.' He left the room and Susan set about the mundane task of making herself something to eat and drink, despite Charlie's insistence that she stop and make a fuss of him every few seconds. Orlando opened one green eye and then closed it again, settling back in his bed as if nothing untoward had occurred. Cats were lucky, Susan thought, as she scraped butter onto a slice of toast; they lived in a self-centred little world where nothing mattered other than their own comfort. How lovely to be like that. She threw the crust to Charlie who swallowed it in one greedy gulp and wagged his tail.

She was washing the dishes when Bob stuck his

head round the door. 'You're wanted in the bar, Susan. That stuck-up bitch who almost got you killed is asking for you. Shall I tell her to take a running jump?'

Susan dropped the dishcloth into the water. 'No. I'll come through.' She dried her hands and followed him into the bar. There were only a handful of customers perched on stools at the bar, and Nutty Slack and Todd seated in their usual places in the snug. Elspeth was standing by the fire. She was still wearing her ATA uniform, and she had a cigarette in one hand and a drink in the other. Susan hurried over to her. 'Is everything all right? Did you get into a lot of trouble?'

Elspeth swallowed a mouthful of gin and tonic. She pulled a face. 'Hauled over the carpet, darling, which is what I expected. They can't afford to lose a good pilot so it was just a verbal warning. What about you?'

'Lost my job. The super said I was a security risk.'

Elspeth let out a derisive snort of laughter. 'What do they think you'll do? Steal a Spit and take it for a joyride? How ridiculous.' She was suddenly serious. 'But I am sorry, sweetie. You only did it to help me. I was in a blue funk after hearing about Patrick. God knows why, but that's how it hit me. And then there was bloody Colin, the bastard. It all got too much for me, and you came to the rescue.'

'It's okay. I could have refused but if I'm being

totally honest I suppose I wanted the chance to fly again.'

Elspeth sat down by the fire. 'Take a pew, darling. I've got a suggestion to make. I thought of it as I was driving here.'

'If you're offering me my old cleaning job – I'll take it.'

'It's more than that. I owe you one, sweetie. I'm going to pay for you to train as a pilot.' She held up her hand as Susan opened her mouth to protest that it was out of the question. 'I know that the silly old government rules mean that you've got to do war work too. Anyway, I rang Daddy and he's going to tell his personnel officer to give you a job in the munitions factory. I told him to make it a nice easy one where you'll get plenty of spare time for flying lessons. When you've got your pilot's licence you can apply for the ATA. They'll snap you up.'

Susan stared at her in disbelief. 'Why would you do that for me?'

'I told you before, darling. I've been pushing the boundaries ever since I joined the ATA and I wasn't the Head Girl's favourite person in the first place, but flying is my life. It means more to me than anything and that's why I understand what you're going through. I've had it easy ever since I was born. Whatever I wanted, Daddy bought for me, including Patrick.' Her eyes filled with tears and she turned away, taking a drag on her cigarette.

'But he can't buy Colin. That's the real reason for all this, isn't it?'

Exhaling a plume of smoke into the ingle nook, Elspeth shot her a sideways glance. 'Yes. It's as simple as that. Perhaps there is one thing I care about more than flying, but he's a two-timing, double-dealing louse.'

'I'm sorry.' Susan could think of nothing else to say. She could only marvel at the apparent depth of feeling that had caused Elspeth to lose some of her iron-willed self-control.

Finishing her drink, Elspeth set her glass down on the nearest table. She tossed the cigarette butt into the fire. 'Anyway, I take it that you accept my offer?'

'I'd be mad not to. If you're sure, that is.'

'I never say anything I don't mean, sweetie. You of all people should know that. Come to the cottage tomorrow evening after six. I'm only on stand-by at the ferry pool, so I should be there. I'll give you all the details then.' She managed a wintry smile and patted Susan on the shoulder. She breezed out of the pub as though she had not a care in the world, but Susan knew now that it was all an act.

'What did she want?' Bob demanded as she placed the empty glass on the bar counter.

She shook her head. She needed time to think. 'I'll tell you later. I'm going up to change and then I'll give you a hand. It looks as though you might be busy this evening.' The bar was filling up and she made her escape to her room, needing to be alone. Elspeth's offer was generous in the extreme and she would be a fool to turn it down, but if she went to work at the Colby factory she would have to move into lodgings. That would mean leaving Bob and Roz without any help. Even worse, it seemed highly unlikely that she would be able to take Charlie with her. He nudged her hand, gazing up at her with sympathetic brown eyes, and she went down on her knees to give him a cuddle. 'If I accept Elspeth's offer it will only be a temporary thing,' she murmured into his fur. 'I'd never give you up, Charlie. We're a team, you and I.' He licked her face and gave her a paw. She smiled. 'But if I can get my pilot's licence we'd be in clover, old chap. We could have our own place with a garden for you and a spare room if Roz and Jennifer came to stay.' She scrambled to her feet, brushing dog hairs off her work clothes. 'Don't worry, Charlie. I'm sure it will work out.' She began to undress, deciding not to tell Bob or Roz until it was definite.

Wearing her one good frock, she went down to the bar and Charlie took up his place in front of the fire. He had become a popular attraction in the pub and customers made a fuss of him. He was expert at cadging and greeted his special friends with a beer mat in his mouth, which he refused to relinquish unless offered a crisp. Susan was afraid he would get fat but Bob said it was good for trade.

Thanks to Charlie, sales of crisps and arrowroot biscuits had rocketed.

Leaving her greedy dog to work his charms on a group of people who had occupied the ingle nook, Susan collected ashtrays and empty glasses and took them to the bar. It was only then that she spotted Danny sitting in the corner of the snug. She picked up a damp cloth and went round to wipe the tables. 'Hello, Danny.'

He looked up but his expression was carefully guarded. 'You look pleased with yourself.' His tone was sharp and his green eyes snapped fire.

'Why are you angry? Nothing bad happened.'

He grabbed her by the wrist. 'Don't ever do anything like that again.'

'Let me go. You're hurting me.'

He released her with a mumbled apology. 'Have you any idea of the upset you caused here? Roz was in shock after getting the news of Patrick's death and you took off with that mad woman without a thought for anyone else.'

'You don't know anything about it, and Roz wasn't the only one to have bad news. I'd just heard that Tony was missing. He might be dead for all we know.'

'And you were doing your best to join him, I suppose.'

'I don't have to listen to this.' She walked away without giving him a chance to argue and almost bumped into Colin who had come into the bar.

'Hello there, Susan. How's tricks?'

His charming smile might have fooled her when they first met, but now she saw him for what he was. 'I suppose you've heard what happened?'

'Of course. It's all round the aerodrome. Poor old Elspeth, she must have had the devil of a hangover.'

'You really are a callous brute,' Susan said in a low voice. 'She's too good for you and always was.'

He raised an eyebrow. 'I didn't think you were her greatest fan.'

'I wasn't, but I know her a bit better now, and you've really hurt her.'

'She's just miffed because I wasn't going to play pet poodle and roll over and die. Elspeth thinks that her father's money can buy anything and anyone. Well, it's time she learned that it doesn't. I may be a lot of things but I'm not a gigolo. I've never gone after a woman for her money.'

'You'd rather flirt with a nightclub girl than stay with someone who really loves you.'

He chuckled. 'So that's what this is all about. Save your pity for someone who deserves it. Elspeth found out about Sandra and blew her top. She behaved like a lunatic and threw me out.'

'I don't blame her.'

'It was a one night stand. It was fun for me and business for Sandra. That's the way of the world.'

'It's not the way I want my world to be.'

'Grow up, Susan. Would you be so judgemental if it was Tony who had slipped up?'

A spasm of pain shot through her and she gasped, unable to speak.

Colin's face puckered with genuine regret. 'Sorry, kid. Forget I said that. I was out of order, but the rest stands. Elspeth will bounce back. She always does.'

'You couldn't be more wrong. Just go and see her. Tell her what you just told me, that it was just a physical thing and meant nothing. It's up to you.' A wave of exhaustion swept over her and she walked away. She could not muster the energy to continue the argument. She had told him the truth and what he did with it was up to him. She went behind the bar to help Bob, but for the rest of the evening her mind was elsewhere. She struggled to add up rounds of drinks, made mistakes giving change and was relieved when the bell rang for closing time.

'You look done in,' Bob said, placing a tea towel over the hand pull pumps. 'I can finish up here.'

'Thanks. I am a bit tired.' Flashing him a grateful smile, Susan headed for the kitchen.

Roz had just finished feeding Jennifer and she hitched her over her shoulder, patting her back gently. 'She's a greedy little gannet,' she said with a misty smile. 'Patrick would have been so proud of her.'

'She's adorable.' Susan stroked the baby's downy head. 'I'm going to make some tea for your dad and some cocoa for me. Want some?'

'Yes, please.' Roz gave her a searching look.

'What's up? I know you're worried sick about Tony, but this is something else.'

'You know me so well.' Susan filled the kettle and put it on the hob. 'I've got a problem, Roz. I didn't want to burden you with it, but you'll find out soon enough.'

'Fire away. I'm listening.'

When Susan had finished, she glanced anxiously at Roz. 'I don't want to leave you and your dad in a difficult position. You've got a tiny baby to look after and there's the pub to run . . .'

Cradling her sleeping daughter in the crook of her arm, Roz reached out to pat Susan's hand. 'We can manage. I know how much flying means to you and this is an opportunity of a lifetime. Do it, Susan. Accept Elspeth's offer quickly in case she changes her mind.'

'I feel as though I'm betraying you and Patrick if I take her up on it. I'll be working for the man who was responsible for him joining the veterinary corps.'

'He would probably have gone anyway. We talked about it before all of this happened, and I wouldn't have tried to stop him. We can't live in the past. I've got Jennifer to bring up, and you must do what you have to.'

'There's another thing.' Susan patted Charlie's head as he laid it on her lap. 'I couldn't take Charlie into digs. Even if the landlady didn't mind dogs it wouldn't be fair to leave him on his own for hours on end.'

'You and that dog,' Roz shook her head, smiling. 'There's no question about it and I know Dad would agree with me. Charlie stays here. You can come home on your days off and see him.'

'Do you really mean it?'

'Of course I do, silly. Charlie is part of the family. He'll be fine.'

The job at the munitions factory was repetitive and boring, but Elspeth had been as good as her word and had pulled a few strings so that Susan's hours were to some extent flexible. This enabled her to leave work early on the evenings when she had a flying lesson.

Elspeth flew the Moth to Southampton, landing in the grounds surrounding her father's factory. She insisted that she did not want her beloved plane mothballed for the entire duration, laughing at the pun, and pretending to be cross with Susan when she showered her with gratitude. A retired pilot with many hours flying time under his belt was hired to train Susan, and they went up almost daily. In the evenings she studied and next day he tested her on her knowledge of all the subjects she would need to obtain her pilot's licence, once she had completed the requisite hours of flying time.

She had a small room in the attic of an Edwardian terrace house on the outskirts of Southampton. It was sparsely furnished with a single bed, a pine chest of drawers and a bentwood chair, but at least she had it to herself. There were two other girls from the factory who shared a room on the floor below, but they regarded her as something of a freak. At first they tried to persuade Susan to go dancing with them or to the cinema, but eventually they gave up. Neither of them, it seemed, could understand why a pretty young woman wanted to spend all her free time swotting. Susan kept quiet about her flying lessons. Even Mrs Jessop, the landlady, had no idea that this was what her youngest lodger did every day after work. Supper was on the table at six o'clock every evening, and if anyone was late their meal went straight to the pig bin at the end of the road. Susan felt quite sorry for the pigs that had to eat Mrs Jessop's Woolton pie or mock banana pudding.

At weekends, if she was not required to work in the factory, Susan caught the train to Hamble and walked home from the station. Sometimes Danny met her pushing Jennifer in her pram. This always struck Susan as quite hilarious. Danny with his tough ways and uncompromising attitude to life did not seem on the surface to be the paternal type, but he obviously adored Jennifer, and he had an easy-going relationship with Roz. She seemed happy to entrust her precious daughter to his care on these occasions, and Susan was allowed to push the pram back to the pub while Danny carried her overnight bag.

On a particularly beautiful June morning Susan alighted from the train expecting to see Danny standing on the platform, but there was no sign of him. Disappointed but unsurprised she started off in the direction of the High Street. The air was filled with birdsong and the hedgerows were choked with wild flowers, their perfume scenting the air. If it were not for the gasmask case slung over her shoulder and the ever present ache in her heart, she might have been able to forget that there was a war casting its shadow across the world. She felt a guilty sense of pleasure as she listened to a skylark warbling its song above a field of ripening corn, and as she entered the High Street people she knew only slightly greeted her like a long lost friend. There seemed to be a smile on everyone's face, and when she saw the frontage of the Victorious hung with bunting she began to wonder if the war had ended and she was the last to know. Her heart thudded against her ribs and she had butterflies in her stomach as she opened the door and stepped inside. It must be good news for someone but she scarcely dared believe that it was for her. Charlie bounded up to her with his usual rapturous greeting, and having calmed him down she looked round, blinking as her eyes grew accustomed to the dimness after the bright sunshine outside. Bob was in his usual position behind the bar, but unusually for this early in the day there were a lot of familiar faces grouped around the room. Mrs Delaney had abandoned her mop and bucket and was standing next to her son Terry. His cheeky face was split in a wide grin but when he opened his mouth to speak he was quelled by a stern look from his mother. Nutty and Todd emerged from the snug clutching their pint glasses, and, most surprisingly of all, Susan saw Roz seated in the ingle nook with Jennifer cradled in her arms, something she would never have done on a normal day. Danny was sitting beside her and then she spotted Dave. He leapt to his feet and came towards her with his arms outstretched and a smile almost splitting his face in two. 'Susan, ducks. I had to come in person. I couldn't tell you over the phone.'

Her knees were trembling and each breath was an effort. 'What? Tell me, please.'

'He's alive. Tony's in a prisoner of war camp. I had the telegram last night. I'd have come then but it was too late. He's not dead, Susan. Our boy is safe.'

She did not know whether to laugh or cry. She returned the hug and then moved away, overcome with emotion and too choked to speak. Roz passed Jennifer to Danny and rose swiftly to her feet. She put her arms around Susan and held her. 'It's all right. Bawl if you want to. No one will mind.' She fumbled in her pocket and brought out a crumpled hanky. She wrinkled her nose. 'Er – maybe not. Sorry, Sue, it's covered in Jennifer's upchuck.'

Susan wiped her eyes on the back of her hand. 'Thanks, but I'm okay. I'm just so happy I don't know what to say.'

The sound of a cork popping made everyone turn

to look at Bob. He held up a bottle of champagne. 'I was saving this for the end of the war, but this seems like as good a time as any. We haven't had much to celebrate recently, so let's drink to young Tony.'

Roz gave Susan's hand a squeeze. 'I'll pass them round,' she said, making her way to the bar. 'I think you'll need another bottle, Dad.' Balancing a tray on one hand she served Dave and Susan first. 'Why don't you take your drinks out in the garden? It's a gorgeous day and I'm sure you've a lot to talk about.'

Dave nodded. 'I'd like that. Is it all right with you, Susan? I mean, you've only just arrived home, and it's all been a bit of a shock for you.'

She slipped her hand through the crook of his arm. 'It's the best sort of shock, but I'm afraid I might be dreaming.'

Roz pinched her, chuckling when Susan yelped with pain. 'Just to prove you're wide awake and it's true. I'm so happy for you.'

'Thanks. That means a lot to me.' Susan felt a shiver run up her spine as she met Roz's smiling gaze. She could feel the sadness beneath that generous smile and she could only imagine what Roz must be feeling at this moment. She glanced at Jennifer, sound asleep in Danny's arms, and when he gave Roz an encouraging smile it came to Susan in an intuitive flash that these three were meant to be together. Roz might not know it yet and Danny was perhaps not fully aware of the depth of his feelings for Roz, but Susan could see quite clearly that they were falling in love with each other.

'Come on, ducks,' Dave said gently. 'Let's go outside and get some sunshine and you can tell me all about your flying lessons. Roz said that you flew a Mosquito all by yourself. By golly, Tony will be proud of you. I know I am.'

Any last trace of embarrassment that Susan felt in Dave's company faded away as they sat in the beer garden and chatted over their drinks. He was once again the father figure that she had longed for all her life. He listened to her intently, making appropriate comments and applauding her actions with warmth and genuine sincerity. His pale eyes flashed with anger when she told him how Colin had treated Elspeth.

'She didn't deserve that,' he said, nodding his bald head. 'She may be a bit of a madam but she's been good to you, Susan. That makes her all right in my book. I'd like to meet her and shake her hand.'

Susan angled her head. 'Would you really, Dave?'

'I just said so, didn't I?' He swallowed the rest of his half-pint of shandy, which he had substituted for the champagne saying that it gave him heartburn. 'We'll invite her to the wedding. Let's hope it won't be long before Tony's home with us again.'

Susan raised her glass. 'I'll drink to that, Dad.' She hesitated, realising what she had just said. 'Do you mind if I call you dad? I never felt quite comfortable calling you Dave.'

His eyes misted behind the thick lenses of his glasses. 'Nothing could make me happier. I always wanted a daughter as well as a son.' He reached across the rustic wooden table and laid his hand over hers. 'I'm so glad you've forgiven me for making a complete fool of myself.'

She smiled. 'Forgiven and forgotten.'

There was a festive atmosphere in the bar that night. Everyone knew by now that Tony Richards was safe, even if he did have to suffer the rigours of a prison camp. It touched Susan to realise how popular he was with the locals. By the end of the evening she had listened to many stories of small kindnesses that he had done for people with whom he had just a fleeting acquaintance, whether it was a lift to town on a cold and wet day, or the loan of ten bob to Nutty Slack when he was short of the rent. Tony was remembered with genuine affection and she wondered, with a wry smile, if his ears were burning.

Dave seemed to be enjoying himself. He sat on a bar stool chatting to Bob as if they were old friends and Charlie positioned himself at his feet, getting in the way of customers waiting to be served but nobody seemed to mind climbing over a large, well-fed Labrador to get to the bar.

Susan could scarcely stop smiling. She felt as though her face was set in a rictus grin that would last forever. Tony was alive; that was all that mattered. She even managed to forget that the first of her theory exams for a pilot's licence were starting on Monday. In the excitement of learning that Tony had survived she had not had the time or the inclination to tell Roz or Bob that she was taking the examinations that could change her life forever. She had, however, confided in Dave and now he met her eyes across the bar and gave her an encouraging wink and a smile. She smiled back, knowing that he had gone through the same thing with Tony when he applied for his pilot's licence, and that Dave understood exactly how she was feeling. She vowed silently that she would not let either of them down. Tony had believed in her and that was why he had risked his job to take her up in a Mosquito. She felt a lump in her throat as she remembered that time which seemed so long ago now, and suddenly she needed to get away from the crowded bar. She wanted a few moments on her own. She tapped Bob on the shoulder. 'Do you mind if I go for a break?'

He beamed at her. 'Of course not, love. If you're making a pot of tea make mine milk and two sugars.' He turned back to Dave. 'You'll stay tonight, of course. You've missed the last train anyway.'

Susan did not wait to hear his response. She left the crowded bar and went through to the kitchen with Charlie relinquishing his post at Dave's feet to follow her. She put the kettle on but she had the sudden need for a breath of fresh air, and she went out into the garden. The sun had long since set and the light was fading fast. The warm summer air was fragrant with the scent of honeysuckle and roses. Most of the garden had been dug over and planted with vegetables, but the pergolas were still heavy with flowers and foliage. She could hear the chickens clucking as they made ready to roost in the hen house, and starlings swooped overhead in noisy black clouds. She strolled across the yard, stepping carefully to avoid bumping into kegs and crates of empty bottles, and Charlie ran round sniffing scents that were only discernible to a dog.

She came to a sudden halt as she heard voices, realising that she was not alone in the garden. A pale moon was visible overhead and in its silver light she saw a couple standing under the sycamore tree, they were so close that their bodies merged into one. She recognised Roz by her colourful cotton frock, and as the man bent his head to kiss her she saw that it was Danny who held her in such a tender embrace. Susan backed away, calling Charlie to heel. She gazed up at the evening stars and wished that the war would end soon so that she could be reunited with the man she loved. She retreated to the kitchen feeling slightly envious. She was happy of course that Danny had found someone worthy of his love, and delighted to know that Roz would not have to raise her child alone, but seeing them together had also made her feel sad. The heartache caused by separation had never seemed more acute than it did at this moment. Tony was somewhere in Germany, incarcerated in a prison camp, the like of which she could not begin to imagine. She could only hope and pray that he would survive.

She made the tea and took a cup through to the bar for Bob. She was smiling, but inwardly she was crying.

On Monday she had been allowed time off work to sit her first theory examination. The rest were spread out over the week and in between she had to undergo a medical. She had clocked up the requisite number of flying hours and done everything that was required for a private pilot's licence, and now she waited for the result. She had gone to the factory as usual but it was almost impossible to settle down to the boring routine tasks that she was given daily. She knew that she had passed the medical examination but she was worried about the theory. She was sweeping the factory floor when the supervisor came up to her and told her she was to go to the boss's office. 'What have you done, Banks? Looks like you're in big trouble. Best get a move on.'

What had she done? Susan could think of nothing apart from taking time off to sit her exams, but she had been doing so with permission from her manager. With some trepidation she made her way through the factory to the suite of offices where Mr Colby held court. No one from the works was allowed into this area without permission, and her knees were trembling as she raised her hand to knock on the door.

Chapter Twenty-Two

She was ushered into the most palatial office that she could ever have imagined. Her feet sank into the deep pile of the midnight-blue carpet and the scent of expensive aftershave and cologne wafted round her in a cloud. She had only seen Cyril Colby from a distance, but she recognised him now as he sat in his throne-like chair behind a huge mahogany desk. His craggy features cracked into a semblance of a smile. 'So this is your protégée, Elspeth.'

Susan had been dimly aware that they were not alone, but she had been too nervous to look at the two people who were seated in white leather armchairs with their backs to her. She stifled a gasp of surprise as Elspeth rose to her feet and came towards her, hands outstretched. 'Congratulations, darling.' She handed Susan a manila envelope. 'I simply had to give it to you myself.'

'What is it?'

'Darling, it's your pilot's licence, of course. I bypassed the official channels because I wanted to see your face when you opened it.'

'I've passed?'

'With flying colours. I'm so proud of you, Susan.'

She opened the envelope with shaking hands, but the print on the enclosed document danced before her eyes like tadpoles swimming in a pond. This was something she had wanted so much. It was almost impossible to believe that her hard work had paid off. It simply could not be happening to a girl from her disadvantaged background.

'Congratulations, Miss Banks.' Cyril Colby rose from his seat and came towards her. He shook her hand. 'I admire pluck and determination. You've done well.'

'She certainly has.' Elspeth beckoned to her companion. 'There's someone I want you to meet, sweetie.'

Any moment now she would wake up in bed and it would all have been a dream. 'Really?' Even to her own ears her voice sounded strained and far away.

Elspeth held out her hand to a tall, attractive woman in ATA uniform. 'I'm sure you know who this is, Susan?'

Susan gulped and swallowed. She had seen Pauline Gower several times, but only in the distance. She nodded, unable to speak.

'Pauline, this is Susan Banks, the girl I told you about,' Elspeth said, suddenly serious. 'She's just about scraped two hundred hours' flying time in my Tiger Moth and she's just been granted her pilot's licence. What do you think?'

'I think she's wasted working in my factory,' Cyril

Colby said before Pauline had a chance to respond. 'Elspeth bullied me into taking her on, but I'd be grateful if you would take her off my hands so that I can fill her place with someone whose head isn't quite literally in the clouds.'

Pauline threw back her head and laughed. 'Now why do I feel that I'm being press-ganged into this?'

'It's entirely up to you, ma'am,' Elspeth said, holding up her hands in a submissive gesture. 'I wouldn't dream of using Daddy's friendship with Pop d'Erlanger to influence you in any way.'

Cyril shook his head, smiling. 'Don't take any notice of her, Pauline. The decision is, of course, entirely yours.'

'I think that Susan and I need to have a serious talk,' Pauline said calmly. 'In private, if that's possible.'

'Of course. Take as long as you like.' Cyril seized Elspeth by the arm and guided her towards the door. 'We'll go for a walk. We've things to mull over anyway.'

'She'll make a fine pilot,' Elspeth insisted as she left the room. 'With a few weeks' training she'll be one of the best. Oh, Daddy, stop pulling my arm. I'm coming.'

The door closed on them and Susan was left face to face with the woman who, next to Amy Johnson, was her idol.

'Sit down, Susan. Tell me why you want to join the Air Transport Auxiliary.'

At the end of her initial training, Susan joined number 15 ferry pool at Hamble. She received a friendly enough welcome but she sensed the reserve behind some of the smiling faces. She decided to keep her head down and work hard. Respect was something that had to be earned; that was a lesson she had learned long ago.

In some ways being in the mess waiting for the delivery chits seemed like being back in school. Everything was run to a strict timetable and there were definite cliques. The other women came from diverse backgrounds and many different countries, some of them barely speaking English, but all with the one purpose: to fly any and every aircraft assigned to them. Susan was very much the new girl but she worked hard, studied and never complained. She learned how to fly everything from a Hurricane to a Lancaster, but her proudest moment came when she flew her first Spitfire. At last her lifelong ambition was achieved when she delivered a Spitfire to Cosford.

On some occasions she flew a four-engine bomber with nothing but a ring-bound set of handling notes tucked in her flying boot to give her the critical statistics and notations necessary to fly that par-ticular aircraft, and later the same day she might be assigned to flying a Mosquito or a Spitfire. It was not always easy and the weather played a huge part in the day to day job of the ferry pilots. It was lonely work and extremely dangerous. They flew unarmed and without radios. There were fatalities amongst both male and female pilots and Susan was well aware that she risked her life daily, but she would not have changed her job for anything in the world.

Even with her busy schedule she still spent her spare time helping out in the pub. Some of the wealthier society girls in the ATA lived much less mundane lives, driving up to London and dining out in expensive nightclubs, dancing until dawn but still managing to be ready for work at nine o'clock sharp. Sometimes Susan envied them, thinking they were like exotic birds of paradise and she was a Jenny wren, but mostly she was glad to get back to the comforting ordinariness of the pub, with nappies hung out to dry on the washing line and chats with the locals over the bar.

Time was measured now by the milestones in Jennifer's life: her first smile, her first word, and all too soon she took her first tentative steps. Susan was happy to be a proud auntie, and even happier when in the summer of 1944 she was bridesmaid at Roz and Danny's wedding. It was a quiet affair and of necessity less than lavish. Roz had saved up all her coupons to buy a new dress, but there was no question of a white wedding. Her gown was made of peach-coloured rayon with a sweetheart neckline, fitted tightly to the waist and flaring gently to just below her knees. She wore her hair in a victory roll, and a perky little hat decorated with a silk rose donated by Elspeth. Susan had learned to sew in the children's home and she had made a floral summer frock for herself which complemented Roz's rather plain outfit but did not detract from it. She too had borrowed a hat from Elspeth, a rather fetching straw picture hat which made her feel glamorous, like Veronica Lake or Anna Neagle.

Elspeth herself was sporting an indecently large diamond engagement ring, and had Colin well and truly in tow. They were guests at the wedding, which would have seemed quite odd in peacetime. Bob had demurred when Roz said she was going to invite Patrick's widow and her boyfriend to her wedding, but Roz had insisted that it was all water under the bridge. Elspeth was Susan's friend, and it had been through her auspices that Susan had learned to fly and gained admission to the ATA. Life was too short, she said, to hold grudges. If Elspeth had moved on then so could she.

Roz and Danny were married in the village church, with Jennifer toddling up the aisle clutching a posy of rosebuds and Susan following her like a nervous mother hen whose chick had turned out to be a duckling and had taken to the water. Dave came down from London for the occasion and Bob was every inch the proud father as he gave his daughter away. Susan's fears that he might start drinking again after a prolonged dry spell were unfounded, and at the reception in the pub the only alcoholic beverage that passed his lips was a glass of champagne to toast the happy couple.

The wedding cake had been made by Mrs Delaney who had been hoarding dried fruit for months, and even then there was more carrot and grated apple in the mixture than raisins or sultanas, but disguised by a cardboard cover of imitation icing borrowed from the baker's shop the cake looked as though it had been made by a professional chef. Roz was thrilled with it anyway, and that to Susan was the main thing. After a wedding breakfast of meat paste sandwiches, sausage rolls and Mrs Delaney's rock cakes, the bride and groom set off for their one night honeymoon in a Southampton hotel. Susan was left in charge of Jennifer, who was exhausted by six o'clock and ready for bed. After reading her a fairy story, Susan tucked her in and went downstairs to make supper for Bob and Dave, who had been invited to stay for the night rather than taking the last train back to London.

When the pub closed and Bob retired to bed, Susan and Dave sat in the kitchen chatting to each other over mugs of cocoa. They compared the brief communications they had received from Tony in the prison camp somewhere in Germany. There were only a few of them and each one was highly censored, but seeing his handwriting and holding a flimsy piece of paper that he had once held, made him seem closer. Their shared love for him had made a strong bond between them, and they had at last achieved an easy-going relationship that boded well for the future. Next morning Dave left early, walking to the station in order to catch the first train to London.

Susan stood on the doorstep waving until he was out of sight. She was genuinely sad to see him go. He was the only person who could understand how deeply she loved his son. She had been afraid that she might forget Tony, but the passing of time had only deepened her feelings for him. Some women separated from their fiancé's or husbands took solace in the arms of another man, especially when they were exposed to the undoubted charms of the American soldiers and airmen who were stationed locally. Susan might feel her heart flutter appreciatively when she went to the pictures on her night off to see a film starring Alan Ladd or Errol Flynn, but she knew that Tony was the love of her life. He might not be handsome or dashing like the actors on the silver screen, but he was good-looking in an understated way; he was kind and thoroughly decent. He was the sort of man she could trust. He would love her no matter what. He would never leave her. That was the most important thing. He had suffered loss at an early age, and he knew what it was like to grow up without a mother. They needed each other. She would wait for him forever, if necessary.

She went back indoors to get Jennifer up and give her breakfast before she had to leave for the aerodrome. Mrs Delaney would arrive at eight thirty and she would take care of her until the honeymooners arrived home later that morning. Susan went upstairs to get dressed before going into Jennifer's bedroom and lifting her from her cot. It was only then that the reality of the situation hit her. Danny had given notice at his digs and was moving in today. Nothing had been said, but if Roz conceived as quickly as she had in her one night of passion with Patrick, it was quite possible that she would be pregnant again in the near future. It would not happen overnight, of course, but Susan could see her days at the pub coming to an end. Until now she had lived as one of the family, but now that Roz had a husband and a child, Susan realised sadly that there would soon be no room for her, even though no one would dream of asking her to go.

She was still mulling this over when she sat in a corner of the mess, waiting for the delivery chits. She did not notice Elspeth until she sat down beside her.

'What ho, old thing? You look down in the dumps.'

Susan looked up with a start. 'I'm okay.'

'Not with a face like a fiddle. Come on, sweetie. Tell Auntie Elspeth what's wrong.'

'I was just thinking that it was time to make a move. I mean from the pub, not the ferry pool.'

Elspeth fished in her handbag for her silver cigarette case. 'Darling, you had me worried for a moment. What brought this on?' She extracted a cigarette and tapped it on the back of the case before lighting it and inhaling with a sigh of pleasure. 'Come on, sweetie. After all we've been through together you know that you can tell me anything.'

Susan gazed out of the window at the aircraft lined up on the tarmac waiting for their pilots, the sunlight bouncing off their silver wings. She sighed. 'Roz and Danny don't need a third party acting as gooseberry. They'll want to have kids of their own and I'll just be in the way.'

'That's all that's bothering you?' Elspeth flicked ash into the ashtray. 'Darling, I've got the perfect answer. I was going to let the cottage but you can have it for a peppercorn rent. I know you'll keep it spick and span, whereas, some of them,' she lowered her voice to a conspiratorial whisper, 'some of the others live like pigs.'

Susan stared at her in amazement. 'You're leaving the cottage?'

'I've decided to move back into my old home. Now that Colin and I are officially a couple I don't see why we should shack up in relative poverty while my beautiful mansion is empty. The tenant moved out a month ago.'

'So you're going to marry him?'

Elspeth studied the ring on her left hand. 'Yes. Probably, I don't know, but he's on trial. If he misbehaves in the near future he'll be out on his ear. I've laid the law down, Susan.'

'And he accepts it?'

'He hasn't much choice, sweetie. If he wants me and all the fringe benefits, then he's got to behave. Anyway, that's not your problem. You can have the cottage for as long as you want.'

'It's a very generous offer.'

'Nonsense. You'll be doing me a favour by keeping the place clean and aired. This war is going to end soon and your boyfriend will come home. You'll need somewhere to live.' She stubbed out her cigarette and rose to her feet as her name was called. 'Think about it, Susan.' She strolled off to collect her chit.

Despite Roz and Bob's pleas for her to stay, Susan moved into the cottage by the river at the end of July. At first she was lonely and missed the hustle and bustle of the pub, but she continued to help out at weekends when she was not on duty, and Roz often brought Jennifer to the cottage to play with Charlie who had become her much loved friend and protector. When Susan was off on a long flight, Danny took Charlie back to the pub where he was petted and spoilt by the regulars and the family alike. He definitely had the best of both worlds.

The war that had seemed never ending was slowly drawing to a close. Victory was in sight as the Allies pressed on through France and into Germany. The battles were bloody and Susan could only be thankful that Tony was in the comparative safety of the prison camp. She dared not dwell on the possibility that he was malnourished and sick; she could only fix her hopes on a speedy end to the war and his release from years of imprisonment.

Christmas came and went. Susan stayed at the pub over the festive season but her time off was short and aeroplanes still had to be ferried across country and abroad. She was so accustomed to flying Spitfires that the cockpit felt like a second skin, although she had now flown almost every aircraft in operation and sometimes up to five flights a day. She was now an accepted member of the ferry pool. Her enthusiasm and willingness to take on any task had earned her the respect of her colleagues, but she kept herself to herself. She could never quite shake off the feeling that she did not belong in any particular social group. Not knowing who her parents were was a cross that she would have to bear for the rest of her life. When she was much younger she had often imagined that one or both of her parents would come back to claim her, but now she knew that was never going to happen. Perhaps she should be grateful that her life was a blank slate on which she could write her own destiny. When she was alone in the cottage she sat by the fire on winter evenings, stroking Charlie and listening to the wireless. Soon she would be reunited with Tony, but it still seemed a long way off.

It was finally over. The conflict in Europe was at an

end. The newscaster on the wireless announced that the prisoners had been released from the German camps, but now it was a matter of getting the men home. Thousands of prisoners and soldiers alike waited on the coast of France for passage to England on troop ships. Overjoyed and buzzing with excitement, Susan set off immediately riding her bicycle and weaving through the crowds of people who were literally dancing in the street. A carnival atmosphere prevailed and everyone was hugging and kissing, waving flags and singing. Charlie bounced along beside Susan, his eyes shining as if he understood that something remarkable had happened. As she reached the pub she could see Bob up a ladder putting out the bunting and when she entered the bar she found it was packed with locals. Danny and Roz were serving behind the bar and Jennifer was sitting on Mrs Delaney's lap eating a biscuit, which Charlie immediately spotted. He threw himself down beside her watching every crumb as it disappeared into her mouth with his tongue hanging out. Susan made her way to the bar.

Roz finished serving Nutty with a pint of mild. She turned to Susan with an ecstatic smile. 'Isn't it wonderful? What are you drinking?'

'I'll have a glass of cider as I'm off duty.'

'Dave wants you to telephone. He says he's got good news.'

'Tony,' Susan breathed. 'Never mind the cider.

I'll have it later.' She edged through the crowd making her way to the door marked 'Private'. In the comparative quiet of the hallway she waited for the operator to put her through to the cycle shop.

Dave answered almost immediately. 'Susan. I knew it would be you. I've just heard from Tony. He's in Dover. They brought them home on a troop ship and he's waiting to get a train to London, but there are hundreds of soldiers there all desperate to get home. He doesn't know when he'll be able to get here.'

For a moment Susan could not speak. Her lips moved but somehow she could not voice the words that flooded her brain.

'Susan, can you hear me, love?'

She nodded her head. 'Yes. Yes. I'll go there and get him.'

'Hang on, ducks. Calm down and give it some thought. Wait for him to get on a train. Come to London by all means but—'

'No.' She almost shouted the word down the mouthpiece. 'I've waited years for this moment. I'll go and meet him even if I have to steal a plane.' She replaced the receiver, dropping it onto its cradle. She stood for a moment, too stunned to move, but then the adrenalin started to flow and she hurried into the bar. She leaned across the counter, catching Roz by the sleeve. 'Look after Charlie for me. I'm going to pick up Tony. He's back in England. Isn't it simply wonderful?' Without giving Roz the chance to argue she raced out of the pub and picking up her bicycle she pedalled as fast as she could back to the aerodrome.

She almost ran Elspeth and Colin down as they walked arm in arm through the gates. 'Here, hold on. Where's the fire?' Colin caught the handlebars as she was about to ride past them. 'Where are you going?'

'Help me, Colin. Tony's just got off a troop ship in Dover. He'll have to wait days for transport to London. I must get to him.'

'Sweetie, calm down,' Elspeth said, exchanging worried glances with Colin. 'You're not going to do anything silly, are you?'

Susan grabbed Colin by the arm. 'I need your help. You know the new two-seater Spitfire trainers? I want one. I can fly to Dover and be back before dark, but I need you to authorise it as a training flight.'

He stared at her as if she had gone mad. 'You can't do that.'

'I'd do the same for you, darling,' Elspeth said sweetly. 'Get her past security and let her fly the Spit. You know she's perfectly capable. It's little enough to ask for a woman who's risked her life for her country time and time again.'

'I'll be arrested and put in the Tower.'

Elspeth gave him a gentle shove towards the hangar. 'Shut up and help the girl. Where's your spirit of romance?'

'I wish I'd stuck to bloody Highland Mary or whatever her name was.'

'No you don't, darling. Do this and I'll name the day. We'll be married in the register office and honeymoon at Daddy's villa in Monte.'

'You drive a hard bargain, Elspeth.'

'Come on,' Susan said, abandoning her bike. 'Please, Colin. You're Tony's friend. Please do this for us.'

Flying the Spitfire trainer was the easy part. Finding somewhere to land near Dover was the difficult bit. In the end she opted for the American air base in the former municipal airport. She executed a perfect landing and was immediately surrounded by army personnel brandishing weapons. Their astonishment on seeing a girl climb out of the cockpit momentarily overcame their suspicions, but she was escorted under guard to the CO's office where she was met by a bemused American officer. Breathless but determined she explained her mission. 'You can arrest me if you like, but I need to get into Dover and find my fiancé. He's an RAF pilot who was shot down over Germany and has been in a prison camp for three years. I don't know what sort of state he'll be in and he might have to wait days for a train to take him to London. Please let me go and find him. I've got to get the Spit back to Hamble or there'll be hell to pay and not just for me. Please give me a couple of hours and then we'll leave here and no one will be the wiser.'

He stared at her for a long moment and then a slow smile spread across his face. 'Well, if that don't beat all. I've never heard a tale like that,' he stared at the gold bands on her sleeve. 'Flight Lieutenant.'

'First Officer, actually, sir. I'm in the Air Transport Auxiliary.'

He whistled through his teeth. 'I've a great admiration for the work that you and your colleagues have done both here and in the States. I guess it would be unpatriotic of me to turn you over to the authorities, especially today.'

Acting on impulse, Susan stood on tiptoe and kissed him on his clean-shaven cheek. 'Thank you, sir. I'm truly grateful.'

He flushed and cleared his throat, shooting a sideways glance at his sergeant who stood to attention by the door. 'Er, yeah. Well, we can't have you wandering about on what is technically US property so the sergeant will organise a jeep to take you to the port and bring you and your fiancé back here, should you find him, of course.'

'I will,' Susan said firmly. 'I most definitely will.'

The town was packed with military personnel. Susan's heart sank. The chances of finding Tony amongst thousands of returning soldiers and prisoners of war were almost nil. There was noise and confusion and after two long hours of searching she was no nearer finding Tony than she had been at the start.

The American soldier who had driven the jeep had stayed with her. He was sympathetic but sceptical. 'I guess we'd better think about getting back to the base, ma'am.'

She clutched his arm. 'Please, just another half an hour. I know he's somewhere near. I can feel it.'

'Half an hour it is, but that's all, ma'am.'

'I'm going to the station,' Susan said firmly. 'Wait here, private. If I don't find him in that time I'll come straight back.' Without giving him a chance to argue she set off for the station, asking for directions from passers-by and then following the sound of the engines letting off steam. She knew it would be like looking for a needle in a haystack, but all she could do was hope for a miracle, and then, as if in answer to her prayers, she saw him standing at the end of a queue outside a telephone box. His uniform was tattered and dirty and it hung on him like the clothes on a scarecrow, but there was no mistaking the straight profile even if it was half concealed by several days' stubble. She would have known him anywhere. She called his name and he turned, shading his eyes against the sunlight. As if in slow motion they made their way towards each other. Measured steps, never faltering, they walked into each other's arms.

When at last they drew apart, breathless and smiling, Tony traced the outline of her face with his fingertips. 'You were always pretty, Susan. But now you're beautiful, and you smell heavenly.'

She swallowed hard as she fought back the tears that threatened to overcome her. 'I wish I could say the same of you, Tony, darling. You smell awful.'

When he laughed he was the old Tony that she loved to desperation. 'I know I do. I'm not fit for human company.'

She linked her hand through his arm. 'You'll do for now. Come on. I promised the private that I wouldn't be long.'

'How did you get here? How did you find me?'

She met his puzzled gaze with a smile. 'I stole a Spitfire.'

With the aeroplane returned to its hangar and no questions asked, Colin having covered up for her with the efficiency of a secret agent, Susan took Tony to the riverside cottage. Bathed, shaved and wearing one of Colin's suits that had been left in the wardrobe thanks to Elspeth's casual attitude to packing, Tony came downstairs looking much more like his old self.

Susan was setting the table but she stopped when she heard his footsteps on the stairs and walked towards him holding out her arms. 'That's more like it. How do you feel?'

He swept her off her feet and carried her to the sofa, sitting down with her on his lap. 'I'm happier than I ever imagined I could be, darling. I can't believe what you just did for me, and I'm so proud of you for what you've achieved. There aren't enough words to tell you how much I love you, Susan.'

She answered him with a kiss that went on and on until she realised that the pan of soup was boiling over on the stove. She clambered off his knee with an apologetic chuckle. 'First things first. You must eat.'

He caught her by the hand. 'I can think of other things I'd like to do.'

She kissed his fingers before twisting free from his grasp. 'I'll bet, but soup first.' She hurried into the kitchen to take the pan off the heat. 'And you'd better phone your dad. He'll be going out of his mind wondering what's happened to you.'

'You're right, of course.'

She glanced through the doorway and smiled to herself as Tony reached for the telephone. She could hardly believe that he was home and safe at last. She had to keep looking at him in order to reassure herself that it was not just a dream. She yelped as she burnt her finger on the hot saucepan, but the pain was as nothing compared to the agonies she had suffered while he was in the prisoner of war camp. She said a silent prayer of thanks for his safe deliverance, and she smiled as she listened to him explaining the situation to his father. She waited for the conversation to end before taking the food in and putting it on the table.

'He's fine,' Tony said, getting to his feet and wrapping his arms around her. 'I'll go and see him on my way back to my squadron.'

She stared at him in dismay. 'What d'you mean? The war's over.'

'But I'm still in the RAF. I'm under orders and you're still in the ATA. You'll go to work as usual tomorrow and so will I.' He laid his finger on her lips as she was about to protest. 'I'm sure I'll get some leave and then I'll be right back. Nothing will keep me away from you for any longer than absolutely necessary.'

She nodded dully. 'I suppose you're right.'

'And we've got an occasion to organise, unless you've changed your mind.'

'What's that?'

He took her left hand and held it, stroking her ring finger. 'We're engaged, aren't we? That usually leads to a wedding, or have things changed since I went away?'

'Are you proposing to me, Tony Richards?'

'I thought I had already, but if you insist.' He went down on one knee. 'Susan, I love you with all my heart and soul. Will you marry me?'

She sank down on her knees and slipped her arms around his neck. 'You'd better tell your squadron leader that I've been waiting for three years for this moment, and he's got to give you leave very soon, because tonight I'm going to lose my reputation.'

'Is that a yes?'

She answered him with a kiss. 'Yes, yes, yes.'

Susan was a summer bride. Bob gave her away and Roz was her matron of honour. Jennifer was a proud bridesmaid and Charlie wore a bow in his collar. Susan wore a long white wedding dress, which was her present from Elspeth and Colin who planned to be married in the register office the following month. The village church was redolent with the scent of roses, honeysuckle and mock orange blossom, and it was packed with guests. Almost everyone in the village had come and to Susan's surprise and pleasure most of Number 15 ferry pool turned up to wish her well.

Dave had travelled from London with his sister, and although Susan had been nervous about meeting Aunt Maida again she was pleasantly surprised to find the redoubtable woman was much more amenable now. Perhaps the war had softened her, or maybe it was because Susan had proved herself to be a worthy adversary. Whatever it was, Susan was relieved and delighted.

After the ceremony they set off for the short walk to the pub. Everyone crowded into the bar for champagne and cucumber sandwiches, followed by jam tarts and one of Mrs Delaney's wedding cakes, the cardboard cover ageing and slightly battered but still in use. The party spilled out into the flower scented garden where Bob had strung paper lanterns in the trees and bushes. For Susan it was the happiest day of her life. She still had to stop and pinch herself from time to time just to make certain she was not dreaming.

That evening, when the pub finally closed, Dave drew Susan and Tony aside as they were about to leave for the cottage, where they had opted to spend their wedding night before setting off next day for a brief honeymoon in Devon. He cleared his throat, gazing at them with a misty smile. 'I expect you're wondering what I could possibly add to the wonderful things that have already been said about you both.' He led Susan towards the settle in the ingle nook. 'You'd better sit down, my dear. I've got something very important that I've been saving up until the guests had gone.'

She sank down on the hard wooden seat, glancing up at Tony. 'We're not in a hurry, are we, darling?'

He grinned, taking her hand and sitting down beside her. 'Of course not. What is it, Dad?'

Dave stood with his back to the empty fireplace. He ran his finger round the inside of his collar, gazing at Susan with a nervous smile. 'You told me a long time ago that your dearest wish was to find out about your parents.'

She nodded her head, tightening her grasp on Tony's hand. 'It was, but it doesn't matter so much now. You and Tony are my family. I don't need anyone else.'

'That's as maybe, love, but I'm sure you'd like

some answers.' He shot a sideways glance at his sister, who had come into the bar clutching a cup of tea. She gave him an encouraging nod.

'Get on with it, David.'

He cleared his throat again. 'With Maida's help I took it upon myself to find out about your mother, Susan. I drew a blank at the children's home. They couldn't or wouldn't tell me anything, so I decided to go and see Mrs Kemp. I thought she must have had some knowledge of your background before she took you on – but she told me where to go in no uncertain terms.'

Susan pulled a face. 'That sounds like the old bat.'

'Exactly so. Anyway, I was just leaving when her housekeeper drew me aside. It was Mrs Wilson, the woman who was kind to you in the early days, Susan. She'd decided to return to her old job because she couldn't stand living with relations. To cut a long story short, she told me that Mrs Kemp had had a younger sister who died giving birth to an illegitimate baby twenty-three years ago.'

Susan stared at him, puzzled. 'That's all very well, but what has it got to do with me?'

'Mrs Wilson said that the child's grandmother was distraught, and she named the baby Susan, in memory of her dead daughter. She wanted to raise the infant herself, but the rest of the family would have none of it. They hushed up the affair and, as far as Mrs Wilson knew, the baby was put out for adoption.'

Leaning against Tony, Susan felt his arm tighten around her shoulders. She reached into her pocket for a hanky. 'That's so sad.'

'But it's not the end of it,' Dave said, smiling. 'The name and the date seemed to tally, so I took a chance and went to Somerset House requesting a copy of the birth certificate of Susan Scantlebery, which was Mrs Kemp's maiden name.' He put his hand into his breast pocket and took out a slip of paper, handing it to Susan. 'You weren't lying when you told Tony that you belonged in that house, my dear. Your unfortunate mother was Mrs Kemp's sister, and your father was a young man who worked as a clerk in her father's business.'

'I can't take this in.' Susan stared at the birth certificate, shaking her head. 'My mother was Susan Scantlebery and my father was Frank Baylis.' She looked up at Dave, her hand trembling as she clutched the document. 'Did you find him? Does he know about me?'

'I'm sorry, love.' Dave shook his head. 'Frank was killed in a motorcycle accident six months before you were born. He never had the chance to make things right for your mum.'

Tony slipped his arm around her waist. 'Are you all right, Susan?'

She shook her head, dazed but happy. 'I don't know what to say. I can't believe it. I wasn't abandoned because my mum and dad didn't want me.' She frowned, even more confused now than before. 'But why did Mrs Kemp take me from the orphanage? I don't understand.'

'The old battleaxe must have had second thoughts,' Dave said slowly. 'Maybe she regretted what she'd done, or perhaps she simply wanted to keep an eye on you so that you had no chance of finding out your true identity. You were a living reminder of an old family scandal and she wanted it kept in the past.'

Tony squeezed her hand. 'If you want to go back there and face her, I'll come with you, darling. I won't let the old cow bully you.'

Susan was silent for a moment. She could feel the tension in the bar as everyone stopped talking and waited for her answer. She took a deep breath. 'I know you would, Tony, but I never want to see that awful woman again, or her hateful daughters.' She leapt to her feet and threw her arms around Dave's neck. 'But thank you, Dad. I can't believe you went to all that trouble just for me.'

He flushed and gave her a gentle hug before extricating himself from her grasp. 'It was the least I could do for my new daughter.'

She sank back onto the settle. 'I'd like to find out more about my mother and Frank, of course, but maybe it's best if I just leave them in peace. At least they're together for all eternity, and perhaps that's where I should let them lie.'

'Very wise, my darling.' Tony drew her into the circle of his arms. 'I love you with all my heart,

Susan. I'll never let anyone hurt you again.'

She smiled up into his eyes, knowing that this was the man with whom she wanted to spend the rest of her life. 'I love you too, and I've got all the family I need.' She glanced over her shoulder at Bob, Roz and Danny gathered round the bar with Aunt Maida. 'I came home a long time ago.' She chuckled as Charlie laid his head on her lap, looking up at her with adoring eyes and wagging tail. 'And of course I love you, Charlie. If it hadn't been for you, none of this would have happened. I'm so happy, I could cry.'

'No tears, Susan.' Bob stepped forward, raising his glass. 'I want to propose a toast to the happy couple – and in particular to our very own Spitfire Girl!'